The Common Law

Other books by Robert W. Chambers:

The Common Law
The Adventures of a Modest Man
Ailsa Paige
The Danger Mark
Special Messenger
The Firing Line
The Younger Set
The Fighting Chance
Some Ladies in Haste
The Tree of Heaven
The Tracer of Lost Persons
A Young Man in a Hurry
Lorraine
Maids of Paradise
Ashes of Empire
The Red Republic
Outsiders
The Green Mouse
Iole
The Reckoning
The Maid-at-Arms
Cardigan
The Haunts of Men
The Mystery of Choice
The Cambric Mask
The Maker of Moons
The King in Yellow
In Search of the Unknown
The Conspirators
A King and a Few Dukes
In the Quarter

Books for Children:

Garden-Land
Forest-Land
River-Land
Mountain-Land
Orchard-Land
Outdoor-Land
Hide and Seek in Forest-Land

The Common Law

Robert W. Chambers

ÆGYPAN PRESS

Text from the 1911
D. Appleton and Company edition.

The Common Law
A publication of
ÆGYPAN PRESS

www.aegypan.com

To Charles Dana Gibson
A Friend of Many Years

Chapter I

*T*here was a long, brisk, decisive ring at the door. He continued working. After an interval the bell rang again, briefly, as though the light touch on the electric button had lost its assurance.

"Somebody's confidence has departed," he thought to himself, busy with a lead-weighted string and a stick of soft charcoal wrapped in silver foil. For a few moments he continued working, not inclined to trouble himself to answer the door, but the hesitating timidity of a third appeal amused him, and he walked out into the hallway and opened the door. In the dim light a departing figure turned from the stairway:

"Do you wish a model?" she asked in an unsteady voice.

"No," he said, vexed.

"Then — I beg your pardon for disturbing you —"

"Who gave you my name?" he demanded.

"Why — nobody —"

"Who sent you to me? Didn't anybody send you?"

"No."

"But how did you get in?"

"I — walked in."

There was a scarcely perceptible pause; then she turned away in the dim light of the corridor.

"You know," he said, "models are not supposed to come here unless sent for. It isn't done in this building." He pointed to a black and white sign on his door which bore the words: "No Admittance."

"I am very sorry. I didn't understand —"

"Oh, it's all right; only, I don't see how you got up here at all. Didn't the elevator boy question you? It's his business."

"I didn't come up on the elevator."

"You didn't *walk* up!"

"Yes."

"Twelve stories!"

"Both elevators happened to be in service. Besides, I was not quite certain that models were expected to use the elevators."

"Good Lord!" he exclaimed, "you must have wanted an engagement pretty badly."

"Yes, I did."

He stared: "I suppose you do, still,"

"If you would care to try me."

"I'll take your name and address, anyhow. Twelve flights! For the love of — oh, come in anyway and rest."

It was dusky in the private hallway through which he preceded her, but there was light enough in the great studio. Through the vast sheets of glass fleecy clouds showed blue sky between. The morning was clearing.

He went over to an ornate Louis XV table, picked up a note book, motioned her to be seated, dropped into a chair himself, and began to sharpen a pencil. As yet he had scarcely glanced at her, and now, while he leisurely shaved the cedar and scraped the lead to a point, he absent-mindedly and good-humoredly admonished her:

"You models have your own guild, your club, your regular routine, and it would make it much easier for us if you'd all register and quietly wait until we send for you.

"You see we painters know what we want and we know where to apply for it. But if you all go wandering over studio buildings in search of engagements, we won't have any leisure to employ you because it will take all our time to answer the bell. And it will end by our not answering it at all. And that's why it is fit and proper for good little models to remain *chez eux.*"

He had achieved a point to his pencil. Now he opened his model book, looked up at her with his absent smile, and remained looking.

"Aren't you going to remove your veil?"

"Oh — I beg your pardon!" Slender gloved fingers flew up, were nervously busy a moment. She removed her veil and sat as though awaiting his comment. None came.

After a moment's pause she said: "Did you wish — my name and address?"

He nodded, still looking intently at her.

"Miss West," she said, calmly. He wrote it down.

"Is that all? Just 'Miss West'?"

"Valerie West — if that is custom — necessary."

He wrote "Valerie West"; and, as she gave it to him, he noted her address.

"Head and shoulders?" he asked, quietly.

"Yes," very confidently.

"Figure?"

"Yes," — less confidently.

"Draped or undraped?"

When he looked up again, for an instant he thought her skin even whiter than it had been; perhaps not, for, except the vivid lips and a carnation tint in the cheeks, the snowy beauty of her face and neck had already preoccupied him.

"Do you pose undraped?" he repeated, interested.

"I — expect to do — what is — required of — models."

"Sensible," he commented, noting the detail in his book. "Now, Miss West, for whom have you recently posed?"

And, as she made no reply, he looked up amiably, balancing his pencil in his hand and repeating the question.

"Is it necessary to — tell you?"

"Not at all. One usually asks that question, probably because you models are always so everlastingly anxious to tell us — particularly when the men for whom you have posed are more famous than the poor devil who offers you an engagement."

There was something very good humored in his smile, and she strove to smile, too, but her calmness was now all forced, and her heart was beating very fast, and her black-gloved fingers were closing and doubling till the hands that rested on the arms of the gilded antique chair lay tightly clenched.

He was leisurely writing in his note book under her name:

"Height, medium; eyes, a dark brown; hair, thick, lustrous, and brown; head, unusually beautiful; throat and neck, perfect —"

He stopped writing and lifted his eyes:

"How much of your time is taken ahead, I wonder?"

"What?"

"How many engagements have you? Is your time all cut up — as I fancy it is?"

"N-no."

"Could you give me what time I might require?"

"I think so."

"What I mean, Miss West, is this: suppose that your figure is what I have an idea it is; could you give me a lot of time ahead?"

She remained silent so long that he had started to write, "probably unreliable," under his notes; but, as his pencil began to move, her lips unclosed with, a low, breathless sound that became a ghost of a voice:

"I will do what you require of me. I meant to answer."

"Do you mean that you are in a position to make a time contract with me? — provided you prove to be what I need?"

She nodded uncertainly.

"I'm beginning the ceiling, lunettes, and panels for the Byzantine Theater," he added, sternly stroking his short mustache, "and under those circumstances I suppose you know what a contract between us means."

She nodded again, but in her eyes was bewilderment, and in her heart, fear.

"Yes," she managed to say, "I think I understand."

"Very well. I merely want to say that a model threw me down hard in the very middle of the Bimmington's ballroom. Max Schindler put on a show, and she put for the spot-light. She'd better stay put," he added grimly: "she'll never have another chance in your guild."

Then the frown vanished, and the exceedingly engaging smile glimmered in his eyes:

"You wouldn't do such a thing as that to me," he added; "would you, Miss West?"

"Oh, no," she replied, not clearly comprehending the enormity of the Schindler recruit's behavior.

"And you'll stand by me if our engagement goes through?"

"Yes, I — will try to."

"Good business! Now, if you really are what I have an idea you are, I'll know pretty quick whether I can use you for the Byzantine job." He rose, walked over to a pair of closed folding doors and opened them. "You can undress in there," he said. "I think you will find everything you need."

For a second she sat rigid, her black-gloved hands doubled, her eyes fastened on him as though fascinated. He had already turned and sauntered over to one of several easels where he picked up the lump of charcoal in its silver foil.

The color began to come back into her face — swifter, more swiftly: the vast blank window with its amber curtains stared at her; she lifted her tragic gaze and saw the sheet of glass above swimming in crystal light. Through it clouds were dissolving in the bluest of skies; against it a spider web of pendant cords drooped from the high ceiling; and she saw the looming mystery of huge canvases beside which stepladders rose surmounted by little crow's-nests where the graceful oval of palettes curved, tinted with scraped brilliancy.

"What a dreamer you are!" he called across the studio to her. "The light is fine, now. Hadn't we better take advantage of it?"

She managed to find her footing; contrived to rise, to move with apparent self-possession toward the folding doors.

"Better hurry," he said, pleasantly. "If you're what I need we might start things now. I am all ready for the sort of figure I expect you have."

She stepped inside the room and became desperately busy for a moment trying to close the doors; but either her hands had suddenly become powerless or they shook too much; and when he turned, almost impatiently, from his easel to see what all that rattling meant, she shrank hastily aside into the room beyond, keeping out of his view.

The room was charming — not like the studio, but modern and fresh and dainty with chintz and flowered wall-paper and the graceful white furniture of a bedroom. There was a flowered screen there, too. Behind it stood a chair, and onto this she sank, laid her hands for an instant against her burning face, then stooped and, scarcely knowing what she was about, began to untie her patent-leather shoes.

He remained standing at his easel, very busy with his string and lump of charcoal; but after a while it occurred to him that she was taking an annoyingly long time about a simple matter.

"What on earth is the trouble?" he called. "Do you realize you've been in there a quarter of an hour?"

She made no answer. A second later he thought he heard an indistinct sound — and it disquieted him.

"Miss West?"

There was no reply.

Impatient, a little disturbed, he walked across to the folding doors; and the same low, suppressed sound caught his ear.

"What in the name of —" he began, walking into the room; and halted, amazed.

She sat all huddled together behind the screen, partly undressed, her face hidden in her hands; and between the slender fingers tears ran down brightly.

"Are you ill?" he asked, anxiously.

After a moment she slowly shook her head.

"Then — what in the name of Mike —"

"P-please forgive me. I — I will be ready in a in-moment — if you wouldn't mind going out —"

"*Are* you ill? Answer me?"

"N-no."

"Has anything disturbed you so that you don't feel up to posing today?"

"No. . . . I — am — almost ready — if you will go out —"

He considered her, uneasy and perplexed. Then:

"All right," he said, briefly. "Take your own time, Miss West."

At his easel, fussing with yard-stick and crayon, he began to square off his canvas, muttering to himself:

"What the deuce is the matter with that girl? Nice moment to nurse secret sorrows or blighted affections. There's always something wrong with the best lookers. . . . And she is a real beauty — or I miss my guess." He went on ruling off, measuring, grumbling, until slowly there came over him the sense of the nearness of another person. He had not heard her enter, but he turned around, knowing she was there.

She stood silent, motionless, as though motion terrified her and inertia were salvation. Her dark hair rippled to her waist; her white arms hung limp, yet the fingers had curled till every delicate nail was pressed deep into the pink palm. She was trying to look at him. Her face was as white as a flower.

"All right," he said under his breath, "you're practically faultless. I suppose you realize it!"

A scarcely perceptible shiver passed over her entire body, then, as he stepped back, his keen artist's gaze narrowing, there stole over her a delicate flush, faintly staining her from brow to ankle, transfiguring the pallor exquisitely, enchantingly. And her small head drooped forward, shadowed by her hair.

"You're what I want," he said. "You're about everything I require in color and form and texture."

She neither spoke nor moved as much as an eyelash.

"Look here, Miss West," he said in a slightly excited voice, "let's go about this thing intelligently." He swung another easel on its rollers, displaying a sketch in soft, brilliant colors — a multitude of figures amid a swirl of sunset-tinted clouds and patches of azure sky.

"You're intelligent," he went on with animation, — "I saw that — somehow or other — though you haven't said very much." He laughed, and laid his hand on the painted canvas beside him:

"You're a model, and it's not necessary to inform you that this Is only a preliminary sketch. Your experience tells you that. But it is necessary to tell you that it's the final composition. I've decided on this arrangement for the ceiling: You see for yourself that you're perfectly fitted to stand or sit for all these floating, drifting, cloud-cradled goddesses. You're an inspiration in yourself — for the perfections of Olympus!" he added, laughing, "and that's no idle compliment. But of course other artists have often told you this before — as though you didn't have eyes of your own I And beautiful ones at that!" He laughed again, turned and dragged a two-storied model-stand across the floor, tossed up one or two silk cushions, and nodded to her.

"Don't be afraid; it's rickety but safe. It will hold us both. Are you ready?"

As in a dream she set one little barefoot on the steps, mounted, balancing with arms extended and the tips of her fingers resting on his outstretched hand.

Standing on the steps he arranged the cushions, told her where to be seated, how to recline, placed the wedges and blocks to support her feet, chalked the bases, marked positions with arrows, and wedged and blocked up her elbow. Then he threw over her a soft, white, wool robe, swathing her from throat to feet, descended the steps, touched an electric bell, and picking up a huge clean palette began to squeeze out coils of color from a dozen plump tubes.

Presently a short, squarely built man entered. He wore a blue jumper; there were traces of paint on it, on his large square hands, on his square, serious face.

"O'Hara?"

"Sorr?"

"We're going to begin *now!* — thank Heaven. So if you'll be kind enough to help move forward the ceiling canvas —"

O'Hara glanced up carelessly at the swathed and motionless figure above, then calmly spat upon his hands and laid hold of one side of the huge canvas indicated. The painter took the other side.

"Now, O'Hara, careful! Back off a little! — don't let it sway! There — that's where I want it. Get a ladder and clamp the tops. Pitch it a little forward — more! — stop! Fix those pulley ropes; I'll make things snug below."

For ten minutes they worked deftly, rapidly, making fast the great blank canvas which had been squared and set with an enormous oval in heavy outline.

From her lofty aerie she looked down at them as in a dream while they shifted other enormous framed canvases and settled the oval one into place. Everything below seemed to be on rubber wheels or casters, easels, stepladders, color cabinets, even the great base where the oval set canvas rested.

She looked up at the blue sky. Sparrows dropped out of the brilliant void into unseen canons far below from whence came the softened roar of traffic. Northward the city spread away between its rivers, glittering under the early April sun; the Park lay like a grey and green map set with, the irregular silver of water; beyond, the huge unfinished cathedral loomed dark against the big white hospital of St. Luke; farther still a lilac-tinted haze hung along the edges of the Bronx.

"All right, O'Hara. Much obliged. I won't need you again."

"Very good, Sorr."

The short, broad Irishman went out with another incurious glance aloft, and closed the outer door.

High up on her perch she watched the man below. He calmly removed coat and waistcoat, pulled a painter's linen blouse over his curly head, lighted a cigarette, picked up his palette, fastened a tin cup to the edge, filled it from a bottle, took a handful of brushes and a bunch of cheese cloth, and began to climb up a stepladder opposite her, lugging his sketch in the other hand.

He fastened the little sketch to an upright and stood on the ladder halfway up, one leg higher than the other.

"Now, Miss West," he said decisively.

At the sound of his voice fear again leaped through her like a flame, burning her face as she let slip the white wool robe.

"All right," he said. "Don't move while I'm drawing unless you have to."

She could see him working. He seemed to be drawing with a brush, rapidly, and with, a kind of assurance that appeared almost careless.

At first she could make out little of the lines. They were all dark in tint, thin, tinged with plum color. There seemed to be no curves in them — and at first she could not comprehend that he was drawing her figure. But after a little while curves appeared; long delicate outlines began to emerge as rounded surfaces in monochrome, casting definite shadows on other surfaces. She could recognize the shape of a human head; saw it gradually become a colorless drawing; saw shoulders, arms, a body emerging into shadowy shape; saw the long fine limbs appear, the slender indication of feet.

Then flat on the cheek lay a patch of brilliant color, another on the mouth. A great swirl of cloud forms sprang into view high piled in a corner of the canvas.

And now he seemed to be eternally running up and down his ladder, shifting it here and there across the vast white background of canvas, drawing great meaningless lines in distant expanses of the texture, then, always consulting her with his keen, impersonal gaze, he pushed back his ladder, mounted, wiped the big brushes, selected others smaller and flatter, considering her in penetrating silence between every brush, stroke.

She saw a face and hair growing lovely under her eyes, bathed in an iris-tinted light; saw little exquisite flecks of color set here and there on the white expanse; watched all so intently, so wonderingly, that the numbness of her body became a throbbing pain before she was aware that she was enduring torture.

She strove to move, gave a little gasp; and he was down from his ladder and up on hers before her half-paralyzed body had swayed to the edge of danger.

"Why didn't you say so?" he asked, sharply. "I can't keep track of time when I'm working!"

With arms and fingers that scarcely obeyed her she contrived to gather the white wool covering around her shoulders and limbs and lay back.

"You know," he said, "that it's foolish to act this way. I don't want to kill you, Miss West."

She only lowered her head amid its lovely crown of hair.

"You know your own limits," he said, resentfully. He looked down at the big clock: "It's a full hour. You had only to speak. Why didn't you?"

"I — I didn't know what to say."

"Didn't know!" He paused, astonished. Then: "Well, you felt yourself getting numb, didn't you?"

"Y-yes. But I thought it was — to be expected" — she blushed vividly under his astonished gaze: "I think I had better tell you that — that this is — the first time."

"The first time!"

"Yes. . . . I ought to have told you. I was afraid you might not want me."

"Lord above!" he breathed. "You poor — poor little thing!"

She began to cry silently; he saw the drops fall shining on the white wool robe, and leaned one elbow on the ladder, watching them. After a while they ceased, but she still held her head low, and her face was bent in the warm shadow of her hair.

"How could I understand?" he asked very gently.

"I — should have told you. I was afraid."

He said: "I'm terribly sorry. It must have been perfect torture for you to undress — to come into the studio. If you'd only given me an idea of how matters stood I could have made it a little easier. I'm afraid I was brusque — taking it for granted that you were a model and knew your business. . . . I'm terribly sorry."

She lifted her head, looked at him, with the tears still clinging to her lashes.

"You have been very nice to me. It is all my own fault."

He smiled. "Then it's all right, now that we understand. Isn't it?"

"Yes."

"You make a stunning model," he said frankly.

"Do I? Then you will let me come again?"

"*Let* you!" He laughed; "I'll be more likely to beg you."

"Oh, you won't have to," she said; "I'll come as long as you want me."

"That is simply angelic of you. Tell me, do you wish to descend to terra firma?"

She glanced below, doubtfully:

"N-no, thank you. If I could only stretch my — legs —"

"Stretch away," he said, much amused, "but don't tumble off and break into pieces. I like you better as you are than as an antique and limbless Venus."

She cautiously and daintily extended first one leg then the other under the wool robe, then eased the cramped muscles of her back, straightening her body and flexing her arms with a little sigh of relief. As her shy sidelong gaze reverted to him she saw to her relief that he was not noticing her. A slight sense of warmth, suffused her body, and she stretched herself again, more confidently, and ventured to glance around.

"Speaking of terms," he said in an absent way, apparently preoccupied with the palette which he was carefully scraping, "do you happen to know what is the usual recompense for a model's service?"

She said that she had heard, and added with quick diffidence that she could not expect so much, being only a beginner.

He polished the surface of the palette with a handful of cheese cloth:

"Don't you think that you are worth it?"

"How can *I* be until I know how to pose for you?"

"You will never have to learn how to pose, Miss West."

"I don't know exactly what you mean."

"I mean that some models never learn. Some know how already — you, for example."

She flushed slightly: "Do you really mean that?"

"Oh, I wouldn't say so if I didn't. It's merely necessary for you to accustom yourself to holding a pose; the rest you already know instinctively."

"What is the rest?" she ventured to ask. "I don't quite understand what you see in me —"

"Well," he said placidly, "you are beautifully made. That is nine-tenths of the matter. Your head is set logically on your neck, and your neck is correctly placed on your spine, and your legs and arms are properly attached to your torso — your entire body, anatomically speaking, is hinged, hung, supported, developed as the ideal body should be. It's undeformed, unmarred, unspoiled, and that's partly luck, partly inheritance, and mostly decent habits and digestion."

She was listening intently, interested, surprised, her pink lips slightly parted.

"Another point," he continued; "you seem unable to move or rest ungracefully. Few women are so built that an ungraceful motion is impossible for them. You are one of the few. It's all a matter of anatomy."

She remained silent, watching him curiously.

He said: "But the final clincher to your qualifications is that you are intelligent. I have known pretty women," he added with, sarcasm, "who were not what learned men would call precisely intelligent. But you are. I showed you my sketch, indicated in a general way what I wanted, and instinctively and intelligently you assumed the proper attitude. I didn't have to take you by the chin and twist your head as though you were a lay figure; I didn't have to pull you about and flex and bend and twist you. You knew that I wanted you to look like some sort of an ethereal immortality, deliciously relaxed, adrift in sunset clouds. And you *were* it — somehow or other."

She looked down, thoughtfully, nestling to the chin in the white wool folds. A smile, almost imperceptible, curved her lips.

"You are making it very easy for me," she said.

"You make it easy for yourself."

"I was horribly afraid," she said thoughtfully.

"I have no doubt of it."

"Oh, you don't know — nobody can know — no man can understand the terror of — of the first time —"

"It must be a ghastly experience."

"It is! — I don't mean that you have not done everything to make it easier — but — there in the little room — my courage left me — I almost died. I'd have run away only — I was afraid you wouldn't let me —"

He began to laugh; she tried to, but the terror of it all was as yet too recent.

"At first," she said, "I was afraid I wouldn't do for a model — not exactly afraid of my — my appearance, but because I was a novice; and I imagined that one had to know exactly how to pose —"

"I think," he interrupted smilingly, "that you might take the pose again if you are rested. Go on talking; I don't mind it."

She sat erect, loosened the white wool robe and dropped it from her with less consciousness and effort than before. Very carefully she set her feet on the blocks, fitting the shapely heels to the chalked outlines; found the mark for her elbow, adjusted her slim, smooth body and looked at him, flushing.

"All right," he said briefly; "go ahead and talk to me."

"Do you wish me to?"

"Yes; I'd rather."

"I don't know exactly what to say."

"Say anything," he returned absently, selecting a flat brush with a very long handle.

She thought a moment, then, lifting her eyes:

"I might ask you your name."

"What? Don't you know it? Oh, Lord! Oh, Vanity! I thought you'd heard of me."

She blushed, confused by her ignorance and what she feared was annoyance on his part; then perceived that he was merely amused; and her face cleared.

"We folk who create concrete amusement for the public always imagine ourselves much better known to that public than we are, Miss West. It's our little vanity — rather harmless after all. We're a pretty decent lot, sometimes absurd, especially in our tragic moments; sometimes emotional, usually illogical, often impulsive, frequently tender-hearted as well as supersensitive.

"Now it was a pleasant little vanity for me to take it for granted that somehow you had heard of me and had climbed twelve flights of stairs for the privilege of sitting for me."

He laughed so frankly that the shy, responsive smile made her face enchanting; and he coolly took advantage of it, and while exciting and stimulating it, affixed it immortally on the exquisite creature he was painting.

"So you didn't climb those twelve flights solely for the privilege of having me paint you?"

"No," she admitted, laughingly, "I was merely going to begin at the top and apply for work all the way down until somebody took me — or nobody took me."

"But why begin at the top?"

"It is easier to bear disappointment going down," she said, seriously; "if two or three artists had refused me on the first and second floors, my legs would not have carried me up very far."

"Bad logic," he commented. "We mount by experience, using our wrecked hopes as footholds."

"You don't know how much a girl can endure. There comes a time-after years of steady descent — when misfortune and disappointment become endurable; when hope deferred no longer sickens. It is in rising toward better things that disappointments hurt most cruelly."

He turned his head in surprise; then went on painting:

"Your philosophy is the philosophy of submission."

"Do you call a struggle of years, submission?"

"But it was giving up after all — acquiescence, despondency, a *laissez faire* policy."

"One may tire of fighting."

"One may. Another may not."

"I think you have never had to fight very hard."

He turned his head abruptly; after a moment's silent survey of her, he resumed his painting with a sharp, impersonal glance before every swift and decisive brush stroke:

"No; I have never had to fight, Miss West. . . . It was keen of you to recognize it. I have never had to fight at all. Things come easily to me — things have a habit of coming my way. . . . I suppose I'm not exactly the man to lecture anybody on the art of fighting fortune. She's always been decent to me. . . . Sometimes I'm afraid — I have an instinct that she's too friendly. . . . And it troubles me. Do you understand what I mean?"

"Yes."

He looked up at her: "Are you sure?"

"I think so. I have been watching you painting. I never imagined anybody could draw so swiftly, so easily — paint so surely, so accurately — that every brush stroke could be so — so significant, so decisive. . . . Is it not unusual? And is not that what is called facility?"

"Lord in Heaven!" he said; "what kind of a girl am I dealing with? — or what kind of a girl is dealing so unmercifully with me?"

"I — I didn't mean —"

"Yes, you did. Those very lovely and wonderfully shaped eyes of yours are not entirely for ornament. Inside that pretty head there's an apparatus designed for thinking; and it isn't idle."

He laughed gaily, a trifle defiantly:

"You've said it. You've found the fly in the amber. I'm cursed with facility. Worse still it gives me keenest pleasure to employ it. It does scare me occasionally — has for years — makes me miserable at intervals — fills me full of all kinds of fears and doubts."

He turned toward her, standing on his ladder, the big palette curving up over his left shoulder, a wet brush extended in his right hand:

"What shall I do!" he exclaimed so earnestly that she sat up straight, startled, forgetting her pose. "Ought I to stifle the vigor, the energy, the restless desire that drives me to express myself — that will not tolerate the inertia of calculation and ponderous reflection? Ought I to check myself, consider, worry, entangle myself in psychologies, seek for subtleties where none exist — split hairs, relapse into introspective philosophy when my fingers itch for a lump of charcoal and every color on my set palette yells at me to be about my business?"

He passed the flat tip of his wet brush through the mass of rags in his left hand with a graceful motion like one unsheathing a sword:

"I tell you I do the things which I do, as easily, as naturally, as happily as any fool of a dicky-bird does his infernal twittering on an April morning. God knows whether there's anything in my work or in his twitter; but neither he nor I are likely to improve our output by pondering and cogitation. . . . Please resume the pose."

She did so, her dark young eyes on him; and he continued painting and talking in his clear, rapid, decisive manner:

"My name is Louis Neville. They call me Kelly — my friends do," he added, laughing. "Have you ever seen any of my work?"

"Yes."

He laughed again: "That's more soothing. However, I suppose you saw that big canvas of mine for the ceiling of the Metropolitan Museum's new northwest wing. The entire town saw it."

"Yes, I saw it."

"Did you care for it?"

She had cared for it too intensely to give him any adequate answer. Never before had her sense of color and form and beauty been so exquisitely satisfied by the painted magic of any living painter. So this was the man who had enveloped her, swayed her senses, whirled her upward into his ocean of limpid light! This was the man who had done that miracle before which, all day long, crowds of the sober, decent, unimaginative — the solid, essentials of the nation — had lingered fascinated! This was the man — across there on a stepladder. And he was evidently not yet thirty; and his name was Neville and his friends called him Kelly.

"Yes," she said, diffidently, "I cared for it."

"Really?"

He caught her eye, laughed, and went on with his work.

"The critics were savage," he said. "Lord! It hurts, too. But I've simply got to be busy. What good would it do me to sit down and draw casts with a thin, needle-pointed stick of hard charcoal. Not that they say I can't draw. They admit that I can. They admit that I can paint, too."

He laughed, stretched his arms:

"Draw! A blank canvas sets me mad. When I look at one I feel like covering it with a thousand figures twisted into every intricacy and difficulty of foreshortening! I wish I were like that Hindu god with a dozen arms; and even then I couldn't paint fast enough to satisfy what my eyes and brain have already evoked upon an untouched canvas.... It's a sort of intoxication that gets hold of me; I'm perfectly cool, too, which seems a paradox but isn't. And all the while, inside me, is a constant, hushed kind of laughter, bubbling, which accompanies every brush stroke with an 'I told you so!' — if you know what I'm trying to say — *do* you?"

"N-not exactly. But I suppose you mean that you are self-confident."

"Lord! Listen to this girl say in a dozen words what I'm trying to say in a volume so that it won't scare me! Yes! That's it. I am confident. And it's that self-confidence which some-times scares me half to death."

From his ladder he pointed with his brush to the prelimi-nary sketch that faced her, touching figure after figure:

"I'm going to draw them in, now," he said; "first this one. Can you catch the pose? It's going to be hard; I'll block up your heels, later; that's it! Stand up straight, stretch as though the next moment you were going to rise on tiptoe and float upward without an effort —"

He was working like lightning in long, beautiful, clean outline strokes, brushed here and there with shadow shapes and masses. And time flew at first, then went slowly, more slowly, until it dragged at her delicate body and set every nerve aching.

"I — may I rest a moment?"

"Sure thing!" he said, cordially, laying aside palette and brushes. "Come on, Miss West, and we'll have luncheon."

She hastily swathed herself in the wool robe.

"Do you mean — here?"

"Yes. There's a dumb-waiter. I'll ring for the card."

"I'd like to," she said, "but do you think I had better?"

"Why not?"

"You mean — take lunch with you?"

"Why not?"

"Is it customary?"

"No, it isn't."

"Then I think I will go out to lunch somewhere —"

"I'm not going to let you get away," he said, laughing. "You're too good to be real; I'm worried half to death for fear that you'll vanish in a golden cloud, or something equally futile and inconsiderate. No, I want you to stay. You don't mind, do you?"

He was aiding her to descend from her aerie, her little white hand balanced on his arm. When she set foot on the floor she looked up at him gravely:

"You wouldn't let me do anything that I ought not to, would you, Mr. Kelly — I mean Mr. Neville?" she added in confusion.

"No. Anyway I don't know what you ought or ought not to do. Luncheon is a simple matter of routine. It's sole significance is two empty stomachs. I suppose if you go out you *will* come back, but — I'd rather you'd remain."

"Why?"

"Well," he admitted with a laugh, "it's probably because I like to hear myself talk to you. Besides, I've always the hope that you'll suddenly become conversational, and that's a possibility exciting enough to give anybody an appetite."

"But I *have* conversed with you," she said.

"Only a little. What you said acted like a cocktail to inspire me for a desire for more."

"I am afraid that you were not named Kelly in vain."

"You mean blarney? No, it's merely frankness. Let me get you some bath-slippers —"

"Oh — but if I am to lunch here — I can't do it this way!" she exclaimed in flushed consternation.

"Indeed you must learn to do that without embarrassment, Miss West. Tie up your robe at the throat, tuck up your sleeves, slip your feet into a nice pair of brand-new bath-slippers, and I'll ring for luncheon."

"I — don't — want to —" she began; but he went away into the hall, rang, and presently she heard the ascending clatter of a dumb-waiter. From it he took the luncheon card and returned to where she was sitting at a rococo table. She blushed as he laid the card before her, and would have nothing to do with it. The result was that he did the ordering, sent the dumb-waiter down with his scribbled memorandum, and came wandering back with long, cool glances at his canvas and the work he had done on it.

"I mean to make a stunning thing of it," he remarked, eying the huge chassis critically. "All this — deviltry — whatever it is inside of me — must come out somehow. And that canvas is the place for it." He laughed and sat down opposite her:

"Man is born to folly, Miss West — born full of it. I get rid of mine on canvas. It's a safer outlet for original sin than some other ways."

She lay back in her antique gilded chair, hands extended along the arms, looking at him with a smile that was still shy.

"My idea of you — of an artist — was so different," she said.

"There are all kinds, mostly the seriously inspired and humorless variety who makes a mystic religion of a very respectable profession. This world is full of pale, enraptured artists; full of muscular, thumb-smearing artists; full of dreamy weavers of visions, usually deficient in spinal process; full of unwashed little inverts to whom the world really resembles a kaleidoscope full of things that wiggle —"

They began to laugh, he with a singular delight in her comprehension of his idle, irresponsible chatter, she from sheer pleasure in listening and looking at this man who was so different from anybody she had ever known — and, thank God! — so young.

And when the bell rang and the clatter announced the
advent of luncheon, she settled in her chair with a little shiver
of happiness, blushing at her capacity for it, and at her
acquiescence in the strangest conditions in which she had
ever found herself in all her life, — conditions so bizarre, so
grotesque, so impossible that there was no use in trying to
consider them — alas! no point in blushing now.

Mechanically she settled her little naked feet deep into the
big bath-slippers, tucked up her white wool sleeves to the
dimpled elbow, and surveyed the soup which he had placed
before her to serve.

"I know perfectly well that this isn't right," she said, helping him and then herself. "But I am wondering what there is
about it that isn't right."

"Isn't it demoralizing!" he said, amused.

"I — wonder if it is?"

He laughed: "Such ideas are nonsense, Miss West. Listen
to me: you and I — everybody except those with whom
something is physically wrong — are born with a full and
healthy capacity for demoralization and mischief. Mischief
is only one form of energy. If lightning flies about unguided
it's likely to do somebody some damage; if it's conducted
properly to a safe terminal there's no damage done and
probably a little good."

"Your brushes are your lightning-rods?" she suggested,
laughing.

"Certainly. I only demoralize canvas. What outlet have you
for your perfectly normal deviltry?"

"I haven't any."

"Any deviltry?"

"Any outlet."

"You ought to have."

"Ought I?"

"Certainly. You are as full of restless energy as I am."

"Oh, I don't think I am."

"You are. Look at yourself! I never saw anybody so sound,
so superbly healthy, so" — he laughed — "adapted to dynam-
ics. You've got to have an outlet. Or there'll be the deuce to
pay."

She looked at her fruit salad gravely, tasted it, and glanced up at him:

"I have never in all my life had any outlet — never even any outlook, Mr. Neville."

"You should have had both," he grumbled, annoyed at himself for the interest her words had for him; uneasy, now that she had responded, yet curious to learn something about this fair young girl, approximately his intellectual equal, who came to his door looking for work as a model. He thought to himself that probably it was some distressing tale which he couldn't help, and the recital of which would do neither of them any good. Of stories of models' lives he was tired, satiated. There was no use encouraging her to family revelations; an easy, pleasant footing was far more amusing to maintain. The other hinted of intimacy; and that he had never tolerated in his employees.

Yet, looking now across the table at her, a not unkind curiosity began to prod him. He could easily have left matters where they were, maintained the *status quo* indefinitely — or as long as he needed her services.

"Outlets are necessary," he said, cautiously. "Otherwise we go to the bow-wows."

"Or — die."

"What?" sharply.

She looked up without a trace of self-consciousness or the least hint of the dramatic:

"I would die unless I had an outlet. This is almost one. At least it gives me something to do with my life."

"Posing?"

"Yes."

"I don't quite understand you."

"Why, I only mean that — the other" — she smiled — "what you call the bow-wows, would not have been an outlet for me. . . . I was a show-girl for two months last winter; I ought to know. And I'd rather have died than —"

"I see," he said; "that outlet was too stupid to have attracted you."

She nodded. "Besides, I have principles," she said, candidly.

"Which effectually blocked that outlet. They sometimes kill, too, as you say. Youth stifled too long means death — the

death of youth at least. Outlets mean life. The idea is to find
a safe one."

She flushed in quick, sensitive response:

"*That* is it; that is what I meant. Mr. Neville, I am twenty-
one; and do you know I never had a childhood? And I am
simply wild for it — for the girlhood and the playtime that I
never had —"

She checked herself, looking across at him uncertainly.

"Go on," he nodded.

"That is all."

"No; tell me the rest."

She sat with head bent, slender fingers picking at her
napkin; then, without raising her troubled eyes:

"Life has been — curious. My mother was bedridden. My
childhood and girlhood were passed caring for her. That is
all I ever did until — a year ago," she added, her voice falling
so low he could scarcely hear her.

"She died, then?"

"A year ago last February."

"You went to school. You must have made friends there."

"I went to a public school for a year. After that mother
taught me."

"She must have been extremely cultivated."

The girl nodded, looking absently at the cloth. Then,
glancing up:

"I wonder whether you will understand me when I tell you
why I decided to ask employment of artists."

"I'll try to," he said, smiling.

"It was an intense desire to be among cultivated people —
if only for a few hours. Besides, I had read about artists; and
their lives seemed so young, so gay, so worth living — please
don't think me foolish and immature, Mr. Neville — but I
was so stifled, so cut off from such people, so uninspired, so
— so starved for a little gaiety — and I needed youthful
companionship — surroundings where people of my own age
and intelligence sometimes entered — and I had never had
it —"

She looked at him with a strained, wistful expression as
though begging him to understand her:

"I couldn't remain at the theater," she said. "I had little talent — no chance except chances I would not tolerate; no companionship except what I was unfitted for by education and inclination. . . . The men were — impossible. There may have been girls I could have liked — but I did not meet them. So, as I had to do something — and my years of seclusion with mother had unfitted me for any business — for office work or shop work — I thought that artists might care to employ me — might give me — or let me see — be near — something of the gayer, brighter, more pleasant and youthful side of life —"

She ceased, bent her head thoughtfully.

"You want — friends? Young ones — with intellects? You want to combine these with a chance of making a decent living?"

"Yes." She looked up candidly: "I am simply starved for it. You must believe that when you see what I have submitted to — gone through with in your studio" — she blushed vividly — "in a — a desperate attempt to escape the — the loneliness, the silence and isolation" — she raised her dark eyes — "the isolation of the poor," she said. "You don't know what that means."

After a moment she added, level-eyed: "For which there is supposed to be but one outlet — if a girl is attractive."

He rose, walked to and fro for a few moments, then, halting:

"All memory of the initial terror and distress and uncertainty aside, have you not enjoyed this morning, Miss West?"

"Yes, I — have. I — you have no idea what it has meant to me."

"It has given you an outlook, anyway."

"Yes. . . . Only — I'm terrified at the idea of going through it again — with another man —"

He laughed, and she tried to, saying:

"But if all artists are as kind and considerate —"

"Plenty of 'em are more so. There are a few bounders, a moderate number of beasts. You'll find them everywhere in the world from the purlieus to the pulpit. . . . I'm going to make a contract with you. After that, regretfully, I'll see that you meet the men who will be valuable to you. . . . I wish there was some way I could box you up in a jeweler's case so that nobody else could have you and I could find you when I needed you!"

She laughed shyly, extended her slim white hand for him to support her while she mounted to her aerie. Then, erect, delicately flushed, she let the robe fall from her and stood looking down at him in silence.

Chapter II

Spring came unusually early that year. By the first of the month a few willows and thorn bushes in the Park had turned green; then, in a single day, the entire Park became lovely with golden bell-flowers, and the first mowing machine clinked over the greenswards leaving a fragrance of clipped verdure in its wake.

Under a characteristic blue sky April unfolded its myriad leaves beneath which robins ran over shaven lawns and purple grackle bustled busily about, and the water fowl quacked and whistled and rushed through the water nipping and chasing one another or, sidling alongside, began that nodding, bowing, bobbing acquaintance preliminary to aquatic courtship.

Many of the wild birds had mated; many were mating; amorous caterwauling on back fences made night an inferno; pigeons cooed and bubbled and made endless nuisances of themselves all day long.

In lofts, offices, and shops youthful faces, whitened by the winter's pallor, appeared at open windows gazing into the blue above, or, with, pretty, inscrutable eyes, studied the passing throng till the lifted eyes of youth below completed the occult circuit with a smile.

And the spring sunshine grew hot, and sprinkling carts appeared, and the metropolis molted its overcoats, and the derby became a burden, and the annual spring exhibition of the National Academy of Design remained uncrowded.

Neville, lunching at the Syrinx Club, carelessly caught the ball of conversation tossed toward him and contributed his final comment:

"Burleson — and you, Sam Ogilvy — and you, Annan, all say that the exhibition is rotten. You say so every year; so does the majority of people. And the majority will continue saying the same thing throughout the coming decades as long as there are any exhibitions to damn.

"It is the same thing in other countries. For a hundred years the majority has pronounced every Salon rotten. And it will so continue.

"But the facts are these: the average does not vary much. A mediocrity, not disagreeable, always rules; supremity has been, is, and always will be the stick in the riffle around which the little whirlpool will always center. This year it happens to be José Querida who stems the sparkling mediocrity and sticks up from the bottom gravel making a fine little swirl. Next year — or next decade it may be anybody — you, Annan, or Sam — perhaps," he added with a slight smile, "it might be I. *Quand même.* The exhibitions are no rottener than they have ever been; and it's up to us to go about our business. And I'm going. Good-bye."

He rose from the table, laid aside the remains of his cigar, nodded good-humoredly to the others, and went out with that quick, graceful, elastic step which was noticed by everybody and envied by many.

"Hell," observed John Burleson, hitching his broad shoulders forward and swallowing a goblet of claret at a single gulp, "it's all right for Kelly Neville to shed sweetness and light over a rotten exhibition where half the people are crowded around his own picture."

"What a success he's having," mused Ogilvy, looking sideways out of the window at a pretty girl across the street.

Annan nodded: "He works hard enough for it."

"He works all the time," grumbled Burleson, "but, does he work *hard?*"

"A cat scrambling in a molasses barrel works hard," observed Ogilvy — "if you see any merit in that, John."

Burleson reared his huge frame and his symmetrical features became more bovine than ever:

"What the devil has a cat in a molasses barrel to do with the subject?" he demanded.

Annan laughed: "Poor old honest, literal John," he said, lazily. "Listen; from my back window in the country, yesterday, I observed one of my hens scratching her ear with her foot. How would you like to be able to accomplish that, John?"

"I wouldn't like it at all!" roared Burleson in serious disapproval.

"That's because you're a sculptor and a Unitarian," said Annan, gravely.

"My God!" shouted Burleson, "what's that got to do with a hen scratching herself!"

Ogilvy was too weak with laughter to continue the favorite pastime of "touching up John"; and Burleson who, under provocation, never exhibited any emotion except impatient wonder at the foolishness of others, emptied his claret bottle with unruffled confidence in his own common-sense and the futility of his friends.

"Kelly, they say, is making a stunning lot of stuff for that Byzantine Theater," he said in his honest, resonant voice. "I wish to Heaven I could paint like him."

Annan passed his delicate hand over his pale, handsome face: "Kelly Neville is, without exception, the most gifted man I ever knew."

"No, the most skillful," suggested Ogilvy. "I have known more gifted men who never became skillful."

"What hair is that you're splitting, Sam?" demanded Burleson. "Don't you like Kelly's work?"

"Sure I do."

"What's the matter with it, then?"

There was a silence. One or two men at neighboring tables turned partly around to listen. There seemed to be something in the very simple and honest question of John Burleson that arrested the attention of every man at the Syrinx Club who had heard it. Because, for the first time, the question which every man there had silently, involuntarily asked himself had been uttered aloud at last by John Burleson — voiced in utter good faith and with all confidence that the answer could be only that there was nothing whatever the matter with Louis Neville's work. And his answer had been a universal silence.

Clive Gail, lately admitted to the Academy said: "I have never in my life seen or believed possible such facility as is Louis Neville's."

"Sure thing," grunted Burleson.

"His personal manner of doing his work — which the critics and public term 'tek — nee — ee — eek,'" laughed Annan, "is simply gloriously bewildering. There is a sweeping splendor to it — and *what* color!"

There ensued murmured and emphatic approbation; and another silence.

Ogilvy's dark, pleasant face was troubled when he broke the quiet, and everybody turned toward him:

"Then," he said, slowly, "what *is* the matter with Neville?"

Somebody said: "He *does* convince you; it isn't that, is it?"

A voice replied: "Does he convince himself?"

"There is — there always has been something lacking in all that big, glorious, splendid work. It only needs that one thing — whatever it is," said Ogilvy, quietly. "Kelly is too sure, too powerfully perfect, too omniscient —"

"And we mortals can't stand that," commented Annan, laughing. "'Raus mit Neville!' He paints joy and sorrow as though he'd never known either —"

And his voice checked itself of its own instinct in the startled silence.

"That man, Neville, has never known the pain of work," said Gail, deliberately. "When he has passed through it and it has made his hand less steady, less omnipotent —"

"That's right. We can't love a man who has never endured what we have," said another. "No genius can hide his own immunity. That man paints with an unscarred soul. A little hell for his — and no living painter could stand beside him."

"Piffle," observed John Burleson.

Ogilvy said: "It is true, I think, that out of human suffering a quality is distilled which affects everything one does. Those who have known sorrow can best depict it — not perhaps most plausibly, but most convincingly — and with fewer accessories, more reticence, and — better taste."

"Why do you want to paint tragedies?" demanded Burleson.

"One need not paint them, John, but one needs to understand them to paint anything else — needs to have lived them, perhaps, to become a master of pictured happiness, physical or spiritual."

"That's piffle, too!" said Burleson in his rumbling bass — "like that damn hen you lugged in —"

A shout of laughter relieved everybody.

"Do you want a fellow to go and poke his head into trouble and get himself mixed up in a tragedy so that he can paint better?" insisted Burleson, scornfully.

"There's usually no necessity to hunt trouble," said Annan.

"But you say that Kelly never had any and that he'd paint better if he had."

"Trouble *might* be the making of Kelly Neville," mused Ogilvy, "and it might not. It depends, John, not on the amount and quality of the hell, but on the man who's frying on the gridiron."

Annan said: "Personally I don't see how Kelly *could* paint happiness or sorrow or wonder or fear into any of his creations anymore convincingly than he does. And yet — and yet — sometimes we love men for their shortcomings — for the sincerity of their blunders — for the fallible humanity in them. That after all is where love starts. The rest — what Kelly shows us — evokes wonder, delight, awe, enthusiasm. . . . If he could only make us love him —"

"*I* love him!" said Burleson.

"We all are inclined to — if we could get near enough to him," said Annan with a faint smile.

"Him — or his work?"

"Both, John. There's a vast amount of nonsense talked about the necessity of separation between a man and his work — that the public has no business with the creator, only with his creations. It is partly true. Still, no man ever created anything in which he did not include a sample of himself — if not what he himself is, at least what he would like to be and what he likes and dislikes in others. No creator who shows his work can hope to remain entirely anonymous. And — I am not yet certain that the public has no right to make its comments on the man who did the work as well as on the work which it is asked to judge."

"The man is nothing; the work everything," quoted Burleson, heavily.

"So I've heard," observed Annan, blandly. "It's rather a precious thought, isn't it, John?"

"Do you consider that statement to be pure piffle?"

"Partly, dear friend. But I'm one of those nobodies who cherish a degenerate belief that man comes first, and then his works, and that the main idea is to get through life as happily as possible with the minimum of inconvenience to others. Human happiness is what I venture to consider more important than the gimcracks created by those same humans. Man first, then man's work, that's the order of mundane importance to me. And if you've got to criticize the work, for God's sake do it with your hand on the man's shoulder."

"Our little socialist," said Ogilvy, patting Annan's blonde head. "He wants to love everybody and everybody to love him, especially when they're ornamental and feminine. Yes? No?" he asked, fondly coddling Annan, who submitted with a bored air and tried to kick his shins.

Later, standing in a chance group on the sidewalk before scattering to their several occupations, Burleson said:

"That's a winner of a model — that Miss West. I used her for the fountain I'm doing for Cardemon's sunken garden. I never saw a model put together as she is. And that's going some."

"She's a dream," said Ogilvy — "*un peu sauvage* — no inclination to socialism there, Annan. I know because I was considering the advisability of bestowing upon her one of those innocent, inadvertent, and fascinatingly chaste salutes — just to break the formality. She wouldn't have it. I'd taken her to the theater, too. Girls are astonishing problems."

"You're a joyous beast, aren't you, Sam?" observed Burleson.

"I may be a trifle joyous. I tried to explain that to her, but she wouldn't listen. Heaven knows my intentions are childlike. I liked her because she's the sort of girl you can take anywhere and not queer yourself if you collide with your fiancée — visiting relative from 'Frisco, you know. She's equipped to impersonate anything from the younger set to the prune and pickle class."

"She certainly is a looker," nodded Annan.

"She can deliver the cultivated goods, too, and make a perfectly good play at the unsophisticated intellectual," said Ogilvy with conviction. "And it's a rare combination to find a dream that looks as real at the Opera as it does in a lobster palace. But she's no socialist, Harry — she'll ride in a taxi with you and sit up half the night with you, but it's nix for getting closer, and the frozen Fownes for the chaste embrace — that's all."

"She's a curious kind of girl," mused Burleson; — "seems perfectly willing to go about with you; — enjoys it like one of those bread-and-butter objects that the department shops call a 'Miss.'"

Annan said: "The girl is unusual, everyway. You don't know where to place her. She's a girl without a caste. I like her. I made some studies from her; Kelly let me."

"Does Kelly own her?" asked Burleson, puffing out his chest.

"He discovered her. He has first call."

Allaire, who had come up, caught the drift of the conversation.

"Oh, hell," he said, in his loud, careless voice, "anybody can take Valerie West to supper. The town's full of her kind."

"Have you taken her anywhere?" asked Annan, casually.

Allaire flushed up: "I haven't had time." He added something which changed the fixed smile on his symmetrical, highly colored face into an expression not entirely agreeable.

"The girl's all right," said Burleson, reddening. "She's damn decent to everybody. What are you talking about, Allaire? Kelly will put a head on you!"

Allaire, careless and assertive, shrugged away the rebuke with a laugh:

"Neville is one of those professional virgins we read about in our neatly manicured fiction. He's what is known as the original mark. Jezebel and Potiphar's wife in combination with Salome and the daughters of Lot couldn't disturb his confidence in them or in himself. And — in my opinion — he paints that way, too." And he went away laughing and swinging his athletic shoulders and twirling his cane, his hat not mathematically straight on his handsome, curly head.

"There strides a joyous bounder," observed Ogilvy.

"Curious," mused Annan. "His family is oldest New York. You see 'em that way, at times."

Burleson, who came from New England, grunted his scorn for Manhattan, ancient or recent, and, nodding a brusque adieu, walked away with ponderous and powerful strides. And the others followed, presently, each in pursuit of his own vocation, Annan and Ogilvy remaining together as their common destination was the big new studio building which they as well as Neville inhabited.

Passing Neville's door they saw it still ajar, and heard laughter and a piano and gay voices.

"Hi!" exclaimed Ogilvy, softly, "let's assist at the festivities. Probably we're not wanted, but does that matter, Harry?"

"It merely adds piquancy to our indiscretion," said Annan, gravely, following him in unannounced — "Oh, hello, Miss West! Was that you playing? Hello, Rita" — greeting a handsome blonde young girl who stretched out a gloved hand to them both and nodded amiably. Then she glanced upward where, perched on his ladder, big palette curving over his left elbow, Neville stood undisturbed by the noise below, outlining great masses of clouds on a canvas where a celestial company, sketched in from models, soared, floated, or hung suspended, cradled in mid air with a vast confusion of wide wings spreading, fluttering, hovering, beating the vast ethereal void, all in pursuit of a single exquisite shape darting up into space.

"What's all that, Kelly? Leda chased by swans?" asked Ogilvy, with all the disrespect of cordial appreciation.

"It's the classic game of follow my Leda," observed Annan.

"Oh — oh!" exclaimed Valerie West, laughing; "such a wretched witticism, Mr. Annan!"

"Your composition is one magnificent vista of legs, Kelly," insisted Ogilvy. "Put pants on those swans."

Neville merely turned and threw an empty paint tube at him, and continued his cloud outlining with undisturbed composure.

"Where have you been, Rita?" asked Ogilvy, dropping into a chair. "Nobody sees you anymore."

"That's because nobody went to the show, and that's why they took it off," said Rita Tevis, resentfully. "I had a perfectly good part which nobody crabbed because nobody wanted it, which suited me beautifully because I hate to have anything that others want. Now there's nothing doing in the millinery line and I'm ready for suggestions."

"Dinner with me," said Ogilvy, fondly. But she turned up her dainty nose:

"Have *you* anything more interesting to offer, Mr. Annan?"

"Only my heart, hand, and Ogilvy's fortune," said Annan, regretfully. "But I believe Archie Allaire was looking for a model of your type —"

"I don't want to pose for Mr. Allaire," said the girl, pouting and twirling the handle of her parasol.

But neither Annan nor Ogilvy could use her then; and Neville had just finished a solid week of her.

"What I'll do," she said with decision, "will be to telephone John Burleson. I never knew him to fail a girl in search of an engagement."

"Isn't he a dear," said Valerie, smiling. "I adore him."

She sat at the piano, running her fingers lightly over the keyboard, listening to what was being said, watching with happy interest everything that was going on around her, and casting an occasional glance over her shoulder and upward to where Neville stood at work.

"John Burleson," observed Rita, looking fixedly at Ogilvy, "is easily the nicest man I know."

"Help!" said Ogilvy, feebly.

Valerie glanced across the top of the piano, laughing, while her hands passed idly here and there over the keys:

"Sam *can* be very nice, Rita; but you've got to make him," she said.

"Did you ever know a really interesting man who didn't require watching?" inquired Annan, mildly.

Rita surveyed him with disdain: "Plenty."

"Don't believe it. No girl has any very enthusiastic use for a man in whom she has perfect confidence."

"Here's another profound observation," added Ogilvy; "when a woman loses confidence in a man she finds a brand-new interest in him. But when a man once really loses confidence in a woman, he never regains it, and it's the beginning of the end. What do you think about that, Miss West?"

Valerie, still smiling, struck a light chord or two, considering:

"I don't know how it would be," she said, "to lose confidence in a man you really care much about. I should think it would break a girl's heart."

"It doesn't," said Rita, with supreme contempt. "You become accustomed to it."

Valerie leaned forward against the keyboard, laughing:

"Oh, Rita!" she said, "what a confession!"

"You silly child," retorted Rita, "I'm twenty-two. Do you think I have the audacity to pretend I've never been in love?"

Ogilvy said with a grin: "How about you, Miss West?" — hoping to embarrass her; but she only smiled gaily and continued to play a light accompaniment to the fugitive air that was running through her head.

"Don't be selfish with your experiences," urged Ogilvy. "Come on, Miss West! 'Raus mit 'em!'"

"What do you wish me to say, Sam?"

"That you've been in love several times."

"But I haven't."

"Not once?"

Her lowered face was still smiling, as her pliant fingers drifted into Grieg's "Spring Song."

"Not one pretty amourette to cheer those twenty-one years of yours?" insisted Ogilvy.

But his only answer was her lowered head and the faint smile edging her lips, and the "Spring Song," low, clear, exquisitely persistent in the hush.

When the last note died out in the stillness Rita emphasized the finish with the ferrule of her parasol and rose with decision:

"I require several new frocks," she said, "and how am I to acquire them unless I pose for somebody? Good-bye, Mr. Neville — bye-bye! Sam — good-bye, Mr. Annan — good-bye, dear," — to Valerie — "if you've nothing better on hand drop in this evening. I've a duck of a new hat."

The girl nodded, and, as Rita Tevis walked out, turning up her nose at Ogilvy who opened the door for her, Valerie glanced up over her shoulder at Neville:

"I don't believe you are going to need me today after all, are you?" she asked.

"No," he said, absently. "I've a lot of things to do. You needn't stay, Miss West."

"Now will you be good!" said Annan, smiling at her with his humorous, bantering air. And to his surprise and discomfiture he saw the least trace of annoyance in her dark eyes.

"Come up to the studio and have a julep," he said with hasty cordiality. "And suppose we dine together at Arrowhead — if you've nothing else on hand —"

She shook her head — the movement was scarcely perceptible. The smile had returned to her lips.

"Won't you, Miss West?"

"Isn't it like you to ask me when you heard Rita's invitation? You're a fraud, Mr. Annan."

"Are you going to sit in that boarding-house parlor and examine Rita's new bonnet all this glorious evening?"

She laughed: "Is there any man on earth who can prophesy what any woman on earth is likely to do? If *you* can, please begin."

Ogilvy, hands clasped behind him, balancing alternately on heels and toes, stood regarding Neville's work. Annan looked up, too, watching Neville where he stood on the scaffolding, busy as always, with the only recreation he cared anything for — work.

"I wish to Heaven I were infected with the bacillus of industry," broke out Ogilvy. "I never come into this place but I see Kelly busily doing something."

"You're an inhuman sort of brute, Kelly!" added Annan. "What do you work that way for — money? If I had my way I'd spend three quarters of my time shooting and fishing and one quarter painting — and I'm as devotedly stuck on art as any healthy man ought to be."

"Art's a bum mistress if she makes you hustle like that!" commented Ogilvy. "Shake her, Kelly. She's a wampire mit a sarpint's tongue!"

"The worst of Kelly is that he'd *rather* paint," said Annan, hopelessly. "It's sufficient to sicken the proverbial cat."

"Get a machine and take us all out to Woodmanston?" suggested Ogilvy. "It's a bee — u — tiful day, dearie!"

"Get out of here!" retorted Neville, painting composedly.

"Your industry saddens us," insisted Annan. "It's only in mediocrity that you encounter industry. Genius frivols; talent takes numerous vacations on itself —"

"And at its own expense," added Valerie, demurely. "I knew a man who couldn't finish his 'Spring Academy' in time: and he had all winter to finish it. But he didn't. Did you ever hear about that man, Sam?"

"Me," said Ogilvy, bowing with hand on heart. "And with that cruel jab from *you* — false fair one — I'll continue heavenward in the elevator. Come on, Harry."

Annan took an elaborate farewell of Valerie which she met in the same mock-serious manner; then she waved a gay and dainty adieu to Ogilvy, and reseated herself after their departure. But this time she settled down into a great armchair facing Neville and his canvas, and lay back extending her arms and resting the back of her head on the cushions.

Whether or not Neville was conscious of her presence below she could not determine, so preoccupied did he appear to be with the work in hand. She lay there in the pleasant, mellow light of the great windows, watching him, at first intently, then, soothed by the soft spring wind that fitfully stirred the hair at her temples, she relaxed her attention, idly contented, happy without any particular reason.

Now and then a pigeon flashed by the windows, sheering away high above the sunlit city. Once, wind-caught, or wandering into unaccustomed heights, high in the blue a white butterfly glimmered, still mounting to infinite altitudes, fluttering, breeze-blown, a silvery speck adrift.

"Like a poor soul aspiring," she thought listlessly, watching with dark eyes over which the lids dropped lazily at moments, only to lift again as her gaze reverted to the man above.

She thought about him, too; she usually did — about his niceness to her, his never-to-be-forgotten kindness; her own gratitude to him for her never-to-be-forgotten initiation.

It seemed scarcely possible that two months had passed
since her novitiate — that two months ago she still knew
nothing of the people, the friendships, the interest, the surcease from loneliness and hopeless apathy, that these new
conditions had brought to her.

Had she known Louis Neville only two months? Did all
this new buoyancy date from two short months' experience
— this quickened interest in life, this happy development of
intelligence so long starved, this unfolding of youth in the
atmosphere of youth? She found it difficult to realize, lying
there so contentedly, so happily, following, with an interest
and appreciation always developing, the progress of the work.

Already, to herself, she could interpret much that she saw
in this new world. Cant phrases, bits of studio lore, artists'
patter, their ways of looking at things, their manners of
expression, their mannerisms, their little vanities, their ideas,
ideals, aspirations, were fast becoming familiar to her. Also
she was beginning to notice and secretly to reflect on their
generic characteristics — their profoundly serious convictions
concerning themselves and their art modified by surface
individualities; their composite lack of humor — exceptions
like Ogilvy and Annan, and even Neville only proving the
rule; their simplicity, running the entire gamut from candor
to stupidity; their patience which was half courage, half a
capacity for suffering; and, in the latter, more womanlike
than like a man.

Simplicity, courage, lack of humor — those appeared to be
the fundamentals characterizing the ensemble — supple-
mented by the extremes of restless intelligence and grim
conservatism.

And the whole fabric seemed to be founded not on industry but on impulse born of sentiment. In this new, busy,
inspiring, delightful world logic became a synthesis erected
upon some inceptive absurdity, carried solemnly to a pictur-
esque and erroneous conclusion.

She had been aware, in stage folk, of the tendency to
sentimental impulse; and she again discovered it in this new
world, in a form slightly modified by the higher average of
reasoning power. In both professions the heart played the
dominant part in creator and creation. The exceptions to the

rule were the few in either profession who might be called distinguished.

Neville had once said to her: "Nothing that amounts to anything in art is ever done accidentally or merely because the person who creates it loves to do it."

She was thinking of this, now, as she lay there watching him.

He had added: "Enthusiasm is excellent while you're dressing for breakfast; but good pictures are painted in cold blood. Go out into the back yard and yell your appreciation of the universe if you want to; but the studio is a silent place; and a blank canvas a mathematical proposition."

Could this be true? Was all the beauty, all the joyous charm, all the splendor of shape and color the result of working out a mathematical proposition? Was this exquisite surety of touch and handling, of mass and line composition, all these lovely depths and vast ethereal spaces superbly peopled, merely the logical result of solving that problem? Was it all clear, limpid, steady, nerveless intelligence; and was nothing due to the chance and hazard of inspiration?

Gladys, the cat, walked in, gently flourishing her tail, hesitated, looked around with narrowing green-jeweled eyes, and, ignoring the whispered invitation and the outstretched hand, leaped lightly to a chair and settled down on a silken cushion, paws and tail folded under her jet-black body.

Valerie reproached her in a whisper, reminding her of past caresses and attentions, but the cat only blinked at her pleasantly.

On a low revolving stand at Valerie's elbow lay a large lump of green modeling wax. This wax Neville sometimes used to fashion, with his facile hands, little figures sketched from his models. These he arranged in groups as though to verify the composition on the canvas before him, and this work and the pliant material which he employed had for her a particular and never-flagging interest. And now, without thinking, purely instinctively, she leaned forward and laid her hand caressingly on the lump of wax. There was something about the yielding, velvety texture that fascinated her, as though in her slim fingers some delicate nerves were responding to the pleasure of contact.

For a while she molded little cubes and pyramids, pinched out bread-crumb chickens and pigs and cats.

"*What* do you think of this little wax kitten, Gladys?" she whispered, holding it up for the cat's inspection. Gladys regarded it without interest and resumed her pleasant contemplation of space.

Valerie, elbows on knees, seated at the revolving stool with all the naïve absorption of a child constructing mud pies, began to make out of the fascinating green wax an image of Gladys dozing.

Time fled away in the studio; intent, absorbed, she pinched little morsels of wax from the lump and pushed them into place with a snowy, pink-tipped thumb, or with the delicate nail of her forefinger removed superfluous material.

Stepping noiselessly so not to disturb Neville she made frequent journeys around to the other side of the cat, sometimes passing sensitive fingers over silky feline contours, which, research inspired a loud purring.

As she worked sometimes she talked under her breath to herself, to Gladys, to Neville:

"I am making a perfectly good cat, Valerie," she whispered. "Gladys, aren't you a little bit flattered? I suppose you think it's honor enough to belong to that man up there on the scaffolding. I imagine it is; he is a very wonderful man, Gladys, very high above us in intellect as he is in body. He doesn't pay very much attention to you and me down here on the floor; he's just satisfied to own us and be amiable to us when he thinks about us.

"I don't mean that in any critical or reproachful sense, Gladys. Don't you dare think I do — not for one moment! Do you hear me? Well then! If you are stupid enough to misunderstand me I'll put a perfectly horrid pair of ears on you. . .! I've made a very dainty pair of ears for you, dear; I only said that to frighten you. You and I like that man up there — tremendously, don't we? And we're very grateful to him for — for a great many happy moments — and for his unfailing kindness and consideration. . . . You don't mind posing for me; *you* wear fur. But I didn't wear anything, dear, when I first sat to him as a novice; and, kitty, I was a fortunate

girl in my choice of the man before whom I was to make a
début. And I —"

The rattle of brushes and the creak of the scaffolding
arrested her: Neville was coming down for a view of his work.

"Hello," he said, pleasantly, noticing for the first time that
she was still in the studio.

"Have I disturbed you, Mr. Neville?"

"Not a bit. You never do anymore than does Gladys." He
glanced absently at the cat, then, facing his canvas, backed
away from it, palette in hand.

For ten minutes he examined his work, shifting his position from minute to minute, until the change of positions
brought him backed up beside Valerie, and his thigh brushing
her arm made him aware of her. Glancing down with smiling
apology his eye fell on the wax, and was arrested. Then he
bent over the work she had done, examining it, twirled the
top of the stool, and inspected it carefully from every side.

"Have you ever studied modeling, Miss West?"

"No," she said, blushing, "you must know that I haven't."
And looked up expecting to see laughter in his eyes; and saw
only the curiosity of interest.

"How did you know how to start this?"

"I have often watched you."

"Is that all the instruction you've ever had in modeling?"

She could not quite bring herself to believe in his pleasant
seriousness:

"Y-yes," she admitted, "except when I have watched John
Burleson. But — this is simply rotten — childish — isn't it?"

"No," he said in a matter of fact tone, "it's interesting."

"Do you really think — mean —"

He looked down at her, considering her while the smile
that she knew and liked best and thought best suited to his
face, began to glimmer; that amused, boyish, bantering smile
hinting of experience and wisdom delightfully beyond her.

"I really think that you're a very unusual girl," he said. "I
don't want to spoil you by telling you so every minute."

"You don't spoil me by telling me so. Sometimes I think
you may spoil me by not telling me so."

"Miss West! You're spoiled already! I'm throwing bouquets at you every minute! You're about the only girl who ever sat for me with whom I talk unreservedly and incessantly."

"Really, Mr. Neville?"

"Yes — really, Mr. Neville," he repeated, laughing — "you bad, spoiled little beauty! You know devilish well that if there's any intellectual space between you and me it's purely a matter of circumstance and opportunity."

"Do you think me silly enough to believe that!"

"I think you clever enough to know it without my telling you."

"I wish you wouldn't say that."

She was still smiling but in the depths of her eyes he felt that the smile was not genuine.

"See here," he said, "I don't want you to think that I don't mean what I say. I do. You're as intelligent a woman as I ever knew. I've known girls more cultivated in general and in particular, but, I say again, that is the hazard of circumstance. Is all clear between us now, Miss West?"

"Yes."

He held out his hand; she glanced up, smiled, and laid her own in it. And they shook hands heartily.

"Good business," he said with satisfaction. "Don't ever let anything threaten our very charming accord. The moment you don't approve of anything I say or do come straight to me and complain — and don't let me divine it in your eyes, Miss West."

"Did you?"

"Certainly I did. Your lips were smiling but in your eyes was something that did not corroborate your lips."

"Yes. . . . But how could you see it?"

"After all," he said, "it's part of my business to notice such things." He seated himself on the arm of her chair and bent over the wax model, his shoulder against hers. And the chance contact meant nothing to either: but what he said about men and things in the world was inevitably arousing the intelligence in her to a gratitude, a happiness, at first timid, then stirring subtly, tremulously, toward passionate response.

No man can do that to a girl and leave the higher side of her indifferent or unresponsive. What he had aroused — what he was awakening every day in her was what he must some day reckon with. Loyalty is born of the spirit, devotion of the mind; and spiritual intelligence arouses fiercer passions than the sensuous emotions born of the flesh.

Leaning there above the table, shoulder to shoulder, his light fingertips caressing the wax model which she had begun, he told her clearly, and with the engaging candor which she already had begun to adore in him, all about what she had achieved in the interesting trifle before them — explained to her wherein she had failed not only to accomplish but to see correctly — wherein she had seen clearly and wrought intelligently.

He might have been talking to a brother sculptor — and therein lay the fascination of this man — for her — that, and the pains he always took with her — which courtesy was only part of him — part of the wonder of this man; of his unerring goodness in all things to her.

Listening, absorbed in all that he said she still was conscious of a parallel thread of thought accompanying — a tiny filament of innocent praise in her heart that chance had given her this man to listen to and to heed and talk to and to think about.

"I won't touch what you've done, Miss West," he said, smilingly; "but just take a pinch of wax — *that* way! — and accent that relaxed flank muscle. . . ! Don't be afraid; watch the shape of the shadows. . . . That's it! Do you see? Never be afraid of dealing vigorously with your subject. Every modification of the first vigorous touch is bound to weaken and sometimes to emasculate. . . . I don't mean for you to parade crudity and bunches of exaggerated muscle as an ultimate expression of vigor. Only the devotee of the obvious is satisfied with that sort of result; and our exhibitions reek with them. But there is no reason why the satin skin and smooth contour of a naked child shouldn't express virility and vigor — no reason why the flawless delicacy of Venus herself should not, if necessary, express violence unexaggerated and without either distortion or lack of finish."

He glanced across at the dozing cat:

"Under that silky black fur there are bones and fibers and muscles. Don't exaggerate them and call your task finished;

merely remember always that they're there framing and pad-
ding the velvet skin. More is done by skillful inference than
by parading every abstract fact you know and translating the
sum-accumulative of your knowledge into the overaccented
concrete. Reticence is a kind of vigor. It can even approach
violence. The mentally garrulous kill their own inspiration.
Inadequacy loves to lump things and gamble with chance for
effective results."

He rose, walked over and examined Gladys, touched her
contemplatively with the button of his mahl-stick, and listened absently to her responsive purr. Then, palette still in
hand, he sat down opposite Valerie, gazing at her in that
detached manner which some mistook for indifference:

"There are, I think, two reasons for failure in art," he said,
"excess of creative emotion, excess of psychological hair-split-
ting. The one produces the normal and lovable failures which,
decorate our art exhibitions; the other results in those curious
products which amuse the public to good-humored contempt
— I mean those pictures full of violent color laid on in streaks,
in great sweeps, in patches, in dots. The painter has turned
half theorist, half scientist; the theories of the juxtaposition
of color, and the science of complementary colors, engrosses
his attention. He is no longer an artist; he is a chemist and
physiologist and an artisan.

"Every now and then there is a revolt from the accepted
order of things. New groups form, sometimes damning what
they call the artificial lighting of the studio, sometimes ex-
claiming against the carnival of harmonious or crude color
generally known as 'plein air.' Impressionists scorn the classic,
and *vice versa*. But, Miss West, as a matter of fact, all schools
are as good as all religions.

"To speak of studio lighting as artificial and unworthy is
silly. It is pretty hard to find anything really artificial in the
world, indoors, or out, or even in the glare of the footlights.
I think the main idea is that a man should prefer doing what
the public calls his work, to any other form of recreation —
should use enough reason — not too much — enough inspiration — but watching himself at every brush stroke; and
finally should feel physically unfettered — that is, have the *a
b c*, the drudgery, the artisan's part of the work at his finger-

tips. Then, if he does what makes him happy, whether in a spirit of realism or romanticism, he can safely leave the rest to Fate."

He looked at her, curiously for a moment, then a smile wholly involuntary broke over his face:

"Lord! What a lecture! And you listened to all that non-sense like an angel!"

The dreamy absorption died out in her eyes; she clasped her hands on her knee, looked down, then up at him almost irritably:

"Please go on, Mr. Neville."

"Not much. I've a few stunts to execute aloft there —"

He contemplated her in amused silence, which became more serious:

"You have talent, Miss West. Artistic talent is not unusual among Americans, but patience is. That is one reason why talent accomplishes so little in this country."

"Isn't another reason that patience is too expensive to be indulged in by talent?"

He laughed: "That is perfectly true. The majority of us have to make a living before we know how."

"Did you have to do that?"

"No, I didn't."

"You were fortunate?"

"Yes. I was — perhaps. . . . I'm not sure."

She touched the lump of green wax gravely, absently. He remained looking at her, busy with his own reflections.

"Would you like to have a chance to study?" he asked.

"Study? What?"

"Sculpture — any old thing! Would you like to try?"

"What chance have I for such expensive amusements as study?" she laughed.

"I'll be responsible for you."

"You?" — in blank surprise.

"I'll attend to the material part of it, if you like. I'll see that you can afford the — patience."

"Mr. Neville, I don't understand."

"What don't you understand?" he asked, lazily humorous.

"Do you mean — that you offer me — an opportunity —"

"Yes; an opportunity to exercise patience. It's an offer, Miss West. But I'm perfectly certain you won't take it."

For a long while she sat, her cheek resting on one palm, looking fixedly into space. Then she stirred, glanced up, blushed vividly, sprang to her feet and crossed to where he sat.

"I've been considering your offer," she said, striving to speak without effort.

"I'll bet you won't accept it!"

"You win your wager, Mr. Neville."

"I wonder why?" he said with his bantering smile: "but I think I know. Talent in America is seldom intellectually ambitious."

To his amazement and vexation tears sprang to her eyes; she said, biting her lower lip: "My ambition is humble. I care — more than anything in the world — to be of use to — to your career."

Taken completely by surprise he said, "Nonsense," and rose to confront her where she stood wholly charming in her nervous, flushed emotion:

"It isn't nonsense, Mr. Neville; it is my happiness.

"I don't believe you realize what your career means to me. I would not willingly consider anything that might interrupt my humble part in it — in this happy companionship. . . . After all, happiness is the essential. You said so once. I am happier here than I possibly could be in an isolation where I might perhaps study — learn —" Her voice broke deliciously as he met her gaze in cool, curious disapproval.

"You *can't* understand it!" she said, flushing almost fiercely. "You can't comprehend what the daily intimacy with a man of your sort has done — is doing for me every moment of my life. How can you understand? You, who have your own place in the world — in life — in this country — in this city! You, who have family, friends, clubs, your social life in city and country, and abroad. Life is very full for you — has always been. But — what I am now learning in contact with you and with the people to whom you have introduced me — is utterly new to me — and — very — pleasant. . . . I have tasted it; I cannot live without it now."

She drew a deep quick breath, then, looking up at him with a tremulous smile:

"What would you think if I told you that, until Sam took me, I had never even been inside a theater except when I was engaged by Schindler? It is perfectly true. Mother did not approve. Until I went with John Burleson I had never ever been in a restaurant; until I was engaged by Schindler I had never seen the city lighted at night — I mean where the theaters and cafés and hotels are. . . . And, Mr. Neville, until I came here to you, I had never had an opportunity to talk to a cultivated man of my own age — I mean the kind of man you are."

She dropped her eyes, considering, while the smile still played faintly with the edges of her lips; then:

"Is it very hard for you to realize that what is an ordinary matter of course to the young of my age is, to me, all a delightful novelty? — that I am enjoying to a perfectly heavenly degree what to you and others may be commonplace and uninteresting? All I ask is to be permitted to enjoy it while I am still young enough. I — I *must!* I really need it, Mr. Neville. It seems, at moments, as if I could never have enough — after the years — where I had — nothing."

Neville had begun walking to and fro in front of her with the quick, decisive step that characterized his movements; but his restlessness seemed only to emphasize the attention he concentrated on every word she spoke; and, though he merely glanced at her from moment to moment, she was conscious that the man now understood, and was responding more directly to her than ever before in their brief and superficial acquaintance.

"I don't want to go away and study," she said. "It is perfectly dear of you to offer it — I — there is no use in trying to thank you —"

"Valerie!"

"What!" she said, startled by his use of her given name for the first time in their acquaintance.

He said, smilingly grave: "You didn't think there was a string attached to anything I offered?"

"A — a string?"

"Did you?"

She blushed hotly: "No, of course not."

"It's all right then," he nodded; but she began to think of that new idea in a confused, startled, helpless sort of way.

"How could you think *that* of me?" she faltered.

"I didn't —"

"You — it must have been in your mind —"

"I wanted to be sure it wasn't in *yours* —"

"You ought to have known! Haven't you learned anything at all about me in two months?"

"Do you think any man can learn anything about anybody in two months?" he asked, lightly.

"Yes, I do. I've learned a good deal about you — enough, anyway, not to attribute anything — unworthy —"

"You silly child; you've learned nothing about me if that's what you think you've discovered."

"I *have* discovered it!" she retorted, tremulously; "I've learned horrid things about other men, too — and they're not like you!"

"Valerie! Valerie! I'm precisely like all the rest — my selfishness is a little more concentrated than theirs, that's the only difference. For God's sake don't make a god of me."

She sat down on the head of the sofa, looking straight at him, pretty head lowered a trifle so that her gaze was accented by the lovely level of her brows:

"I've long wanted to have a thorough talk with you," she said. "Have you got time now?"

He hesitated, controlling his secret amusement under an anxious gravity as he consulted the clock.

"Suppose you give me an hour on those figures up there? The light will be too poor to work by in another hour. Then we'll have tea and 'thorough talks.'"

"All right," she said, calmly.

He picked up palette and mahl-stick and mounted to his perch on the scaffolding; she walked slowly into the farther room, stood motionless a moment, then raising both arms she began to unhook the collar of her gown.

When she was ready she stepped into her sandals, threw the white wool robe over her body, and tossed one end across her bare shoulder.

He descended, aided her aloft to her own aerie, walked across the planking to his own, and resumed palette and brushes in excellent humor with himself, talking gaily while he was working:

"I'm devoured by curiosity to know what that 'thorough talk' of yours is going to be about. You and I, in our briefly connected careers, have discussed every subject on earth, gravely or flippantly, and what in the world this 'thorough talk' is going to resemble is beyond me —"

"It might have to do with your lack of ceremony — a few minutes ago," she said, laughing at him.

"My — what?"

"Lack of ceremony. You called me Valerie."

"You can easily revenge that presumption, you know."

"I think I will — Kelly."

He smiled as he painted:

"I don't know why the devil they call me Kelly," he mused. "No episode that I ever heard of is responsible for that Milesian misnomer. *Quand même!* It sounds prettier from you than it ever did before. I'd rather hear you call me Kelly than Caruso sing my name as Algernon."

"Shall I really call you Kelly?"

"Sure thing! Why not?"

"I don't know. You're rather celebrated — to have a girl call you Kelly."

He puffed out his chest in pretence of pompous satisfaction:

"True, child. Good men are scarce — but the good and great are too nearly extinct for such familiarity. Call me *Mr.* Kelly."

"I won't. You are only a big boy, anyway — Louis Neville — and sometimes I shall call you Kelly, and sometimes Louis, and very occasionally Mr. Neville."

"All right," he said, absently — "only hold that distractingly ornamental head and those incomparable shoulders a trifle more steady, please — rest solidly on the left leg — let the right hip fall into its natural position — *that's* it. Thank you."

Holding the pose her eyes wandered from him and his canvas to the evening tinted clouds already edged with deeper gold. Through the sheet of glass above she saw a shred of white fleece in mid-heaven turn to a pale pink.

"I wonder why you asked me to tea?" she mused.

"What?" He turned around to look at her.

"You never before asked me to do such a thing," she said, candidly. "You're an absent-minded man, Mr. Neville."

"It never occurred to me," he retorted, amused. "Tea is weak-minded."

"It occurred to me. That's what part of my 'thorough talk' is to be about; your carelessness in noticing me except professionally."

He continued working, rapidly now; and it seemed to her as though something — a hint of the somber — had come into his face — nothing definite — but the smile was no longer there, and the brows were slightly knitted.

Later he glanced up impatiently at the sky: the summer clouds wore a deeper rose and gold.

"We'd better have our foolish tea," he said, abruptly, driving his brushes into a bowl of black soap and laying aside his palette for his servant to clean later.

For a while, not noticing her, he fussed about his canvas, using a knife here, a rag there, passing to and fro across the scaffolding, oblivious of the flight of time, until at length the waning light began to prophesy dusk, and he came to himself with a guilty start.

Below, in the studio, Valerie sat, fully dressed except for hat and gloves, head resting in the padded depths of an armchair, watching him in silence.

"I declare," he said, looking down at her contritely, "I never meant to keep you all this time. Good Lord! Have I been puttering up here for an hour and a half! It's nearly eight o'clock! Why on earth didn't you speak to me, Valerie?"

"It's a braver girl than I am who'll venture to interrupt you at work, Kelly," she said, laughingly. "I'm a little afraid of you."

"Nonsense! I wasn't doing anything. My Heaven! — *can* it be eight o'clock?"

"It is. . . . You *said* we were going to have tea."

"Tea! Child, you can't have tea at eight o'clock! I'm terribly sorry" — he came down the ladder, vexed with himself, wiping the paint from his hands with a bunch of cheese cloth — "I'm humiliated and ashamed, Miss West. Wait a moment —"

He walked hastily through the next room into his small
suite of apartments, washed his hands, changed his painter's
linen blouse for his street coat, and came back into the dim
studio.

"I'm really sorry, Valerie," he said. "It was rotten rude of
me."

"So am I sorry. It's absurd, but I feel like a perfectly
unreasonable kid about it. . . . You never before asked me —
and I — wanted to — stay — so much —"

"Why didn't you remind me, you foolish child!"

"Somehow I couldn't. . . . I wanted *you* to think of it."

"Well, I'm a chump. . . ." He stood before her in the dim
light; she still reclined in the armchair, not looking at him,
one arm crook'd over her head and the fingers closed tightly
over the rosy palm which was turned outward, resting across
her forehead.

For a few moments neither spoke; then:

"I'm horridly lonely tonight," she said, abruptly.

"Why, Valerie! What a — an unusual —"

"I want to talk to you. . . . I suppose you are too hungry
to want to talk now."

"N-no, I'm not." He began to laugh: "What's the matter,
Valerie? What is on your mind? Have you any serious fidgets,
or are you just a spoiled, pretty girl?"

"Spoiled, Kelly. There's nothing really the matter. I just felt
like — what you asked me to do —"

She jumped up suddenly, biting her lips with vexation: "I
don't know what I'm saying — except that it's rather rude of
me — and I've got to go home. Good-night — I think my hat
is in the dressing-room —"

He stood uneasily watching her pin it before the mirror;
he could just see her profile and the slender, busy hands white
in the dusk.

When she returned, slowly drawing on her long gloves, she
said to him with composure:

"Some day ask me again. I really would like it — if you
would."

"Do you really think that you could stand the excitement
of taking a cup of weak tea with me," he said, jestingly —

"after all those jolly dinners and suppers and theaters and motor parties that I hear about?"

She nodded and held out her hand with decision:

"Good-night."

He retained her hand a moment, not meaning to — not really intending to ask her what he did ask her. And she raised her velvet eyes gravely:

"Do you really want me?"

"Yes. . . . I don't know why I never asked you before —"

"It was absurd not to," she said, impulsively; "I'd have gone anywhere with you the first day I ever knew you! Besides, I dress well enough for you not to be ashamed of me."

He began to laugh: "Valerie, you funny little thing! You funny, funny little thing!"

"Not in the slightest," she retorted, sedately. "I'm having a heavenly time for the first time in my life, and I have so wanted you to be part of it . . . of course you *are* part of it," she added, hastily — "most of it! I only meant that I — I'd like to be a little in your other life — have you enter mine, a little — just so I can remember, in years to come, an evening with you now and then — to see things going on around us — to hear what you think of things that we see together. . . . Because, with you, I feel so divinely free, so unembarrassed, so entirely off my guard. . . . I don't mean to say that I don't have a splendid time with the others even when I have to watch them; I do — and even the watching is fun —"

The childlike audacity and laughing frankness, the confidence of her attitude toward him were delightfully refreshing. He looked into her pretty, eager, engaging face, smiling, captivated.

"Valerie," he said, "tell me something — will you?"

"Yes, if I can."

"I'm more or less of a painting machine. I've made myself so, deliberately — to the exclusion of other interests. I wonder" — he looked at her musingly — "whether I'm carrying it too far for my own good."

"I don't understand."

"I mean — is there anything machine-made about my work? Does it lack — does it lack anything?"

"No!" she said, indignantly loyal. "Why do you ask me that?"

"People — some people say it does lack — a certain quality."

She said with supreme contempt: "You must not believe them. I also hear things — and I know it is an unworthy jealousy that —"

"What have you heard?" he interrupted.

"Absurdities. I don't wish even to think of them —"

"I wish you to. Please. Such things are sometimes significant."

"But — is there any significance in what a few envious artists say — or a few silly models —"

"More significance in what they say than in a whole chorus of professional critics."

"Are you serious?" she asked, astonished.

"Perfectly. Without naming anybody or betraying any confidence, what have you heard in criticism of my work? It's from models and brother painters that the real truth comes — usually distorted, half told, maliciously hinted sometimes — but usually the germ of truth is to be found in what they say, however they may choose to say it."

Valerie leaned back against the door, hands clasped behind her, eyebrows bent slightly inward in an unwilling effort to remember.

Finally she said impatiently: "They don't know what they're talking about. They all say, substantially, the same thing —"

"What is that thing?"

"Why — oh, it's too silly to repeat — but they say there is nothing lovable about your work — that it's inhumanly and coldly perfect — too — too —" she flushed and laughed uncertainly — "'too damn omniscient' is what one celebrated man said. And I could have boxed his large, thin, celebrated ears for him!"

"Go on," he nodded; "what else do they say?"

"Nothing. That's all they can find to say — all they dare say. You know what they are — what other men are — and some of the younger girls, too. Not that I don't like them — and they are very sweet to me — only they're not like you —"

"They're more human. Is that it, Valerie?"

"No, I don't mean that!"

"Yes, you do. You mean that the others take life in a perfectly human manner — find enjoyment, amusement in each other, in a hundred things outside of their work. They act like men and women, not like a painting machine; if they experience impulses and emotions they don't entirely stifle 'em. They have time and leisure to foregather, laugh, be silly, discuss, banter, flirt, make love, and cut up all the various harmless capers that humanity is heir to. *That's* what you mean, but you don't realize it. And you think, and they think, that my solemn and owlish self-suppression is drying me up, squeezing out of me the essence of that warm, lovable humanity in which, they say, my work is deficient. They say, too, that my inspiration is lacking in that it is not founded on personal experience; that I have never known any deep emotion, any suffering, any of the sterner, darker regrets — anything of that passion which I sometimes depict. They say that the personal and convincing element is totally absent because I have not lived" — he laughed — "and loved; that my work lacks the one thing which only the self-knowledge of great happiness and great pain can lend to it. . . . And — I think they are right, Valerie. What do you think?"

The girl stood silent, with lowered eyes, reflecting for a moment. Then she looked up curiously.

"*Have* you never been very unhappy?"

"I had a toothache once."

She said, unsmiling: "Haven't you ever suffered mentally?"

"No — not seriously. Oh, I've regretted little secret meannesses — bad temper, jealousy —"

"Nothing else? Have you never experienced deep unhappiness — through death, for example?"

"No, thank God. My father and mother and sister are living. . . . It is rather strange," he added, partly to himself, "that the usual troubles and sorrows have so far passed me by. I am twenty-seven; there has never been a death in my family, or among my intimate friends."

"Have you any intimate friends?"

"Well — perhaps not — in the strict sense. I don't confide."

"Have you never cared, very much, for anybody — any woman?"

"Not sentimentally," he returned, laughing. "Do you think that a good course of modern flirtation — a thorough schooling in the old-fashioned misfortunes of true love would inject into my canvases that elusively occult quality they're all howling for?"

She remained smilingly silent.

"Perhaps something less strenuous would do," he said, mischievously — "a pretty amourette? — just one of those gay, frivolous, Louis XV affairs with some daintily receptive girl, not really improper, but only ultra fashionable. Do you think *that* would help some, Valerie?"

She raised her eyes, still smiling, a little incredulous, very slightly embarrassed:

"I don't think your painting requires any such sacrifices of you, Mr. Neville. . . . Are you going to take me somewhere to dinner? I'm dreadfully hungry."

"You poor little girl, of course I am. Besides, you must be suffering under the terrible suppression of that 'thorough talk' which you —"

"It doesn't really require a thorough talk," she said; "I'll tell you now what I had to say. No, don't interrupt, please! I want to — please let me — so that nothing will mar our enjoyment of each other and of the gay world around us when we are dining. . . . It is this: Sometimes — once in a while — I become absurdly lonely, which makes me a fool, temporarily. And — will you let me telephone you at such times? — just to talk to you — perhaps see you for a minute?"

"Of course. You know my telephone number. Call me up whenever you like."

"*Could* I see you at such moments? I — there's a — some — a kind of sentiment about me — when I'm *very* lonely; and I've been foolish enough to let one or two men see it — in fact I've been rather indiscreet — silly — with a man — several men — now and then. A lonely girl is easily sympathized with — and rather likes it; and is inclined to let herself go a little. . . . I don't want to. . . . And at times I've done it. . . . Sam Ogilvy nearly kissed me, which really doesn't count — does it? But I let Harry Annan do it, once. . . . If I'm weak enough to drift into such silliness I'd better find a safeguard. I've been thinking — thinking — that it really does originate in a sort of foolish loneliness . . . not in anything worse. So I thought I'd have a thorough talk with you about it. I'm twenty-one — with all my experience of life and of men crowded into a single winter and spring. I have as friends only the few people I have met through you. I have nobody to see unless I see them — nowhere to go unless I go where they ask me. . . . So I thought I'd ask you to let me depend a little on you, sometimes — as a refuge from isolation and morbid thinking now and then. And from other mischief — for which I apparently have a capacity — to judge by what I've done — and what I've let men do already."

She laid her hand lightly on his arm in sudden and impulsive confidence:

"That's my 'thorough talk.' I haven't anyone else to tell it to. And I've told you the worst." She smiled at him adorably: "And now I am ready to go out with you," she said, — "go anywhere in the world with you, Kelly. And I am going to be perfectly happy — if you are."

Chapter III

One day toward the middle of June Valerie did not arrive on time at the studio. She had never before been late.

About two o'clock Sam Ogilvy sauntered in, a skull pipe in his mouth, his hair rumpled:

"It's that damn mermaid of mine," he said, "can't you come up and look at her and tell me what's the trouble, Kelly?"

"Not now. Who's posing?"

"Rita. She's in a volatile humor, too — fidgets; denies fidgeting; reproaches me for making her keep quiet; says I draw like a bum chimney — no wonder my work's rotten! Besides, she's in a tub of water, wearing that suit of fish-scales I had made for Violet Cliland, and she says it's too tight and she's tired of the job, anyway. Fancy my mental condition."

"Oh, she won't throw you down. Rita is a good sport," said Neville.

"I hope so. It's an important picture. Really, Kelly, it's great stuff — a still, turquoise-tinted pool among wet rocks; ebb tide; a corking little mermaid caught in a pool left by the receding waves — all tones and subtle values," he declared, waving his arm.

"Don't paint things in the air with your thumb," said Neville, coldly. "No wonder Rita is nervous."

"Rita is nervous," said Ogilvy, "because she's been on a bat and supped somewhere until the coy and rosy dawn chased her homeward. And your pretty paragon, Miss West, was with the party —"

"What?" said Neville, sharply.

"Sure thing! Harry Annan, Rita, Burleson, Valerie — and I don't know who else. They feasted somewhere east of Coney — where the best is like the würst — and ultimately became full of green corn, clams, watermelon, and assorted fidgets. . . . Can't you come up and look at my picture?"

Neville got up, frowning, and followed Ogilvy upstairs.

Rita Tevis, swathed in a blanket from which protruded a dripping tinseled fish's tail, sat disconsolately on a chair, knitting a red-silk necktie for some party of the second part, as yet unidentified.

"Mr. Neville," she said, "Sam has been quarreling with me every minute while I'm doing my best in that horrid tub of water. If anybody thinks it's a comfortable pose, let them try it! I wish — I *wish* I could have the happiness of seeing Sam afloat in this old fish-scale suit with every spangle sticking into him and his legs cramped into this unspeakable tail!"

She extended a bare arm, shook hands, pulled up her blanket wrap, and resumed her knitting with a fierce glance at Ogilvy, who had attempted an appealing smile.

Neville stood stock-still before the canvas. The picture promised well; it was really beautiful — the combined result of several outdoor studies now being cleverly worked up. But Ogilvy's pictures never kept their promise.

"Also," observed Rita, reproachfully, "*I* posed *en plein air* for those rainbow sketches of his — and though it was a lonely cove with a cunningly secluded little crescent beach, I was horribly afraid of somebody coming — and besides I got most cruelly sunburned —"

"Rita! You *said* you enjoyed that excursion!" exclaimed Ogilvy, with pathos.

"I said it to flatter that enormous vanity of yours, Sam. I had a perfectly wretched time."

"What sort of a time did you have last evening?" inquired Neville, turning from the picture.

"Horrid. Everybody ate too much, and Valerie spooned with a new man — I don't remember his name. She went out in a canoe with him and they sang 'She kissed him on the gangplank when the boat moved out.'"

Neville, silent, turned to the picture once more. In a low rapid voice he indicated to Ogilvy where matters might be differently treated, stepped back a few paces, nodded decisively, and turned again to Rita:

"I've been waiting for Miss West," he said. "Have you any reason to think that she might not keep her appointment this morning?"

"She had a headache when we got home," said Rita. "She stayed with me last night. I left her asleep. Why don't you ring her up. You know my number."

"All right," said Neville, shortly, and went out.

When he first tried to ring her up the wire was busy. It was a party wire, yet a curious uneasiness set him pacing the studio, smoking, brows knitted, until he decided it was time to try again.

This time he recognized her distant voice: "Hello — hello! *Is* that you, Mr. Neville?"

"Valerie!"

"Oh, it *is* you, Kelly? I hoped you would call me up. I *knew* it must be *you!*"

"Yes, it is. What the deuce is the matter? Are you ill?"

"Oh, dear, no.'"

"What, then?"

"I was *so* sleepy, Kelly. Please forgive me. We had such a late party — and it was daylight before I went to bed. Please forgive me; won't you?"

"When I called you a few minutes ago your wire was busy. Were you conversing?"

"Yes. I was talking to José Querida."

"H'm!"

"José was with us last evening. . . . I went canoeing with him. He just called me up to ask how I felt."

"Hunh!"

"What?"

"Nothing."

"Are you annoyed, Louis?"

"No!"

"Oh, I thought it sounded as though you were irritated. I am so ashamed at having overslept. Who told you I was here? Oh, Rita, I suppose. Poor child, she was more faithful than I. The alarm clock woke her and she was plucky enough to

get up — and I only yawned and thought of you, and I was
so sleepy! Are you sure you do forgive me?"

"Of course."

"You don't say it very kindly."

"I mean it cordially," he snapped. He could hear her sigh:
"I suppose you do." Then she added:

"I am dressing, Kelly. I don't wish for any breakfast, and
I'll come to the studio as soon as I can —"

"Take your breakfast first!"

"No, I really don't care for —"

"All right. Come ahead."

"I will. Good-bye, Kelly, dear."

He rang off, picked up the telephone again, called the great
Hotel Regina, and ordered breakfast sent to his studio immediately.

When Valerie arrived she found silver, crystal, and snowy
linen awaiting her with chilled grapefruit, African melon,
fragrant coffee, toast, and pigeon's eggs poached on Astra-
khan caviar.

"Oh, Louis!" she exclaimed, enraptured; "I don't deserve
this — but it is perfectly dear of you — and I *am* hungry. . . !
Good-morning," she added, shyly extending a fresh cool
hand; "I am really none the worse for wear you see."

That was plain enough. In her fresh and youthful beauty
the only sign of the night's unwisdom was in the scarcely
perceptible violet tint under her thick lashes. Her skin was
clear and white and dewy fresh, her dark eyes unwearied —
her gracefully slender presence fairly fragrant with health and
vigor.

She seated herself — offered to share with him in dumb
appeal, urged him in delicious pantomime, and smiled en-
couragingly as he reluctantly found a chair beside her and
divided the magnificent melon.

"Did you have a good time?" he asked, trying not to speak
ungraciously.

"Y-yes. . . . It was a silly sort of a time."

"Silly?"

"I was rather sentimental — with Querida."

He said nothing — grimly.

"I told you last night, Louis. Why couldn't you see me?"

"I was dining out; I couldn't."

She sipped her chilled grapefruit meditatively:

"I hadn't seen you for a week," she laughed, glancing sideways at him, "and that lonely feeling began about five o'clock; and I called you up at seven because I couldn't stand it. . . . But you wouldn't see me; and so when Rita and the others came in a big touring car — do you blame me very much for going with them?"

"No."

Her expression became serious, a trifle appealing:

"My room isn't very attractive," she said, timidly. "It is scarcely big enough for the iron bed and one chair — and I get so tired trying to read or sew every evening by the gas — and it's very hot in there."

"Are you making excuses for going?"

"I do not know. . . . Unless people ask me, I have nowhere to go except to my room; and when a girl sits there evening after evening alone it — it is not very gay."

She tried the rich, luscious melon with much content, and presently her smile came back:

"Louis, it was a funny party. To begin we had one of those terrible clambakes — like a huge, horrid feast of the Middle Ages — and it did not agree with everybody — or perhaps it was because we weren't middle-aged — or perhaps it was just the beer. I drank water; so did the beautiful José Querida. . . . I think he is pretty nearly the handsomest man I ever saw; don't you?"

"He's handsome, cultivated, a charming conversationalist, and a really great painter," said Neville, dryly.

She looked absently at the melon; tasted it: "He is very romantic . . . when he laughs and shows those beautiful, even teeth. . . . He's really quite adorable, Kelly — and so gentle and considerate —"

"That's the Latin in him."

"His parents were born in New York."

She sipped her coffee, tried a pigeon egg, inquired what it was, ate it, enchanted.

"How thoroughly nice you always are to me, Kelly!" she said, looking up in the engagingly fearless way characteristic of her when with him.

"Isn't everybody nice to you?" he said with a shrug which escaped her notice.

"Nice?" She colored a trifle and laughed. "Not in *your* way, Kelly. In the sillier sense they are — some of them."

"Even Querida?" he said, carelessly.

"Oh, just like other men — generously ready for any event. What self-sacrificing opportunists men are! After all, Kelly," she added, slipping easily into the vernacular, "it's always up to the girl."

"Is it?"

"Yes, I think so. I knew perfectly well that I had no business to let Querida's arm remain around me. But — there was a moon, Kelly."

"Certainly."

"Why do you say 'certainly'?"

"Because there *was* one."

"But you say it in a manner —" She hesitated, continued her breakfast in leisurely reflection for a while, then:

"Louis?"

"Yes."

"Am I too frank with you?"

"Why?"

"I don't know; I was just thinking. I tell you pretty nearly everything. If I didn't have you to tell — have somebody —" She considered, with brows slightly knitted — "if I didn't have *somebody* to talk to, it wouldn't be very good for me. I realize that."

"You need a grandmother," he said, dryly; "and I'm the closest resemblance to one procurable."

The imagery struck her as humorous and she laughed.

"Poor Kelly," she said aloud to herself, "he is used and abused and imposed upon, and in revenge he offers his ungrateful tormentor delicious breakfasts. *What* shall his reward be? — or must he await it in Paradise where he truly belongs amid the martyrs and the blessed saints!"

Neville grunted.

"Oh, *oh!* such a post-Raphaelite scowl! Job won't bow to you when you go aloft, Kelly. Besides, polite martyrs smile pleasantly while enduring torment. . . . What are you going to do with me today?" she added, glancing around with frank curiosity at an easel which was set with a full-length virgin canvas.

"Portrait," he replied, tersely.

"Oh," she said, surprised. He had never before painted her clothed.

From moment to moment, as she leisurely breakfasted, she glanced around at the canvas, interested in the new idea of his painting her draped; a trifle perplexed, too.

"Louis," she said, "I don't quite see how you're ever going to find a purchaser for just a plain portrait of me."

He said, irritably: "I don't have to work for a living *every* minute, do I? For Heaven's sake give me a day off to study."

"But — it seems like wasted time —"

"What is wasted time?"

"Why just to paint a portrait of me as I am. Isn't it?" She looked up smilingly, perfectly innocent of any self-consciousness. "In the big canvases for the Byzantine Theater you always made my features too radiant, too glorious for portraits. It seems rather a slump to paint me as I am — just a girl in street clothes."

A singular expression passed over his face.

"Yes," he said, after a moment — "just a girl in street clothes. No clouds, no sky, no diaphanous draperies of silk; no folds of cloth of gold; no gemmed girdles, no jewels. Nothing of the old glamour, the old glory; no sunburst laced with mist; no 'light that never was on sea or land' . . . Just a young girl standing in the half light of my studio. . . . And by God! — if I can not do it — the rest is worthless."

Amazed at his tone and expression she turned quickly, set back her cup, remained gazing at him, bewildered by the first note of bitterness she had ever heard in his voice.

He had risen and walked to his easel, back partly turned. She saw him fussing with his palette, colors, and brushes, watched him for a few moments, then she went away into the farther room where she had a glass shelf to herself with toilet requisites — a casual and dainty gift from him.

When she returned he was still bending over his color-table; and she walked up and laid her hand on his shoulder — not quite understanding why she did it.

He straightened up to his full stature, surprised, turning his head to meet a very clear, very sweetly disturbed gaze.

"Kelly, dear, are you unhappy?"

"Why — no."

"You seem to be a little discontented."

"I hope I am. It's a healthy sign."

"Healthy?"

"Certainly. The satisfied never get anywhere. . . . That Byzanite business has begun to wear on my nerves."

"Thousands and thousands of people have gone to see it, and have praised it. You know what the papers have been saying —"

Under her light hand she felt the impatient movement of his shoulders, and her hand fell away.

"Don't you care for it, now that it's finished?" she asked, wondering.

"I'm devilish sick of it," he said, so savagely that every nerve in her recoiled with a tiny shock. She remained silent, motionless, awaiting his pleasure. He set his palette, frowning. She had never before seen him like this.

After a while she said, quietly: "If you are waiting for me, please tell me what you expect me to do, because I don't know, Kelly."

"Oh, just stand over there," he said, vaguely; "just walk about and stop anywhere when you feel like stopping."

She walked a few steps at hazard, partly turned to look back at him with a movement adorable in its hesitation.

"Don't budge!" he said, brusquely.

"Am I to remain like this?"

"Exactly."

He picked up a bit of white chalk, went over to her, knelt down, and traced on the floor the outline of her shoes.

Then he went back, and, with his superbly cool assurance, began to draw with his brush upon the untouched canvas.

From where she stood, and as far as she could determine, he seemed, however, to work less rapidly than usual — with a trifle less decision — less precision. Another thing she noticed; the calm had vanished from his face. The vivid animation, the cool self-confidence, the half indolent relapse into careless certainty — all familiar phases of the man as she had so often seen him painting — were now not perceptible. There seemed to be, too, a curious lack of authority about his brush strokes at intervals — moments of grave perplexity, indecision almost resembling the hesitation of inexperience — and for the first time she saw in his grey eyes the narrowing concentration of mental uncertainty.

It seemed to her sometimes as though she were looking at a total stranger. She had never thought of him as having any capacity for the ordinary and lesser ills, vanities, and vexations — the trivial worries that beset other artists.

"Louis?" she said, full of curiosity.

"What?" he demanded, ungraciously.

"You are not one bit like yourself today."

He made no comment. She ventured again:

"Do I hold the pose properly?"

"Yes, thanks," he said, absently.

"May I talk?"

"I'd rather you didn't, Valerie, just at present."

"All right," she rejoined, cheerfully; but her pretty eyes watched him very earnestly, a little troubled.

When she was tired the pose ended; that had been their rule; but long after her neck and back and thighs and limbs begged for relief, she held the pose, reluctant to interrupt him. When at last she could endure it no longer she moved; but her right leg had lost not only all sense of feeling but all power to support her; and down she came with a surprised and frightened little exclamation — and he sprang to her and swung her to her feet again.

"Valerie! You bad little thing! Don't you know enough to stop when you're tired?"

"I — didn't know I was so utterly gone," she said, bewildered.

He passed his arm around her and supported her to the sofa where she sat, demure, a little surprised at her collapse, yet shyly enjoying his disconcerted attentions to her.

"It's your fault, Kelly. You had such a queer expression — not at all like you — that I tried harder than ever to help you — and fell down for my pains."

"You're an angel," he said, contritely, "but a silly one."

"A scared one, Kelly — and a fallen one." She laughed, flexing the muscles of her benumbed leg: "Your expression intimidated me. I didn't recognize you; I could not form any opinion of what was going on inside that very stern and frowning head of yours. If you look like that I'll never dare call you Kelly."

"Did I seem inhuman?"

"N-no. On the contrary — very human — ordinary — like the usual ill-tempered artist man, with whom I have learned how to deal. You know," she added, teasingly, "that you are calm and godlike, usually — and when you suddenly became a mere mortal —"

"I'll tell you what I'll do with you," he said; "I'll pick you up and put you to bed."

"I wish you would, Kelly. I haven't had half enough sleep."

He sat down beside her on the sofa: "Don't talk anymore of that godlike business," he growled, "or I'll find the proper punishment."

"Would *you* punish *me*, Kelly?"

"I sure would."

"If I displeased you?"

"You bet."

"Really?" She turned partly toward him, half in earnest. "Suppose — suppose —" but she stopped suddenly, with a light little laugh that lingered pleasantly in the vast, still room.

She said: "I begin to think that there are two Kellys — no, *one* Kelly and *one* Louis. Kelly is familiar to me; I seem to have known him all my life — the happy part of my life. Louis I have just seen for the first time — there at the easel, painting, peering from me to his canvas with Kelly's good-looking eyes all narrow with worry —"

"What on earth are you chattering about, Valerie?"

"You and Kelly. . . . I don't quite know which I like best — the dear, sweet, kind, clever, brilliant, impersonal, godlike Kelly, or this new Louis — so very abrupt in speaking to me —"

"Valerie, dear! Forgive me. I'm out of sorts somehow. It began — I don't know — waiting for you — wondering if you could be ill — all alone. Then that ass, Sam Ogilvy — oh, it's just oversmoking I guess, or — I don't know what."

She sat regarding him, head tipped unconsciously on one side in an attitude suggesting a mind concocting malice.

"Louis?"

"What?"

"You're very attractive when you're godlike —"

"You little wretch!"

"But — you're positively dangerous when you're human."

"Valerie! I'll —"

"The great god Kelly, or the fascinating, fearsome, erring Louis! Which is it to be? I've an idea that the time is come to decide!"

Fairly radiating a charming aura of malice she sat back, nursing one knee, distractingly pretty and defiant, saying: "I *will* call you a god if I like!"

"I'll tell you what, Valerie," he said, half in earnest; "I've played grandmother to you long enough, by Heck!"

"Oh, Kelly, be lofty and Olympian! Be a god and shame the rest of us!"

"I'll shamefully resemble one of 'em in another moment if you continue tormenting me!"

"Which one, great one?"

"Jupiter, little lady. He was the boss philanderer you know."

"What is a philanderer, my Olympian friend?"

"Oh, one of those Olympian divinities who always began the day by kissing the girls all around."

"Before breakfast?"

"Certainly."

"It's — after breakfast, Kelly."

"Luncheon and dinner still impend."

"Besides — I'm not a bit lonely today. . . . I'm afraid I wouldn't let you, Kel — I mean Louis."

"Why didn't you say 'Kelly'?"

"Kelly is too godlike to kiss."

"Oh! So *that's* the difference! Kelly isn't human; Louis is."

"Kelly, to me," she admitted, "is practically kissless. . . . I haven't thought about Louis in that regard."

"Consider the matter thoroughly."

"Do you wish me to?" She bent her head, smiling. Then, looking up with enchanting audacity:

"I really don't know, Mr. Neville. Some day when I'm lonely — and if Louis is at home and Kelly is out — you and I might spend an evening together on a moonlit lake and see how much of a human being Louis can be."

She laughed, watching him under the dark lashes, charming mouth mocking him in every curve.

"Do you think you're likely to be lonely tonight?" he asked, surprised at the slight acceleration of his pulses.

"No, I don't. Besides, you'd be only the great god Kelly to me this evening. Besides that I'm going to dinner with Querida, and afterward we're going to see the 'Joy of the Town' at the Folly Theater."

"I didn't know," he said, curtly. For a few moments he sat there, looking interestedly at a familiar door-knob. Then rising: "Do you feel all right for posing?"

"Yes."

"Alors —"

"Allons, mon dieu!" she laughed.

Work began. She thought, watching him with sudden and unexpected shyness, that he seemed even more aloof, more preoccupied, more worried, more intent than before. In this new phase the man she had known as a friend was now entirely gone, vanished! Here stood an utter stranger, very human, very determined, very deeply perplexed, very much in earnest. Everything about this man was unknown to her. There seemed to be nothing about him that particularly appealed to her confidence, either; yet the very uncertainty was interesting her now — intensely.

This other phase of his dual personality had been so completely a surprise that, captivated, curious, she could keep neither her gaze from him nor her thoughts. Was it that she was going to miss in him the other charm, lose the delight in his speech, his impersonal and kindly manner, miss the comfortable security she had enjoyed with him, perhaps after some half gay, half sentimental conflict with lesser men?

What was she to expect from this brand-new incarnation of Louis Neville? The delightful indifference, fascinating absent-mindedness and personal neglect of the other phase? Would he be god enough to be less to her, now? Man enough to be more than other men? For a moment she had a little shrinking, a miniature panic lest this man turn too much like other men. But she let her eyes rest on him, and knew he would not. Whatever Protean changes might yet be reserved for her to witness, she came to the conclusion that this man was a man apart, different, and would not disappoint her no matter what he turned into.

She thought to herself: "If I want Kelly to lean on, he'll surely appear, godlike, impersonally nice, and kindly as ever; if I want Louis to torment and provoke and flirt with — a little — a very little — I'm quite sure he'll come, too. Whatever else is contained in Mr. Neville I don't know; but I like him separately and compositely, and I'm happy when I'm with him."

With which healthy conclusion she asked if she might rest, and came around to look at the canvas.

As she had stood in silence for some time, he asked her, a little nervously, what she thought of it.

"Louis — I don't know."

"Is your opinion unfavorable?"

"N-no. I *am* like that, am I not?"

"In a shadowy way. It *will* be like you."

"Am I as — interesting?"

"More so," he said.

"Are you going to make me — beautiful?"

"Yes — or cut this canvas into shreds."

"Oh-h!" she exclaimed with a soft intake of breath; "would you have the heart to destroy me after you've made me?"

"I don't know what I'd do, Valerie. I never felt just this way about anything. If I can't paint you — a human, breathing *you* — with all of you there on the canvas — *all* of you, soul, mind, and body — all of your beauty, your youth, your sadness, happiness — your errors, your nobility — *you*, Valerie! — then there's no telling what I'll do."

She said nothing. Presently she resumed the pose and he his painting.

It became very still in the sunny studio.

Chapter IV

*I*n that month of June, for the first time in his deliberately active career, Neville experienced a disinclination to paint. And when he realized that it was disinclination, it appalled him. Something – he didn't understand what – had suddenly left him satiated – and with all the uneasiness and discontent of satiation he forced matters until he could force no further.

He had commissions, several, and valuable; and let them lie. For the first time in all his life the blank canvas of an unexecuted commission left him untempted, unresponsive, weary.

He had, also, his portrait of Valerie to continue. He continued it mentally, at intervals; but for several days, now, he had not laid a brush to it.

"It's funny," he said to Querida, going out on the train to his sister's country home one delicious morning – "it's confoundedly odd that I should turn lazy in my old age. Do you think I'm worked out?" He gulped down a sudden throb of fear smilingly.

"Lie fallow," said Querida, gently. "No soil is deep enough to yield without rest."

"Yours does."

"Oh, for me," said Querida, showing his snowy teeth, "I often sicken of my fat sunlight, frying everything to an iridescent omelet." He shrugged, laughed: "I turn lazy for months every year. Try it, my friend. Don't you even keep *mi-carême?*"

Neville stared out of the window at the station platform past which they were gliding, and rose with Querida as the train stopped. His sister's touring car was waiting; into it stepped Querida, and he followed; and away they sped over the beautiful rolling country, where handsome cattle tried to behave like genuine Troyon's, and silvery sheep attempted to imitate Mauve, and even the trees, separately or in groups, did their best to look like sections of Rousseau, Diaz, and even Corot — but succeeded only in resembling questionable imitations.

"There's to be quite a week-end party?" inquired Querida.

"I don't know. My sister telephoned me to fill in. I fancy the party is for you."

"For *me!*" exclaimed Querida with delightful enthusiasm. "That is most charming of Mrs. Collis."

"They'll all think it charming of you. Lord, what a rage you've become and what a furor you've aroused. . . ! And you deserve it," added Neville, coolly.

Querida looked at him, calm intelligence in his dark gaze; and understood the honesty of the comment.

"That," he said, "if you permit the vigor of expression, is damn nice of you, Neville. But you can afford to be generous to other painters."

"Can I?" Neville turned and gazed at Querida, grey eyes clear in their searching inquiry. Then he laughed a little and looked out over the sunny landscape.

Querida's olive cheeks had reddened a trifle.

Neville said: "What *is* the trouble with my work, anyway? Is it what some of you fellows say?"

Querida did not pretend to misunderstand:

"You're really a great painter, Neville. And you know it. Must you have *everything?*"

"Well — I'm going after it."

"Surely — surely. I, also. God knows my work lacks many, many things —"

"But it doesn't lack that one essential which mine lacks. *What* is it?"

Querida laughed: "I can't explain. For me — your Byzantine canvas — there is in it something not intimate —"

"Austere?"

"Yes — even in those divine and lovely throngs. There is, perhaps, an aloofness — even a self-denial —" He laughed again: "I deny myself nothing — on canvas — even I have the audacity to try to draw as you do!"

Neville sat thinking, watching the landscape speed away on either side in a running riot of green.

"Self-denial — too much of it — separates you from your kind," said Querida. "The solitary fasters are never personally pleasant; hermits are the world's public admiration and private abomination. Oh, the good world dearly loves to rub elbows with a talented sinner and patronize him and sentimentalize over him — one whose miracles don't hurt their eyes enough to blind them to the pleasant discovery that his halo is tarnished in spots and needs polishing, and that there's a patch on the seat of his carefully creased toga."

Neville laughed. Presently he said: "Until recently I've cherished theories. One of 'em was to subordinate everything in life to the enjoyment of a single pleasure — the pleasure of work. . . . I guess experience is putting that theory on the blink."

"Surely. You might as well make an entire meal of one favorite dish. For a day you could stand it, even like it, perhaps. After that —" he shrugged.

"But — I'd *rather* spend my time painting — if I could stand the diet."

"Would you? I don't know what I'd rather do. I like almost everything. It makes me paint better to talk to a pretty woman, for example. To kiss her inspires a masterpiece."

"Does it?" said Neville, thoughtfully.

"Of course. A week or two of motoring — riding, dancing, white flannel idleness — all these I adore. And," tapping his carefully pinned lilac tie — "inside of me I know that every pleasant experience, every pleasure I offer myself, is going to make me a better painter!"

"Experience," repeated the other.

"By all means and every means — experience in pleasure, in idleness, in love, in sorrow — but experience! — always experience, by hook or by crook, and at any cost. That is the main idea, Neville — *my* main idea — like the luscious agglomeration of juicy green things which that cow is eating; they all go to make good milk. Bah! — that's a stupid simile," he added, reddening.

Neville laughed. Presently he pointed across the meadows.

"Is *that* your sister's place?" asked Querida with enthusiasm, interested and disappointed. "What a charming house!"

"That is Ashuelyn, my sister's house. Beyond is El Naúar, Cardemon's place. . . . Here we are."

The small touring car stopped; the young men descended to a grassy terrace where a few people in white flannels had gathered after breakfast. A slender woman, small of bone and built like an undeveloped girl, came forward, the sun shining on her thick chestnut hair.

"Hello, Lily," said Neville.

"Hello, Louis. Thank you for coming, Mr. Querida — it is exceedingly nice of you to come —" She gave him her firm, cool hand, smiled on him with unfeigned approval, turned and presented him to the others — Miss Aulne, Miss Swift, Miss Annan, a Mr. Cameron, and, a moment later, to her husband, Gordon Collis, a good-looking, deeply sunburned young man whose only passion, except his wife and baby, was Ashuelyn, the home of his father.

But it was a quiet passion which bored nobody, not even his wife.

When conversation became general, with Querida as the center around which it eddied, Neville, who had seated himself on the grey stone parapet near his sister, said in a low voice:

"Well, how goes it, Lily?"

"All right," she replied with boyish directness, but in the same low tone. "Mother and father have spent a week with us. You saw them in town?"

"Of course. I'll run up to Spindrift House to see them as often as I can this summer. . . . How's the kid?"

"Fine. Do you want to see him?"

"Yes, I'd like to."

His sister caught his hand, jumped up, and led him into the house to the nursery where a normal and in nowise extraordinary specimen of infancy reposed in a cradle, pink with slumber, one thumb inserted in its mouth.

"Isn't he a wonder," murmured Neville, venturing to release the thumb.

The young mother bent over, examining her offspring in all the eloquent silence of pride unutterable. After a little while she said: "I've got to feed him. Go back to the others, Louis, and say I'll be down after a while."

He sauntered back through the comfortable but modest house, glancing absently about him on his way to the terrace, nodding to familiar faces among the servants, stopping to inspect a sketch of his own which he had done long ago and which his sister loved and he hated.

"Rotten," he murmured — "it has an innocence about it that is actually more offensive than stupidity."

On the terrace Stephanie Swift came over to him:

"Do you want a single at tennis, Louis? The others are hot for Bridge — except Gordon Collis — and he is going to dicker with a farmer over some land he wants to buy."

Neville looked at the others:

"Do you mean to say that you people are going to sit here all hunched up around a table on a glorious day like this?"

"We are," said Alexander Cameron, calmly breaking the seal of two fresh, packs. "You artists have nothing to do for a living except to paint pretty models, and when the week end comes you're in fine shape to caper and cut up didoes. But we business men are too tired to go galumphing over the greensward when Saturday arrives. It's a wicker chair and a 'high one,' and peaceful and improving cards for ours."

Alice Annan laughed and glanced at Querida degrees Cameron's idea was her idea of what her brother Harry was doing for a living; but she wasn't sure that Querida would think it either flattering or humorous.

But Jose Querida laughed, too, saying: "Quite right, Mr. Cameron. It's only bluff with, us; we never work. Life is one continual comic opera."

"It's a cinch," murmured Cameron. "Stocks and bonds are exciting, but *your* business puts it all over us. Nobody would have to drive me to business every morning if there was a pretty model in a cozy studio awaiting me."

"Sandy, you're rather horrid," said Miss Aulne, watching him sort out the jokers from the new packs and, with a skillful flip, send them scaling out, across the grass, for somebody to pick up.

Cameron said: "How about this Trilby business, anyway, Miss Annan? You have a brother in it. Is the world of art full of pretty models clad in ballet skirts — when they wear anything? Is it all one mad, joyous mélange of high-brow conversation discreetly peppered with low-brow revelry? Yes? No? Inform an art lover, please — as they say in the *Times Saturday Review.*"

"I don't know," said Miss Annan, laughing. "Harry never has anybody interesting in the studio when he lets me take tea there."

Rose Aulne said: "I saw some photographs of a very beautiful girl in Sam Ogilvy's studio — a model. What is her name, Alice? — the one Sam and Harry are always raving over?"

"They call her Valerie, I believe."

"Yes, that's the one — Valerie West, isn't it? *Is* it, Louis? You know her, of course."

Neville nodded coolly.

"Introduce me," murmured Cameron, spreading a pack for cutting. "Perhaps she'd like to see the Stock Exchange when I'm at my best."

"Is she such a beauty? Do you know her, too, Mr. Querida?" asked Rose Aulne.

Querida laughed: "I do. Miss West is a most engaging, most amiable and cultivated girl, and truly very beautiful."

"Oh! They *are* sometimes educated?" asked Stephanie, surprised.

"Sometimes they are even equipped to enter almost any drawing room in New York. It doesn't always require the very highest equipment to do that," he added, laughing.

"That sounds like romantic fiction," observed Alice Annan. "You are a poet, Mr. Querida."

"Oh, it's not often a girl like Valerie West crosses our path. I admit that. Now and then such a comet passes across our sky — or is reported. I never before saw any except this one."

"If she's as much of a winner as all that," began Cameron with decision, "I want to meet her immediately —"

"Mere brokers are out of it," said Alice. . . . "Cut, please."

Rose Aulne said: "If you painters only knew it, your stupid studio teas would be far more interesting if you'd have a girl like this Valerie West to pour for you . . . and for us to see."

"Yes," added Alice; "but they're a vain lot. They think we are unsophisticated enough to want to go to their old studios and be perfectly satisfied to look at their precious pictures, and listen to their art patter. I've told Harry that what we want is to see something of the real studio life; and he tries to convince me that it's about as exciting as a lawyer's life when he dictates to his stenographer."

"Is it?" asked Stephanie of Neville.

"Just about as exciting. Some few business men may smirk at their stenographers; some few painters may behave in the same way to their models. I fancy it's the exception to the rule in any kind of business — isn't it, Sandy?"

"Certainly," said Cameron, hastily. "I never winked at my stenographer — never! never! Will you deal, Mr. Querida?" he asked, courteously.

"I should think a girl like that would be interesting to know," said Lily Collis, who had come up behind her brother and Stephanie Swift and stood, a hand on each of their shoulders, listening and looking on at the card game.

"That is what I wanted to say, too," nodded Stephanie. "I'd like to meet a really nice girl who is courageous enough, and romantic enough to pose for artists —"

"You mean poor enough, don't you?" said Neville. "They don't do it because it's romantic."

"It must be romantic work."

"It isn't, I assure you. It's drudgery — and sometimes torture."

Stephanie laughed: "I believe it's easy work and a gay existence full of romance. Don't undeceive me, Louis. And I think you're selfish not to let us meet your beautiful Valerie at tea."

"Why not?" added his sister. "I'd like to see her myself."

"Oh, Lily, you know perfectly well that oil and water don't mix," he said with a weary shrug.

"I suppose we're the oil," remarked Rose Aulne — "horrid, smooth, insinuating stuff. And his beautiful Valerie is the clear, crystalline, uncontaminated fountain of inspiration."

Lily Collis dropped her hands from Stephanie's and her brother's shoulders:

"Do ask us to tea to meet her, Louis," she coaxed.

"We've never seen a model —"

"Do you want me to exhibit a sensitive girl as a museum freak?" he asked, impatiently.

"Don't you suppose we know how to behave toward her? Really, Louis, you —"

"Probably you know how to behave. And I can assure you that she knows perfectly well how to behave toward anybody. But that isn't the question. You want to see her out of curiosity. You wouldn't make a friend of her — or even an acquaintance. And I tell you, frankly, I don't think it's square to her and I won't do it. Women are nuisances in studios, anyway."

"What a charming way your brother has of explaining things," laughed Stephanie, passing her arm through Lily's: "Shall we reveal to him that he was seen with his Valerie at the St. Regis a week ago?"

"Why not?" he said, coolly, but inwardly exasperated. "She's as ornamental as anybody who dines there."

"I don't do *that* with *my* stenographers!" called out Cameron gleefully, cleaning up three odd in spades. "Oh, don't talk to me, Louis! You're a gay bunch all right! — you're qualified, every one of you, artists and models, to join the merry, merry!"

Stephanie dropped Lily's arm with a light laugh, swung her tennis bat, tossed a ball into the sunshine, and knocked it over toward the tennis court.

"I'll take you on if you like, Louis!" she called back over her shoulder, then continued her swift, graceful pace, white serge skirts swinging above her ankles, bright hair wind-blown — a lithe, full, wholesome figure, very comforting to look at.

"Come upstairs; I'll show you where Gordon's shoes are," said his sister.

Gordon's white shoes fitted him, also his white trousers. When he was dressed he came out of the room and joined his sister, who was seated on the stairs, balancing his racquet across her knees.

"Louis," she said, "how about the good taste of taking that model of yours to the St. Regis?"

"It was perfectly good taste," he said, carelessly.

"Stephanie took it like an angel," mused his sister.

"Why shouldn't she? If there was anything queer about it, you don't suppose I'd select the St. Regis, do you?"

"Nobody supposed there was anything queer."

"Well, then," he demanded, impatiently, "what's the row?"

"There is no row. Stephanie doesn't make what you call rows. Neither does anybody in your immediate family. I was merely questioning the wisdom of your public appearance — under the circumstances."

"What circumstances?"

His sister looked at him calmly:

"The circumstances of your understanding with Stephanie. . . . An understanding of years, which, in her mind at least, amounts to a tacit engagement."

"I'm glad you said that," he began, after a moment's steady thinking. "If that is the way that Stephanie and you still regard a college affair —"

"A — what!"

"A boy-and-girl preference which became an undergraduate romance — and has never amounted to anything more —"

"Louis!"

"What?"

"Don't you *care* for her?"

"Certainly; as much as I ever did — as much, as she really and actually cares for me," he answered, defiantly. "You know perfectly well what such affairs ever amount to — in the sentimental-ever-after line. Infant sweethearts almost never marry. She has no more idea of it than have I. We are fond of each other; neither of us has happened, so far, to encounter the real thing. But as soon as the right man comes along Stephanie will spread her wings and take flight —"

"You don't know her! Well — of all faithless wretches — your inconstancy makes me positively ill!"

"Inconstancy! I'm not inconstant. I never saw a girl I liked better than Stephanie. I'm not likely to. But that doesn't mean that I want to marry her —"

"For shame!"

"Nonsense! Why do you talk about inconstancy? It's a ridiculous word. What is constancy in love? Either an accident or a fortunate state of mind. To promise constancy in love is promising to continue in a state of mind over which your will has no control. It's never an honest promise; it can be only an honest hope. Love comes and goes and no man can stay it, and no man is its prophet. Coming unasked, sometimes undesired, often unwelcome, it goes unbidden, without reason, without logic, as inexorably as it came, governed by laws that no man has ever yet understood —"

"Louis!" exclaimed his sister, bewildered; "what in the world are you lecturing about? Why, to hear you expound the anatomy of love —"

He began to laugh, caught her hands, and kissed her:

"Little goose, that was all impromptu and horribly trite and commonplace. Only it was new to me because I never before took the trouble to consider it. But it's true, even if it is trite. People love or they don't love, and a regard for ethics controls only what they do about it."

"That's another Tupperesque truism, isn't it, dear?"

"Sure thing. Who am I to mock at the Proverbial One when I've never yet evolved anything better. . . ? Listen; you don't want me to marry Stephanie, do you?"

"Yes, I do."

"No, you don't. You think you do —"

"I do, I do, Louis! She's the sweetest, finest, most generous, most suitable —"

"Sure," he said, hastily, "she's all that except 'suitable' — and she isn't that, and I'm not, either. For the love of Mike, Lily, let me go on admiring her, even loving her in a perfectly harmless —"

"It *isn't* harmless to caress a girl —"

"Why — you can't call it caressing —"

"What do you call it?"

"Nothing. We've always been on an intimate footing. She's perfectly unembarrassed about — whatever impulsive — er — fugitive impulses —"

"You *do* kiss her!"

"Seldom — very seldom. At moments the conditions happen accidentally to — suggest — some slight demonstration — of a very warm friendship —"

"You positively sicken me! Do you think a nice girl is going to let a man paw her if she doesn't consider him pledged to her?"

"I don't think anything about it. Nice girls have done madder things than their eulogists admit. As a plain matter of fact you can't tell what anybody nice is going to do under theoretical circumstances. And the nicer they are the bigger the gamble — particularly if they're endowed with brains —"

"*That's* cynicism. You seem to be developing several streaks —"

"Polite blinking of facts never changes them. Conforming to conventional and accepted theories never yet appealed to intelligence. I'm not going to be dishonest with myself; that's one of the streaks I've developed. You ask me if I love Stephanie enough to marry her, and I say I don't. What's the good of blinking it? I don't love anybody enough to marry 'em; but I like a number of girls well enough to spoon with them."

"*That* is disgusting!"

"No, it isn't," he said, with smiling weariness; "it's the unvarnished truth about the average man. Why wink at it? The average man can like a lot of girls enough to spoon and sentimentalize with them. It's the pure accident of circumstance and environment that chooses for him the one he marries. There are myriads of others in the world with whom, under proper circumstances and environment, he'd have been just as happy — often happier. Choice is a mystery, constancy a gamble, discontent the one best bet. It isn't pleasant; it isn't nice fiction and delightful romance; it isn't poetry or precept as it is popularly inculcated; it's the brutal truth about the average man. . . . And I'm going to find Stephanie. Have you any objection?"

"Louis — I'm terribly disappointed in you —"

"I'm disappointed, too. Until you spoke to me so plainly a few minutes ago I never clearly understood that I couldn't marry Stephanie. When I thought of it at all it seemed a vague and shadowy something, too far away to be really impending — threatening — like death —"

"Oh!" cried his sister in revolt. "I shall make it my business to see that Stephanie understands you thoroughly before this goes any farther —"

"I wish to heaven you would," he said, so heartily that his sister, exasperated, turned her back and marched away to the nursery.

When he went out to the tennis court he found Stephanie idly batting the balls across the net with Cameron, who, being dummy, had strolled down to gibe at her — a pastime both enjoyed:

"Here comes your Alonzo, fair lady — lightly skipping o'er the green — yes, yes — wearing the panties of his brother-in-law!" He fell into an admiring attitude and contemplated Neville with a simper, his ruddy, prematurely bald head cocked on one side:

"Oh, girls! *Ain't* he just grand!" he exclaimed. "Honest, Stephanie, your young man has me in the ditch with two blow-outs and the gas afire!"

"Get out of this court," said Neville, hurling a ball at him.

"Isn't he the jealous old thing!" cried Cameron, flouncing away with an affectation of feminine indignation. And presently the tennis balls began to fly, and the little jets of white dust floated away on the June breeze.

They were very evenly matched; they always had been, never asking odds or offering handicaps in anything. It had always been so; at the traps she could break as many clay birds as he could; she rode as well, drove as well; their averages usually balanced. From the beginning — even as children — it had been always give and take and no favor.

And so it was now; sets were even; it was a matter of service.

Luncheon interrupted a drawn game; Stephanie, flushed, smiling, came around to his side of the net to join him on the way to the house:

"How do you keep up your game, Louis? Or do I never improve? It's curious, isn't it, that we are always deadlocked."

Bare-armed, bright hair in charming disorder, she swung along beside him with that quick, buoyant step so characteristic of a spirit ever undaunted, saluting the others on the terrace with high-lifted racquet.

"Nobody won," she said. "Come on, Alice, if you're going to scrub before luncheon. Thank you, Louis; I've had a splendid game —" She stretched out a frank hand to him, going, and the tips of her fingers just brushed his.

His sister gave him a tragic look, which he ignored, and a little later luncheon was on and Cameron garrulous, and Querida his own gentle, expressive, fascinating self, devotedly receptive to any woman who was inclined to talk to him or to listen.

That evening Neville said to his sister: "There's a train at midnight; I don't think I'll stay over —"

"Why?"

"I want to be in town early."

"Why?"

"The early light is the best."

"I thought you'd stopped painting for a while."

"I have, practically. There's one thing I keep on with, in a desultory sort of way —"

"What is it?"

"Oh, nothing of importance —" he hesitated — "that Is, it may be important. I can't be sure, yet."

"Will you tell me what it is?"

"Why, yes. It's a portrait — a study —"

"Of whom, dear?"

"Oh, of nobody you know —"

"Is it a portrait of Valerie West?"

"Yes," he said, carelessly.

There was a silence; in the starlight his shadowy face was not clearly visible to his sister.

"Are you leaving just to continue that portrait?"

"Yes. I'm interested in it."

"Don't go," she said, in a low voice.

"Don't be silly," he returned shortly.

"Dear, I am not silly, but I suspect you are beginning to be. And over a model!"

"Lily, you little idiot," he laughed, exasperated; "what in the world is worrying you?"

"Your taking that girl to the St. Regis. It isn't like you."

"Good Lord! How many girls do you suppose I've taken to various places?"

"Not many," she said, smiling at him. "Your reputation for gallantries is not alarming."

Ho reddened. "You're perfectly right. That sort of thing never appealed to me."

"Then why does it appeal to you now?"

"It doesn't. Can't you understand that this girl is entirely different —"

"Yes, I understand. And that is what worries me."

"It needn't. It's precisely like taking any girl you know and like —"

"Then let me know her — if you mean to decorate public places with her."

They looked at one another steadily.

"Louis," she said, "this pretty Valerie is not your sister's sort, or you wouldn't hesitate."

"I — hesitate — yes, certainly I do. It's absurd on the face of it. She's too fine a nature to be patronized — too inexperienced in the things of your world — too ignorant of petty conventions and formalities — too free and fearless and confident and independent to appeal to the world you live in."

"Isn't that a rather scornful indictment against my world, dear?"

"No. Your world is all right in its way. You and I were brought up in it. I got out of it. There are other worlds. The one I now inhabit is more interesting to me. It's purely a matter of personal taste, dear. Valerie West inhabits a world that suits her."

"Has she had any choice in the matter?"

"I — yes. She's had the sense and the courage to keep out of the various unsafe planets where electric light furnishes the principal illumination."

"But has she had a chance for choosing a better planet than the one you say she prefers? Your choice was free. Was hers?"

"Look here, Lily! Why on earth are you so significant about a girl you never saw — scarcely ever heard of —"

"Dear, I have not told you everything. I *have* heard of her — of her charm, her beauty, her apparent innocence — yes, her audacity, her popularity with men. . . . Such things are not unobserved and unreported between your new planet and mine. Harry Annan is frankly crazy about her, and his sister Alice is scared to death. Mr. Ogilvy, Mr. Burleson, Clive Gail, dozens of men I know are quite mad about her. . . . If it was she whom you used as model for the figures in the Byzantine decorations, she is divine — the loveliest creature to look at! And I don't care, Louis; I don't care a straw one way or the other except that I know you have never bothered with the more or less Innocently irregular gaieties which attract many men of your age and temperament. And so — when I hear that you are frequently seen —"

"Frequently?"

"Is that St. Regis affair the only one?"

"No, of course not. But, as for my being with her frequently —"

"Well?"

He was silent for a moment, then, looking up with a laugh:

"I like her immensely. Until this moment I didn't realize how much I do like her — how pleasant it is to be with a girl who is absolutely fearless, clever, witty, intelligent, and unspoiled."

"Are there no girls in your own set who conform to this standard?"

"Plenty. But their very environment and conventional traditions kill them — make them a nuisance."

"Louis!"

"That's more plain truth, which no woman likes. Will you tell me what girl in your world, who approaches the qualitative standard set by Valerie West, would go about by day or evening with any man except her brother? Valerie does. What girl would be fearless enough to ignore the cast-iron fetters of her caste? Valerie West is a law unto herself — a law as sweet and good and excellent and as inflexible as any law made by men to restrain women's liberty, arouse them to unhappy self-consciousness and infect them with suspicion. Every one of you are the terrified slaves of custom, and you know it. Most men like it. I don't. I'm no tea drinker, no cruncher of macaroons, no gabbler at receptions, no top-hatted haunter of weddings, no social graduate of the Ecole Turvydrop. And these places — if I want to find companionship in any girl of your world — must frequent. And I won't. And so there you are."

His sister came up to him and placed her arms around his neck.

"Such — a — wrong-headed — illogical — boy," she sighed, kissing him leisurely to punctuate her words. "If you marry a girl you love you can have all the roaming and unrestrained companionship you want. Did that ever occur to you?"

"At that price," he said, laughing, "I'll do without it."

"Wrong head, handsome head! I'm in despair about you. Why in the world cannot artists conform to the recognized customs of a perfectly pleasant and respectable world? Don't answer me! You'll make me very unhappy. . . . Now go and talk to Stephanie. The child won't understand your going tonight, but make the best of it to her."

"Good Lord, Lily! I haven't a string tied to me. It doesn't matter to Stephanie what I do — why I go or remain. You're all wrong. Stephanie and I understand each other."

"I'll see that she understands *you*" said his sister, sorrowfully.

He laughed and kissed her again, impatient. But why he was impatient he himself did not know. Certainly it was not to find Stephanie, for whom he started to look — and, on the way, glanced at his watch, determined not to miss the train that would bring him into town in time to talk to Valerie West over the telephone.

Passing the lighted and open windows, he saw Querida and Alice absorbed in a tête-à-tête, ensconced in a corner of the big living room; saw Gordon playing with Heinz, the dog — named Heinz because of the celebrated "57 varieties" of dog in his pedigree — saw Miss Aulne at solitaire, exchanging lively civilities with Sandy Cameron at the piano between charming bits of a classic ballad which he was inclined to sing:

"I'd share my pottage
    With you, dear, but
True love in a cottage
    Is hell in a hut."

"Is that you, Stephanie?" he asked, as a dark figure, seated on the veranda, turned a shadowy head toward him.

"Yes. Isn't this starlight magnificent? I've been up to the nursery looking at the infant wonder — just wild to hug him; but he's asleep, and his nurse glared at me. So I thought I'd come and look at something else as unattainable — the stars, Louis," she added, laughing — "not you."

"Sure," he said, smiling, "I'm always obtainable. Unlike the infant upon whom you had designs," he added, "I'm neither asleep nor will any nurse glare at you if you care to steal a kiss from me."

"I've no inclination to transfer my instinctively maternal transports to you," she said, serenely, "though, maternal solicitude might not be amiss concerning you."

"Do you think I need moral supervision?"

"Not by me."

"By whom?"

"Ask me an easier one, Louis. And — I didn't *say* you needed it at all, did I?"

He sat beside her, silent, head lifted, examining the stars.

"I'm going back on the midnight," he remarked, casually.

"Oh, I'm sorry!" she exclaimed, with her winning frankness.

"I'm — there's something I have to attend to in town —"

"Work?"

"It has to do with my work — indirectly —"

She glanced sideways at him, and remained for a moment curiously observant.

"How is the work going, anyway?" she asked.

He hesitated. "I've apparently come up slap against a blank wall. It isn't easy to explain how I feel — but I've no confidence in myself —"

"*You!* No confidence? How absurd!"

"It's true," he said a little sullenly.

"You are having a spasm of progressive development," she said, calmly. "You take it as a child takes teething — with a squirm and a mental howl instead of a physical yell."

He laughed. "I suppose it's something of that sort. But there's more — a self-distrust amounting to self-disgust at moments. . . . Stephanie, I *want* to do something good —"

"You have — dozens of times."

"People say so. The world forgets what is really good —" he made a nervous gesture — "always before us poor twentieth-century men looms the goal guarded by the vast, austere, menacing phantoms of the Masters."

"Nobody ever won a race looking behind him," she Said, gaily; "let 'em menace and loom!"

He laughed in a half-hearted fashion, then his head fell again slowly, and he sat there brooding, silent.

"Louis, why are you always dissatisfied?"

"I always will be, I suppose." His discontented gaze grew more vague.

"Can you never learn to enjoy the moment?"

"It goes too quickly, and there are so many others which promise more, and will never fulfill their promise; I know it. We painters know it when we dare to think clearly. It is better not to think too clearly — better to go on and pretend to expect attainment. . . . Stephanie, sometimes I wish I were in an honest business — selling, buying — and could close up shop and go home to pleasant dreams."

"Can't you?"

"No. It's eternal obsession. A painter's work is never ended. It goes on with some after they are asleep; and then they go crazy," he added, and laughed and laid his hand lightly and unthinkingly over hers where it rested on the arm of her chair. And he remained unaware of her delicate response to the contact.

The stars were clear and liquid-bright, swarming in myriads in the June sky. A big meteor fell, leaving an incandescent arc which faded instantly.

"I wonder what time it is," Be said.

"You mustn't miss your train, must you?"

"No." . . . Suddenly it struck him that it would be one o'clock before he could get to the studio and call up Valerie. That would be too late. He couldn't awake her just for the pleasure of talking to her. Besides, he was sure to see her in the morning when she came to him for her portrait. . . . Yet — yet — he wanted to talk to her. . . . There seemed to be no particular reason for this desire.

"I think I'll just step to the telephone a moment." He rose, and her fingers dropped from his hand. "You don't mind, do you?"

"Not at all," she smiled. "The stars are very faithful friends. I'll be well guarded until you come back, Louis."

What she said, for some reason, made him slightly uncomfortable. He was thinking of her words as he called up "long distance" and waited. Presently Central called him with a brisk "Here's your party!" And very far away he heard her voice:

"I know it is *you*. Is it?"

"Who?"

"It is! I recognize your voice. But *which* is it — Kelly or Louis or Mr. Neville?"

"All three," he replied, laughing.

"But which gentleman is in the ascendant? The godlike one? Or the conventional Mr. Neville? Or — the bad and very lovable and very human Louis?"

"Stop talking-nonsense, Valerie. What are you doing?"

"Conversing with an abrupt gentleman called Louis Neville. I *was* reading."

"All alone in your room?"

"Naturally. Two people *couldn't* get into it unless one of them also got into bed."

"You poor child! What are you reading?"

"Will you promise not to laugh?"

"Yes, I will."

"Then — I was reading the nineteenth psalm."

"It's a beauty, isn't it," he said.

"Oh, Louis, it is glorious! — I don't know what in it appeals most thrillingly to me — the wisdom or the beauty of the verse — but I love it."

"It is fine," he said. ". . . And are you there in your room all alone this beautiful starry night, reading the psalms of old King David?"

"Yes. What are you doing? Where are you?"

"At Ashuelyn, my sister's home."

"Oh! Well, it is perfectly sweet of you to think of me and to call me up —"

"I usually — I — well, naturally I think of you. I thought I'd just call you up to say good night. You see my train doesn't get in until one this morning; and of course I couldn't wake you —"

"Yes, you could. I am perfectly willing to have you wake me."

"But that would be the limit!"

"Is *that* your limit, Louis? If it is you will never disturb my peace of mind." He heard her laughing at the other end of the wire, delighted with her own audacity.

He said: "Shall I call you up at one o'clock when I get into town?"

"Try it. I may awake."

"Very well then. I'll make them ring till daylight."

"Oh, they won't have to do that! I always know, about five minutes before you call me, that you are going to."

"You uncanny little thing! You've said that before."

"It's true. I knew before you called me that you would. It's a vague feeling — a — I don't know. . . . And oh, Louis, it *is* hot in this room! Are you cool out there in the country?"

"Yes; and I hate to be when I think of you —"

"I'm glad you are. It's one comfort, anyway. John Burleson called me up and asked me to go to Manhattan Beach, but somehow it didn't appeal to me. . . . I've rather missed you."

"Have you?"

"Really."

"Well, I'll admit I've missed you."

"Really?"

"Sure thing! I wish to heaven I were in town now. We would go somewhere."

"Oh, I wish so, too."

"Isn't it the limit!"

"It is, Kelly. Can't you be a real god for a moment and come floating into my room in a golden cloud?"

"Shall I try?"

"Please do."

"All right. I'll do my godlike best. And anyway I'll call you up at one. Good night."

"Good night."

He went back to the girl waiting for him in the starlight.

"Well," she said, smiling at his altered expression, "you certainly have recovered your spirits."

He laughed and took her unreluctant fingers and kissed them — a boyishly impulsive expression of the gay spirits which might have perplexed him or worried him to account for if he had tried to analyze them. But he didn't; he was merely conscious of a sudden inrush of high spirits — of a warm feeling for all the world — this star-set world, so still and sweet-scented.

"Stephanie, dear," he said, smiling, "you know perfectly well that I think — always have thought — that there was nobody like you. You know that, don't you?"

She laughed, but her pulses quickened a little.

"Well, then," he went on. "I take it for granted that our understanding is as delightfully thorough as it has always been — a warm, cordial intimacy which leaves us perfectly unembarrassed — perfectly free to express our affection for each other without fear of being misunderstood."

The girl lifted her blue eyes: "Of course."

"That's what I told Lily," he nodded, delighted. I told her that you and I understood each other — that it was silly of her to suspect anything sentimental in our comradeship; that whenever the real thing put in an appearance and came tagging down the pike after you, you'd sink the gaff into him — "

"The — what?"

"Rope him and paste your monogram all over him."

"I certainly will," she said, laughing. Eyes and lips and voice were steady; but the tumult in her brain confused her.

"That is exactly what I told Lily," he said. "She seems to think that if two people frankly enjoy each other's society they want to marry each other. All married women are that way. Like clever decoys they take genuine pleasure in bringing the passing string under the guns."

He laughed and kissed her pretty fingers again:

"Don't you listen to my sister. Freedom's a good thing; and people are selfish when happy; they don't set up a racket to attract others into their private paradise."

"Oh, Louis, that is really horrid of you. Don't you think Lily is happy?"

"Sure — in a way. You can't have a perfectly good husband and baby, and have the fun of being courted by other aspirants, too. Of course married women are happy; but they give up a lot. And sometimes it slightly irritates them to remember it when they see the unmarried innocently frisking as they once frisked. And it's their instinct to call out 'Come in! Matrimony's fine! You don't know what you are missing!'"

Stephanie laughed and lay back in her steamer chair, her hand abandoned to him. And when her mirth had passed a slight sense of fatigue left her silent, inert, staring at nothing.

When the time came to say *adieu* he kissed her as he sometimes did, with a smiling and impersonal tenderness — not conscious of the source of all this happy, demonstrative, half impatient animation which seemed to possess him in every fiber.

"Good-bye, you dear girl," he said, as the lights of the motor lit up the drive. "I've had a bully time, and I'll see you soon again."

"Come when you can, Louis. There is no man I would rather see."

"And no girl I would rather go to," he said, warmly, scarcely thinking what he was saying.

Their clasped hands relaxed, fell apart. He went in to take leave of Lily and Gordon and their guests, then emerged hastily and sprang into the car.

Overhead the June stars watched him as he sped through the fragrant darkness. But with him, time lagged; even the train crawled as he timed it to the ticking seconds of his opened watch.

In the city a taxi swallowed him and his haste; and it seemed as though he would never get to his studio and to the telephone; but at last he heard her voice — a demure, laughing little voice:

"I didn't think you'd be brute enough to do it!"

"But you said I might call you —"

"There are many things that a girl says from which she expects a man to infer, tactfully and mercifully, the contrary."

"Did I wake you, Valerie? I'm terribly sorry —"

"If you are sorry I'll retire to my pillow —"

"I'll ring you up again!"

"Oh, if you employ threats I think I'd better listen to you. What have you to say to me?"

"What were you doing when I rang you up?"

"I Wish I could say that I was asleep. But I can't. And if I tell the truth I've got to flatter you. So I refuse to answer."

"You were not waiting up for —"

"Kelly! I refuse to answer! Anyway you didn't keep your word to me."

"How do you mean?"

"You promised to appear in a golden cloud!"

"Something went wrong with the Olympian machinery," he explained, "and I was obliged to take the train. . . . What are you doing there, anyway?"

"Now?"

"Yes, now."

"Why, I'm sitting at the telephone in my night-dress talking to an exceedingly inquisitive gentleman —"

"I mean were you reading more psalms?"

"No. If you must know, I was reading 'Bocaccio'"

He could hear her laughing.

"I was meaning to ask you how you'd spent the day," he began. "Haven't you been out at all?"

"Oh, yes. I'm not under vows, Kelly."

"Where?"

"Now I wonder whether I'm expected to account for every minute when I'm not with you? I'm beginning to believe that it's a sort of monstrous vanity that incites you to such questions. And I'm going to inform you that I did *not* spend the day sitting by the window and thinking about you."

"What *did* you do?"

"I motored in the Park. I lunched at Woodmanston with a perfectly good young man. I enjoyed it."

"Who was the man?"

"Sam."

"Oh," said Neville, laughing.

"You make me perfectly furious by laughing," she exclaimed. "I wish I could tell you that I'd been to Niagara Falls with José Querida!"

"I wouldn't believe it, anyway."

"I wouldn't believe it myself, even if I had done it," she said, naïvely. There was a pause; then:

"I'm going to retire. Good night."

"Good night, Valerie."

"Louis!"

"What?"

"You say the golden-cloud machinery isn't working?"

"It seems to have slipped a cog."

"Oh! I thought you might have mended it and that — perhaps — I had better not leave my window open."

"That cloud is warranted to float through solid masonry."

"You alarm me, Kelly."

"I'm sorry, but the gods never announce their visits."

"I know it. . . . And I suppose I must sleep in a dinner gown. When one receives a god it's a full-dress affair, isn't it?"

He laughed, not mistaking her innocent audacity.

"Unexpected Olympians must take their chances," he said. ". . . Are you sleepy?"

"Fearfully."

"Then I won't keep you —"

"But I hope you won't be rude enough to dismiss me before I have a chance to give you your *congé!*"

"You blessed child. I could stay here all night listening to you —"

"Could you? That's a temptation."

"To you, Valerie?"

"Yes — a temptation to make a splendid exit. Every girl adores being regretted. So I'll hang up the receiver, I think. . . . Good night, Kelly, dear. . . . Good night, Louis. *À demain! — non — pardon! à bien tôt! — parceque il est deux heures de matin! Et — vous m'avez rendu bien heureuse.*"

Chapter V

*T*oward the last of June Neville left town to spend a month with his father and mother at their summer Lome near Portsmouth. Valerie had already gone to the mountains with Rita Tevis, gaily refusing her address to everybody. And, packing their steamer trunks and satchels, the two young girls departed triumphantly for the unindicated but modest boarding-house tucked away somewhere amid the hills of Delaware County, determined to enjoy every minute of a vacation well earned, and a surcease from the round of urban and suburban gaiety which the advent of July made a labor instead of a relaxation.

From some caprice or other Valerie had decided that her whereabouts should remain unknown even to Neville. And for a week it suited her perfectly. She swam in the stump-pond with Rita, drove a buckboard with Rita, fished industriously with Rita, played tennis on a rutty court, danced rural dances at a "platform," went to church and giggled like a schoolgirl, and rocked madly on the veranda in a rickety rocking-chair, demurely tolerant of the adoration of two boys working their way through, college, a smartly dressed and very confident drummer doing his two weeks, and several assorted and ardent young men who, at odd moments, had persuaded her to straw rides and soda at the village druggists.

And all the while she giggled with Rita in a most shameless and undignified fashion, went about hatless, with hair blowing and sleeves rolled up; decorated a donation party at the local minister's and flirted with him till his gold-rimmed eye-glasses protruded; behaved like a thoughtful and consid-

erate angel to the old, uninteresting and infirm; romped like
a young goddess with the adoring children of the boarders,
and was fiercely detested by the crocheting spinsters rocking
in acidulated rows on the piazza.

The table was meager and awful and pruneful; but she ate
with an appetite that amazed Rita, whose sophisticated palate
was grossly insulted thrice daily.

"How on earth you can contrive to eat that hash," she said,
resentfully, "I don't understand. When my Maillard's give
out I'll quietly starve in a daisy field somewhere."

"Close your eyes and pretend you and Sam are dining at
the Knickerbocker," suggested Valerie, cheerfully. "That's
what I do when the food doesn't appeal to me."

"With whom do you pretend you are dining?"

"Sometimes with Louis Neville, sometimes with Querida,"
she, said, frankly. "It helps the hash wonderfully. Try it, dear.
Close your eyes and visualize some agreeable man, and the
food isn't so very awful."

Rita laughed: "I'm not as fond of men as that."

"Aren't you? I am. I do like an agreeable man, and I don't
mind saying so."

"I've observed that," said Rita, still laughing.

"Of course you have. I've spent too many years without
them not to enjoy them now — bless their funny hearts!"

"I'm glad there are no men here," observed Rita.

"But there are men here," said Valerie, innocently.

"Substitutes. Lemons."

"The minister is superficially educated —"

"He's a muff."

"A nice muff. I let him pat my gloved hand."

"You wicked child. He's married."

"He only patted it in spiritual emphasis, dear. Married or
single he's more agreeable to me than that multi-colored
drummer. I let the creature drive me to the post office in a
buckboard, and he continued to sit closer until I took the
reins, snapped the whip, and drove at a gallop over that
terrible stony road. And he is so fat that it nearly killed him.
It killed all sentiment in him, anyway."

Rita, stretched lazily in a hammock and displaying a perfectly shod foot and silken ankle to the rage of the crocheters on the veranda, said dreamily:

"The unfortunate thing about us is that we know too much to like the only sort of men who are likely to want to marry us."

"What of it?" laughed Valerie. "We don't want to marry them — or anybody. Do we?"

"Don't you?"

"Don't I what?"

"Want to get married?"

"I should think not."

"Never?"

"Not if I feel about it as I do now. I've never had enough play, Rita. I've missed all those years that you've had — that most girls have had. I never had any boys to play with. That's really all I am doing now — playing with grown-up boys. That's all I am — merely a grown-up girl with a child's heart."

"A heart of gold," murmured Rita, "you darling."

"Oh, it isn't all gold by any means! It's full of silver whims and brassy selfishness and tin meannesses and senseless ideas — full of fiery, coppery mischief, too; and, sometimes, I think, a little malice — perhaps a kind of diluted deviltry. But it's a hungry heart, dear, hungry for laughter and companionship and friendship — with a capacity for happiness! Ah, you don't know, dear — you never can know how capable I am of friendship and happiness!"

"And — sentiment?"

"I — don't — know."

"Better watch out, sweetness!"

"I do."

Rita said thoughtfully, swinging in her hammock:

"Sentiment, for us, is no good. I've learned that."

"You?"

"Of course."

"How?"

"Experience," said Rita, carelessly. "Every girl is bound to have it. She doesn't have to hunt for it, either."

"Were you ever in — love?" asked Valerie, curiously.

"Now, dear, if I ever had been happily in love is it likely you wouldn't know it?"

"I suppose so," said Valerie. . . . She added, musingly:

"I wonder what will become of me if I ever fall in love."

"If you'll take my advice you'll run."

"Run? Where? For goodness' sake!"

"Anywhere until you became convalescent."

"That would be a ridiculous idea," remarked Valerie so seriously that Rita began to laugh:

"You sweet thing," she said, "it's a million chances that you'd be contented only with the sort of man who wouldn't marry you."

"Because I'm poor, you mean? Or because I am working for my living?"

"Both — and then some."

"What else?"

"Why, the only sort of men who'd attract you have come out of their own world of their own accord to play about for a while in our world. They can go back; that is the law. But they can't take us with them."

"They'd be ashamed, you mean?"

"Perhaps not. A man is likely enough to try. But alas! for us, if we're silly enough to go. I tell you, Valerie, that their world is full of mothers and sisters and feminine relatives and friends who could no more endure us than they would permit us to endure them. It takes courage for a man to ask us to go into that world with him; it takes more for us to do it. And our courage is vain. We stand no chance. It means a rupture of all his relations; and a drifting — not into our world, not into his, but into a horrible midway void, peopled by derelicts. . . . I know, dear, believe me. And I say that to fall in love is no good, no use, for us. We've been spoiled for what we might once have found satisfactory. We are people without a class, you and I."

Valerie laughed: "That gives us the more liberty, doesn't it?"

"It's up to us, dear. We are our own law, social and spiritual. If we live inside it we are not going to be any too happy. If we live without it — I don't know. Sometimes I wonder whether some of the pretty girls you and I see at Rector's —"

"I've wondered, too. . . . They *look* happy — some of them."

"I suppose they are — for a while. . . . But the worst of it is that it never lasts."

"I suppose not." Valerie pondered, grave, velvet-eyed, idly twisting a grass stem.

"After all," she said, "perhaps a brief happiness — with love — is worth the consequences."

"Many women risk it. . . . I wonder how many men, if social conditions were reversed, would risk it? Not many, Valerie."

They remained silent; Rita lay in the shadow of the maples, eyes closed; Valerie plaited her grass stems with absent-minded industry.

"I never yet wished to marry a man," she observed, presently.

Rita made no response.

"Because," continued the girl with quaint precision, "I never yet wanted anything that was not offered freely; even friendship. I think — I don't know — but I think — if any man offered me love — and I found that I could respond — I *think* that, if I took it, I'd be contented with love — and ask nothing further — wish nothing else — unless he wanted it, too."

Rita opened her eyes.

Valerie, plaiting her grass very deftly, smiled to herself.

"I don't know much about love, Rita; but I believe it is supreme contentment. And if it is — what is the use of asking for more than contents one?"

"It's safer."

"Oh — I know that. . . . I've read enough newspapers and novels and real literature to know that. Incidentally the Scriptures treat of it. . . . But, after all, love is love. You can't make it more than it is by law and custom; you can't make it less; you can't summon it; you can't dismiss it. . . . And I believe that I'd be inclined to take it, however offered, if it were really love."

"That is unmoral, dear," said Rita, smiling.

"I'm not unmoral, am I?"

"Well — your philosophy sounds Pagan."

"Does it? Then, as you say, perhaps I'd better run if anything resembling love threatens me."

"The nymphs ran — in Pagan times."

"And the gods ran after them," returned Valerie, laughing. "I've a very fine specimen of god as a friend, by the way — a Protean gentleman with three quick-change stunts. He's a perfectly good god, too, but he never ran after me or tried to kiss me."

"You *don't* mean Querida, then."

"No. He's no god."

"Demigod."

"Not even that," said Valerie; "he's a sentimental shepherd who likes to lie with his handsome head in a girl's lap and make lazy eyes at her."

"I know," nodded Rita. "Look out for that shepherd."

"Does he bite?"

"No; there's the trouble. Anybody can pet him."

Valerie laughed, turned over, and lay at length on her stomach in the grass, exploring the verdure for a four-leaf clover.

"I never yet found one," she said, cheerfully. "But then I've never before seen much grass except in the Park."

"Didn't you ever go to the country?"

"No. Mother was a widow and bedridden. We had a tiny income; I have it now. But it wasn't enough to take us to the country."

"Didn't you work?"

"I couldn't leave mother. Besides, she wished to educate me."

"Didn't you go to school?"

"Only a few months. We had father's books. We managed to buy a few more — or borrow them from the library. And that is how I was educated, Rita — in a room with a bedridden mother."

"She must have been well educated."

"I should think so. She was a college graduate. . . . When I was fifteen I took the examinations for Barnard — knowing, of course, that I couldn't go — and passed in everything. . . . If mother could have spared me I could have had a scholarship."

"That was hard luck, wasn't it, dear?"

"N-no. I had mother — as long as she lived. After she died I had what she had given me — and she had the education of a cultivated woman; she was a lover of the best in literature and in art, a woman gently bred, familiar with sorrow and privation."

"If you choose," said Rita, "you are equipped for a governess — or a lady's companion — or a secretary —"

"I suppose I am. Before I signed with Schindler I advertised, offering myself as a teacher. How many replies do you suppose I received?"

"How many?"

"Not one."

Rita sighed. "I suppose you couldn't afford to go on advertising."

"No, and I couldn't afford to wait. . . . Mother's burial took all the little income. I was glad enough when Schindler signed me. . . . But a girl can't remain long with Schindler."

"I know."

Valerie plucked a grass blade and bit it in two reflectively.

"It's a funny sort of a world, isn't it, Rita?"

"Very humorous — if you look at it that way."

"Don't you?"

"Not entirely."

Valerie glanced up at the hammock.

"How did *you* happen to become a model, Rita?"

"I'm a clergyman's daughter; what do you expect?" she said, with smiling bitterness.

"You!"

"From Massachusetts, dear. . . . The blue-light elders got on my nerves. I wanted to study music, too, with a view to opera." She laughed unpleasantly.

"Was your home life unhappy, dear?"

"Does a girl leave happiness?"

"You didn't run away, did you?"

"I did — straight to the metropolis as a moth to its candle."

Valerie waited, then, timidly: "Did you care to tell me anymore, dear? I thought perhaps you might like me to ask you. It isn't curiosity."

"I know it isn't — you blessed child! I'll tell you — some day — perhaps. . . . Pull the rope and set me swinging, please. . . . Isn't this sky delicious — glimpsed through the green leaves? Fancy you're not knowing the happiness of the country! I've always known it. Perhaps the trouble was I had too much of it. My town was an ancient, respectable, revolutionary relic set in a very beautiful rolling country near the sea; but I suppose I caught the infection — the country rolled, the breakers rolled, and finally I rolled out of it all — over and over plump into Gotham! And I didn't land on my feet, either. . . . You are correct, Valerie; there is something humorous about this world. . . . There's one of the jokes, now!" as a native passed, hunched up on the dashboard, driving a horse and a heifer in double harness.

"Shall we go to the post office with him?" cried Valerie, jumping to her feet.

"Now, dear, what is the use of our going to the post office when nobody knows our address and we never could possibly expect a letter!"

"That is true," said Valerie, pensively. "Rita, I'm beginning to think I'd like to have a letter. I believe — believe that I'll write to — to somebody."

"That is more than I'll do," yawned Rita, closing her eyes. She opened them presently and said:

"I've a nice little writing case in my trunk. Sam presented it. Bring it out here if you're going to write."

The next time she unclosed her eyes Valerie sat cross-legged on the grass by the hammock, the writing case on her lap, scribbling away as though she really enjoyed it.

The letter was to Neville. It ran on:

"Rita is asleep in a hammock; she's too pretty for words. I love her. Why? Because she loves me, silly!

"I'm a very responsive individual, Kelly, and a pat on the head elicits purrs.

"I want you to write to me. Also, pray be flattered; you are the only person on earth who now has my address. I *may* send it to José Querida; but that is none of your business. When I saw the new moon on the stump-pond last night I certainly did wish for Querida and a canoe. He can sing very charmingly.

"Now I suppose you want to know under what circumstances I have permitted myself to wish for you. If you talk to a man about another man he always attempts to divert the conversation to himself. Yes, he does. And you are no better than other men, Louis — not exempt from their vanities and cunning little weaknesses. Are you?

"Well, then, as you admit that you are thoroughly masculine, I'll admit that deep in a corner of my heart I've wished for you a hundred times. The moon suggests Querida; but about everything suggests you. Now are you flattered?

"Anyway, I do want you. I like you, Louis! I like you, Mr. Neville! And oh, Kelly, I worship you, without sentiment or any nonsense in reserve. You are life, you are happiness, you are gaiety, you are inspiration, you are contentment.

"I wonder if it would be possible for you to come up here for a day or two after your visit to your parents is ended. I'd adore it. You'd probably hate it. Such food! Such beds! Such people! But — could you — would you come — just to walk in the heavenly green with me? I wonder.

"And, Louis, I'd row you about on the majestic expanse of the stump-pond, and we'd listen to the frogs. Can you desire anything more romantic?

"The trouble with you is that you're romantic only on canvas. Anyway, I can't stir you to sentiment. Can I? True, I never tried. But if you come here, and conditions are favorable, and you are so inclined, and I am feeling lonely, nobody can tell what might happen in a flat scow on the stump-pond.

"To be serious for a moment, Louis, I'd really love to have you come. You know I never before saw the real country; I'm a novice in the woods and fields, and, somehow, I'd like to have you share my novitiate in this — as you did when I first came to you. It is a curious feeling I have about anything new; I wish you to experience it with me.

"Rita is awake and exploring the box of Maillard's which is about empty. Be a Samaritan and send me some assorted chocolates. Be a god, and send me something to read — anything, please, from Jacobs to James. There's latitude for you. Be a man, and send me yourself. You have no idea how welcome you'd be. The chances are that I'd seize you and embrace you. But if you're willing to run that risk, take your courage in both hands and come.

"Your friend,

"Valerie West"

The second week of her sojourn she caught a small pickerel — the only fish she had ever caught in all her life. And she tearfully begged the yokel who was rowing her to replace the fish in its native element. But it was too late; and she and Rita ate her victim, sadly, for dinner.

At the end of the week an enormous box of bonbons came for her. Neither she nor Rita were very well next day, but a letter from Neville did wonders to restore abused digestion.

Other letters, at intervals, cheered her immensely, as did baskets of fruit and boxes of chocolates and a huge case of books of all kinds.

"Never," she said to Rita, "did I ever hear of such an angel as Louis Neville. When he comes the first of August I wish you to keep tight hold of me, because, if he flees my demonstrations, I feel quite equal to running him down."

But, curiously enough, it was a rather silent and subdued young girl in white who offered Neville a shy and sun-tanned hand as he descended from the train and came forward, straw hat under one arm, to greet her.

"How well you look!" he exclaimed, laughingly; "I never saw such a flawless specimen of healthy perfection!"

"Oh, I know I look like a milk-maid, Kelly; I've behaved like one, too. Did you ever see such a skin? Do you suppose this sunburn will ever come off?"

"Instead of snow and roses you're strawberries and cream," he said — "and it's just as fetching, Valerie. How are you, anyway?"

"Barely able to sit up and take nourishment," she admitted, demurely. ". . . I don't think you look particularly vigorous," she added, more seriously. "You are brown but thin."

"Thin as a scorched pancake," he nodded. "The ocean was like a vast plate of clam soup in which I simmered several times a day until I've become as leathery and attenuated as a punctured pod of kelp. . . . Where's the rig we depart in, Valerie?" he concluded, looking around the sun-scorched, wooden platform with smiling interest.

"I drove down to meet you in a buck-board."

"Splendid! Is there room for my suit case?"

"Plenty. I brought yards of rope."

They walked to the rear of the station where buckboard and horse stood tethered to a tree. He fastened his suit case to the rear of the vehicle, swathing it securely in, fathoms of rope; she sprang in, he followed; but she begged him to let her drive, and pulled on a pair of weather-faded gloves with a businesslike air which was enchanting.

So he yielded seat and rusty reins to her; whip in hand, she steered the fat horse through the wilderness of arriving and departing carriages of every rural style and description — stages, surreys, mountain-wagons, buck-boards — drove across the railroad track, and turned up a mountain road — a gradual ascent bordered heavily by blackberry, raspberry, thimble berry and wild grape, and flanked by young growths of beech and maple set here and there with hemlock and white pine. But the characteristic foliage was laurel and rhododendron — endless stretches of the glossy undergrowth fringing every woodland, every diamond-clear water-course.

"It must be charming when it's in blossom," he said, drawing the sweet air of the uplands deep into his lungs. "These streams look exceedingly like trout, too. How high are we?"

"Two thousand feet in the pass, Kelly. The hills are much higher. You need blankets at night. . . ." She turned her head and smilingly considered him:

"I can't yet believe you are here."

"I've been trying to realize it, too."

"Did you come in your favorite cloud?"

"No; on an exceedingly dirty train."

"You've a cinder mark on your nose."

"Thanks." He gave her his handkerchief and she wiped away the smear.

"How long can you stay? — Oh, don't answer! Please forget I asked you. When you've got to go just tell me a few minutes before your departure.... The main thing in life is to shorten unhappiness as much as possible. That is Rita's philosophy."

"Is Rita well?"

"Perfectly — thanks to your bonbons. She doesn't precisely banquet on the fare here — poor dear! But then," she added, philosophically, "what can a girl expect on eight dollars a week? Besides, Rita has been spoiled. I am not unaccustomed to fasting when what is offered does not interest me."

"You mean that boarding house of yours in town?"

"Yes. Also, when mother and I kept house with an oil stove and two rooms the odor of medicine and my own cooking left me rather indifferent to the pleasures of Lucullus."

"You poor child!"

"Not at all to be pitied — as long as I had mother," she said, with a quiet gravity that silenced him.

Up, up, and still up they climbed, the fat horse walking leisurely, nipping at blackberry leaves here, snatching at tender maple twigs there. The winged mountain beauties — Diana's butterflies — bearing on their velvety, blue-black pinions the silver bow of the goddess, flitted ahead of the horse — celestial pilots to the tree-clad heights beyond.

Save for the noise of the horse's feet and the crunch of narrow, iron-tired wheels, the stillness was absolute under the azure splendor of the heavens.

"I am not yet quite at my ease — quite accustomed to it," she said.

"To what, Valerie?"

"To the stillness; to the remote horizons.... At night the vastness of things, the height of the stars, fascinate me to the edge of uneasiness. And sometimes I go and sit in my room for a while — to reassure myself.... You see I am used to an enclosure — the walls of a room — the walled-in streets of New York.... It's like suddenly stepping out of a cellar to the edge of eternal space, and looking down into nothing."

"Is that the way these rolling hillocks of Delaware County impress you?" he asked, laughing.

"Yes, Kelly. If I ever found myself in the Alps I believe the happiness would so utterly overawe me that I'd remain in my hotel under the bed. What are you laughing at? *Voluptates commendat rarior usus.*"

"*Sit tua cura sequi, me duce tutus eris!*" he laughed, mischievously testing her limit of Latin.

"*Plus e medico quam e morbo periculi!*" she answered, saucily.

"You cunning little thing!" he exclaimed: "*vix a te videor posse tenere manus!*"

"*Di melius, quam nos moneamus talia quenquam!*" she said, demurely; "Louis, we are becoming silly! Besides, I probably know more Latin than you do — as it was my mother's favorite relaxation to teach me to speak it. And I imagine that your limit was your last year at Harvard."

"Upon my word!" he exclaimed; "I never was so snubbed and patronized in all my life!"

"Beware, then!" she retorted, with an enchanting sideway glance: "*noli me tangere!*" At the same instant he was aware of her arm in light, friendly contact against his, and heard her musing aloud in deep contentment:

"Such perfect satisfaction to have you again, Louis. The world is a grey void without the gods."

And so, leisurely, they breasted the ascent and came out across the height-of-land. Here and there a silvery ghost of the shorn forest stood, now almost mercifully hidden in the green foliage of hard wood — worthlessly young as yet but beautiful.

From tree to tree flickered the brilliant woodpeckers — they of the solid crimson head and ivory-barred wings. The great vermilion-tufted cock-o'-the-woods called querulously; over the steel-blue stump-ponds the blue kingfishers soared against the blue. It was a sky world of breezy bushes and ruffled waters, of pathless fields and dense young woodlands, of limpid streams clattering over greenish white rocks, pouring into waterfalls, spreading through wild meadows set with iris and pink azalea.

"How is the work going, Louis?" she asked, glancing at him askance.

"It's stopped."

"*A cause de* — ?"

"*Je n'en sais rien, Valerie.*"

She flicked the harness with her whip, absently. He also leaned back, thoughtfully intent on the blue hills in the distance.

"Has not your desire to paint returned?"

"No."

"Do you know why?"

"Partly. I am up against a solid wall. There is no thorough-fare."

"Make one."

"Through the wall?"

"Straight through it."

"Ah, yes" — he murmured — "but what lies beyond?"

"It would spoil the pleasures of anticipation to know beforehand."

He turned to her: "You are good for me. Do you know it?"

"Querida said that, too. He said that I was an experience; and that all good work is made up of experiences that concern it only indirectly."

"Do you like Querida?" he asked, curiously.

"Sometimes."

"Not always?"

"Oh, yes, always more or less. But sometimes" — she was silent, her dark eyes dreaming, lips softly parted.

"What do you mean by that?" he inquired, carelessly.

"By what, Louis?" she asked, naïvely, interrupted in her daydream.

"By hinting — that sometimes you like Querida — more than at others?"

"Why, I do," she said, frankly. "Besides, I don't hint things; I say them." She had turned her head to look at him. Their eyes met in silence for a few moments.

"You are funny about Querida," she said. "Don't you like him?"

"I have no reason to dislike him."

"Oh! Is it the case of Sabidius? *'Non amo te, Sabidi, nec possum dicere quare!'*"

He laughed uneasily: "Oh, no, I think not. . . . You and he are such excellent friends that I certainly ought to like him anyway."

But she remained silent, musing; and on the edge of her upcurled lip he saw the faint smile lingering, then fading, leaving the oval face almost expressionless.

So they drove past the one-story post office where a group of young people stood awaiting the arrival of the stage with its battered mailbags; past the stump-pond where Valerie had caught her first and only fish, past a few weather-beaten farm houses, a whitewashed church, a boarding house or two, a village store, a watering-trough, and then drove up to the wooden veranda where Rita rose from a rocker and came forward with hand outstretched.

"Hello, Rita!" he said, giving her hand a friendly shake. "Why didn't you drive down with Valerie?"

"I? That child would have burst into tears at such a suggestion."

"Probably," said Valerie, calmly: "I wanted him for myself. Now that I've had him I'll share him."

She sprang lightly to the veranda ignoring Neville's offered hand with a smile. A hired man took away the horse; a boy picked up his suit case and led the way.

"I'll be back in a moment," he said to Valerie and Rita.

That evening at supper, a weird rite where the burned offering was rice pudding and the stewed sacrifice was prunes, Neville was presented to an interesting assemblage of the free-born.

There was the clerk, the drummer, the sales-lady, and ladies unsaleable and damaged by carping years; city-wearied fathers of youngsters who called their parents "pop" and "mom"; young mothers prematurely aged and neglectful of their coiffure and shoe-heels; simpering maidenhood, acid maidenhood, sophisticated maidenhood; shirt-waisted manhood, flippant manhood, full of strange slang and double negatives unresponsively suspicious manhood, and manhood disillusioned, prematurely tired, burned out with the weariness of a sordid Harlem struggle.

Here in the height-of-land among scant pastures and the green charity which a spindling second-growth spread over the nakedness of rotting forest bones — here amid the wasted uplands and into this flimsy wooden building came the rank and file of the metropolis in search of air, of green, of sky, for ten days' surcease from toil and heat and the sad perplexities of those with slender means.

Neville, seated on the veranda with Valerie and Rita in the long summer twilight, looked around him at scenes quite new to him.

On the lumpy croquet ground where battered wickets and stakes awry constituted the center of social activity after supper, some young girls were playing in partnership with young men, hatless, striped of shirt, and very, very yellow of foot-gear.

A social favorite, very jolly and corporeally redundant, sat in the hammock fanning herself and uttering screams of laughter at jests emanating from the boarding-house cut-up — a blonde young man with rah-rah hair and a brier pipe.

Children, neither very clean nor very dirty, tumbled noisily about the remains of a tennis court or played base-ball in the dusty road. Ominous sounds arose from the parlor piano, where a gaunt maiden lady rested one spare hand among the keys while the other languidly pawed the music of the "Holy City."

Somewhere in the house a baby was being spanked and sent to bed. There came the clatter of dishes from the wrecks of the rite in the kitchen, accompanied by the warm perfume of dishwater.

But, little by little the high stars came out, and the grey veil fell gently over unloveliness and squalor; little by little the raucous voices were hushed; the scuffle and clatter and the stringy noise of the piano died away, till, distantly, the wind awoke in the woods, and very far away the rushing music of a little brook sweetened the silence.

Rita, who had been reading yesterday's paper by the lamp-light which streamed over her shoulder from the open parlor-window, sighed, stifled a yawn, laid the paper aside, and drew her pretty wrap around her shoulders.

"It's absurd," she said, plaintively, "but in this place I become horribly sleepy by nine o'clock. You won't mind if I go up, will you?"

"Not if you feel that way about it," he said, smiling.

"Oh, Rita!" said Valerie, reproachfully, "I thought we were going to row Louis about on the stump-pond!"

"I am too sleepy; I'd merely fall overboard," said Rita, simply, gathering up her bonbons. "Louis, you'll forgive me, won't you? I don't understand why, but that child never sleeps."

They rose to bid her good night. Valerie's fingertips rested a moment on Neville's sleeve in a light gesture of excuse for leaving him and of promise to return. Then she went away with Rita.

When she returned, the piazza was deserted except for Neville, who stood on the steps smoking and looking out across the misty waste.

"I usually go up with Rita," she said. "Rita is a dear. But do you know, I believe she is not a particularly happy girl."

"Why?"

"I don't know why. . . . After all, such a life — hers and mine — is only happy if you make it so. . . . And I don't believe she tries to make it so. Perhaps she doesn't care. She is very young — and very pretty — too young and pretty to be so indifferent — so tired."

She stood on the step behind and above him, looking down at his back and his well-set shoulders. They were inviting, those firm, broad, young shoulders of his; and she laid both hands on them.

"Shall I row you about in the flat-boat, Louis?"

"I'll do the paddling —"

"Not by any means. I like to row, if you please. I have cold cream and a pair of gloves, so that I shall acquire no blisters."

They walked together out to the road and along it, she holding to her skirts and his arm, until the star-lit pond came into view.

Afloat in the ancient, weedy craft he watched her slender strength mastering the clumsy oars — watched her, idly charmed with her beauty and the quaint, childish pleasure that she took in maneuvering among the shoreward lily pads and stumps till clear water was reached and the little misty wavelets came slap! slap! against the bow.

"If you were Querida you'd sing in an exceedingly agreeable tenor," she observed.

"Not being Querida, and laboring further under the disadvantage of a baritone, I won't," he said.

"Please, Louis."

"Oh, very well — if you feel as romantic as that." And he began to sing:

"My wife's gone to the country,
        Hurrah! Hurrah!"

"Louis! Stop it! Do you know you are positively corrupt to do such a thing at such a time as this?"

"Well, it's all I know, Valerie —"

"I could cry!" she said, indignantly, and maintained a dangerous silence until they drifted into the still waters of the outlet where the starlight silvered the sedge-grass and feathery foliage formed a roof above.

Into the leafy tunnel they floated, oars shipped; she, cheek on hand, watching the fireflies on the water; he, rid of his cigarette, motionless in the stern.

After they had drifted half a mile she seemed disinclined to resume the oars; so he crossed with her, swung the boat, and drove it foaming against the silent current.

On the return they said very little. She stood pensive, distraite, as he tied the boat, then — for the road was dark and uneven — took his arm and turned away beside him.

"I'm afraid I haven't been very amusing company," he ventured.

She tightened her arm in his — a momentary, gentle pressure:

"I'm merely too happy to talk," she said. "Does that answer satisfy you?"

Touched deeply, he took her hand which rested so lightly on his sleeve — a hand so soft and fine of texture — so cool and fresh and slender that the youth and fragrance of it drew his lips to it. Then he reversed it and kissed the palm.

"Why, Louis," she said, "I didn't think you could be so sentimental."

"Is that sentimental?"

"Isn't it?"

"It rather looks like it, doesn't it?"

"Rather."

"Did you mind?"

"No. . . . Only — you and I — it seems — superfluous. I don't think anything you do could make me like you more than I do."

"You sweet little thing!"

"No, only loyal, Kelly. I can never alter toward you."

"What's that? A vow!"

"Yes — of constancy and of friendship eternal."

"*Nomen amicitia est; nomen inane fides!* — Friendship is only a name; constancy an empty title,'" he quoted.

"Do you believe that?"

"Constancy is an honest wish, but a dishonest promise," he said. "You know it lies with the gods, Valerie."

"So they say. But I know myself. And I know that, however I may ever care for anybody else, it can never be at your expense — at the cost of one atom of my regard for you. As I care for you now, so have I from the beginning; so will I to the end; care more for you, perhaps; but never less, Louis. And that I know."

More deeply moved than he perhaps cared to be, he walked on slowly in silence, measuring his step to hers. In the peace of the midnight world, in the peace of her presence, he was aware of a tranquility, a rest that he had not known in weeks. Vaguely first, then uneasily, he remembered that he had not known it since her departure, and shook off the revelation with instinctive recoil — dismissed it, smiled at it to have done with it. For such things could not happen.

The woods were fragrant as they passed; a little rill, swelling from the thicket of tangled jewel-weed, welled up, bubbling in the starlight. She knelt down and drank from her cupped hands, and offered him the same sweet cup, holding it fragrantly to his lips.

And there, on their knees under the stars, he touched her full childlike lips with his; and, laughing, she let him kiss her again — but not a third time, swaying back from her knees to avoid him, then rising lithely to her feet.

"The poor nymph and the great god Kelly!" she said; "a new hero for the pantheon: a new dryad to weep over. Kelly, I believe your story of your golden cloud, now."

"Didn't you credit it before?"

"No."

"But now that I've kissed you, you do believe it?"

"Y-yes."

"Then to fix that belief more firmly —"

"Oh, no, you mustn't, Kelly —" she cried, her soft voice hinting of hidden laughter. "I'm quite sure that my belief is very firmly fixed. Hear me recite my creed. Credo! I believe that you are the great god Kelly, perfectly capable of traveling about wrapped in a golden cloud —"

"You are mocking at the gods!"

"No, I'm not. Who am I to affront Olympus. . . ? Wh-what are you going to do, Kelly? Fly to the sacred mount with me?"

But she suffered his arm to remain around her waist as they moved slowly on through the darkness.

"How long are you going to stay? Tell me, Louis. I'm as tragically curious as Pandora and Psyche and Bluebeard's wife, melted into the one and eternal feminine."

"I'm going tomorrow."

"Oh-h," she said, softly.

He was silent. They walked on, she with her head bent a little.

"Didn't you want me to?" he asked at length.

"Not if you care to stay. . . . I never want what those I care for are indifferent about."

"I am not indifferent. I think I had better go."

"Is the reason important?"

"I don't know, Valerie — I don't really know."

He was thinking of this new and sweet familiarity — something suddenly born into being under the wide stars — something that had not been a moment since, and now was — something invoked by the vastness of earth and sky — something confirmed by the wind in the forest.

"I had better go," he said.

Her silence acquiesced; they turned into the ragged lawn, ascended the dew-wet steps; and then he released her waist.

The hallways were dark and deserted as they mounted the stairs side by side.

"This is my door," she said.

"Mine is on the next floor."

"Then — good night, Louis."

He took her hand in silence. After a moment she released it; laid both hands lightly on his shoulders, lifted her face and kissed him.

"Good night," she said. "You have made this a very happy day in my life. Shall I see you in the morning?"

"I'm afraid not. I left word to have a horse ready at daylight. It is not far from that, now."

"Then I shall not see you again?"

"Not until you come to New York."

"Couldn't you come back for a day? Querida is coming. Sammy and Harry Annan are coming up over Sunday. Couldn't you?"

"Valerie, dear, I *could*" — he checked himself; thought for a while until the strain of his set teeth aroused him to consciousness of his own emotion.

Rather white he looked at her, searching for the best phrase — for it was already threatening to be a matter of phrases now — of forced smiles — and some breathing spot fit for the leisure of self-examination.

"I'm going back to paint," he said. "Those commissions have waited long enough."

He strove to visualize his studio, to summon up the calm routine of the old regime — as though the colorless placidity of the past could steady him.

"Will you need me?" she asked.

"Later — of course. Just now I've a lot of men's figures to deal with — that symbolical affair for the new court house."

"Then you don't need me?"

"No."

She thought a moment, slim fingers resting on the knob of her door, standing partly turned away from him. Then, opening her door, she stepped inside, hesitated, looked back:

"Good-bye, Louis, dear," she said, gently.

Chapter VI

*N*eville had begun to see less and less of Valerie West. When she first returned from the country in September she had come to the studio and had given him three or four mornings on the portrait which he had begun during the previous summer. But the painting of it involved him in difficulties entirely foreign to him — difficulties born of technical timidity of the increasing and inexplicable lack of self-confidence. And deeply worried, he laid it aside, A dull, unreasoning anxiety possessed him. Those who had given him commissions to execute were commencing to importune him for results. He had never before disappointed any client. Valerie could be of very little service to him in the big mural decorations which, almost in despair, he had abruptly started. Here and there, in the imposing compositions designed for the Court House, a female figure, or group of figures, was required, but, in the main, male figures filled the preliminary cartoons — great law-givers and law-defenders of all ages and all lands, in robes and gowns of silks; in armor, in skins, in velvet and ermine — men wearing doublet, jack-coat, pourpoint; men in turban and caftan, men covered with mail of all kinds — armor of leather, of fiber, of lacquer, of quilted silk, of linked steel, Milanaise, iron cuirass; the emblazoned panoply of the Mongol paladins; Timour Melek's greaves of virgin gold; men of all nations and of all ages who fashioned or executed human law, from Moses to Caesar, from Mohammed to Genghis Kahn and the Golden Emperor, from Charlemagne to Napoleon, and down through those who made and upheld the laws in the Western world, beginning with

Hiawatha, creator of the Iroquois Confederacy — the Great League.

His studio was a confusion of silks, cut velvets, tapestries, embroideries, carpets of the East, lay figures glittering with replicas of priceless armor. Delicate fabrics trailed over chair and floor almost under foot; inlaid and gem-hilted weapons, illuminated missals, glass-cased papyri, gilded zones, filets, girdles, robes of fur, hoods, wallets, helmets, hats, lay piled up, everywhere in methodical disorder. And into and out of the studio passed male models of all statures, all ages, venerable, bearded men, men in their prime, men with the hard-hammered features and thick, sinewy necks of gladiators, men slender and pallid as dreaming scholars, youths that might have worn the gold-red elf-locks and the shoulder cloak of Venice, youth chiseled in a beauty as dark and fierce as David wore when the mailed giant went crashing earthward under the smooth round pebble from his sling.

Valerie's turn in this splendid panoply was soon over. Even had she been so inclined there was, of course, no place for her to visit now, no place to sit and watch him among all these men. After hours, once or twice, she came in to tea — to gossip a little with the old-time ease, and barter with him epigram for jest, nonsense for inconsequence. Yet, subtly — after she had gone home — she felt the effort. Either he or she had imperceptibly changed; she knew not which was guilty; but she knew.

Besides, she herself was now in universal demand — and in the furor of her popularity she had been, from the beginning, forced to choose among a very few with whom she personally felt herself at ease, and to whom she had become confidently accustomed. Also, from the beginning, she had not found it necessary to sit undraped for many — a sculptor or two — Burleson and Gary Graves — Sam Ogilvy with his eternal mermaidens, Querida — nobody else. The other engagements had been for costume or, at most, for head and shoulders. Illustrators now clamored for her in modish garments of the moment — in dinner gown, ball gown, afternoon, carriage, motor, walking, tennis, golf, riding costumes; poster artists made her pretty features popular; photographs of her in every style of indoor and outdoor garb decorated advertisements

in the backs of monthly magazines. She was seen turning on
the water in model bathtubs, offering the admiring reader a
box of bonbons, demurely displaying a brand of hosiery,
recommending cold cream, baked beans, railroad routes,
tooth powder, and real-estate on Long Island.

Her beauty, the innocent loveliness of her features, her
dainty modest charm, the enchanting outline and mold of
her figure were beginning to make her celebrated. Already
people about town — at the play, in the park, on avenue and
street, in hotels and restaurants, were beginning to recognize
her, follow her with approving or hostile eyes, turn their
heads to watch her.

Theatrical agents wrote her, making attractive offers for an
engagement where showgirls were the ornamental caryatids
which upheld the three tottering unities along Broadway. She
also had chances to wear very wonderful model gowns for
next season at the Countess of Severn's new dressmaking,
drawing rooms whither all snobdom crowded and shoved to
get near the trade-marked coronet, and where bewildering
young ladies strolled haughtily about all day long, displaying
to agitated Gotham the most startling gowns in the extrava-
gant metropolis.

She had other opportunities, too — such as meeting several
varieties of fashionable men of various ages — gentlemen
prominently identified with the arts and sciences — the art of
killing time and the science of enjoying the assassination.
And some of these assorted gentlemen maintained extensive
stables and drove tandems, spikes, and fours; and some were
celebrated for their yachts, or motors, or prima-donnas, or
business acumen, or charitable extravagances. . . . Yes, truly,
Valerie West was beginning to have many opportunities in
this generously philanthropic world. And she was making a
great deal of money — for her — but nothing like what she
might very easily have made. And she knew it, young as she
was. For it does not take very long to learn about such things
when a girl is attempting to earn her living in this altruistic
world.

"She'll spread her wings and go one of these days," observed Archie Allaire to Rita Tevis, who was posing as Psyche
for one of his clever, thinly brushed, high-keyed studies very

much after the manner and palette of Chaplin when they resembled neither Chartrain nor Zier, nor any other artist temporarily in vogue. For he was an adaptable man, facile, adroit, a master navigator in trimming sail to the fitful breeze of popular favor. And his work was in great demand.

"She'll be decorating the tonneau of some big touring car with crested panels — and there'll be a bunch of orchids in the crystal holder, and a Chow dog beside her, defying the traffic squad —"

"No, she won't!" snapped Rita. "She's as likely to do that as she is to dine with you again."

Allaire, caught off his guard, scowled with unfeigned annoyance. Repeated essays to ingratiate himself with Valerie had finally resulted in a dinner at the Astor, and in her firm, polite, but uncompromising declination of all future invitations from him, either to sit for him or beside him under any circumstances and any conditions whatever.

"So that's your opinion, is it, Rita?" he inquired, keeping his light-blue eyes and his thin wet brush busy on his canvas. "Well, sister, take it from muh, she thinks she's the big noise in the Great White Alley; but they're giving her the giggle behind her back."

"That giggle may be directed at you, Archie," observed Rita, scornfully; "you're usually behind her back, you know, hoisting the C.Q.D."

"Which is all right, too," he said, apparently undisturbed; "but when she goes to Atlantic City with Querida —"

"That is an utter falsehood," retorted Rita, calmly. "Whoever told you that she went there with Querida, lied."

"You think so?"

"I know so! She went alone."

"Then we'll let it go at that," said Allaire so unpleasantly that Rita took fiery offence.

"There is not a man living who has the right to look sideways at Valerie West! Everybody knows it — Neville, Querida, Sam, John Burleson — even you know it! If a man or two has touched her fingertips — her waist — her lips, perhaps — no man has obtained more than that of her — dared more than that! I have never heard that any man has ever even ventured to offend her ears, unless" — she added with malice, "that is the reason that she accepts no more invitations from you and your intimate friends."

Allaire managed to smile and continue to paint. But later he found use for his palette knife — which was unusual in a painter as clever as he and whose pride was in his technical skill with materials used and applied *premier coup*.

With October came the opening of many theaters; a premature gaiety animated the hotels and restaurants; winter fabrics, hats, furs, gowns, appeared in shops; the glittering windows along Fifth Avenue reflected more limousines and fewer touring bodies passing. Later top hats reappeared on street and in lobby; and when the Opera reopened, Long Island, Jersey, and Westchester were already beginning to pour in cityward, followed later by Newport, Lenox, and Bar Harbor. The police put on their new winter uniforms; furs were displayed in carriages, automobiles, and theaters; the beauty of the florist's windows became mellower, richer, and more splendid; the jewelry in the restaurants more gorgeous. Gotham was beginning to be its own again, jacked up by the Horse Show, the New Theater, and the Opera; and by that energetic Advertising Trust Company with its branches, dependencies, and mergers, which is called Society, and which is a matter of eternal vigilance and desperate business instead of the relaxation of cultivated security in an accepted and acceptable order of things.

Among other minor incidents, almost local in character, the Academy and Society of American Artists opened its doors. And the exhibition averaged as well as it ever will, as badly as it ever had averaged. Allaire showed two portraits of fashionable women, done, this time, in the manner of Zorn, and quite as clever on the streaky surface. Sam Ogilvy proudly displayed another mermaid — Rita in the tub — and two babies from photographs and "chic" — very bad; but as usual it was very quickly marked sold.

Annan had a portrait of his sister Alice, poorly painted and even recognized by some of her more intimate friends. Clive Gail offered one of his marines — waves splashing and dashing all over the canvas so realistically that women instinctively stepped back and lifted their skirts, and men looked vaguely around for a waiter — at least Ogilvy said so. As for

Neville, he had a single study to show — a full length — just
the back and head and the soft contour of limbs melting into
a luminously somber background — a masterpiece in technical perfection, which was instantly purchased by a wise and
Western millionaire, and which left the public staring but
unmoved.

But it was José Querida who dominated the whole show,
flooding everything with the splendor of his sunshine so that
all else in the same room looked cold or tawdry or washed
out. His canvas, with its superbly vigorous drawing, at once
became the sensation of the exhibition. Sunday supplements
reproduced it with a photograph of Querida looking amiably
at a statuette of Venus which he held in his long, tapering
fingers; magazines tried to print it in two colors, in three, in
dozens, and made fireworks of it to Querida's inwardly suppressed agony, and their own satisfaction. Serious young men
wrote "appreciations" about it; serious young women published instructive discourses concerning it in the daily papers.
Somebody in the valuable columns of the *Tribune* inquired
whether Querida's painting was meant to be symbolical;
somebody in the *Nation* said yes; somebody in the *Sun* said
no; somebody in something or other explained its psychological subtleties; somebody in something else screamed,
"bosh!"

Meanwhile the discussion was a god-send to fashionable
diners-out and to those cultivated leaders of society who
prefer to talk through the Opera and philharmonic.

In what the educated daily press calls the "world of art"
and the "realm of literature," Querida's picture was discussed
intelligently and otherwise, but it *was* discussed — from the
squalid table d'hôte, where unmanicured genius punctures
the air with patois and punches holes in it with frenzied
thumbs, to quiet, cultivated homes, where community of
taste restricts the calling lists — from the noisy studio, where
pianos and girls make evenings lively, to the austere bare
boards or the velvet elegance of studios where authority and
preciousness, and occasionally attainment, reside, and sometimes do not.

Cognatis maculis similis fera.

Neville was busy, but not too busy to go about in the evening among his own kind, and among other kinds, too. This unexpected resurgence within him of the social instinct, he made no attempt to account for to others or to himself. He had developed a mental and physical restlessness, which was not yet entirely nervous, but it had become sufficiently itching to stir him out of fatigue when the long day's work had ended — enough to drive him out of the studio — at first merely to roam about at hazard through the livelier sections of the city. But to the lonely, there is no lonelier place than a lively one; and the false brilliancy and gaiety drove him back upon himself and into his lair again, where for a while he remained meditating amid the somber menace of looming canvases and the heavy futility of dull-gold hangings, and the mischievous malice of starlight splintering into a million incandescent rainbow rays through the sheet of glass above.

Out of this, after some days, he emerged, set in motion by his increasing restlessness. And it shoved him in the direction of his kind once more — and in the direction of other kinds.

He dined at his sister's in Seventy-ninth Street near Madison Avenue; he dined with the Grandcourts on Fifth Avenue; he decorated a few dances, embellished an opera box now and then, went to Lakewood and Tuxedo for week ends, rode for a few days at Hot Springs, frequented his clubs, frequented Stephanie, frequented Maxim's.

And all the while it seemed to him as though he were temporarily enduring something which required patience, which could not last forever, which must one day end in a great change, a complete transformation for himself, of himself, of the world around him and of his aim and hope and purpose in living. At moments, too, an odd sensation of expectancy came over him — the sense of waiting, of suppressed excitement. And he could not account for it.

Perhaps it concerned the finishing of his great mural frieze for the Court House — that is, the completion of the section begun in September. For, when it was done, and cleared out of his studio, and had been set in its place, framed by the rose and gold of marble and ormolu, a heavy reaction of relief set in, leaving him listless and indifferent at first, then idle, disinclined to begin the companion frieze; then again restless, discontented, tired, and lonely in that strange solitude which seemed to be growing wider and wider around him in rings of silence. Men praised and lauded the great frieze; and he strove to respond, to believe them — to believe in the work and in himself — strove to shake off the terrible discouragement invading him, lurking always near to reach out and touch him, slinking at his heels from street to street, from room to room, skulking always just beyond the shadows that his reading lamp cast.

Without envy, yet with profound sadness, he stood and faced the splendor of Querida's canvas. He had gone to Querida and taken him by both of his thin, olive-skinned hands, and had praised the work with a heart clean of anything unworthy. And Querida had laughed and displayed his handsome teeth, and returned compliment for compliment. . . . And Neville had seen, on his dresser, a photograph of Valerie, signed in her long, girlish, angular hand — "To José from Valerie"; and the date was of mid-winter.

Christmas came; he sent Valerie some furs and a note, and, before he went to Aiken to spend the holidays with his father and mother, he tried to get her on the telephone — tried half a dozen times. But she was either busy with business or with pleasure somewhere or other — and he never found her at home; so he went South without hearing from her.

After he arrived, it is true, he received from her a cigarette case and a very gay and frank Christmas greeting — happy and untroubled apparently, brimming with gossip, inconsequences, and nonsense. In it she thanked him for his letter and his gift, hoped he was happy with his parents, and expressed an almost conventional desire to see him on his return.

Then his parents came back to New York with him. Two days before New Year's Day they went to Spindrift House instead of sailing for Egypt, where for some years now they had been accustomed to spend the winters shivering at Shepherd's. And he and his sister and brother-in-law and Stephanie dined together that evening. But the plans they made to include him for a New Year's Eve home party remained uncertain as far as he was concerned. He was vague — could not promise — he himself knew not why. And they ceased to press him.

"You're growing thin and white," said Lily. "I believe you're getting painter's colic."

"House painters acquire that," he said, smiling. "I'm not a member of their union yet."

"Well, you must use as much white lead as they do on those enormous canvases of yours. Why don't you start on a trip around the world, Louis?"

He laughed.

Later, after he had taken his leave, the suggestion reoccurred to him. He took enough trouble to think about it the next morning; sent out his servant to amass a number of folders advertising world girdling tours of various attractions, read them while lunching, and sat and pondered. Why not? It might help. Because he certainly began to need help. He had gone quite stale. Querida was right; he ought to lie fallow. No ground could yield eternally without rest. Querida was clever enough to know that; and he had been stupid enough to ignore it — even disbelieve it, contemptuous of precept and proverb and wise saw, buoyed above apprehension by consciousness and faith in his own inexhaustible energy.

And, after all, something really seemed to have happened to him. He almost admitted it now for the first time — considered the proposition silently, wearily, without any definite idea of analyzing it, without even the desire to solve it.

Somehow, at some time, he had lost pleasure in his powers, faith in his capacity, desire for the future. What had satisfied him yesterday, today became contemptible. Farther than ever, farther than the farthest, stars receded the phantoms of the great Masters. What they believed and endured and wrought and achieved seemed now not only hopelessly beyond any comprehension or attainment of his, but even beyond hope of humble discipleship.

And always, horribly, like an obsession, was creeping over him in these days the conviction of some similarity between his work and the thin, clear, clever brush-work of Allaire — with all its mastery of ways and means, all its triumph over technical difficulties, all its tricks and subtle appeals, and its falsity, and its glamour.

Reflection, retrospection sickened him. It was snowing and growing late when he wrote to a steamship agent making inquiries and asking for plans of staterooms.

Then he had tea, alone there in the early winter dusk, with the firelight playing over Gladys who sat in the full heat of the blaze, licking her only kitten, embracing its neck with one maternal paw.

He dressed about six, intending to dine somewhere alone that New Year's Eve. The somewhere, as usual, ended at the Syrinx Club — or rather at the snowy portal — for there he collided with Samuel Strathclyde Ogilvy and Henry Knickerbocker Annan, and was seized and compelled to perform with them on the snowy sidewalk, a kind of round dance resembling a powwow, which utterly scandalized the perfectly respectable club porter, and immensely interested the chauffeurs of a row of taxicabs in waiting.

"Come! Let up! This isn't the most dignified performance I ever assisted at," he protested.

"Who said it was dignified?" demanded Ogilvy. "We're not hunting for dignity. Harry and I came here in a hurry to find an undignified substitute for John Burleson. You're the man!"

"Certainly," said Annan, "you're the sort of cheerful ass we need in our business. Come on! Some of these taxis belong to us —"

"Where do you want me to go, you crazy —"

"Now be nice, Louis," he said, soothingly; "play pretty and don't kick and scream. Burleson was going with us to see the old year out at the Café Gigolette, but he's got laryngitis or some similar species of pip —"

"I don't want to go —"

"You've got to, dear friend. We've engaged a table for six —"

"Six!"

"Sure, dearie. In the college of experience coeducation is a necessary evil. Step lively, son!"

"Who is going?"

"One dream, one vision, one hallucination —" he wafted three kisses from his gloved fingertips in the general direction of Broadway — "and you, and Samuel, and I. Me lord, the taxi waits!"

"Now, Harry, I'm not feeling particularly cheerful —"

"But you will, dear friend; you will soon be feeling the Fifty-seven Varieties of cheerfulness. All kinds of society will be at the Gigolette — good, bad, fashionable, semi-fashionable — all imbued with the intellectual and commendable curiosity to see somebody 'start something.' And," he added, modestly, "Sam and I are going to see what can be accomplished —"

"No; I won't go —"

But they fell upon him and fairly slid him into a taxi, beckoning two other similar vehicles to follow in procession.

"Now, dearie," simpered Sam, "don't you feel better?"

Neville laughed and smoothed out the nap of his top hat.

They made three stops at three imposing looking apartment hotels between Sixth Avenue and Broadway — The Daisy, The Gwendolyn, The Sans Souci — where Negro porters and hallboys were gorgeously conspicuous and the clerk at the desk seemed to be unusually popular with the guests. And after every stop there ensued a shifting of passengers in the taxicabs, until Neville found himself occupying the rear taxi in the procession accompanied by a lively young lady in pink silk and swansdown — a piquant face and pretty figure, white and smooth and inclined to a plumpness so far successfully contended with by her corset maker.

"I have on my very oldest gown," she explained with violet-eyed animation, patting her freshly dressed hair with two smooth little hands loaded with diamonds and turquoises. "I'm afraid somebody will start something and then they'll throw confetti, and somebody will think it's funny to aim champagne corks at you. So I've come prepared," she added, looking up at him with a challenge to deny her beauty. "By the way," she said, "I'm Mazie Grey. Nobody had the civility to tell you, did they?"

"They said something. . . . I'm Louis Neville," he replied, smiling.

"Are you?" she laughed. "Well, you may take it from mother that you're as cute as your name, Louis. Who was it they had all framed up to give me my cues? That big Burleson gentleman who'd starve if he had to laugh for a living, wasn't it? Can you laugh, child?"

"A few, Mazie. It is my only Sunday accomplishment."

"Dearie," she added, correcting him.

"It is my only accomplishment, dearie."

"That will be about all — for a beginning!" She laughed as the cab stopped at the red awning and Neville aided her to descend.

Steps, vestibules, stairs, cloak-rooms were crowded with jolly, clamoring throngs flourishing horns, canes, rattles, and dusters decked with brilliant ribbons. Already some bore marks of premature encounters with confetti and cocktails.

Waiters and headwaiters went gliding and scurrying about, assigning guests to tables reserved months in advance. Pages in flame-colored and gold uniforms lifted the silken rope that stretched its barrier between the impatient crowd and the tables; managers verified offered credentials and escorted laughing parties to spaces bespoken.

Two orchestras, relieving each other, fiddled and tooted continuously; great mounds of flowers, smilax, ropes of evergreens, multi-tinted electroliers made the vast salon gay and filled it with perfume.

Even in the beginning it was lively enough though not yet boisterous in the city where all New York was dining and preparing for eventualities; the eventualities being that noisy mid-winter madness which seizes the metropolis when the birth of the New Year is imminent.

It is a strange evolution, a strange condition, a state of mind not to be logically accounted for. It is not accurate to say that the nicer people, the better sort, hold aloof; because some of them do not. And in this uproarious carnival the better sort are as likely to misbehave as are the worse; and they have done it, and do it, and probably will continue to say and do and tolerate and permit inanities in themselves and in others that, at other moments, they would regard as insanities — and rightly.

*A*round every table, rosily illuminated, laughter rang. White throats and shoulders glimmered, jewels sparkled, the clear crystalline shock of glasses touching glasses rang con-

tinual accompaniment to the music and the breezy confusion
of voices.

Here and there, in premonition of the eventual, the comet-
like passage of streaming confetti was blocked by bare arms
upflung to shield laughing faces; arms that flashed with
splendid jewels on wrist and finger.

Neville, coolly surveying the room, recognized many, responding to recognition with a laugh, a gesture, or with glass
uplifted.

"Stop making goo-goos," cried Mazie, dropping her hand
over his wrist. "Listen, and I'll be imprudent enough to tell
you the very latest toast —" She leaned nearer, opening her
fan with a daring laugh; but Ogilvy wouldn't have it.

"This is no time for single sentiment!" he shouted. "Everybody should be perfectly plural tonight — everything
should be plural, multiple, diffuse, all embracing, general,
polydipsiatic, polygynyatic, polyandryatic!"

"What's   polyandryatic?"   demanded   Mazie   in
astonishment.

"It means everybody is everybody else's! I'm yours and
you're mine but everybody else owns us and we own everybody."

"Hurrah!" shouted Annan. "Hear — hear! Where is the fair
and total stranger who is going to steal the first kiss from me?
Somebody count three before the rush begins —"

A ball of roses struck him squarely on the mouth; a furious
shower of confetti followed. For a few moments the volleys
became general, then the wild interchange of civilities subsided, and the cries of laughter died away and were lost in the
loud animated hum which never ceased under the gay uproar
of the music.

When they played the barcarole from Contes d'Hoffman
everybody sang it and rose to their feet cheering the beautiful
prima donna with whom the song was so closely identified,
and who made one of a gay group at a flower-smothered table.

And she rose and laughingly acknowledged the plaudits;
but they wouldn't let her alone until she mounted her chair
and sang it in solo for them; and then the vast salon went
wild.

Neville, surveying the vicinity, recognized people he never dreamed would have appeared in such a place — here a celebrated architect and his pretty wife entertaining a jolly party, there a well-known lawyer and somebody else's pretty wife; and there were men well known at fashionable clubs and women known in fashionable sets, and men and women characteristic of quieter sets, plainly a little uncertain and surprised to find themselves there. And he recognized assorted lights of the "profession," masculine and feminine; and one or two beautiful meteors that were falling athwart the underworld, leaving fading trails of incandescence in their jeweled wake.

The noise began to stun him; he laughed and talked and sang with the others, distinguishing neither his own voice nor the replies. For the tumult grew as the hour advanced toward midnight, gathering steadily in strength, in license, in abandon.

And now, as the minute hands on the big gilded clock twitched nearer and nearer to midnight, the racket became terrific, swelling, roaring into an infernal din as the raucous blast of horns increased in the streets outside and the whistles began to sound over the city from Westchester to the Bay, from Long Island to the Palisades.

Sheer noise, stupefying, abominable, incredible, unending, greeted the birth of the New Year; they were dancing in circles, singing, cheering amid the crash of glasses. Tablecloths, silken gowns, flowers were crushed and trampled under foot; flushed faces looked into strange faces, laughing; eyes strange to other eyes smiled; strange hands exchanged clasps with hands unknown; the whirl had become a madness.

And, suddenly, in its vortex, Neville saw Valerie West. Somebody had set her on a table amid the silver and flowers and splintered crystal. Her face was flushed, eyes and mouth brilliant, her gown almost torn from her left shoulder and fluttering around the lovely arm in wisps and rags of silk and lace. Querida supported her there.

They pelted her with flowers and confetti, and she threw roses back at everybody, snatching her ammunition from a great basket which Querida held for her.

Ogilvy and Annan saw her and opened fire on her with a cheer, and she recognized them and replied with volleys of rosebuds — was in the act of hurling her last blossom — caught sight of Neville where he stood with Mazie on a chair behind him, her arms resting on his shoulders. And the last rose dropped from her hand.

Querida turned, too, inquiringly; recognized Neville; and for a second his olive cheeks reddened; then with a gay laugh he passed his arm around Valerie and, coolly facing the bombardment of confetti and flowers, swung her from the table to the floor.

A furious little battle of flowers began at his own table, but Neville was already lost in the throng, making his way toward the door, pelted, shouldered, blocked, tormented — but, indifferent, unresponsive, forcing his path to the outer air.

Once or twice voices called his name, but he scarcely heard them. Then a hand caught at his; and a breathless voice whispered:

"Are you going?"

"Yes," he said, dully.

"Why?"

"I've had enough — of the New Year."

Breathing fast, the color in her face coming and going, she stood, vivid lips parted, regarding him. Then, in a low voice:

"I didn't know you were to be here, Louis."

"Nor I. It was an accident."

"Who was the — girl —"

"What girl?"

"She stood behind you with her hands on your shoulders."

"How the devil do I know," he said, savagely — "her name's Mazie — something — or — other."

"Did you bring her?"

"Yes. Did Querida bring *you?*" he asked, insolently.

She looked at him in a confused, bewildered way — laid her hand on his sleeve with an impulse as though he had been about to strike her.

He no longer knew what he was doing in the sudden surge of unreasoning anger that possessed him; he shook her hand from his sleeve and turned.

And the next moment, on the stairs, she was beside him again, slender, pale, close to his shoulder, descending the great staircase beside him, one white-gloved hand resting lightly within his arm.

Neither spoke. At the cloak-room she turned and looked at him — stood a moment slowly tearing the orchids from her breast and dropping the crushed petals underfoot.

A maid brought her fur coat — his gift; a page brought his own coat and hat.

"Will you call a cab?"

He turned and spoke to the porter. Then they waited, side by side, in silence.

When the taxicab arrived he turned to give the porter her address, but she had forestalled him. And he entered the narrow vehicle; and they sat through the snowy journey in utter silence until the cab drew up at his door.

Then he said: "Are you not going home?"

"Not yet."

They descended, stood in the falling snow while he settled with the driver, then entered the great building, ascended in the elevator, and stepped out at his door.

He found his latchkey; the door swung slowly open on darkness.

Chapter VII

*A*n electric lamp was burning in the hallway; he threw open the connecting doors of the studio where a light gleamed high on the ceiling, and stood aside for her to pass him.

She stepped across the threshold into the subdued radiance, stood for a moment undecided, then:

"Are you coming in?" she asked, cheerfully, quite aware of his ill-temper. "Because if you are, you may take off my coat for me."

He crossed the threshold in silence, and divested her of the fur garment which was all sparkling with melting snow.

"Do let's enjoy the firelight," she said, turning out the single ceiling lamp; "and please find some nice, big crackly logs for the fire, Kelly! — there's a treasure!"

His frowning visage said: "Don't pretend that it's all perfectly pleasant between us"; but he turned without speaking, cleared a big armchair of its pile of silks, velvets, and antique weapons, and pushed it to the edge of the hearth. Every movement he made, his every attitude was characterized by a sulky dignity which she found rather funny, now that the first inexplicable consternation of meeting him had subsided. And already she was wondering just what it was that had startled her; why she had left the café with him; why *he* had left; why he seemed to be vexed with her. For her conscience, in regard to him, was perfectly clear and serene.

"Now the logs, Kelly, dear," she said, "the kind that catch fire in a second and make frying-pan music, please."

He laid three or four logs of yellow birch across the bed of coals. The blaze caught swiftly, mounting in a broad sheet of yellow flame, making their faces brilliant in the darkness; and the tall shadows leaped across floor and wall and towered, wavering above them from the ruddy ceiling.

"Kelly!"

"What?"

"I wish you a Happy New Year."

"Thank you. I wish you the same."

"Come over here and curl up on the hearth and drop your head back on my knees, and tell me what is the trouble — you sulky boy!"

He did not appear to hear her.

"Please? —" with a slight rising inflection.

"What is the use of pretending?" he said, shortly.

"Pretending!" she repeated, mimicking him delightedly. Then with a clear, frank laugh: "Oh, you great, big infant! The idea of *you* being the famous painter Louis Neville! I wish there was a nursery here. I'd place you in it and let you pout!"

"That's more pretence," he said, "and you know it."

"What silly things you do say, Louis! As though people could find life endurable if they did not pretend. Of course I'm pretending. And if a girl pretends hard enough it sometimes comes true."

"What comes true?"

"Ah! — you ask me too much. . . . Well, for example, if I pretend I don't mind your ill-temper it *may* come true that you will be amiable to me before I go home."

There was no smile from him, no response. The warmth of the burning logs deepened the color in her cold cheeks. Snow crystals on her dark hair melted into iris-rayed drops. She stretched her arms to the fire, and her eyes fell on Gladys and her kitten, slumbering, softly embraced.

"Oh, do look, Kelly! How perfectly sweet and cunning! Gladys has her front paws right around the kitten's neck."

Impulsively she knelt down, burying her face in the fluffy heap; the kitten partly opened its bluish eyes; the mother-cat stretched her legs, yawned, glanced up, and began to lick the kitten, purring loudly.

For a moment or two the girl caressed the drowsy cats, then, rising, she resumed her seat, sinking back deeply into the armchair and casting a sidelong and uncertain glance at Neville.

The flames burned steadily, noiselessly, now; nothing else stirred in the studio; there was no sound save the ghostly whisper of driving snow blotting the glass roof above.

Her gaze wandered over the silken disorder in the studio, arrested here and there as the firelight gleamed on bits of armor — on polished corselet and helmet and the tall hilts of swords. Then she looked upward where the high canvas loomed a vast expanse of grey, untouched except for the brushed-in outlines of men in shadowy processional.

She watched Neville, who had begun to prowl about in the disorder of the place, stepping over trailing velvets, avoiding manikins armed cap-a-pie, moving restlessly, aimlessly. And her eyes followed his indecision with a smile that gradually became perplexed and then a little troubled.

For even in the uncertain firelight she was aware of the change in his face — of features once boyish and familiar that seemed now to have settled into a sterner, darker mold — a visage that was too lean for his age — a face already haunted of shadows; a mature face — the face of a man who had known unhappiness.

He had paused, now, head lifted, eyes fixed on vast canvas above. And for a long while he stood there leaning sideways against a ladder, apparently oblivious of her.

Time lagged, halted — then sped forward, slyly robbing him of minutes of which his senses possessed no record. But minutes had come and gone while he stood there thinking, unconscious of the trick time played him — for the fire was already burning low again and the tall clock in the shadows pointed with stiff and ancient hands to the death of another hour and the birth of yet another; and the old-time bell chimed impartially for both with a shift and slide of creaking weights and wheels.

He lifted his head abruptly and looked at Valerie, who lay curled up in her chair, eyes closed, dark lashes resting on her cheeks.

As he passed her chair and returned to place more logs on the fire she opened her eyes and looked up at him. The curve of her mouth grew softly humorous.

"I'd much prefer my own bed," she said, "if this is all you have to say to me."

"Had you anything to say to me?" he asked, unsmiling.

"About what, Kelly, dear?"

"God knows; I don't."

"Listen to this very cross and cranky young man!" she exclaimed, sitting up and winking her eyes in the rushing brilliancy of the blaze. "He is neither a very gracious host, nor a very reasonable one; nor yet particularly nice to a girl who left a perfectly good party for an hour with him."

She stole a glance at him, and her gaze softened:

"Perhaps," she said aloud to herself, "he is not really very cross; perhaps he is only tired — or in trouble. Otherwise his voice and manners are scarcely pardonable — even by me."

He stood regarding the flames with narrowing gaze for a few moments, then, hands in his pockets, walked over to his chair once more and dropped into it.

A slight flush stole into her cheeks; but it went as it came. She rose, crossed to where he sat and stood looking down at him.

"What *is* the matter?"

"With me?" in crude pretence of surprise.

"Of course. I am happy enough. What troubles *you?*"

"Absolutely nothing."

"Then — what troubles *us?*" she persisted. "What has gone wrong between us, Kelly, dear? Because we mustn't let it, you know," she added, slowly, shaking her head.

"Has anything gone wrong with us?" he asked, sullenly.

"Evidently. I don't know what it is. I'm keeping my composure and controlling my temper until I find out. You know what that dreadful temper of mine can be?" She added, smiling: "Well, then, please beware of it unless you are ready to talk sensibly. Are you?"

"What is it you wish me to say?"

"How perfectly horrid you can be!" she exclaimed, "I never knew you could be like this? Do you want a girl to go on her knees to you? I care enough for our friendship to do it — but I won't!"

Her mood was altering:

"You're a brute, Kelly, to make me miserable. I was having such a good time at the Gigolette when I suddenly saw you — your expression — and — I don't even yet know why, but every bit of joy went out of everything for me —"

"*I* was going out, too," he said, laughing. "Why didn't you remain? Your gay spirits would have returned untroubled after my departure."

There was an ugly sound to his laugh which checked her, left her silent for a moment. Then:

"Did you disapprove of me?" she asked, curiously. "Was that it?"

"No. You can take care of yourself, I fancy."

"I have had to," she said, gravely.

He was silent.

She added with a light laugh not perfectly genuine:

"I suppose I am experiencing with you what all mortals experience when they become entangled with the gods."

"What is that?"

"Unhappiness. All the others experienced it — Proserpine, Helen, poor little Psyche — every nice girl who ever became mixed up with the Olympians had a bad half hour of it sooner or later. And tonight the great god Kelly has veiled his face from me, and I'm on my knees at his altar sacrificing every shred of sweet temper to propitiate him. Now, mighty and sulky oracle! *what* has happened to displease you?"

He said: "If there seems to be any constraint — if anything has altered our pleasant intimacy, I don't know what it is anymore than you do, Valerie."

"Then there *is* something!"

"I have not said so."

"Well, then, I say so," she said, impatiently. "And I say, also, that whatever threatens our excellent understanding ought to be hunted out and destroyed. Shall we do it together, Louis?"

He said nothing.

"Come to the fire and talk it over like two sensible people. Will you? And please pull that sofa around to the blaze for me. Thank you. This, Kelly, is our bed of justice."

She drew the cushions under her head and nestled down in the full warmth of the hearth.

"*Le lit de justice,*" she repeated, gaily. "Here I preside, possessing inquisitorial power and prerogative, and exercising here tonight the high justice, the middle, and the low. Now hale before me those skulking knaves, Doubt, Suspicion, and Distrust, and you and I will make short work of them. Pull 'em along by their ears, Louis! This Court means to sit all night if necessary!"

She laughed merrily, raised herself on one arm, and looked him straight in the eyes:

"Louis!"

"What?"

"Do you doubt me?"

"Doubt what?"

"That my friendship for you is as warm as the moment it began?"

He said, unsmiling: "People meet as we met, become friends — very good, very close friends — in that sort of friendship which is governed by chance and environment. The hazard that throws two people into each other's company is the same hazard that separates them. It is not significant either way. . . . I liked you — missed you. . . . Our companionship had been pleasant."

"Very," she said, quietly.

He nodded: "Then chance became busy; your duties led you elsewhere — mine set me adrift in channels once familiar —"

"Is that all you see in our estrangement?"

"What?" he asked, abruptly.

"Estrangement," she repeated, tranquilly. "That is the real word for it. Because the old intimacy is gone. And now we both admit it."

"We have had no opportunity to be together this —"

"We once *made* opportunities."

"We have had no time —"

"We halted time, hastened it, dictated to it, ruled it — once."

"Then explain it otherwise if you can."

"I am trying to — with God's help. Will you aid me, too?"

Her sudden seriousness and emotion startled him.

"Louis, if our estrangement is important enough for us to notice at all, it is important enough to analyze, isn't it?"

"I have analyzed the reasons —"

"Truthfully?"

"I think so — as far as I have gone —"

"Let us go farther, then — to the end."

"But there is no particular significance —"

"Isn't there?"

"I don't know. After all, *why* did you leave that café? Why did *I*? Why are we together, now — here in your studio, and utterly miserable at one o'clock of the New Year's morning? For you and I are unhappy and ill at ease; and you and I are talking at cross purposes, groping, evading, fencing with words. If there is nothing significant in the friendship we gave each other from the hour we met — it is not worth the self-deception you are content with."

"Self-deception!" he repeated, flushing up.

"Yes. Because you do care more for me than what you have said about our friendship indicates. . . . And I care more for your regard than you seem willing to recognize —"

"I am very glad to —"

"Listen, Kelly. Can't we be honest with ourselves and with each other? Because — our being here, now — my leaving that place in the way I did — surprises me. I want to find out why there has been confusion, constraint, somewhere — there is *something* to clear up between us — I have felt that, vaguely, at moments; now I *know* it. Let us try to find out what it is, what is steadily undermining our friendship."

"Nothing, Valerie," he said, smiling. "I am as fond of you as ever. Only you have found time for other friendships. Your life has become more interesting, fuller, happier —"

"Not happier. I realize that, now, as you say it." She glanced around her; swiftly her dark eyes passed over things familiar. "I was happier here than I have ever been in all my life," she said. "I love this room — and everything in it. You know I do, Louis. But I couldn't very well come here when you were using all those models. If you think that I have neglected you, it is a silly and unfair thing to think. If I did neglect you I couldn't help it. And you didn't seem to care."

He shrugged and looked up at the outlined men's figures partly covering the canvas above them. Her gaze followed his, then again she raised herself on one elbow and looked around her, searching with quick eyes among the shadows.

"Where is my portrait?"

"Behind the tapestry."

"Have you abandoned it?"

"I don't know."

Her smile became tremulous: "Are you going to abandon the original, too?"

"I never possessed very much of you, did I?" he said, sulkily; and looked up at her quick exclamation of anger and surprise.

"What do you mean? You had all of me worth having —" there came a quick catch, in her throat — "you had all there is to me — confidence in you, gratitude for your friendship, deep, happy response to your every mood — my unquestioning love and esteem —"

"Your *love?*" he repeated, with an unpleasant laugh.

"What else do you call it?" she demanded, fiercely. "Is there a name less hackneyed for it? If there is, teach it to me. Yet — if ever a girl truly loved a man, I have loved you. And I do love you, dearly, honestly, cleanly, without other excuse than that, until tonight, you have been sweet to me and made me happier and better than I have ever been."

He sprang to his feet confused, deeply moved, suddenly ashamed of his own inexplicable attitude that seemed to be driving him into a bitterness that had no reason.

"Valerie," he began, but she interrupted him:

"I ask you, Kelly, to look back with me over our brief and happy companionship — over the hours together, over all you have done for me —"

"Have you done less for me?"

"I? What have I done?"

"You say you have given me — love."

"I have — with all my heart and soul. And, now that I think of it, I have given you more — I have given you all that goes with love — an unselfish admiration; a quick sympathy in your perplexities; quiet solicitude in your silences, in your aloof and troubled moments." She leaned nearer, a brighter flush on either cheek:

"Louis, I have given you more than that; I gave you my bodily self for your work — gave it to *you* first of all — came first of all to you — came as a novice, ignorant, frightened — and what you did for me then — what you were to me at that time — I can never, never forget. And that is why I overlook your injustice to me now!"

She sat up on the sofa's edge balanced forward between her arms, fingers nervously working at the silken edges of the upholstery.

"You ought never to have doubted my interest and affection," she said. "In my heart I have not doubted yours — never — except tonight. And it makes me perfectly wretched."

"I did not mean —"

"Yes, you did! There was something about you — your expression — when you saw me throwing roses at everybody — that hurt me — and you meant to."

"With Querida's arm around you, did you expect me to smile?" he asked, savagely.

"Was it *that?*" she demanded, astonished.

"What?"

"Querida's arm —" She hesitated, gazing straight into his eyes in utter amazement.

"It wasn't *that?*" she repeated. "Was it. . . ? You never cared about such petty things, did you? *Did* you? *Do* you care? Because I never dreamed that you cared. . . . What has a little imprudence — a little silly mischief — to do with our friendship? *Has* it anything to do with it? You've never said anything — and . . . I've flirted — I've been spoons on men — you knew it. Besides, I've nearly always told you. I've told you without thinking it could possibly matter to you — to *you* of all men! What do you care what I do? — as long as I am to you what I have always been?"

"I — *don't* — care."

"Of course not. How *can* you?" She leaned nearer, dark and curious gaze searching his. Then, with a nervous laugh voicing the impossible — "*You* are not in love with me — that way. Are you?" she asked, scarcely realizing what she was saying.

"No," he said, forcing a smile. "Are you with *me?*"

She flushed scarlet:

"Kelly, I never thought — dreamed — hoped —" Her voice caught in her throat a moment; "I — such a matter has not occurred to me." She looked at him partly dismayed, partly confused, unable now to understand him — or even herself.

"You know — that kind of love —" she began — "*real* love, never has happened to me. You didn't think *that*, did you? — because — just because I did flirt a little with you? It didn't mean anything serious — anything of *that* kind. Kelly, dear, *have* you mistaken me? Is *that* what annoys you? Were you afraid I was silly enough, mad enough to — to really think of you — in that way?"

"No."

"Oh, I was sure you couldn't believe it of me. See how perfectly frank and honest I have been with you. Why, you never were sentimental — and a girl isn't unless a man begins it! You never kissed me — except last summer when you were going away — and both of our hearts were pretty full —"

"Wait," he said, suddenly exasperated, "are you trying to make me understand that you haven't the slightest real emotion concerning me — concerning me as a *man* — like other men?"

She looked at him, still confused and distressed, still determined he should not misunderstand her:

"I don't know what you mean; truly I don't. I'm only trying to make you believe that I am not guilty of thinking — wishing — of pretending that in our frank companionship there lay concealed anything of — of deeper significance —"

"Suppose — it were true?" he said.

"But it is *not* true!" she retorted angrily — and looked up, caught his gaze, and her breath failed her.

"Suppose it were true — for example," he repeated. "Suppose you did find that you or I were capable of — deeper —"

"Louis! Louis! Do you realize what you are saying to me? Do you understand what you are doing to the old order of things between us — to the old confidences, the old content, the happiness, the — the innocence of our life together? *Do* you? Do you even *care?*"

"Care? Yes — I care."

"Because," she said, excitedly, "if it is to be — *that* way with you — I — I can not help you — be of use to you here in the studio as I have been. . . . *Am* I taking you too seriously? You do not mean that you *really* could ever love me, or I you, do you? You mean that — that you just want me back again — as I was — as we were — perfectly content to be together. That is what you mean, isn't it, Kelly, dear?" she asked, piteously.

He looked into her flushed and distressed face:

"Yes," he said, "that is exactly what I mean, Valerie — you dear, generous, clear-seeing girl! I just wanted you back again; I miss you; I am perfectly wretched without you, and that is all the trouble. Will you come?"

"I — don't — know. Why did you say such a thing?"

"Forgive me, dear!"

She slowly shook her head:

"You've made me think of — things," she said. "You shouldn't ever have done it."

"Done what, Valerie?"

"What you did — what you said — which makes it impossible for me to — to ever again be what I have been to you — even pose for you — as I did —"

"You mean that you won't pose for me anymore?" he asked, aghast.

"Only — in costume." She sat on the edge of the sofa, head averted, looking steadily down at the hearth below. There was a pink spot on either cheek.

He thought a moment. "Valerie," he said, "I believe we had better finish what we have only begun to say."

"Is there — anything more?" she asked, unsmiling.

"Ask yourself. Do you suppose things can be left this way between us — all the happiness and the confidence — and the innocence, as you say, destroyed?"

"What more is there to say," she demanded, coldly.

"Shall — I — say it?" he stammered.

She looked up, startled, scarcely recognizing the voice as his — scarcely now recognizing his altered features.

"What *is* the matter with you?" she exclaimed nervously.

"Good God," he said, hoarsely, "can't you see I've gone quite mad about you!"

"About — *me!*" she repeated, blankly.

"About *you* — Valerie West. Can't you see it? Didn't you know it? Hasn't it been plain enough to you — even if it hasn't been to me?"

"Louis! Louis!" she cried in hurt astonishment, "what have you said to me?"

"That I'm mad about you, and I am. And it's been so — for months — always — ever since the very first! I must have been crazy not to realize it. I've been fool enough not to understand what has been the matter. Now you know the truth, Valerie!" He sprang to his feet, took a short turn or two before the hearth, then, catching sight of her face in its colorless dismay and consternation:

"I suppose you don't care a damn for me — that way!" he said, with a mirthless laugh.

"What!" she whispered, bewildered by his violence. Then: "Do you mean that you are in *love* with me!"

"Utterly, hopelessly —" his voice broke and he stood with hands clenched, unable to utter a word.

She sat up very straight and pale, the firelight gleaming on her neck and shoulders. After a moment his voice came back to his choked throat:

"I love you better than anything in the world." he said in unsteady tones. "And *that* is what has come between us. Do you think it is something we had better hunt down and destroy — this love that has come between us?"

"Is — is that *true?*" she asked in the awed voice of a child.

"It seems to be," he managed to say. She slid stiffly to the floor and stood leaning against the sofa's edge, looking at him wide-eyed as a schoolgirl.

"It never occurred to you what the real trouble might be," he asked, "did it?"

She shook her head mechanically.

"Well, we know now. Your court of inquiry has brought out the truth after all."

She only stared at him, fascinated. No color had returned to her cheeks.

He began to pace the hearth again, lip caught savagely between his teeth.

"You are no more amazed than I am to learn the truth," he said. "I never supposed it was that. . . . And it's been that from the moment I laid eyes on you. I know it now. I'm learning, you see — learning not to lie to myself or to you. . . .

Learning other things, too — God knows what — if this is love — this utter — suffering —"

He swung on his heel and began to pace the glimmering tiles toward her:

"Discontent, apathy, unhappiness, loneliness — the hidden ache which merely meant I missed you when you were not here — when I was not beside you — all these are now explained before your bed of justice. Your court has heard the truth tonight; and you, Valerie, are armed with justice — the high, the middle, and the low."

Pale, mute, she raised her dark eyes and met his gaze.

In the throbbing silence he heard his heart heavy in his breast; and now she heard her own, rapid, terrifying her, hurrying her she knew not whither. And again, trembling, she covered her eyes with her hands.

"Valerie," he said, in anguish, "come back to me. I will not ask you to love me if you cannot. Only come back. I — can't — endure it — without you."

There was no response.

He stepped nearer, touched her hands, drew them from her face — revealing its pallid loveliness — pressed them to his lips, to his face; drew them against his own shoulders — closer, till they fell limply around his neck.

She uttered a low cry: "Louis!" Then:

"It — it is all over — with us," she faltered. "I — had never thought of you — this way."

"Can you think of me this way, now?"

"I — can't help it."

"Dearest — dearest —" he stammered, and kissed her unresponsive lips, her throat, her hair. She only gazed silently at the man whose arms held her tightly imprisoned.

Under the torn lace and silk one bare shoulder glimmered; and he kissed it, touched the pale veins with his lips, drew the arm from his neck and kissed elbow, wrist, and palm, and every slender finger; and still she looked at him as though dazed. A lassitude, heavy, agreeable to endure, possessed her. She yielded to the sense of fatigue — to the confused sweetness that invaded her; every pulse in her body beat its assent, every breath consented.

"Will you try to care for me, Valerie?"

"You know I will."

"With all your heart?" he asked, trembling.

"I do already."

"Will you give yourself to me?"

There was a second's hesitation; then with a sudden movement she dropped her face on his shoulder. After a moment her voice came, very small, smothered:

"What did you mean, Louis?"

"By what — my darling?"

"By — my giving myself — to you?"

"I mean that I want you always," he said in a happy, excited voice that thrilled her. But she looked up at him, still unenlightened.

"I don't quite understand," she said — "but —" and her voice fell so low he could scarcely hear it — "I am — not afraid — to love you."

"Afraid!" He stood silent a moment, then: "What did you think I meant, Valerie? I want you to *marry* me!"

She flushed and laid her cheek against his shoulder, striving to think amid the excited disorder of her mind, the delicious bewilderment of her senses — strove to keep clear one paramount thought from the heavenly confusion that was invading her, carrying her away, sweeping her into paradise — struggled to keep that thought intact, uninfluenced, and cling to it through everything that threatened to overwhelm her.

Her slim hands resting in his, her flushed face on his breast, his words ringing in her ears, she strove hard, hard! to steady herself. Because already she knew what her decision must be — what her love for him had always meant in the days when that love had been as innocent as friendship. And even now there was little in it except innocence; little yet of passion. It was still only a confused, heavenly surprise, unvexed, and, alas! unterrified. The involuntary glimpse of any future for it or for her left her gaze dreamy, curious, but unalarmed. The future he had offered her she would never accept; no other future frightened her.

"Louis?"

"Dearest," he whispered, his lips to hers.

"It is sweet of you, it is perfectly dear of you to wish me to be your — wife. But — let us decide such questions later —"

"Valerie! What do you mean?"

"I didn't mean that I don't love you," she said, tremulously. "I believe you scarcely understand how truly I do love you. . . . As a matter of fact, I have always been in love with you without knowing it. You are not the only fool," she said, with a confused little laugh.

"You darling!"

She smiled again uncertainly and shook her head:

"I truly believe I have always been in love with you. . . . Now that I look back and consider, I am sure of it." She lifted her pretty head and gazed at him, then with a gay little laugh of sheer happiness almost defiant: "You see I am not afraid to love you," she said.

"Afraid? Why should you be?" he repeated, watching her expression.

"Because — I am not going to marry you," she announced, gaily.

He stared at her, stunned.

"Listen, you funny boy," she added, framing his face with her hands and smiling confidently into his troubled eyes: "I am not afraid to love you because I never was afraid to face the inevitable. And the inevitable confronts me now. And I know it. But I will not marry you, Louis. It is good of you, dear of you to ask it. But it is too utterly unwise. And I will not."

"Why?"

"Because," she said, frankly, "I love you better than I do myself." She forced another laugh, adding: "Unlike the gods, whom I love I do not destroy."

"That is a queer answer, dear —"

"Is it? Because I say I love you better than I do myself? Why, Louis, all the history of my friendship for you has been only that. Have you ever seen anything selfish in my affection for you?."

"Of course not, but —"

"Well, then! There isn't one atom of it in my love for you, either. And I love you dearly — dearly! But I'm not selfish enough to marry you. Don't scowl and try to persuade me,

Louis, I've a perfectly healthy mind of my own, and you know it — and it's absolutely clear on that subject. You must be satisfied with what I offer — every bit of love that is in me —" She hesitated, level eyed and self-possessed, considering him with the calm gaze of a young goddess:

"Dear," she went on, slowly, "let us end this marriage question once and for all. You can't take me out of my world into yours without suffering for it. Because your world is full of women of your own kind — mothers, sisters, relatives, friends. . . . And all your loyalty, all your tact, all *their* tact and philosophy, too, could not ease one moment in life for you if I were unwise enough to go with you into that world and let you try to force them to accept me."

"*I tell you,*" he began, excitedly, "that they must accept —"

"Hush!" she smiled, placing her hand gently across his lips; "with all your man's experience you are only a man; but I *know* how it is with women. I have no illusions, Louis. Even by your side, and with the well-meant kindness of your family to me, you would suffer; and I have not the courage to let you — even for love's sake."

"You are entirely mistaken —" he broke out; but she silenced him with a pretty gesture, intimate, appealing, a little proud.

"No, I am not mistaken, nor am I likely to deceive myself that any woman of your world could ever consider me of it — or could ever forgive you for taking me there. And that means spoiling life for you. And I will not!"

"Then they can eliminate me, also!" he said, impatiently.

"What logic! When I have tried *so* hard to make you understand that I will not accept any sacrifice from you!"

"It is no sacrifice for me to give up such a —"

"You say very foolish and very sweet things to me, Louis, but I could not love you enough to make up to you your unhappiness at seeing me in your world and not a part of it. Ah, the living ghosts of that world, Louis! Yet *I* could endure it for myself — a woman can endure anything when she loves; and find happiness, too — if only the man she loves is happy. But, for a man, the woman is never entirely sufficient. My position in your world would anger you, humiliate you, finally embitter you. And I could not live if sorrow came to you through me."

"You are bringing sorrow on me with every word —"

"No, dear. It hurts for a moment. Then wisdom will heal it. You do not believe what I say. But you must believe this, that through me you shall never know real unhappiness if I can prevent it."

"And I say to you, Valerie, that I want you for my wife. And if my family and my friends hesitate to receive you, it means severing my relations with them until they come to their senses —"

"*That* is *exactly* what I will not do to your life, Louis! *Can't* you understand? Is your mother less dear to you than was mine to me? I will *not* break your heart! I will not humiliate either you or her; I will not ask her to endure — or any of your family — or one man or woman in that world where you belong. . . . I am too proud — and too merciful to you!"

"I am my own master!" he broke out, angrily —

"I am my own mistress — and incidentally yours," she added in a low voice.

"Valerie!"

"Am I not?" she asked, quietly.

"How can you say such a thing, child!"

"Because it is true — or will be. Won't it?" She lifted her clear eyes to his, unshrinking — deep brown wells of truth untroubled by the shallows of sham and pretence.

His face burned a deep red; she confronted him, slender, calm eyed, composed: "I am not the kind of woman who loves twice. I love you so dearly that I will not marry you. That is settled. I love you so deeply that I can be happy with you unmarried. And if this is true, is it not better for me to tell you? I ask nothing except love; I give all I have — myself."

She dropped her arms, palms outward, gazing serenely at him; then blushed vividly as he caught her to him in a close embrace, her delicate, full lips crushed to his.

"Dearest — dearest," he whispered, "you will change your ideas when you understand me better —"

"I can love you no more than I do. Could I love you more if I were your wife?"

"Yes, you willful, silly child!"

She laughed, her lips still touching his. "I don't believe it, Louis. I *know* I couldn't. Besides, there is no use thinking about it."

"Valerie, your logic and your ethics are terribly twisted —"

"Perhaps. All I know is that I love you. I'd rather talk of that —"

"Than talk of marrying me!"

"Yes, dear."

"But you'd make me so happy, so proud —"

"You darling! to say so. Think so always, Louis, because I promise to make you happy, anyway —"

He had encircled her waist with one arm, and they were slowly pacing the floor before the hearth, she with her charming young head bent, eyes downcast, measuring her steps to his.

She said, thoughtfully: "I have my own ideas concerning life. One of them is to go through it without giving pain to others. To me, the only real wickedness is the willful infliction of unhappiness. That covers all guilt. . . . Other matters seem so trivial in comparison — I mean the forms and observances — the formalism of sect and creed. . . . To me they mean nothing — these petty laws designed to govern those who are willing to endure them. So I ignore them," she concluded, smilingly; and touched her lips to his hand.

"Do you include the marriage law?" he asked, curiously.

"In our case, yes. . . . I don't think it would do for everybody to ignore it."

"You think we may, safely?"

"Don't you, Louis?" she asked, flushing. "It leaves you free in your own world."

"How would it leave you?"

She looked up, smiling adorably at his thought of her:

"Free as I am now, dearest of men — free to be with you when you wish for me, free to relieve you of myself when you need that relief, free to come and go and earn my living as independently as you gain yours. It would leave me absolutely tranquil in body and mind. . . ." She laid her flushed face against his. "Only my heart would remain fettered. And that is now inevitable."

He kissed her and drew her closer:

"You are so very, very wrong, dear. The girl who gives herself without benefit of clergy walks the earth with her lover in heavier chains than ever were forged at any earthly altar."

She bent her head thoughtfully; they paced the floor for a while in silence.

Presently she looked up: "You once said that love comes unasked and goes unbidden. Do vows at an altar help matters? Is divorce more decent because lawful? Is love more decent when it has been officially and clerically catalogued?"

"It is safer."

"For whom?"

"For the community."

"Perhaps." She considered as she timed her slow pace to his:

"But, Louis, I can't marry you and I love you! What am I to do? Live out life without you? Let you live out life without me? When my loving you would not harm you or me? When I love you dearly — more dearly, more deeply every minute? When life itself is — is beginning to be nothing in this world except you? What are we to do?"

And, as he made no answer:

"Dear," she said, hesitating a little, "I am perfectly unconscious of any guilt in loving you. I am glad I love you. I wish to be part of you before I die. I wish it more than anything in the world! How can an unselfish girl who loves you harm you or herself or the world if she gives herself to you — without asking benefit of clergy and the bureau of licenses?"

Standing before the fire, her head resting against his shoulder, they watched the fading embers for a while in silence. Then, irresistibly drawn by the same impulse, they turned toward one another, trembling:

"I'll marry you that way — if it's the only way," he said.

"It is the — only way."

She laid a soft hand in his; he bent and kissed it, then touched her mouth with his lips.

"Do you give yourself to me, Valerie?"

"Yes."

"From this moment?" he whispered.

Her face paled. She stood resting her cheek on his shoulder, eyes distrait thinking. Then, in a voice so low and tremulous he scarce could understand:

"Yes, *now,*" she said, "I — give — myself."

He drew her closer: she relaxed in his embrace; her face, white as a flower, upturned to his, her dark eyes looking blindly into his.

There was no sound save the feathery rush of snow against the panes — the fall of an ember amid whitening ashes — a sigh — silence.

Twice logs fell from the andirons, showering the chimney with sparks; presently a little flame broke out amid the débris, lighting up the studio with a fitful radiance; and the single shadow cast by them wavered high on wall and ceiling.

His arms were around her; his lips rested on her face where it lay against his shoulder. The ruddy resurgence of firelight stole under the lashes on her cheeks, and her eyes slowly unclosed.

Standing there gathered close in his embrace, she turned her head and watched the flame growing brighter among the cinders. Thought, which had ceased when her lips met his in the first quick throb of passion, stirred vaguely, and awoke. And, far within her, somewhere in confused obscurity, her half-stunned senses began groping again toward reason.

"Louis!"

"Dearest one!"

"I ought to go. Will you take me home? It is morning — do you realize it?"

She lifted her head, cleared her eyes with one slender wrist, pushing back the disordered hair. Then gently disengaging herself from his arms, and still busy with her tumbled hair, she looked up at the dial of the ancient clock which glimmered red in the firelight.

"Morning — and a strange new year," she said aloud, to herself. She moved nearer to the clock, watching the stiff, jerking revolution of the second hand around its lesser dial.

Hearing him come forward behind her, she dropped her head back against him without turning.

"Do you see what Time is doing to us? — Time, the incurable, killing us by seconds, Louis — eating steadily into the

New Year, devouring it hour by hour — the hours that we thought belonged to us." She added, musingly: "I wonder how many hours of the future remain for us."

He answered in a low voice:

"That is for you to decide."

"I know it," she murmured. She lifted one ringless hand and still without looking at him, pressed the third finger backward against his lips.

"So much for the betrothal," she said. "My ring-finger is consecrated."

"Will you not wear any ring?" he asked.

"No. Your kiss is enough."

"Yet — if we are — are —"

"Engaged?" she suggested, calmly. "Yes, call it that. I really am engaged to give myself to you — *ex cathedra — extra muros.*"

"When?" he said under his breath.

"I don't know. . . . I must think. A girl who is going to break all conventions ought to have time to consider the consequences —" She smiled, faintly — "a little time to prepare herself for the — the great change. . . . I think we ought to remain engaged for a while — don't you?"

"Dearest!" he broke out, pleadingly, "the old way *is* the best way! I cannot bear to take you — to have you promise yourself without formality or sanction —"

"But I have already consented, Louis. *Volenti non fit injuria,*" she added with a faint smile. *"Voluntas non potest cogi* — dearest — dearest of lovers! I love you dearly for what you offer me — I adore you for it. And — *how* long do you think you ought to wait for me?"

She disengaged herself from his arm, walked slowly toward the tall old clock, turned her back to it and faced him with clear level eyes. After a moment she laughed lightly:

"Did ever an engaged gentleman face the prospect of impending happiness with such a long face as this suitor of mine is wearing!"

His voice broke in the protest wrung from his lips.

"You *must* be my wife. I tell you! For God's sake marry me and let the future take care of itself!"

"You say so many sweet, confusing, and foolish things to me, Louis, that while you are saying them I almost believe them. And then that clear, pitiless reasoning power of mine awakens me; and I turn my gaze inward and read written on my heart that irrevocable law of mine, that no unhappiness shall ever come to you through me."

Her face, sweetly serious, brightened slowly to a smile.

"Now I am going home, monsieur — home to think over my mad and incredible promise to you . . . and I'm wondering whether I'll wake up scared to death. . . . Daylight is a chilly shower-bath. No doubt at all that I'll be pretty well frightened over what I've said and done tonight. . . . Louis, dear, you simply *must* take me home this very minute!" She came up to him, placed both hands on his shoulders, kissed him lightly, looked at him for a moment, humorously grave:

"Some day," she said, "a big comet will hit this law-ridden, man-regulated earth — or the earth will slip a cog and go wabbling out of its orbit into interstellar space and side-wipe another planet — or it will ultimately freeze up like the moon. And who will care then *how* Valerie West loved Louis Neville? — or what letters in a forgotten language spelled 'wife' and what letters spelled 'mistress'? After all, I am not afraid of words. Nor do I fear what is in my heart. God reads it as I stand here; and he can see no selfishness in it. So if merely loving you all my life — and proving it — is an evil thing to do, I shall be punished; but I'm going to do it and find out what celestial justice really thinks about it."

Chapter VIII

*V*alerie was busy — exceedingly busy arranging matters, in view of the great change impending.

She began by balancing her check book, comparing stubs with canceled checks, adding and verifying sums total, filing away paid bills and paying the remainder — a financial operation which did not require much time, but to which she applied herself with all the seriousness of a wealthy man hunting through a check book which will not balance, for a few pennies that ought to be his.

For since she had any accounts at all to keep, she had kept them with method and determination. Her genius for order was inherent: even when she possessed nothing except the clothes she wore, she had always kept them in perfect condition. And now that her popularity in business gave her a bank balance and permitted some of the intimate little luxuries that make for a woman's self-respect, a perfect passion for order and method possessed her.

The tiny bedroom which she inhabited, and the adjoining bathroom, were always immaculate. Every week she made an inventory of her few but pretty garments, added or subtracted from her memorandum, went over her laundry list, noted and laid aside whatever clothing needed repairs.

Once a week, too, she inspected her hats, foot-wear, furs; dusted the three rows of books, emptied and cleaned the globe in which a solitary goldfish swam, goggling his eyes in the sunshine, and scrubbed the porcelain perching pole on which her parrot sat all day in the bathroom window making limited observations in French, Spanish, and English, and splitting red peppers and dried watermelon seeds with his heavy curved beak. He was a gorgeous bird, with crimson and turquoise blue on him, and a capacity for deviltry restrained only by a silver anklet and chain, gifts from Querida, as was also the parrot.

So Valerie, in view of the great change impending, began to put her earthly house in order — without any particular reason, however, because the great change would not affect her quarters or her living in them. Nor could she afford to permit it to interfere with her business career for which perfect independence was necessary.

She had had it out with Neville one stormy afternoon in January, stopping in for tea after posing for John Burleson's Psyche fountain ordered by Penrhyn Cardemon. She had demanded from Neville acquiescence in her perfect freedom of action, absolute independence; had modestly requested non-interference in her business affairs and the liberty to support herself.

"There is no other way, Louis," she explained very sweetly. "I do not think I am going to lose any self-respect in giving myself to you — but there would not be one shred of it left to cover me if I were not as free as you are to make the world pay me fairly for what I give it."

And, another time, she had said to him: "It is better not to tell me all about your personal, private, and financial affairs — better that I do not tell you about mine. Is it necessary to burst into financial and trivial confidences when one is in love?

"I have an idea that that is what spoils most marriages. To me there is a certain respectability in reticence when a girl is very much in love. I would no more open my personal and private archives in all their petty disorder to your inspection than I would let you see me dress — even if we had been married for hundreds of years."

And still, on another occasion, when he had fought her for hours in an obstinate determination to make her say she would marry him — and when, beaten, chagrined, baffled, he had lost his temper, she won him back with her childlike candor and self-control.

"Your logic," he said, "is unbaked, unmature, unfledged. It's squab-logic, I tell you, Valerie; and it is not very easy for me to listen to it."

"I'm afraid that I am not destined to be entirely easy for you, dear, even with love as the only tie with which to bind you. The arbitrary laws of a false civilization are going to impose on you what you think are duties and obligations to me and to yourself — until I explain them away. You must come to me in your perplexity, Louis, and give me a chance to remind you of the basic and proven proposition that a girl is born into this world as free as any man, and as responsible to herself and to others; and that her title to her own individuality and independence — her liberty of mind, her freedom to give and accept, her capability of taking care of herself, her divine right of considering, re-considering, of meeting the world unafraid — is what really ought to make her lovable."

He had answered: "What rotten books have you been reading?" And it annoyed her, particularly when he had asked her whether she expected to overturn, with the squab-logic of twenty years, the formalisms of a civilization several thousand years old. He had added:

"The runways of wild animals became Indian paths; the Indian paths became settlers' roads, and the roads, in time, city streets. But it was the instinct of wild creatures that surveyed and laid out the present highways of our reasoning civilization. And I tell you, Valerie, that the old ways are the best, for on them is founded every straight highway of modern thought and custom."

She considered:

"Then there is only one way left — to see you no more."

He had thought so, too, infuriated at the idea; and they had passed a very miserable and very stormy afternoon together, which resulted in her crying silently on the way home; and in a sleepless night for two; and in prolonged telephone conversation at daybreak. But it all ended with a ring at his door-bell, a girl in furs all flecked with snow, springing swiftly into his studio; a moment's hesitation — then the girl and her furs in his arms, her cold pink cheeks against his face — a brief moment of utter happiness — for she was on her way to business — a swift, silent caress, then eyes searching eyes in silent promise — in reluctant farewell for an hour or two.

But it left him to face the problems of the day with a new sense of helplessness — the first confused sensation that hers was the stronger nature, the dominant personality — although he did not definitely understand this.

Because, how could he understand it of a young girl so soft, so yielding, so sweet, so shy and silent in the imminence of passion when her consenting lips trembled and grew fragrant in half-awakened response to his.

How could he believe it — conscious of what he had made of himself through sheer will and persistent? How could he credit it — remembering what he already stood for in the world, where he stood, how he had arrived by the rigid road of self-denial; how he had mounted, steadily, undismayed, unperturbed, undeterred by the clamor of envy, of hostility, unseduced by the honey of flattery?

Upright, calm, self-confident, he had forged on straight ahead, following nobody — battled steadily along the upward path until — out of the void, suddenly he had come up against a blank wall.

That wall which had halted, perplexed, troubled, dismayed, terrified him because he was beginning to believe it to be the boundary which marked his own limitations, suddenly had become a transparent barrier through which he could see. And what he saw on the other side was an endless vista leading into infinity. But the path was guarded; Love stood sentinel there. And that was what he saw ahead of him now, and he knew that he might pass on if Love willed it — and that he would never care to pass on alone. But that he *could* not go forward, ignoring Love, neither occurred to him nor would he have believed it if it had. Yet, at times, an indefinable unease possessed him as though some occult struggle was impending for which he was unprepared.

That struggle had already begun, but he did not know it.

On the contrary all his latent strength and brilliancy had revived, exquisitely virile; and the new canvas on which he began now to work blossomed swiftly into magnificent florescence.

A superb riot of color bewitched the entire composition; never had his brushes swept with such sun-tipped fluency, never had the fresh splendor of his hues and tones approached so closely to convincing himself in the hours of fatigue and coldly sober reaction from the auto-intoxication of his own facility.

That auto-intoxication had always left his mind and his eye steady and watchful, although drugged — like the calm judgment of the intoxicated opportunist at the steering wheel of a racing motor. And a race once run and ended, a deliberate consideration of results usually justified the pleasure of the pace.

Yet that mysterious something which some said he lacked, had not yet appeared. That *something*, according to many, was an elusive quality born of a sympathy for human suffering — an indefinable and delicate bond between the artist and his world — between a master who has suffered, and all humanity who understands.

The world seemed to recognize this subtle bond between themselves and Querida's pictures. Yet in the pictures there was never any sadness. Had Querida ever suffered? Was it in that olive-skinned, soft-voiced young man to suffer? — a man apparently all grace and unruffled surface and gentle charm — a man whose placid brow remained smooth and untroubled by any line of perplexity or of sorrow.

And as Neville studied his own canvas coolly, logically, with an impersonal scrutiny that almost amounted to hostility, he wondered what it was in Querida's work that still remained absent in his. He felt its absence but he could not define what it was that was absent, could not discover the nature of it. He really began to feel the lack of it in his work, but he searched his canvas and his own heart in vain for any vacuum unfilled.

Then, too, had he himself not suffered? What had that restless, miserable winter meant, if it had not meant sorrow? He *had* suffered — blindly it is true until the truth of his love for Valerie had suddenly confronted him. Yet that restless pain — and the intense emotion of their awakening — all the doubts, all the anxieties — the wonder and happiness and sadness in the imminence of that strange future impending

for them both — had altered nothing in his work — brought
into it no new quality — unless, as he thought, it had inten-
sified to a dazzling brilliancy the same qualities which already
had made his work famous.

"It's all talk," he said to himself — "it's sentimental jargon,
precious twaddle — all this mysterious babble about occult
quality and humanity and sympathy. If José Querida has the
capacity of a chipmunk for mental agony, I've lost my bet
that he hasn't."

And all the time he was conscious that there *was* something
about Querida's work which made that work great; and that
it was not in his own work, and that his own work was not
great, and never had been great.

"But it will be," he said rather grimly to himself one day,
turning with a shrug from his amazing canvas and pulling
the unfinished portrait of Valerie into the cold north light.

For a long while he stood before it, searching in it for any
hint of that elusive and mysterious *something,* and found
none.

Moreover there was in the painting of this picture a certain
candor amounting to stupidity — an uncertainty — a naïve,
groping sort of brush work. It seemed to be technically,
almost deliberately, muddled.

There was a tentative timidity about it that surprised his
own technical assurance — almost moved him to contempt.

What had he been trying to do? For what had he been
searching in those slow, laborious, almost painful brush
strokes — in that clumsy groping for values, in the painstaking
reticence, the joyless and mathematical establishment of a
somber and uninspiring key, in the patient plotting of simpler planes where space and quiet reigned unaccented?

"Lord!" he said, biting his lip. "I've been stung by the
microbe of the precious! I'll be talking Art next with both
thumbs and a Vandyke beard."

Still, through his self-disgust, a sensation of respect for the
canvas at which he was scowling, persisted. Nor could he
account for the perfectly unwelcome and involuntary idea
that there was, about the half-finished portrait, something
almost dignified in the very candor of its painting.

John Burleson came striding in while he was still examining it. He usually came about tea time, and the door was left
open after five o'clock.

"O-ho!" he said in his big, unhumorous voice, "what in
hell and the name of Jimmy Whistler have we here?"

"Mud," said Neville, shortly — "like Mr. Whistler's."

"He was muddy — sometimes," said John, seriously, "but
you never were until this."

"Oh, I know it, Johnny. Something infected me. I merely
tried to do what isn't in me. And this is the result. When a
man decides he has a mission, you can never tell what fool
thing he'll be guilty of."

"It's Valerie West, isn't it?" demanded John, bluntly.

"She won't admire you for finding any resemblance," said
Neville, laughing.

The big sculptor rubbed his big nose reflectively.

"After all," he said, "what is so bad about it, Kelly?"

"Oh, everything."

"No, it isn't. There's something about it that's — different
— and interesting —"

"Oh, shut up, John, and fix yourself a drink —"

"Kelly, I'm telling you that it isn't bad — that there's
something terribly solid and sincere about this beginning —"

He looked around with a bovine grunt as Sam Ogilvy and
Harry Annan came mincing in: "I say, you would-be funny
fellows! — come over and tell Kelly Neville that he's got a
pretty good thing here if he only has the brains to develop
it!"

Neville lighted a cigarette and looked on cynically as
Ogilvy and Annan joined Burleson on tiptoe, affecting exaggerated curiosity.

"I think it's rotten," said Annan, after a moment's scrutiny;
"don't you, Sam?"

Ogilvy, fists thrust deep into the pockets of his painting
jacket, eyed the canvas in silence.

"*Don't* you?" repeated Annan. "Or is it a masterpiece
beyond my vulgar ken?"

"Well — no. Kelly was evidently trying to get at something
new — work out some serious idea. No, I don't think it's
rotten at all. I rather like it."

"It looks too much like her; that's why it's rotten," said Annan. "Thank God I've a gift for making pretty women out of my feminine clients, otherwise I'd starve. Kelly, you haven't made Valerie pretty enough. That's the trouble. Besides, it's muddy in spots. Her gown needs dry-cleaning. But my chief criticism is the terrible resemblance to the original."

"Ah-h, what are you talking about!" growled Burleson; "did you ever see a prettier girl than Valerie West?"

Ogilvy said slowly: "She's pretty — to look at in real life. But, somehow, Kelly has managed here to paint her more exactly than we have really ever noticed her. That's Valerie's face and figure all right; and it's more — it reflects what is going on inside her head — all the unbaked, unassimilated ideas of immaturity whirring in a sequence which resembles logic to the young, but isn't."

"What do you mean by such bally stuff?" demanded Burleson, bluntly.

Annan laughed, but Ogilvy said seriously:

"I mean that Kelly has painted something interesting. It's a fascinating head — all soft hair and delicious curves, and the charming indecision of immature contours which ought some day to fall into a nobler firmness. . . . It's as interesting as a satire, I tell you. Look at that perfectly good mouth and its delicate sensitive decision with a hint of puritanical primness in the upper lip — and the full, sensuous under lip mocking the upper and giving the lie to the child's eyes which are still wide with the wonder of men and things. And there's something of an adolescent's mystery in the eyes, too — a hint of languor where the bloom of the cheek touches the lower lid — and those smooth, cool, little hands, scarcely seen in the shadow — did you ever see more purity and innocence — more character and the lack of it — painted into a pair of hands since Van Dyck and Whistler died?"

Neville, astonished, stood looking incredulously at the canvas around which the others had gathered.

Burleson said: "There's something honest and solid about it, anyway; hanged if there isn't."

"Like a hen," suggested Ogilvy, absently.

"Like a hen?" repeated Burleson. "What in hell has a hen got to do with the subject?"

"Like *you,* then, John," said Annan, "honest, solid, but totally unacquainted with the finer phases of contemporary humor —"

"I'm as humorous as anybody!" roared Burleson.

"Sure you are, John — just as humorously contemporaneous as anybody of our anachronistic era," said Ogilvy, soothingly. "You're right; there's nothing funny about a hen."

"And here's a highball for you, John," said Neville, concocting a huge one on the sideboard.

"And here are two charming ladies for you, John," added Sam, as Valerie and Rita Tevis entered the open door and mockingly curtsied to the company.

"We've dissected *your* character," observed Annan to Valerie, pointing to her portrait. "We know all about you now; Sam was the professor who lectured on you, but you can blame Kelly for turning on the searchlight."

"What search-light?" she asked, pivoting from Neville's greeting, letting her gloved hand linger in his for just a second longer than convention required.

"Harry means that portrait of you I started last year," said Neville, vexed. "He pretends to find it full of psychological subtleties."

"Do you?" inquired Valerie. "Have you discovered anything horrid in my character?"

"I haven't finished looking for the character yet," said Sam with an impudent grin. "When I find it I'll investigate it."

"Sam! Come here!"

He came carefully, wincing when she took him by the generous lobes of both ears.

"Now *what* did you say?"

"Help!" he murmured, contritely; "will no kind wayfarer aid me?"

"Answer me!"

"I only said you were beautifully decorative but intellectually impulsive —"

"No, answer me, Sam!"

"Ouch! *I* said you had a pair of baby eyes and an obstinate mouth and an immature mind that came to, conclusions before facts were properly assimilated. In other words I intimated that you were afflicted with incurable femininity and extreme youth," he added with satisfaction, "and if you tweak my ears again I'll kiss you!"

She let him go with a last disdainful tweak, gracefully escaping his charge and taking refuge behind Neville who was mixing another highball for Annan.

"This is a dignified episode," observed Neville, threatening Ogilvy with the siphon.

"Help me make tea, Sam," coaxed Valerie. "Bring out the table; that's an exceedingly nice boy. Rita, you'll have tea, too, won't you, dear?"

Unconsciously she had come to assume the role of hostess in Neville's studio, even among those who had been familiar there long before Neville ever heard of her.

Perfectly unaware herself of her instinctive attitude, other people noticed it. For the world is sharp-eyed, and its attitude is always alert, ears pricked forward even when its tail wags good-naturedly.

Ogilvy watched her curiously as she took her seat at the tea table. Then he glanced at Neville; but could not make up his mind.

It would be funny if there was anything between Valerie and Neville — anything more than there ever had been between the girl and dozens of her men friends. For Ogilvy never allowed himself to make any mistake concerning the informality and freedom of Valerie West in her intimacies with men of his kind. She was a born flirt, a coquette, daring, even indiscreet; but that ended it; and he knew it; and so did every man with whom she came in contact.

Yet — and he looked again at her and then at Neville — there seemed to him to be, lately, something a little different in the attitudes of these two toward each other — nothing that he could name — but it preoccupied him sometimes.

There was a little good-natured malice in Ogilvy; some masculine curiosity, too. Looking from Valerie to Neville, he said very innocently:

"Kelly, you know that peachy dream with whom you cut up so shamefully on New Year's night? Well, she asked me for your telephone number —"

"What are you talking about?" demanded Neville, annoyed.

"Why, I'm talking about Mazie," said Sam, pleasantly. "You remember Mazie Grey? And how crazy you and she became about each other?"

Valerie, who was pouring tea, remained amiably unconcerned; and Ogilvy obtained no satisfaction from her; but Neville's scowl was so hearty and unfeigned that a glimpse of his visage sent Annan into fits of laughter. To relieve which he ran across the floor, like a huge spider. Then Valerie leisurely lifted her tranquil eyes and her eyebrows, too, a trifle.

"Why such unseemly contortions, Harry?" she inquired.

"Sam tormenting Kelly to stir *you* up! He's got a theory that you and Kelly are mutually infatuated."

"What a delightful theory, Sam," said Valerie, smiling so sincerely at Ogilvy that he made up his mind there wasn't anything in it. But the next moment, catching sight of Neville's furious face, his opinion wavered.

Valerie said laughingly to Rita: "They'll never grow up, these two —" nodding her head toward Ogilvy and Annan. And to Neville carelessly — too carelessly: "Will you have a little more tea, Kelly dear?"

Her attitude was amiable and composed; her voice clear and unembarrassed. There may have been a trifle more color in her cheeks; but what preoccupied Rita was in her eyes — a fleeting glimpse of something that suddenly concentrated all of Rita's attention upon the girl across the table.

For a full minute she sat looking at Valerie who seemed pleasantly unconscious of her inspection; then almost stealthily she shifted her gaze to Neville.

Gladys and her kitten came purring around in quest of cream; Rita gathered them into her arms and caressed them and fed them bits of cassava and crumbs of cake. She was unusually silent that afternoon. John Burleson tried to interest her with heavy information of various kinds, but she only smiled absently at that worthy man. Sam Ogilvy and Harry Annan attempted to goad her into one of those lively exchanges of banter in which Rita was entirely capable of taking care of herself. But her smile was spiritless and non-combative; and finally they let her alone and concentrated their torment upon Valerie, who endured it with equanimity and dangerously sparkling eyes, and an occasional lightening retort which kept those young men busy, especially when the epigram was in Latin — which hurt their feelings.

She had just furnished them with a sample of this classical food for thought when the door-bell rang and Neville looked up in astonishment to see José Querida come in.

"Hello," he said, springing up with friendly hand out-stretched — "this is exceedingly good of you, Querida. You have not been here in a very long while."

Querida's smile showed his teeth; he bowed to Valerie and to Rita, bowed to the men in turn, and smiled on Neville.

"In excuse I must plead work, my dear fellow — a poor plea and poorer excuse for the pleasure lost in seeing you —" he nodded to the others — "and in missing many agreeable little gatherings — similar to this, I fancy?"

There was a rising inflection to his voice which made the end of his little speech terminate as a question; and he looked to Valerie for his answer.

"Yes," she said, "we usually have tea in Kelly's studio. And you may have some now, if you wish, José."

He nodded his thanks and placed his chair beside hers.

*T*he conversation had become general; Rita woke up, dumped the cats out of her lap, and made a few viciously verbal passes at Ogilvy. Burleson, earnest and most worthy, engaged Querida's attention for a while; but that intellectu-ally lithe young man evaded the ponderously impending dispute with suave skill, and his gentle smile lingered longer on Valerie than on anybody else. Several times, with an adroit carelessness that seemed to be purposeless, he contrived to draw Valerie out of the general level of conversation by merely lowering his voice; but she seemed to understand the invita-tion; and, answering him as carelessly as he spoke, keyed her replies in harmony with the chatter going on around them.

He drank his tea smilingly; listened to the others; bore his part modestly; and at intervals his handsome eyes wandered about the studio, reverting frequently to the great canvas overhead.

"You know," he said to Neville, showing the eternal edge of teeth under his crisp black beard — "that composition of yours is simply superb. I am all for it, Neville."

"I'm glad you are," nodded Neville, pleasantly, "but it hasn't yet developed into what I hoped it might." His eyes swerved toward Valerie; their glances encountered casually and passed on. Only Rita saw the girl's breath quicken for an instant — saw the scarcely perceptible quiver of Neville's mouth where the smile twitched at his lip for its liberty to tell the whole world that he was in love. But their faces were placid, their expressions well schooled; Querida's half-veiled eyes appeared to notice nothing and for a while he remained smilingly silent.

Later, by accident, he caught sight of Valerie's portrait; he turned sharply in his chair and looked full at the canvas.

Nobody spoke for a moment; Neville, who was passing Valerie, felt the slightest contact as the velvet of her fingers brushed across his.

Then Querida rose and walked over to the portrait and stood before it in silence, biting at his vivid under lip and at the crisp hairs of his beard that framed it.

Without knowing why, Neville began to feel that Querida was finding in that half-finished work something that disturbed him; and that he was not going to acknowledge what it was that he saw there, whether of good or of the contrary.

Nobody spoke and Querida said nothing.

A mild hope entered Neville's mind that the *something,* which had never been in any work of his, might perhaps lie latent in that canvas — that Querida was discovering it — without a pleasure — but with a sensitive clairvoyance which was already warning him of a new banner in the distance, a new trumpet-call from the barriers, another lance in the lists where he, Querida, had ridden so long unchallenged and supreme.

Within him he felt a sudden and secret excitement that he never before had known — a conviction that the unexpressed hostility of Querida's silence was the truest tribute ever paid him — the tribute that at last was arousing hope from its apathy, and setting spurs to his courage.

Rita, watching Querida, yawned and concealed the indiscretion with her hand and a taunting word directed at Ogilvy,
who retorted in kind. And general conversation began again.

Querida turned toward Neville, caught his eye, and
shrugged:

"That portrait is scarcely in your happiest manner, is it?"
he asked with a grimace. "For me —" he touched his breast
with long pale fingers — "I adore your gayer vein — your color,
clarity — the glamour of splendor that you alone can cast over
such works as that —" He waved his hand upward toward the
high canvas looming above. And he smiled at Neville and
seated himself beside Valerie.

A portfolio of new mezzotints attracted Annan; others
gathered around to examine Neville's treasures; the tea table
was deserted for a while except by Querida and Valerie. Then
he deliberately dropped his voice:

"Will you give me another cup of tea, Valerie? And let me
talk to you?"

"With pleasure." She set about preparing it.

"I have not seen you for some time," he said in the same
caressing undertone.

"You haven't required me, José."

"Must it be entirely a matter of business between us?"

"Why, of course," she said in cool surprise. "You know
perfectly well how busy I am — and must be."

"You are sometimes busy — pouring tea, here."

"But it is after hours."

"Yet, after hours, you no longer drop in to chat with me."

"Why, yes, I do —"

"Pardon. Not since — the new year began. . . . Will you
permit me a word?"

She inclined her head with undisturbed composure; he
went on:

"I have asked you to many theaters, invited you to dine
with me, to go with me to many, many places. And, it
appeared, that you had always other engagements. . . . Have
I offended you?"

"Of course not. You know I like you immensely —"

"Immensely," he repeated with a smile. "Once there was more of sentiment in your response, Valerie. There is little sentiment in immensity."

She flushed: "I *was* spoons on you," she said, candidly. "I was silly with you — and very indiscreet. . . . But I'd rather not recall that —"

"*I* can not choose but recall it!"

"Nice men forget such things," she said, hastily.

"How can you speak that way about it?"

"Because I *think* that way, José," she said, looking up at him; but she saw no answering smile in his face, and little color in it; and she remained unquietly conscious of his gaze.

"I will not talk to you if you begin to look at me like that," she began under her breath; "I don't care for it —"

"Can I help it — remembering —"

"You have nothing to remember except my pardon," she interrupted hotly.

"Your pardon — for showing that I cared for you?"

"My pardon for your losing your head."

"We were absolutely frank with one another —"

"I do not understand that you are the sort of man a girl can not be frank with. We imprudently exchanged a few views on life. You —"

"Many," he said — "and particularly views on marriage."

She said, steadily: "I told you that I cared at heart nothing at all for ceremony and form. You said the same. But you misunderstood me. What was there in that silly conversation significant to you or to me other than an impersonal interest in hearing ideas expressed?"

"You knew I was in love with you."

"I did *not!*" she said, sharply.

"You let me touch your hands — kiss you, once —"

"And you behaved like a madman — and frightened me nearly to death! Had you better recall that night, José? I was generous about it; I was even a little sorry for you. And I forgave you."

"Forgave me my loving you?"

"You don't know what love is," she said, reddening.

"Do you, Valerie?"

She sat flushed and silent, looking fixedly at the cups and saucers before her.

"*Do* you?" he repeated in a curious voice. And there seemed to be something of terror in it, for she looked up, startled, to meet his long, handsome eyes looking at her out of a colorless visage.

"José," she said, "what in the world possesses you to speak to me this way? Have you any right to assume this attitude — merely because I flirted with you as harmlessly — or meant it harmlessly —"

She glanced involuntarily across the studio where the others had gathered over the new collection of mezzotints, and at her glance Neville raised his head and smiled at her, and encountered Querida's expressionless gaze.

For a moment Querida turned his head away, and Valerie saw that his face was pale and sinister.

"José," she said, "are you insane to take our innocent affair so seriously? What in the world has come over you? We have been such excellent friends. You have been just as nice as you could be, so gay and inconsequential, so witty, so jolly, such good company! — and now, suddenly, out of a perfectly clear sky·your wrath strikes me like lightning!"

"My anger is like that."

"José!" she exclaimed, incredulously.

He showed the edge of perfect teeth again, but she was not sure that he was smiling. Then he laughed gently.

"Oh," she said in relief — "you really startled me."

"I won't do it again, Valerie." She looked at him, still uncertain, fascinated by her uncertainty.

The color — as much as he ever had — returned to his face; he reached over for a cigarette, lighted it, smiled at her charmingly.

"I was just lonely without you," he said. "Like an unreasonable child I brooded over it and —" he shrugged, "it suddenly went to my head. Will *you* forgive my bad temper?"

"Yes — I will. Only I never knew *you* had a temper. It — astonishes me."

He said nothing, smilingly.

"Of course," she went on, still flushed, "I knew you were impulsive — hotheaded — but I know you like me —"

"I was crazily in love with you," he said, lightly; "and when you let me touch you —"

"Oh, I won't ever again, José!" she exclaimed, half-fearfully; "I supposed you understood that sentiment could be a perfectly meaningless and harmless thing — merely a silly moment — a foolish interlude in a sober friendship. . . . And I *liked* you, José —"

"Can you still like me?"

"Y-yes. Why, of course — if you'll let me."

"Shall we be the same excellent friends, Valerie? And all this ill temper of mine will be forgotten?"

"I'll try. . . . Yes, why not? I *do* like you, and I admire you tremendously."

His eyes rested on her a moment; he inhaled a deep breath from his cigarette, expelled it, nodded.

"I'll try to win back all your friendship for me," he said, pleasantly.

"That will be easy. I want you to like me. I want to be able to like you. . . . I shall have need of friends," she said half to herself, and looked across at Neville with a face tranquil, almost expressionless save for the sensitive beauty of the mouth.

After a moment Querida, too, lifted his head and gazed deliberately at Neville. Then very quietly:

"Are you dining alone this evening?"

"No."

"Oh. Perhaps tomorrow evening, then —"

"I'm afraid not, José."

He smiled: "Not dining alone ever again?"

"Not — for the present."

"I see."

"There is nothing to see," she said calmly. But his smile seemed now so genuine that it disarmed her; and she blushed when he said:

"Am I to wish you happiness, Valerie? Is *that* the trouble?"

"Certainly. Please wish it for me always — as I do for you — and for everybody."

But he continued to laugh, and the color in her face persisted, annoying her intensely.

"Nevertheless," he said, "I do not believe you can be hopelessly in love."

"What ever put such an idea into that cynical head of yours?"

"Chance," he said. "But you are not irrevocably in love. You are ignorant of what love can really mean. Only he who understands it — and who has suffered through it — can ever teach you. And you will never be satisfied until he does."

"Are you *very* wise concerning love, José?" she asked, laughing.

"Perhaps. You will desire to be, too, some day. A good school, an accomplished scholar."

"And the schoolmaster? Oh! José!"

They both were laughing now — he with apparent pleasure in her coquetry and animation, she still a little confused and instinctively on her guard.

Rita came strolling over, a tiny cigarette balanced between her slender fingers:

"Stop flirting, José," she said; "it's too near dinner time. Valerie, child, I'm dining with the unspeakable John again. It's a horrid habit. Can't you prescribe for me? José, what are you doing this evening?"

"Penance," he said; "I'm dining with my family."

"Penance," she repeated with a singular look — "well — that's one way of regarding the pleasure of having any family to dine with — isn't it, Valerie?"

"José didn't mean it that way."

Rita blew a ring from her cigarette's glimmering end.

"Will you be at home this evening, Valerie?"

"Y-yes . . . rather late."

"Too late to see me?"

"No, you dear girl. Come at eleven, anyway. And if I'm a little late you'll forgive me, won't you?"

"No, I won't," said Rita, crossly. "You and I are business women, anyway, and eleven is too late for week days. I'll wait until I can see you, sometime —"

"Was it anything important, dear?"

"Not to me."

Querida rose, took his leave of Valerie and Rita, went over and made his adieux to his host and the others. When he had gone Rita, standing alone with Valerie beside the tea table, said in a low voice:

"Don't do it, Valerie!"

"Do — what?" asked the girl in astonishment.

"Fall in love."

Valerie laughed.

"Do you mean with Querida?"

"No."

"Then — what *do* you mean?"

"You're on the edge of doing it, child. It isn't wise. It won't do for us. . . . I know — I *know*, Valerie, more than you know about — love. Listen to me. Don't! Go away — go somewhere; drop everything and go, if you've any sense left. I'll go with you if you will let me. . . . I'll do anything for you, dear. Only listen to me before it's too late; keep your self-control; keep your mind clear on this one thing, that love is of no use to us — no good to us. And if you think you suspect its presence in your neighborhood, get away from it; pick up your skirts and run, Valerie. . . . You've plenty of time to come back and wonder what you ever could have seen in the man to make you believe you could fall in love with him."

Ogilvy, strolling up, stood looking sentimentally at the two young girls.

"A — perfect — pair — of precious — priceless — peaches," he said; "I'd love to be a Turk with an Oriental smirk and an ornamental dirk, and a tendency to shirk when the others go to work; for the workers I can't bear 'em and I'd rather run a harem —"

"No doubt," said Rita, coldly; "so you need not explain to me the rather lively young lady I met in the corridor looking for studio number ten —"

"Rita! Zuleika! Star of my soul! Jewel of my turban! Do you entertain suspicions —"

"Oh, *you* probably did the entertaining —"

"I? Heaven! How I am misunderstood! John Burleson! Come over here and tell this very charming young lady all about that somewhat conspicuous vision from a local theater who came floating into my studio by accident while in joyous quest of you!"

But Annan only laughed, and Rita shrugged her disdain. But as she nodded adieu to Valerie, the latter saw a pinched look in her face, and did not understand it.

Chapter IX

The world, and his own family, had always been inclined to love Louis Neville, and had advanced no farther than the inclination. There were exceptions.

Archie Allaire, who hated him, discussing him floridly once with Querida at the Thumb-tack Club in the presence of a dozen others, characterized him as "one of those passively selfish snobs whose virtues are all negative and whose modesty is the mental complacency of an underdone capon."

He was sharply rebuked by Ogilvy, Annan, and Burleson; skillfully by Querida — so adroitly indeed that his amiable and smiling apology for the absent painter produced a curiously depressing effect upon Ogilvy and Annan, and even left John Burleson dully uncomfortable, although Allaire had been apparently well drubbed.

"All the same," said Allaire with a sneer to Querida after the others had departed, "Neville is really a most frightful snob. Like a busy bacillus surrounded by a glass tube full of prepared culture, he exists in his own intellectual exudations perfectly oblivious to the miseries and joys of the world around him. He hasn't time for anybody except himself."

Querida laughed: "What has Neville done to you, my friend?"

"To me?" repeated Allaire with a shrug. "Oh, nothing. It isn't that. . . . All the same when I had my exhibition at the Monson Galleries I went to him and said, 'See here, Neville, I've got some Shoe-trust and Button-trust women to pour tea for me. Now you know a lot of fashionable people and I want my tea-pourers to see them, and I want the papers to say that they've been to a private view of my exhibition.'

"He gave me one of those absent-treatment stares and said he'd tell all the really interesting people he knew; and the damnedest lot of scrubby, dowdy, down-at-the-heels tatterdemalions presented his card at my private view that you ever saw outside an artist's rathskeller, a lower Fifth Avenue reception, or a varnishing day! By God, I can go to the bread-line and get that sort of lookers myself — and I don't care whether his bunch came from Tenth Street Colonial stock or the Washington Square nobility or the landed gentry of Chelsea or from the purlieus of the Bronx, which is where they apparently belong! I can get that kind myself. I wanted automobiles and broughams and clothes, and I got one sea-going taxi, and the dirty end of the stick! And to cap the climax he strolled in himself with a girl whose face is familiar to everybody who looks at bath tubs in the back of the magazines — Valerie West! And I want to tell you I couldn't look my Shoe-trust tea-pourers in the face; and they're so mad that I haven't got an order out of them since."

Querida laughed till the tears stood in his big, velvety, almond-shaped eyes.

"Why didn't you come to me?" he said.

"Tell you the truth, Querida, I would have if I'd known then that you were painting portraits of half of upper Fifth Avenue. Besides," he added, naïvely, "that was before I began to see you in the grand tier at the opera every week."

"It was before I sat anywhere except in the gallery," said Querida with a humorous shrug. "Until this winter I knew nobody, either. And very often I washed my own handkerchiefs and dried them on the windowpane. I had only fame for my laundress and notoriety for my butcher."

"Hey?" said Allaire, a trifle out of countenance.

"It is very true. It cost me so much to paint and frame my pictures that the prices they brought scarcely paid for models and materials." He added, pleasantly: "I have dined more often on a box of crackers and a jar of olives than at a table set with silver and spread with linen." He laughed without affectation or bitterness:

"It has been a long road, Allaire — from a stable-loft studio to —" he shrugged — "the 'Van Rypens' grand tier box, for example."

"How in God's name did you do it?" inquired Allaire, awed to the momentary obliteration of envy.

"I — painted," said Querida, smiling.

"Sure. I know that. I suppose it was the hellish row made over your canvases last winter that did the trick."

Querida's eyes were partly closed as though in retrospection. "Also," he said, softly, "I painted a very fashionable woman — for nothing — and to her entire satisfaction."

"That's the *real* thing, isn't it?"

"I'm afraid so. . . . Make two or three unlovely and unlovable old ladies lovely and lovable — on canvas — for nothing. Then society will let you slap its powdered and painted face — yes — permit you — other liberties — if only you will paint it and sign your canvases and ask them a wicked price for what you give them and — for what they yield to you."

Allaire's ruddy face grew ruddier; he grinned and passed a muscular hand over his thick, handsome, fox-tinted hair.

"I wish I could get next," he said with a hard glance at Querida. "I'd sting 'em."

"I would be very glad to introduce you to anybody I know," observed the other.

"Do you mean that?"

"Why not. A man who has waited as I have for opportunity understands what others feel who are still waiting."

"That's damn square of you, Querida."

"Oh, no, not square; just natural. The public table is big enough for everybody."

Allaire thought a moment, slowly caressing his foxy hair.

"After all," he said with a nervous snicker, "you needn't be afraid of anybody. Nobody can paint like you. . . . But I'd like to get a look in, Querida. I've got to make a little money in one way or another —" he added impudently — "and if I can't paint well enough to sting them, there's always the chance of marrying one of 'em."

Querida laughed: "Any man can always marry any woman. There's no trick in getting any *wife* you want."

"Sure," grinned Allaire; "a wife is a cinch; it's the front row that keeps good men guessing." He glanced at Querida, his grey-green eyes brimming with an imprudent malice he could not even now deny himself — "Also the backs of the magazines keep one guessing," he added, carelessly; "and I've the patience of a tom-cat, myself."

Querida's beautifully penciled eyebrows were raised interrogatively.

"Oh, I'll admit that the little West girl kept me sitting on back fences until some other fellow threw a bottle at me," said Allaire with a disagreeable laugh. He had come as near as he dared to taunting Querida and, afraid at the last moment, had turned the edge of it on himself.

Querida lighted a cigarette and blew a whiff of smoke toward the ceiling.

"I've an idea," he said, lazily, "that somebody is trying to marry her."

"Forget it," observed Allaire in contempt. "She wouldn't stand for the sort who marry her kind. She'll land hard on her neck one of these days, and the one best bet will be some long-faced Botticelli with heavenly principles and the moral stability of a tumbler pigeon. Then there'll be hell to pay; but *he* will get over it and she'll get aboard the toboggan. That's the way it ends, Querida."

Querida sipped his coffee and glanced out of the club window. From the window he could see the roof of the studio building where Neville lived. And he wondered how far Valerie was from that building at the present moment, wondered, and sipped his coffee.

He was a man whose career had been builded upon perseverance. He had begun life by slaying every doubt. And his had been a bitter life; but he had suffered smilingly; the sordid struggle along the edges of starvation had hardened nothing of his heart.

Sensitive, sympathetic, ardent, proud, and ambitious with the quiet certainty of a man predestined, he had a woman's capacity for patience, for suffering, and for concealment, but not for mercy. And he cared passionately for love as he did for beauty — had succumbed to both in spirit oftener than in the caprice of some inconsequential amourette.

But never, until he came to know Valerie West, had a living woman meant anything vital to his happiness. Yet, what she aroused in him was that part of his nature to which he himself was a stranger — a restless, sensuous side which her very isolation and exposure to danger seemed to excite the more until desire to control her, to drive others away, to subdue, master, mold her, make her his own, obsessed him. And he had tried it and failed; and had drawn aside, fiercely, still watching and determined.

Some day he meant to marry properly. He had never doubted his ability to do so even in the sordid days. But there was no hurry, and life was young, and so was Valerie West — young enough, beautiful enough to bridge the years with him until his ultimate destiny awaited him.

And all was going well again with him until that New Year's night; and matters had gone ill with him since then — so ill that he could not put the thought of it from him, and her beauty haunted him — and the expression of Neville's eyes! —

But he remained silent, quiet, alert, watching and waiting with all his capacity for enduring. And he had now something else to watch — something that his sensitive intuition had divined in a single unfinished canvas of Neville's.

So far there had been but one man supreme in the new world as a great painter of sunlight and of women. There could not be two. And he already felt the approach of a shadow menacing the glory of his sunlight — already stood alert and fixedly observant of a young man who had painted something disquieting into an unfinished canvas.

*T*hat man and the young girl whom he had painted to the astonishment and inward disturbance of José Querida, were having no easy time in that new world which they had created for themselves.

Embarked upon an enterprise in the management of which they were neither in accord nor ever seemed likely to be, they had, so far, weathered the storms of misunderstandings and the stress of prejudice. Blindly confident in Love, they were certain, so far, that it was Love itself that they worshipped no matter what rites and ceremonies each one observed in its adoration. Yet each was always attempting to convert the other to the true faith; and there were days of trouble and of tears and of telephones.

Neville presented a frightfully complex problem to Valerie West.

His even-tempered indifference to others — an indifference which had always characterized him — had left only a wider and deeper void now filling with his passion for her.

They were passing through a maze of cross-purposes; his ardent and exacting intolerance of any creed and opinion save his own was ever forcing her toward a more formal and literal appreciation of what he was determined must become a genuine and formal engagement — which attitude on his part naturally produced clash after clash between them.

That he entertained so confidently the conviction of her ultimate surrender to convention, at moments vexed her to the verge of anger. At times, too, his disposition to interfere with her liberty tried her patience. Again and again she explained to him the unalterable fundamentals of their pact. These were, first of all, her refusal to alienate him from his family and his own world; second, her right to her own individuality and freedom to support herself without interference or unrequested assistance from him; third, absolute independence of him in material matters and the perfect liberty of managing her own little financial affairs without a hint of dependence on him either before or after the great change.

That she posed only in costume now did not satisfy him. He did not wish her to pose at all; and they discussed various other theaters for her business activity. But she very patiently explained to him that she found, in posing for interesting people, much of the intellectual pleasure that he and other men found in painting; that the life and the environment, and the people she met, made her happy; and that she could not expect to meet cultivated people in any other way.

"I *don't* want to learn stenography and take dictation in a stuffy office, dear," she pleaded. "I *don't* want to sit all day in a library where people whisper about books. I don't want to teach in a public school or read novels to invalids, or learn how to be a trained nurse and place thermometers in people's mouths. I like children pretty well but I don't want to be a governess and teach other people's children; I want to be taught myself; I want to learn — I'm a sort of a child, too, dear; and it's the familiarity with wiser people and brighter people and pleasant surroundings that has made me as happy as I am — given me what I never had as a child. You don't understand, but I'm having my childhood now — nursery, kindergarten, parties, boarding-school, finishing school, début — all concentrated into this happy year of being among gay, clever, animated people."

"Yet you will not let me take you into a world which is still pleasanter —"

And the eternal discussion immediately became inevitable, tiring both with its earnestness and its utter absence of a common ground. Because in him apparently remained every vital germ of convention and of generations of training in every precept of formality; and in her — for with Valerie West adolescence had arrived late — that mystery had been responsible for far-reaching disturbances consequent on the starved years of self-imprisonment, of exaltations suppressed, of fears and doubts and vague desires and dreams ineffable possessing the silence of a lonely soul.

And so, essentially solitary, inevitably lonely, out of her own young heart and an untrained mind she was evolving a code of responsibility to herself and to the world.

Her ethics and her morals were becoming what wide, desultory, and unrestrained reading was making them; her passion for happiness and for truth, her restless intelligence, were prematurely forming her character. There was no one in authority to tell her — check, guide, or direct her in the revolt from dogmatism, pedantry, sophistry and conventionalism. And by this path youthful intelligence inevitably passes, incredulous of snare and pitfall where lie the bones of many a savant under magic blossoms nourished by creeds long dead.

*T*o bring no sorrow to anyone, Louis — that is the way I am trying to live," she said, seriously.

"You are bringing it to me."

"If that is so — then I had better depart as I came and leave you in peace."

"It's too late."

"Perhaps it is not. Shall we try it?"

"Could *you* recover?"

"I don't know. I am willing to try for your sake."

"Do you *want* to?" he asked, almost angrily.

"I am not thinking of myself, Louis."

"I *want* you to. I don't want you *not* to think about yourself all the time."

She made a hopeless gesture, opening her arms and turning her palms outward:

"Kelly Neville! *What* do you suppose loving you means to me?"

"Don't you think of yourself at all when you love me?"

"Why — I suppose I do — in a way. I know I'm fortunate, happy — I —" She glanced up shyly — "I am glad that I am — loved —"

"You darling!"

She let him take her into his arms, suffered his caress, looking at him in silence out of eyes as dark and clear and beautiful as brown pools in a forest.

"You're just a bad, spoiled, perverse little kid, aren't you?" he said, rumpling her hair.

"You say so."

"Breaking my heart because you won't marry me."

"No, breaking my own because you don't really love me enough, yet."

"I love you too much —"

"That is literary bosh, Louis."

"Good God! Can't you ever understand that I'm respectable enough to want you for my wife?"

"You mean that you want me for what I do not wish to be. And you decline to love me unless I turn into a selfish, dependent, conventional nonentity, which you adore because respectable. Is that what you mean?"

"I want the laws of civilization to safeguard you," he persisted patiently.

"I need no more protection than you need. I am not a baby. I am not afraid. Are you?"

"That is not the question —"

"Yes it is, dear. I stand in no fear. Why do you wish to force me to do what I believe would be a wrong to you? Can't you respect my disreputable convictions?"

"They are theories — not convictions —"

"Oh, Kelly, I'm so tired of hearing you say that!"

"I should think you would be, you little imp of perversity!"

"I am. . . . And I wonder how I can love you just as much, as though you were kind and reasonable and — and minded your own business, dear."

"Isn't it my business to tell the girl to whom I'm engaged what I believe to be right?"

"Yes; and it's her business to tell *you*" she said, smiling; and put her arms higher so that they slipped around his neck for a moment, then were quickly withdrawn.

"What a thoroughly obstinate boy you are!" she exclaimed. "We're wasting such lots of time in argument when it's all so very simple. Your soul is your own to develop; mine is mine. *Noli, me tangere!*"

But he was not to be pacified; and presently she went away to pour their tea, and he followed and sat down in an armchair near the fire, brooding gaze fixed on the coals.

They had tea in hostile silence; he lighted a cigarette, but presently flung it into the fire without smoking.

She said: "You know, Louis, if this is really going to be an unhappiness to you, instead of a happiness beyond words, we had better end it now." She added, with an irrepressible laugh, partly nervous, "Your happiness seems to be beyond words already. Your silence is very eloquent. . . . I think I'll take my doll and go home."

She rose, stood still a moment looking at him where he sat, head bent, staring into the coals; then a swift tenderness filled her eyes; her sensitive lips quivered; and she came swiftly to him and took his head into her arms.

"Dear," she whispered, "I only want to do the best for you. Let me try in my own way. It's all for you — everything I do or think or wish or hope is for you. Even I myself was made merely for you."

Sideways on the arm of his chair, she stooped down, laying her cheek against his, drawing his face closer.

"I am so hopelessly in love with you," she murmured; "if I make mistakes, forgive me; remember only that it is because I love you enough to die for you very willingly."

He drew her down into his arms. She was never quick to respond to the deeper emotions in him, but her cheeks and throat were flushed now, and, as his embrace enclosed her, she responded with a sudden flash of blind passion — a moment's impulsive self-surrender to his lips and arms — and drew away from him dazed, trembling, shielding her face with one arm.

All that the swift contact was awakening in him turned on her fiercely now; in his arms again she swayed, breathless, covering her face with desperate hands, striving to comprehend, to steady her senses, to reason while pulses and heart beat wildly and every vein ran fire.

"No —" she stammered — "this is — is wrong — wrong! Louis, I beg you, to remember what I am to you. . . . Don't kiss me again — I ask you not to — I pray that you won't. . . . We are — I am — engaged to you, dear. . . . Oh — it is wrong — wrong, now! — all wrong between us!"

"Valerie," he stammered, "you care nothing for any law — nor do I — now —"

"I *do!* You don't understand me! Let me go. Louis — you don't love me enough. . . . This — this is madness — wickedness! — you can't love me! You don't — you can't!"

"I do love you, Valerie —"

"No — no — or you would let me go! — or you would not kiss me again —"

She freed herself, breathless, crimson with shame and anger, avoiding his eyes, and slipped out of his embrace to her knees, sank down on the rug at his feet, and laid her head against the chair, breathing fast, both small hands pressed to her breast.

For a few minutes he let her lie so; then, stooping over her, white lipped, trembling:

"What can you expect if we sow the wind?"

She began to cry, softly: "You don't understand — you never have understood!"

"I understand this: that I am ready to take you in your way, now. I cannot live without you, and I won't. I care no longer how I take you, or when, or where, as long as I can have you for mine, to keep forever, to love, to watch over, to worship. . . . Dear — will you speak to me?"

She shook her head, desolately, where it lay now against his knees, amid its tumbled hair.

Then he asked again for her forgiveness — almost fiercely, for passion still swayed him with every word. He told her he loved her, adored her, could not endure life without her; that he was only too happy to take her on any terms she offered.

"Louis," she said in a voice made very small and low by the crossed arms muffling her face, "I am wondering whether you will ever know what love is."

"Have I not proved that I love you?"

"I — don't know what it is you have proved. . . . We were engaged to each other — and — and —"

"I thought you cared nothing for such conventions!"

She began to cry again, silently.

"Valerie — darling —"

"No — you don't understand," she sobbed.

"Understand what, dearest — dearest —

"That I thought our love was its own protection — and mine."

He made no answer.

She knelt there silent for a little while, then put her hand up appealingly for his handkerchief.

"I have been very happy in loving you," she faltered; "I have promised you all there is of myself. And you have already had my best self. The rest — whatever it is — whatever happens to me — I have promised — so that there will be nothing of this girl called Valerie West which is not all yours — all, all — every thought, Louis, every pulse-beat — mind, soul, body. . . . But no future day had been set; I had thought of none as yet. Still — since I knew I was to be to you what I am to be, I have been very busy preparing for it — mind, soul, my little earthly possessions, my personal affairs in their small routine. . . . No bride in your world, busy with her trousseau, has been a happier dreamer than have I, Louis. You don't know how true I have tried to be to myself, and to the truth as I understand it — as true as I have been to you in thought and deed. . . . And, somehow, what threatened — a moment since — frightens me, humiliates me —"

She lifted her head and looked up at him with dimmed eyes:

"You were untrue to yourself, Louis — to your own idea of truth. And you were untrue to me. And for the first time I look at you, ashamed and shamed."

"Yes," he said, very white.

"Why did you offer our love such an insult?" she asked.

He made no answer.

"Was it because, in your heart, you hold a girl lightly who promised to give herself to you for your own sake, renouncing the marriage vows?"

"No! Good God —"

"Then — is it because you do not yet love me enough? For I shall not give myself to you until you do."

He hung his head.

"I think that is it," she said, sorrowfully.

"No. I'm no good," he said. "And that's the truth, Valerie." A dark flush stained his face and he turned it away, sitting there in silence, his tense clasp tightening on the arms of the chair. Then he said, still not meeting her eyes:

"Whatever your beliefs are you practice them; you are true to your convictions, loyal to yourself. I am only a miserable, rotten specimen of man who is true to nothing — not even to himself. I'm not worth your trouble, Valerie."

"Louis!"

"Well, what am I?" he demanded in fierce disgust. "I have told you that I believe in the conventions — and I violate every one of them. I'm a spectacle for gods and men!" His face was stern with self-disgust: he forced himself to meet her gaze, wincing under it; but he went on:

"I know well enough that I deserve your contempt; I've acquired plenty of self-contempt already. But I *do* love you,

God knows how or in what manner, but I love you, cur that
I am — and I respect you — oh, more that you understand,
Valerie. And if I ask your mercy on such a man as I am, it is
not because I deserve it."

"My mercy, Louis?"

She rose to her knees and laid both hands on his shoulders.

"You *are* only a man, dear — with all the lovable faults and
sins and contradictions of one. But there is no real depravity
in you anymore than there is in me. Only — I think you are
a little more selfish than I am — you lose self-command —"
she blushed — "but that is because you are only a man after
all. . . . I think, perhaps, that a girl's love is different in many
ways. Dear, my love for you is perfectly honest. You believe
it, don't you? If for one moment I thought it was otherwise,
I'd never let you see me again. If I thought for one moment
that anything spiritual was to be gained for us by denying
that love to you or to myself — or by living out life alone
without you, I have the courage to do it. Do you doubt it?"

"No," he said.

She sighed, and her gaze passed from his and became
remote for a moment, then:

"I want to live my life with you," she said, wistfully; "I want
to be to you all that the woman you love could possibly be.
But to me, the giving of myself to you is to be, in my heart,
a ceremony more solemn than any in the world — and it is
to be a rite at which my soul shall serve on its knees, Louis."

"Dearest — dearest," he breathed, "I know — I understand
— I ask your pardon. And I worship you."

Then a swift, smiling change passed over her face; and, her
hands still resting on his shoulders, kneeling there before
him, she bent forward and kissed him on the forehead.

"Pax," she said. "You are forgiven. Love me enough, Louis.
And when I am quite sure you do, then — then — you may
ask me, and I will answer you."

"I love you now, enough."

"Are you sure?"

"Yes."

"Then — ask," she said, faintly.

His lips moved in a voiceless question, she could not hear
him, but she understood.

"In a year, I think," she answered, forcing her eyes to meet his, but the delicate rose color was playing over her cheeks and throat.

"As long as that?"

"That is not long. Besides, perhaps you won't learn to love me enough even by that time. Do you think you will? If you really think so — perhaps in June —"

She watched him as he pressed her hands together and kissed them; laughed a little, shyly, as she suddenly divined a new tenderness and respect in his eyes — something matching the vague exaltation of her own romantic dreams.

"I will wait all my life if you wish it," he said.

"Do you mean it?"

"You know I do, now."

She considered him, smiling. "If you truly do feel that way — perhaps — perhaps it might really be in June — or in July —"

"You *said* June."

"Listen to the decree of the great god Kelly! He says it must be in June, and he shakes his thunderbolts and frowns."

"June! Say so, Valerie,"

"*You* have said so."

"But there's no use in *my* saying so if —"

"Oh, dear!" she exclaimed, "the great god totters on his pedestal and the oracle falters and I see the mere man looking very humbly around the corner of the shrine at me, whispering, 'June, if you please, dear lady!'"

"Yes," he said, "that's what you see and hear. Now answer me, dear."

"And what am I to say?"

"June, please."

"June — please," she repeated, demurely.

"You darling. . . ! What day?"

"Oh, that's too early to decide —"

"Please, dear!"

"No; I don't want to decide —"

"Dearest!"

"What?"

"Won't you answer me?"

"If you make me answer now, I'll be tempted to fix the first of April."

"All right, fix it."

"It's All Fool's day, you know," she threatened. "Probably it is peculiarly suitable for us. . . . Very well, then, I'll say it."

She was laughing when he caught her hands and looked at her, grave, unsmiling. Suddenly her eyes filled with tears and her lip trembled.

"Forgive me, I meant no mockery," she whispered. "I had already fixed the first day of June for — for the great change in our lives. Are you content?"

"Yes." And before she knew what he was doing a brilliant flashed along her ring finger and clung sparkling to it; and she stared at the gold circlet and the gem flashing in the firelight.

There were tears in her eyes when she kissed it, looking at him while her soft lips rested on the jewel.

Neither spoke for a moment; then, still looking at him, she drew the ring from her finger, touched it again with her lips, and laid it gently in his hand.

"No, dear," she said.

He did not urge her; but she knew he still believed that she would come to think as he thought; and the knowledge edged her lips with tremulous humor. But her eyes were very sweet and tender as she watched him lay away the ring as though it and he were serenely biding their time.

"Such a funny boy," she said, "and such a dear one. He will never, never grow up, will he?"

"Such an idiot, you mean," he said, drawing her into the big chair beside him.

"Yes, I mean that, too," she said, impudently, nose in the air. "Because, if I were you, Louis, I wouldn't waste anymore energy in worrying about a girl who is perfectly able to take care of herself, but transfer it to a boy who apparently is not."

"How do you mean?"

"I mean about your painting. Dear, you've got it into that obstinate head of yours that there's something lacking in your pictures, and there isn't."

"Oh, Valerie! You know there is!"

"No, no, no! There isn't anything lacking in them. They're all of you, Louis — every bit of you — as far as you have lived."

"What!"

"Certainly. As far as you have lived. Now live a little more, and let more things come into your life. You can't paint what isn't in you; and there's nothing in you except what you get out of life."

She laid her soft cheek against his.

"Get a little real love out of life, Louis; a little *real* love. Then surely, surely your canvases can not disguise that you know what life means to us all. Love nobly; and the world will not doubt that love is noble; love mercifully; and the world will understand mercy. For I believe that what you are must show in your work, dear.

"Until now the world has seen in your work only the cold splendor, or dreamy glamour, or the untroubled sweetness and brilliancy of passionless romance. I love your work. It is happiness to look at it; it thrills, bewitches, enthralls. . . ! Dear, forgive me if in it I have not yet found a deeper inspiration. . . . And that inspiration, to be there, must be first in you, my darling — born of a wider interest in your fellow men, a little tenderness for friends — a more generous experience and more real sympathy with humanity — and perhaps you may think it out of place for me to say it — but — a deeper, truer, spiritual conviction.

"Do you think it strange of me to have such convictions? I can't escape them. Those who are merciful, those who are kind, to me are Christlike. Nothing else matters. But to be kind is to be first of all interested in the happiness of others. And you care nothing for people. You *must* care, Louis!

"And, somehow, you who are, at heart, good and kind and merciful, have not really awakened real love in many of those about you. For one thing your work has absorbed you. But if, at the same time, you could pay a little more attention to human beings —"

"Valerie!" he said in astonishment, "I have plenty of friends. Do you mean to say I care nothing for them?"

"How much *do* you care, Louis?"

"Why, I —" He fell silent, troubled gaze searching hers.

She smiled: "Take Sam, for example. The boy adores you. He's a rotten painter, I know — and you don't even pretend to an interest in what he does because you are too honest to praise it. But, Louis, he's a lovable fellow — and he does the best that's in him. You needn't pretend to care for what he does — but if you could show that you do care for and respect the effort —"

"I do, Valerie — when I think about it!"

"Then think about it; and let Sam know that you think about his efforts and himself. And do the same for Harry Annan. He's a worse painter than Sam — but do you think he doesn't know it? Don't you realize what a lot of heartache the monkey-shines of those two boys conceal?"

"I am fond of them," he said, slowly. "I like people, even if I don't show it —"

"Ah, Louis! Louis! That is the world's incurable hurt — the silence that replies to its perplexity — the wistful appeal that remains unanswered. . . . And many, many vex God with the desolation of their endless importunities and complaints when a look, a word, a touch from a human being would relieve them of the heaviest of all burdens — a sad heart's solitude."

He put his arm around her, impulsively:

"You little angel," he said, tenderly.

"No — only a human girl who has learned what solitude can mean."

"I shall make you forget the past," he said.

"No, dear — for that might make me less kind." She put her lips against his cheek, thoughtfully: "And — I think — that you are going to need all the tenderness in me — some day, Louis — as I need all of yours. . . . We shall have much to learn — after the great change. . . . And much to endure. And I think we will need all the kindness that we can give each other — and all that the world can spare us."

Chapter X

*I*t was slowly becoming evident to Neville that Valerie's was the stronger character — not through any genius for tenacity nor on account of any domineering instinct — but because, mistaken or otherwise in her ethical reasoning, she was consistent, true to her belief, and had the courage to live up to it. And this made her convictions almost unassailable.

Slavery to established custom of any kind she smilingly disdained, refusing to submit to restrictions which centuries of social usage had established, when such social restrictions and limitations hampered or annoyed her.

Made conscious by the very conventions designed to safeguard unconsciousness; made wise by the unwisdom of a civilization which required ignorance of innocence, she had as yet lost none of her sweetness and confidence in herself and in a world which she considered a friendly one at best and, at worst, more silly than vicious.

Her life, the experience of a lonely girlhood in the world, wide and varied reading, unwise and otherwise, and an intelligence which needed only experience and training, had hastened to a premature maturity her impatience with the faults of civilization. And in the honest revolt of youth, she forgot that what she rejected was, after all, civilization itself, and that as yet there had been offered no acceptable substitute for its faulty codification.

To do one's best was to be fearlessly true to one's convictions and let God judge; that was her only creed. And from her point of view humanity needed no other.

So she went about the pleasure and happiness of living
with a light heart and a healthy interest, not doubting that
all was right between her and the world, and that the status
quo must endure.

And endless misunderstandings ensued between her and
the man she loved. She was a very busy business girl and he
objected. She went about to theaters and parties and dinners
and concerts with other men; and Neville didn't like it.
Penrhyn Cardemon met her at a theatrical supper and asked
her to be one of his guests on his big yacht, the *Mohave*, fitted
out for the Azores. There were twenty in the party, and she
would have gone had not Neville objected angrily.

It was not his objection but his irritation that confused
her. She could discover no reason for it.

"It can't be that you don't trust me," she said to him, "so
it must be that you're lonely without me, even when you go
to spend two weeks with your parents. I don't mind not going
if you don't wish me to, Louis, and I'll stay here in town while
you visit your father and mother, but it seems a little bit odd
of you not to let me go when I can be of no earthly use to
you."

Her gentleness with him, and her sweet way of reasoning
made him ashamed.

"It's the crowd that's going, Valerie — Cardemon, Querida,
Marianne Valdez — where did you meet her, anyway?"

"In her dressing room at the Opera. She's perfectly sweet.
Isn't she all right?"

"She's Cardemon's mistress," he said, bluntly.

A painful color flushed her face and neck; and at the same
instant he realized what he had said.

Neither spoke for a while; he went on with his painting;
she, standing once more for the full-length portrait, resumed
her pose in silence.

After a while she heard his brushes clatter to the floor, saw
him leave his easel, was aware that he was coming toward her.
And the next moment he had dropped at her feet, kneeling
there, one arm tightening around her knees, his head pressed
close.

Listlessly she looked down at him, dropped one slim hand
on his shoulder, considering him.

"The curious part of it is," she said, "that all the scorn in your voice was for Marianne Valdez and none for Penrhyn Cardemon."

He said nothing.

"Such a queer, topsy-turvy world," she sighed, letting her hand wander from his shoulder to his thick, short hair. She caressed his forehead thoughtfully.

"I suppose some man will say that of me some day. . . . But that is a little matter — compared to making life happy for you. . . . To be your mistress could never make me unhappy."

"To be your husband — and to put an end to all these damnable doubts and misgivings and cross-purposes would make me happy all my life!" he burst out with a violence that startled her.

"Hush, Louis. We must not begin that hopeless argument again."

"Valerie! Valerie! You are breaking my heart!"

"Hush, dear. You know I am not."

She looked down at him; her lip was trembling.

Suddenly she slid down to the floor and knelt there confronting him, her arms around him.

"Dearer than all the world and heaven! — do you think that I am breaking your heart? You *know* I am not. You know what I am doing for your sake, for your family's sake, for my own. I am only giving you a love that can cause them no pain, bring no regret to you. Take it, then, and kiss me."

*B*ut the days were full of little scenes like this — of earnest, fiery discussions, of passionate arguments, of flashes of temper ending in tears and heavenly reconciliation.

He had gone for two weeks to visit his father and mother at their summer home near Portsmouth, and before he went he took her in his arms and told her how ashamed he was of his bad temper at the idea of her going on the *Mohave*, and said that she might go; that he did trust her anywhere, and that he was trying to learn to concede to her the same liberty of action and of choice that any man enjoyed.

But she convinced him very sweetly that she really had no desire to go, and sent him off to Spindrift House happy, and madly in love; which resulted in two letters a day from him, and in her passing long evenings in confidential duets with Rita Tevis.

Rita had taken the bedroom next to Valerie's, and together they had added the luxury of a tiny living room to the suite.

It was the first time that either had ever had anyplace in which to receive anybody; and now, delighted to be able to ask people, they let it be known that their friends could have tea with them.

Ogilvy and Annan had promptly availed themselves.

"This is exceedingly grand," said Ogilvy, examining everything in a tour around the pretty little sitting room. "We can have all kinds of a rough house now." And he got down on his hands and knees in the middle of the rug and very gravely turned a somersault.

"Sam! Behave! Or I'll set my parrot on you!" exclaimed Valerie.

Ogilvy sat up and inspected the parrot.

"You know," he said, "I believe I've seen that parrot somewhere."

"Impossible, my dear friend — unless you've been in my bedroom."

Ogilvy got up, dusted his trousers, and walked over to the parrot.

"Well it looks like a bird I used to know — I — it certainly resembles —" He hesitated, then addressing the bird:

"Hello, Leparello — you old scoundrel!" he said, cautiously.

"Forget it!" muttered the bird, cocking his head and lifting first one slate-colored claw from his perch, then the other; — "forget it! Help! Oh, very well. God bless the ladies!"

"*Where* on earth did you ever before see my parrot?" asked Valerie, astonished. Ogilvy appeared to be a little out of countenance, too.

"Oh, I really don't remember exactly where I did see him," he tried to explain; and nobody believed him.

"Sam! Answer me!"

"Well, where did *you* get him?"

"José Querida gave Leparello to me."

Annan and Ogilvy exchanged the briefest glance — a perfectly blank glance.

"It probably isn't the same bird," said Ogilvy, carelessly. "There are plenty of parrots that talk — plenty of 'em named Leparello, probably."

"Sam, how *can* you be so untruthful! Rita, hold him tightly while I pull his ears!"

It was a form of admonition peculiarly distasteful to Ogilvy, and he made a vain effort to escape.

"Now, Sam, the truth, the whole truth, and nothing but the truth! Quick, or I'll tweak!"

"All right, then," he said, maliciously, "Querida's got relatives in Oporto who send him these kind of parrots occasionally. He names 'em all Leparello, teaches 'em all the same jargon, and — gives 'em to girls!"

"How funny," said Valerie. She looked at Sam, aware of something else in his grin, and gave an uncertain little laugh.

He sat down, rubbing his ear-lobes, the malicious grin still lingering on his countenance. What he had not told her was that Querida's volcanically irregular affairs of the heart always ended with the gift of an Oporto parrot. Marianne Valdez owned one. So did Mazie Grey.

His cynical gaze rested on Valerie reflectively. He had heard plenty of rumors and whispers concerning her; and never believed any of them. He could not believe now that the gift of this crimson, green and sky-blue creature signified anything. Yet Querida had known her as long as anybody except Neville.

"When did he give you this parrot?" he asked, carelessly.

"Oh, one day just before I was going to Atlantic City. He was coming down, too, to stay a fortnight while I was there, and come back with me; and he said that He had intended to give the parrot to me after our return, but that he might as well give it to me before I went."

"I see," said Ogilvy, thoughtfully. A few moments later, as he and Annan were leaving the house, he said:

"It looks to me as though our friend, José, had taken too much for granted."

"It looks like it," nodded Annan, smiling unpleasantly.

"Too sure of conquest," added Ogilvy. "Got the frozen mitt, didn't he?"

"*And* the Grand Cordon of the double cross."

"*And* the hot end of the poker; yes?"

"Sure; and it's still sizzling." Ogilvy cast a gleeful glance back at the house:

"Fine little girl. All white. Yes? No?"

"All white," nodded Annan. . . . "And Neville isn't that kind of a man, anyway."

Ogilvy said: "So *you* think so, too?"

"Oh, yes. He's crazy about her, and she isn't taking Sundays out if it's his day in. . . . Only, what's the use?"

"No use. . . . I guess Kelly Neville has seen as many artists who've married their models as we have. Besides, his people are frightful snobs."

Annan, walking along briskly, swung his stick vigorously:

"She's a sweet little thing," he said.

"I know it. It's going to be hard for her. She can't stand for a mutt — and it's the only sort that will marry her. . . . I don't know — she's a healthy kind of girl — but God help her if she ever really falls in love with one of our sort."

"I think she's done it," said Annan.

"Kelly!"

"Doesn't it look like it?"

"Oh, it will wear off without any harm to either of them. That little girl is smart, all right; she'll never waste an evening screaming for the moon. And Kelly Neville is — is Kelly Neville — a dear fellow, so utterly absorbed in the career of a brilliant and intelligent young artist named Louis Neville, that if the entire earth blew up he'd begin a new canvas the week after. . . . Not that I think him cold-hearted — no, not even selfish as that little bounder Allaire says — but he's a man who has never yet had time to spare."

"They're the most hopeless," observed Annan — "the men who haven't time to spare. Because it takes only a moment to say, 'Hello, old man! How in hell are you?' It takes only a moment to put yourself, mentally, in some less lucky man's shoes; and be friendly and sorry and interested."

"He's a pretty decent sort," murmured Ogilvy. "Anyway, that Valerie child is safe enough in temporarily adoring Kelly Neville."

*T*he "Valerie child," in a loose, rose-silk peignoir, cross-legged on her bed, was sewing industriously on her week's mending. Rita, in dishabille, lay across the foot of the bed nibbling bonbons and reading the evening paper.

They had dined in their living room, a chafing dish aiding. Afterward Valerie went over her weekly accounts and had now taken up her regular mending; and there she sat, sewing away, and singing in her clear, young voice, the old madrigal:

"Let us dry the starting tear
    For the hours are surely fleeting
And the sad sundown is near.
        All must sip the cup of sorrow,
        I today, and thou tomorrow!
This the end of every song,
Ding-dong! Ding-dong!
Yet until the shadows fall
Over one and over all,
Sing a merry madrigal!"

Rita, nibbling a chocolate, glanced up:

"That's a gay little creed," she observed.

"Of course. It's the *only* creed."

Rita shrugged and Valerie went on blithely singing and sewing.

"How long has that young man of yours been away?" inquired Rita, looking up again.

"Thirteen days."

"Oh. Are you sure it isn't fourteen?"

"Perfectly." Then the sarcasm struck her, and she looked around at Rita and laughed:

"Of course I count the days," she said, conscious of the soft color mounting to her cheeks.

Rita sat up and, tucking a pillow under her shoulders, leaned back against the foot-board of the bed, kicking the newspaper to the floor. "Do you know," she said, "that you have come pretty close to falling in love with Kelly Neville?"

Valerie's lips trembled on the edge of a smile as she bent lower over her sewing, but she made no reply.

"I should say," continued Rita, "that it was about time for you to pick up your skirts and run for it."

Still Valerie sewed on in silence.

"Valerie!"

"What?"

"For goodness' sake, say something!"

"What do you want me to say, dear?" asked the girl, laughing.

"That you are *not* in danger of making a silly ninny of yourself over Kelly Neville."

"Oh, I'll say that very cheerfully —"

"Valerie!"

The girl looked at her, calmly amused. Then she said:

"I might as well tell you. I am head over heels in love with him. You knew it, anyway, Rita. You've known it — oh, I don't know how long — but you've known it. Haven't you?"

Rita thought a moment: "Yes, I have known it. . . . What are you going to do?"

"Do?"

"Yes; what do you intend to do about this matter?"

"Love him," said Valerie. "What else can I do?"

"You could try not to."

"I don't want to."

"You had better."

"Why?"

"Because," said Rita, deliberately, "if you really love him you'll either become his wife or his mistress; and it's a pretty rotten choice either way."

Valerie blushed scarlet;

"Rotten — choice?"

"Certainly. You know perfectly well what your position would be when his family and his friends learned that he'd married his model. No girl of any spirit would endure it — no matter how affable his friends might perhaps pretend to be. No girl of any sense would ever put herself in such a false position. . . . I tell you, Valerie, it's only the exceptional man who'll stand by you. No doubt Louis Neville would. But it would cost him every friend he has — and probably the respect of his parents. And that means misery for you both — because he couldn't conceal from you what marrying you was costing him —"

"Rita!"

"Yes."

"There is no use telling me all this. I know it. He knows I know it. I am not going to marry him."

After a silence Rita said, slowly: "Did he ask you to?"

Valerie looked down, passed her needle through the hem once, twice.

"Yes," she said, softly, "he asked me."

"And — you refused?"

"Yes."

Rita said: "I like Kelly Neville . . . and I love you better, dear. But it's not best for you to marry him. . . . Life isn't a very sentimental affair — not nearly as silly a matter as poets and painters and dramas and novels pretend it is. Love really plays a very minor part in life, Don't you know it?"

"Yes. I lived twenty years without it," said Valerie, demurely, yet in her smile Rita divined the hidden tragedy. And she leaned forward and kissed her impulsively.

"Let's swear celibacy," she said, "and live out our lives together in single blessedness! Will you? We can have a perfectly good time until the undertaker knocks."

"I hope he won't knock for a long while," said Valerie, with a slight shiver. "There's so much I want to see first."

"You shall. We'll see everything together. We'll work hard, live frugally if you say so, cut out all frills and nonsense, and save and save until we have enough to retire on respectably. And then, like two nice old ladies, we'll start out to see the world —"

"Oh, Rita! I don't want to see it when I'm too old!"

"You'll enjoy it more —"

"Rita! How ridiculous! You've seen more of the world than I have, anyway. It's all very well for you to say wait till I'm an old maid; but you've been to Paris — haven't you?"

"Yes," said Rita. There was a slight color in her face.

"Well, then! Why must I wait until I'm a dowdy old frump before I go? Why should you and I not be as happy as we can afford to be while we're young and attractive and unspoiled?"

"I want you to be as happy as you can afford to be, Valerie. . . . But you can't afford to fall in love."

"Why?"

"Because it will make you miserable."

"But it doesn't."

"It will if it is love."

"It is, Rita," said the girl, smiling out of her dark eyes — deep brown wells of truth that the other gazed into and saw a young soul there, fearless and doomed.

"Valerie," she said, shivering, "you won't do — *that* — will you?"

"Dear, I cannot marry him, and I love him. What else am I to do?"

"Well, then — then you'd better marry him!" stammered Rita, frightened. "It's better for you! It's better —"

"For *me?* Yes, but how about him?"

"What do you care about him!" burst out Rita, almost incoherent in her fright and anger. "He's a man; he can take care of himself. Don't think of him. It isn't your business to consider him. If he wants to marry you it's his concern after all. Let him do it! Marry him and let him fight it out with his friends! After all what does a man give a girl that compares with what she gives him? Men — men —" she stammered — "they're all alike in the depths of their own hearts. We are incidents to them — no matter how they say they love us. They *can't* love as we do. They're not made for it! We are part of the game to them; they are the whole game to us; we are, at best, an important episode in their careers; they are our whole careers. Oh, Valerie! Valerie! listen to me, child! That man could go on living and painting and eating and drinking and sleeping and getting up to dress and going to bed to sleep, if you lay dead in your grave. But if you loved him, and were his wife — or God forgive me! — his mistress, the day he died *you* would die, though your body might live on. I know — *I* know, Valerie. Death — whether it be his body or his love, ends all for the woman who really loves him. Woman's loss is eternal. But man's loss is only temporary — he is made that way, fashioned so. Now I tell you the exchange is not fair — it has never been fair — never will be, never can be. And I warn you not to give this man the freshness of your youth, the happy years of your life, your innocence, the devotion which he will transmute into passion with his accursed magic! I warn you not to forsake the tranquility of ignorance, the blessed immunity from that devil's paradise that you are already gazing into —"

"Rita! Rita! What are you saying?"

"I scarcely know, child. I am trying to save you from lifelong unhappiness — trying to tell you that — that men are not worth it —"

"How do you know?"

There was a silence, then Rita, very pale and quiet, leaned forward, resting her elbows on her knees and framing her face with her hands.

"I had my lesson," she said.

"You! Oh, my darling — forgive me! I did not know —"

Rita suffered herself to be drawn into the younger girl's impulsive embrace; they both cried a little, arms around each other, faltering out question and answer in unsteady whispers:

"Were you married, dearest?"

"No."

"Oh — I am *so* sorry, dear —"

"So am I. . . . Do you blame me for thinking about men as I do think?"

"Didn't you love — him?"

"I thought I did. . . . I was too young to know. . . . It doesn't matter now —"

"No, no, of course not. You made a ghastly mistake, but it's no more shame to you than it is to him. Besides, you thought you loved him."

"He could have made me. I was young enough. . . . But he let me see how absolutely wicked he was. . . . And then it was too late to ever love him."

"O Rita, Rita! — then you haven't ever even had the happiness of loving? Have you?"

Rita did not answer.

"Have you, darling?"

Then Rita broke down and laid her head on Valerie's knees, crying as though her heart would break.

"That's the terrible part of it," she sobbed — "I really do love a man, now. . . . Not that *first* one . . . and there's nothing to do about it — nothing, Valerie, nothing — because even if he asked me to marry him I can't, now —"

"Because you —"

"Yes."

"And if you had not —"

"God knows what I would do," sobbed Rita, "I love him so, Valerie — I love him so!"

The younger girl looked down at the blond head lying on her knees — looked at the pretty tear-stained face gleaming through the fingers — looked and wondered over the philosophy broken down beside the bowed head and breaking heart.

Terrible her plight; with or without benefit of clergy she dared not give herself. Love was no happiness to her, no confidence, no sacrifice — only a dreadful mockery — a thing that fettered, paralyzed, terrified.

"Does he love you?" whispered Valerie.

"No — I think not."

"If he did he would forgive."

"Do you think so?"

"Of course. Love pardons everything," said the girl in surprise.

"Yes. But never forgets."

*T*hat was the first confidence that ever had passed between Valerie West and Rita Tevis. And after it, Rita, apparently forgetting her own philosophical collapse, never ceased to urge upon Valerie the wisdom, the absolute necessity of self-preservation in considering her future relations with Louis Neville. But, like Neville's logic, Rita's failed before the innocent simplicity of the creed which Valerie had embraced. Valerie was willing that their relations should remain indefinitely as they were if the little gods of convention were to be considered; she had the courage to sever all relations with the man she loved if anybody could convince her that it was better for Neville. Marry him she would not, because she believed it meant inevitable unhappiness for him. But she was not afraid to lay her ringless hands in his forever.

Querida called on them and was very agreeable and lively and fascinating; and when he went away Valerie asked him to come again. He did; and again after that. She and Rita dined with him once or twice; and things gradually slipped back to their old footing; and Querida remained on his best behavior.

Neville had prolonged the visit to the parental roof. He did not explain to her why, but the reason was that he had made up his mind to tell his parents that he wished to marry and to find out once and for all what their attitudes would be toward such a girl as Valerie West. But he had not yet found courage to do it, and he was lingering on, trying to find it and the proper moment to employ it.

His father was a gentleman so utterly devoid of imagination that he had never even ventured into business, but had been emotionlessly content to marry and live upon an income sufficient to maintain the material and intellectual traditions of the house of Neville.

Tall, transparently pale, negative in character, he had made it a life object to get through life without increasing the number of his acquaintances — legacies in the second generation left him by his father, whose father before him had left the grandfathers of these friends as legacies to his son.

It was a pallid and limited society that Henry Neville and his wife frequented — a coterie of elderly, intellectual people, and their prematurely dried-out offspring. And intellectual in-breeding was thinning it to attenuation — to a bloodless meagerness in which they, who composed it, conceived a mournful pride.

Old New Yorkers all, knowing no other city, no other bourne north of Tenth Street or west of Chelsea — silent, serene, drab-toned people, whose drawing rooms were musty with what had been fragrance once, whose science, religion, interests, desires were the beliefs, interests and emotions of a century ago, their colorless existence and passive snobbishness affronted nobody who did not come seeking affront.

To them Theodore Thomas had been the last conductor; his orchestra the last musical expression fit for a cultivated society; the Academy of Music remained their last symphonic temple, Wallack's the last refuge of a drama now dead forever.

Delmonico's had been their northern limit, Stuyvesant Square their eastern, old Trinity their southern, and their western, Chelsea. Outside there was nothing. The blatancy and gilt of the million-voiced metropolis fell on closed eyes, and on ears attuned only to the murmurs of the past. They lived in their ancient houses and went abroad and summered in some simple old-time hamlet hallowed by the headstones of their grandsires, and existed as meaninglessly and blamelessly as the old catalpa trees spreading above their dooryards.

And into this narrow circle Louis Neville and his sister Lily had been born.

It had been a shock to her parents when Lily married Gordon Collis, a mining engineer from Denver. She came to see them with her husband every year; Collis loved her enough to endure it.

As for Louis' career, his achievements, his work, they regarded it without approval. Their last great painters had been Bierstadt and Hart, their last great sculptor, Powers. Blankly they gazed upon the splendors of the mural symphonies achieved by the son and heir of all the Nevilles; they could not comprehend the art of the Uitlanders; their comment was silence and dignity.

To them all had become only shadowy tradition; even affection and human emotion, and the relationship of kin to kin, of friend to friend, had become only part of a negative existence which conformed to precedent, temporal and spiritual, as written in the archives of a worn-out civilization.

So, under the circumstances, it was scarcely to be wondered that Neville hesitated to introduce the subject of Valerie West as he sat in the parlor at Spindrift House with his father and mother, reading the *Tribune* or the *Evening Post* or poring over some ancient tome of travels, or looking out across the cliffs at an icy sea splintering and glittering against a coast of frozen adamant.

At length he could remain no longer; commissions awaited him in town; hunger for Valerie gnawed ceaselessly, unsubdued by his letters or by hers to him.

"Mother," he said, the evening before his departure, "would it surprise you very much if I told you that I wished to marry?"

"No," she said, tranquilly; "you mean Stephanie Swift, I suppose."

His father glanced up over his spectacles, and he hesitated; then, as his father resumed his reading:

"I don't mean Stephanie, mother."

His father laid aside his book and removed, the thin gold-rimmed spectacles.

"I understand from Lily that we are to be prepared to receive Stephanie Swift as your affianced wife," he said. "I shall be gratified. Stephen Swift was my oldest friend."

"Lily was mistaken, father. Stephanie and I are merely very good friends. I have no idea of asking her to marry me."

"I had been given to understand otherwise, Louis. I am disappointed."

Louis Neville looked out of the window, considering, yet conscious of the hopelessness of it all.

"Who is this girl, Louis?" asked his mother, pulling the white-and-lilac wool shawl closer around her thin shoulders.

"Her name is Valerie West."

"One of the Wests of West Eighth Street?" demanded his father.

The humor of it all twitched for a moment at his son's grimly set jaws, then a slight flush mantled his face:

"No, father."

"Do you mean the Chelsea Wests, Louis?"

"No."

"Then we — don't know them," concluded his father with a shrug of his shoulders, which dismissed many, many things from any possibility of further discussion. But his mother's face grew troubled.

"Who is this Miss West?" she asked in a colorless voice.

"She is a very good, very noble, very cultivated, very beautiful young girl — an orphan — who is supporting herself by her own endeavors."

"What!" said his father, astonished.

"Mother, I know how it sounds to you, but you and father have only to meet her to recognize in her every quality that you could possibly wish for in my wife."

"*Who* is she, Louis!" demanded his father, casting aside the evening newspaper and folding up his spectacles.

"I've told you, father."

"I beg to differ with you. Who is this girl? In what description of business is she actually engaged?"

The young fellow's face grew red:

"She *was* engaged in — the drama."

"What!"

"She was an actress," he said, realizing now the utter absurdity of any hope from the beginning, yet now committed and determined to see it through to the bitter end.

"An actress! Louis!" faltered his mother.

There was a silence, cut like a knife by the thin edge of his father's voice:

"If she *was* an actress, what is she now?"

"She has helped me with my painting."

"Helped you? How?"

"By — posing."

"Do you desire me to understand that the girl is an artist's model!"

"Yes."

His father stared at him a moment, then:

"And is this the woman you propose to have your mother meet?"

"Father," he said, hopelessly, "there is no use in my saying anything more. Miss West is a sweet, good, generous young girl, fully my peer in education, my superior in many things. . . . You and mother can never believe that the ideas, standards — even the ideals of civilization change — have changed since your youth — are changing every hour. In your youth the word actress had a dubious significance; today it signifies only what the character of her who wears the title signifies. In your youth it was immodest, unmaidenly, reprehensible, for a woman to be anything except timid, easily abashed, ignorant of vital truths, and submissive to every social convention; today women are neither ignorant nor timid; they are innocent because they choose to be; they are fearless, intelligent, ambitious, and self-reliant — and lose nothing in feminine charm by daring to be themselves instead of admitting their fitness only for the seraglio of some Occidental monogamist —"

"Louis! Your mother is present!"

"Good heavens, father, I know it! Isn't it possible even for a man's own mother to hear a little truth once in a while —"

His father rose in pallid wrath:

"Be silent!" he said, unsteadily; "the subject is definitely ended."

*I*t was ended. His father gave him a thin, chilly hand at parting. But his mother met him at the outer door and laid her trembling lips to his forehead.

"You won't bring this shame on us, Louis, I know. Nor on yourself, nor on the name you bear. . . . It is an honorable name in the land, Louis. . . . I pray God to bless you and counsel you, my son —" She turned away, adding in a whisper — "and — and comfort you."

And so he went away from Spindrift House through a snowstorm, and arrived in New York late that evening; but not too late to call Valerie on the telephone and hear again the dear voice with its happy little cry of greeting — and the promise of tomorrow's meeting before the day of duty should begin.

*L*ove grew as the winter sped glittering toward the far primrose dawn of spring; work filled their days; evening brought the happiness of a reunion eternally charming in its surprises, its endless novelty. New, forever new, love seemed; and youth, too, seemed immortal.

On various occasions when Valerie chanced to be at his studio, pouring tea for him, friends of his sister came unannounced — agreeable women more or less fashionable, who pleaded his sister's sanction of an unceremonious call to see the great painted frieze before it was sent to the Court House.

He was perfectly nice to them; and Valerie was perfectly at ease; and it was very plain that these people were interested and charmed with this lovely Miss West, whom they found pouring tea in the studio of an artist already celebrated; and every one of them expressed themselves and their curiosity to his sister, Mrs. Collis, who, never having heard of Valerie West, prudently conveyed the contrary in smiling but silent acquiescence, and finally wrote to her brother and told him what was being said.

Before he determined to reply, another friend — or rather acquaintance of the Collis family — came in to see the picture — the slim and pretty Countess d'Enver. And went quite mad over Valerie — so much so that she remained for an hour talking to her, almost oblivious of Neville and his picture and of Ogilvy and Annan, who consumed time and cocktails in the modest background.

When she finally went away, and Neville had returned from putting her into her overelaborate carriage, Ogilvy said:

"Gee, Valerie, you sure did make a hit with the lady. What was she trying to make you do?"

"She asked me to come to a reception of the Five-Minute Club with Louis," said Valerie, laughing. "What *is* the Five-Minute Club, Louis?"

"Oh, it's a semi-fashionable, semi-artistic affair — one of the incarnations of the latest group of revolting painters and sculptors and literary people, diluted with a little society and a good deal of near-society."

Later, as they were dining together at Delmonico's, he said:

"Would you care to go, Valerie?"

"Yes — if you think it best for us to accept such invitations together."

"Why not?"

"I don't know. . . . Considering what we are to become to each other — I thought — perhaps the prejudices of your friends —"

He turned a dull red, said nothing for a moment, then, looking up at her, suddenly laid his hand over hers where it rested on the table's edge.

"The world must take us as it finds us," he said.

"I know; but is it quite fair to seek it?"

"You adorable girl! Didn't the Countess seek us — or rather you? — and torment you until you promised to go to the up-to-date doings of her bally club! It's across to her, now. And as half of society has exchanged husbands and half of the remainder doesn't bother to, I don't think a girl like you and a man like myself are likely to meet very many people as innately decent as ourselves."

A reception at the Five-Minute Club was anything but an ordinary affair.

It was the ultra-modern school of positivists where realism was on the cards and romance in the discards; where muscle, biceps, and thumb-punching replaced technical mastery and delicate skill; where inspiration was physical, not intellectual; where writers called a spade a spade, and painters painted all sorts of similar bucolic instruments with candor and an inadequate knowledge of their art; where composers thumped their pianos the harder, the less their raucous inspiration responded, or maundered incapably into interminable incoherency, hunting for themes in greys and mauves and reds and yellows, determined to find in music what does not belong there and never did.

In spite of its apparent vigor and uncompromising modernity, one suspected a sub-stratum of weakness and a perversity slightly vicious.

Color blindness might account for some of the canvases, strabismus for some of the draftsmanship; but not for all. There was an ugly deliberation in the glorification of the raw, the uncouth; there was a callous hardness in the deadly elaboration of ugliness for its own sake. And transcendentalism looked on in approval.

A near-sighted study of various masters, brilliant, morbid, or essentially rotten, was the basis of this cult — not originality. Its devotees were the devotees of Richard Strauss, of Huysmans, of Manet, of Degas, Rops, Louis Le Grand, Forain, Monticelli; its painters painted nakedness in footlight effects with blobs for faces and blue shadows where they were needed to conceal the defects of impudent drawing; its composers maundered with both ears spread wide for stray echoes of Salome; its sculptors, stupefied by Rodin, achieved sections of human anatomy protruding from lumps of clay and marble; its dramatists, drugged by Mallarmé and Maeterlinck, dabbled in dullness, platitude and mediocre psychology; its writers wrote as bloodily, as squalidly, and as immodestly as they dared; its poets blubbered with Verlaine, spat with Aristide Bruant, or leered with the alcoholic muses of the Dead Rat.

They were all young, all in deadly earnest, all imperfectly educated, all hard workers, brave workers, blind, incapable workers sweating and twisting and hammering in their impotence against the changeless laws of truth and beauty. With them it was not a case of a loose screw; all screws had been tightened so brutally that the machinery became deadlocked. They were neither lazy, languid, nor precious; they only thought they knew how and they didn't. All their vigor was sterile; all their courage vain.

Several attractive women exquisitely gowned were receiving; there was just a little something unusual in their prettiness, in their toilets; and also a little something lacking; and its absence was as noticeable in them as it was in the majority of arriving or departing guests.

It could not have been self-possession and breeding which an outsider missed. For the slim Countess d'Enver possessed both, inherited from her Pittsburgh parents; and Mrs. Hind-Willet was born to a social security indisputable; and Latimer Varyck had been in the diplomatic service before he wrote "Unclothed," and the handsome, dark-eyed Mrs. Atherstane divided social Manhattan with a blonder and lovelier rival.

Valerie entering with Neville, slender, self-possessed, a hint of inquiry in her level eyes, heard the man at the door announce them, and was conscious of many people turning as they passed into the big reception room. A woman near her murmured, "What a beauty!" Another added, "How intelligently gowned!" The slim Countess Hélène d'Enver, née Nellie Jackson, held out a perfectly gloved hand and nodded amiably to Neville. Then, smiling fixedly at Valerie:

"My dear, how nice of you," she said. "And you, too, Louis; it is very amusing of you to come. José Querida has just departed. He gave us such a delightful five-minute talk on modernity. Quoting Huneker, he spoke of it as a 'quality' — and 'that nervous, naked vibration' —"

She ended with a capricious gesture which might have meant anything ineffable, or an order for a Bronx cocktail.

"What's a nervous, naked vibration?" demanded Neville, with an impatient shrug. "It sounds like a massage parlor — not," he added with respect, "that Huneker doesn't know what he's talking about. Nobody doubts that. Only art is one delicious bouillabaisse to him."

The Countess d'Enver laughed, still retaining Valerie's hand:

"Your gown is charming — may I add that you are disturbingly beautiful, Miss West? When they have given you some tea, will you find me if I can't find you?"

"Yes, I will," said Valerie.

At the tea table Neville brought her a glass of sherry and a bite of something squashy; a number of people spoke to him and asked to be presented to Valerie. Her poise, her unconsciousness, the winning simplicity of her manner were noticed everywhere, and everywhere commented on. People betrayed a tendency to form groups around her; women, prepared by her unusual beauty for anything between mediocrity and inanity, were a little perplexed at her intelligence and candor.

To Mrs. Hind-Willet's question she replied innocently: "To me there is no modern painter comparable to Mr. Neville, though I dearly love Wilson, Sorella and Querida."

To Latimer Varyck's whimsical insistence she finally was obliged to admit that her reasons for not liking Richard Strauss were because she thought him ugly, uninspired, and disreputable, which unexpected truism practically stunned that harmless dilettante and so delighted Neville that he was obliged to disguise his mirth with a scowl directed at the ceiling.

"Did I say anything very dreadful, Kelly?" she whispered, when opportunity offered.

"No, you darling. I couldn't keep a civil face when you told the truth about Richard Strauss to that rickety old sensualist."

"I don't really know enough to criticize anything. But Mr. Varyck *would* make me answer; and one must say something."

Olaf Dennison, without preliminary, sat down at the piano, tossed aside his heavy hair, and gave a five-minute prelude to the second act of his new opera, "Yvonne of Bannalec." The opera might as well have been called Mamie of Hoboken, for all the music signified to Neville.

Mrs. Hind-Willet, leaning over the chair where Valerie was seated, whispered fervently:

"Isn't it graphic! The music describes an old Breton peasant going to market. You can hear the very click of his sabots and the gurgle of the cider in his jug. And that queer little slap-stick noise is where he's striking palms with another peasant bargaining for his cider."

"But where does Yvonne come in?" inquired Valerie in soft bewilderment.

"He's Yvonne's father," whispered Mrs. Hind-Willet. "The girl doesn't appear during the entire opera. It's a marvelously important advance beyond the tonal and graphic subtleties of Richard Strauss."

Other earnest and worthy people consumed intervals of five minutes now and then; a "discuse," — whom Neville insisted on calling a "disease," — said a coy and rather dirty little French poem directly at her audience, leeringly assisted by an oversophisticated piano accompaniment.

"If that's modernity it's certainly naked and nervous enough," commented Neville, dryly.

"It's — it's perfectly horrid," murmured Valerie, the blush still lingering on cheek and brow. "I can't understand how intelligent people can even think about such things."

"Modernity," repeated Neville. "Hello; there's Carrillo, the young apostle of Bruant, who makes such a hit with the elect."

"How, Kelly?"

"Realism, New York, and the spade business. He saw a sign on a Bowery clothing store, — 'Gents Pants Half Off Today,' and he wrote a poem on it and all Manhattan sat up and welcomed him as a peerless realist; and dear old Dean Williams compared him to Tolstoy and Ed. Harrigan, and there was the deuce to pay artistically and generally. Listen to the Yankee Steinlen in five-minute verse, dear."

Carrillo rose, glanced carelessly at his type-written manuscript and announced its title unconcernedly:

"Mutts In Madison Square

"A sodden tramp sits scratching on a bench,
  The S.C.D. cart trails a lengthening stench
  Where White Wings scrape the asphalt; and a breeze
  Ripples the fountain and the budding trees.
  Now fat old women, waddling like hogs,
  Arrive to exercise their various dogs;
  And 'round and 'round the little mutts all run,
  Grass-maddened, frantic, circling in the sun,
  Wagging and nosing — see! beneath yon tree
  One little mutt meets his affinity:
  And, near, another madly wags his tail
  Inquiringly; but his advances fail,
  And, 'yap-yap-yap!' replies the shrewish tyke,
  So off the other starts upon a hike,
  Rushing at random, crazed with sun and air,
  Circling and barking out his canine prayer:

"'Oh, Lord of dogs who made the Out-of-doors
  And fashioned mutts to gambol on all fours,
  Grant us a respite from the city's stones!
  Grant us a grassy place to bury bones! — A
  grassy spot to roll on now and then,
  Oh, Lord of dogs who also fashioned men,
  Accept our thanks for this brief breath of air,
  And grant, Oh, Lord, a humble mongrel's prayer!'

*

The hoboe, sprawling, scratches in the sun;
  While 'round and 'round the happy mongrels run."

"Good Heavens," breathed Neville, "that sort of thing may be modern and strong, but it's too rank for me, Valerie. Shall we bolt?"

"I — I think we'd better," she said miserably. "I don't think I care for — for these interesting people very much."

They rose and passed slowly along the walls of the room, which were hung with "five-minute sketches," which probably took five seconds to conceive and five hours to execute — here an unclothed woman, chiefly remarkable for an extraordinary development of adipose tissue and house-maid's knee; here a pathological gem that might have aptly illustrated a work on malformations; yonder a dashing dab of balderdash, and next it one of Rackin's masterpieces, flanked by a gem of Stanley Pooks.

In the center of the room, emerging from a chunk of marble, the back and neck and one ear of an unclothed lady protruded; and the sculptured achievement was labeled, "Beatrice Andante."

"Oh, Lord," whispered Neville, repressing a violent desire to laugh. "Beatrice and Aunty! I didn't know he had one."

"Is it Dante's Beatrice, Kelly? Where is Dante and his Aunty?"

"God knows. They made a mess of it anyway, those two — andante — which I suppose this mess in marble symbolizes. Pity he didn't have an aunty to tell him how."

"Louis! How irreverent!" she whispered, eyes sparkling with laughter.

"Shall I try a five-minute fashionable impromptu, dear?" he asked:

"If Dante'd had an Aunty
  Who ante-dated Dante
  And scolded him
  And tolded him
  The way to win a winner,
  It's a cinch or I'm a sinner,
  He'd have taken Trix to dinner,
  He'd have given her the eye
  Of the fish about to die,
  And folded her,
  And molded her
  Like dough within a pie —
  sallow, pallid pie —

And cooked a scheme to marry her,
And hired a hack to carry her
To stately Harlem-by-the-Bronx,
Where now the lonely taxi honks —"

"Kelly!" she gasped.

They both were laughing so that they hastened their steps, fearful of offending, and barely contrived to compose their features when making their adieux to Mrs. Hind-Willet and the Countess d'Enver.

As they walked east along Fifty-ninth Street, breathing in the fresh, sparkling evening air, she said impulsively:

"And to think, Louis, that if I had been wicked enough to marry you I'd have driven you into that kind of society — or into something genetically similar!"

His face sobered:

"You could hold your own in any society."

"Perhaps I could. But they wouldn't let me."

"Are you afraid to fight it out?"

"Yes, dear — at *your* expense. Otherwise —" She gazed smilingly into space, a slight color in either cheek.

Chapter XI

Valerie West was twenty-two years old in February. One year of life lay behind her; her future stretched away into sunlit infinity.

Neville attained his twenty-eighth year in March. Years still lay before him, a few lay behind him; but in a single month he had waded so swiftly forward through the sea of life that the shallows were already passed, the last shoal was deepening rapidly. Only immeasurable and menacing depths remained between him and the horizon — that pale, dead line dividing the noonday of today from the phantom suns of blank eternity.

It was that winter that he began the picture destined to fix definitely his position among the painters of his times — began it humbly, yet somehow aware of what it was to be; afraid, for all his courage, yet conscious of something inevitable impending. It was Destiny; and, instinctively, he arose to meet it.

He called the picture "A Bride." A sapphire sky fading to turquoise, in which great clouds crowded high in argent splendor — a young girl naked of feet, her snowy body cinctured at the waist with straight and silvered folds, standing amid a riot of wild flowers, head slightly dropped back, white arms inert, pendant. And in her eyes' deep velvet depths the mystery of the Annunciation.

All of humanity and of maturity — of adolescence and of divinity was in that face; in the exquisitely sensitive wisdom of the woman's eyes, in the full sweet innocence of the childish mouth — in the smooth little hands so unsoiled, so pure — in the nunlike pallor and slender beauty of the throat.

Whatever had been his inspiration — whether spiritual conviction, or the physical beauty of Valerie, neither he nor she considered very deeply. But that he was embodying and creating something of the existence of which neither he nor she had been aware a month ago, was awaking something within them that had never before stirred or given sign of life.

Since the last section of the mural decoration for the new court house had been shipped to its destination, he had busied himself on two canvases, a portrait of his sister in furs, and the portrait of Valerie.

Lily Collis came in the mornings twice a week to sit for her; and once or twice Stephanie Swift came with her; also Sandy Cameron, ruddy, bald, jovial, scoffing, and insatiably curious.

"Where do you keep all those pretty models, Louis?" he demanded, prying aside the tapestry with the crook of his walking stick, and peeping behind furniture and hangings and big piles of canvases. "Be a sport and introduce us; Stephanie wants to see a few as well as I do."

Neville shrugged and went on painting, which exasperated Cameron.

"It's a fraud," he observed, in a loud, confidential aside to Stephanie; "this studio ought to be full of young men in velvet coats and bunchy ties, singing, 'Oh la — la!' and dexterously balancing on their baggy knees a series of assorted soubrettes. It's a bluff, a hoax, a con game! Are you going to stand for it? I don't see any absinthe either — or even any Vin ordinaire! Only a teapot — a *teapot!*" he repeated in unutterable scorn. "Why, there's more of Bohemia in a Broad Street Trust Company than there is in this Pullman car studio!"

Mrs. Collis was laughing so that her brother had difficulty in going on with her portrait.

"Get out of here, Sandy," he said — "or take Stephanie into the rest of the apartment, somewhere, and tell her your woes."

Stephanie, who had been exploring, turning over piles of chassis and investigating canvases and charcoal studies stacked up here and there against the wainscot, pulled aside an easel which impeded her progress, and in so doing accidentally turned the canvas affixed to it toward the light.

"Hello!" exclaimed Cameron briskly, "who is this?"

Lily turned her small, aristocratic head, and Stephanie looked around.

"What a perfectly beautiful girl!" she exclaimed impulsively; "who is she, Louis?"

"A model," he said calmly; but the careless and casual exposure of the canvas had angered him so suddenly that his own swift emotion astonished him.

Lily had risen from her seat, and now stood looking fixedly at the portrait of Valerie West, her furs trailing from one shoulder to the chair.

"My eye and Betty Martin!" cried Cameron, "I'll take it all back, girls! It's a real studio after all — and this is the real thing! Louis, do you think she's seen the Aquarium? I'm disengaged after three o'clock —"

He began to kiss his hand rapidly in the direction of the portrait, and then, fondly embracing his own walking stick, he took a few jaunty steps in circles, singing "Waltz me around again, Willy."

Lily Collis said: "If your model is as lovely as her portrait, Louis, she is a real beauty. Who is she?"

"A professional model." He could scarcely contain his impatience with his sister, with Cameron's fat humor, with Stephanie's quiet and intent scrutiny — as though, somehow, he had suddenly exposed Valerie herself to the cool and cynically detached curiosity of a world which she knew must always remain unfriendly to her.

He was perfectly aware that his sister had guessed whose portrait confronted them; he supposed, too, that Stephanie probably suspected. And the knowledge irritated him more than the clownishness of Cameron.

"It is a splendid piece of painting," said Stephanie cordially, and turned quietly to a portfolio of drawings at her elbow. She had let her fleeting glance rest on Neville for a second; had divined in a flash that he was enduring and not courting their examination of this picture; that, somehow, her accidental discovery of it had displeased him — was even paining him.

"Sandy," she said cheerfully, "come here and help me look over these sketches."

"Any peaches among 'em?"

"Bushels."

Cameron came with alacrity; Neville waited until Lily reluctantly resumed her seat; then he pushed back the easel, turned Valerie's portrait to the wall, and quietly resumed his painting.

Art in any form was powerless to retain Cameron's attention for very many consecutive minutes at a time; he grew restless, fussed about with portfolios for a little while longer, enlivening the tedium with characteristic observations.

"Well, I've got business down town," he exclaimed, with great pretence of regret. "Come on, Stephanie; we'll go to the Exchange and start something. Shall we? Oh, anything — from a panic to a bull-market! I don't care; go as far as you like. You may wreck a few railroads if you want to. Only I've *got* to go. . . . Awfully good of you to let me — er — see all these — er — interesting and er — m-m-m — things, Louis. Glad I saw that dream of a peacherino, too. What is she on the side? An actorine? If she is I'll take a box for the rest of the season including the road and one-night stands. . . . Good-bye, Mrs. Collis! Good-bye, Stephanie! *Good*-bye, Louis! — I'll come and spend the day with you when you're too busy to see me. Now, Stephanie, child! It's the Stock Exchange or the Little Church around the Corner for you and me, if you say so!"

Stephanie had duties at a different sort of an Exchange; and she also took her leave, thanking Neville warmly for the pleasure she had had, and promising to lunch with Lily at the Continental Club.

When they had departed, Lily said:

"I suppose that is a portrait of your model, Valerie West."

"Yes," he replied shortly.

"Well, Louis, it is perfectly absurd of you to show so plainly that you consider our discovery of it a desecration."

He turned red with surprise and irritation:

"I don't know what you mean."

"I mean exactly what I say. You showed by your expression and your manner that our inspection of the picture and our questions and comments concerning it were unwelcome."

"I'm sorry I showed it. . . . But they *were* unwelcome."

"Will you tell me why?"

"I don't think I know exactly why — unless the portrait was a personal and private affair concerning only myself —"

"Louis! Has it gone as far as that?"

"As far as what? What on earth are you trying to say, Lily?"

"I'm trying to say — as nicely and as gently as I can — that your behavior — in regard to this girl is making us all perfectly wretched."

"Who do you mean by 'us all'?" he demanded sullenly.

"Father and mother and myself. You must have known perfectly well that father would write to me about what you told him at Spindrift House a month ago."

"Did he?"

"Of course he did, Louis! Mother is simply worrying herself ill over you; father is incredulous — at least he pretends to be; but he has written me twice on the subject — and I think you might just as well be told what anxiety and unhappiness your fascination for this girl is causing us all."

Mrs. Collis was leaning far forward in her chair, forgetful of her pose; Neville stood silent, head lowered, absently mixing tints upon his palette without regard to the work under way.

When he had almost covered his palette with useless squares of color he picked up a palette-knife, scraped it clean, smeared the residue on a handful of rags, laid aside brushes and palette, and walked slowly to the window.

It was snowing again. He could hear the feathery whisper of the flakes falling on the glass roof above; and he remembered the night of the new year, and all that it had brought to him — all the wonder and happiness and perplexity of a future utterly unsuspected, undreamed of.

And now it was into that future he was staring with a fixed and blank gaze as his sister's hand fell upon his shoulder and her cheek rested a moment in caress against his.

"Dearest child," she said tremulously, "I did not mean to speak harshly or without sympathy. But, after all, shouldn't a son consider his father and mother in a matter of this kind?"

"I have considered them — tried to."

Mrs. Collis dropped into an armchair. After a few moments he also seated himself listlessly, and sat gazing at nothing out of absent eyes.

She said: "You know what father and mother are. Even I have something left of their old-fashioned conservatism clinging to me — and yet people consider me extremely liberal in my views. But all my liberality, all my modern education since I left the dear old absurdities of our narrow childhood and youth, can not reconcile me to what you threaten us with — with what you are threatened — you, your entire future life."

"What seems to threaten you — and them — is my marriage to the woman with whom I'm in love. Does that shock you?"

"The circumstances shock me."

"I could not control the circumstances."

"You can control yourself, Louis."

"Yes — I can do that. I can break her heart and mine."

"Hearts don't break, Louis. And is anybody to live life through exempt from suffering? If your unhappiness comes early in life to you it will pass the sooner, leaving the future tranquil for you, and you ready for it, unperplexed — made cleaner, purer, braver by a sorrow that came, as comes all sorrow — and that has gone its way, like all sorrows, leaving you the better and the worthier."

"How is it to leave *her?*"

He spoke so naturally, so simply, that for the moment his sister did not recognize in him what had never before been there to recognize — the thought of another before himself. Afterward she remembered it.

She said quietly: "If Valerie West is a girl really sincere and meriting your respect, she will face this matter as you face it."

"Yes — she would do that," he said, thoughtfully.

"Then I think that the sooner you explain matters to her —"

He laughed: "*I* don't have to explain anything to her, Lily."

"What do you mean?"

"She knows how things stand. She is perfectly aware of your world's attitude toward her. She has not the slightest intention of forcing herself on you, or of asking your indulgence or your charity."

"You mean, then, that she desires to separate you from your family — from your friends —"

"No," he said wearily, "she does not desire that, either."

His sister's troubled eyes rested on him in silence for a while; then:

"I know she is beautiful; I am sure she is good, Louis — good in — in her own way — worthy, in her own fashion. But, dear, is that all that you, a Neville, require of the woman who is to bear your name — bear your children?"

"She *is* all I require — and far more."

"Dear, you are utterly blinded by your infatuation!"

"You do not know her."

"Then let me!" exclaimed Mrs. Collis desperately. "Let me meet her, Louis — let me talk with her —"

"No. . . . And I'll tell you why, Lily; it's because she does not care to meet you."

"What!"

"I have told you the plain truth. She sees no reason for knowing you, or for knowing my parents, or any woman in a world that would never tolerate her, never submit to her entrance, never receive her as one of them! — a world that might shrug and smile and endure her as my wife — and embitter my life forever."

As he spoke he was not aware that he merely repeated Valerie's own words; he remained still unconscious that his decision was in fact merely her decision; that his entire attitude had become hers because her nature and her character were as yet the stronger.

But in his words his sister's quick intelligence perceived a logic and a conclusion entirely feminine and utterly foreign to her brother's habit of mind. And she realized with a thrill of fear that she had to do, not with her brother, but with a woman who was to be reckoned with.

"Do you — or does Miss West think it likely that I am a woman to wound, to affront another — no matter who she may be? Surely, Louis, you could have told her very little about me —"

"I never mention you to her."

Lily caught her breath.

"Why?"

"Why should I?"

"That is unfair, Louis! She has the right to know about your own family — otherwise how can she understand the situation?"

"It's like all situations, isn't it? You and father and mother have your own arbitrary customs and traditions and stand-ards of respectability. You rule out whom you choose. Valerie West knows perfectly well that you would rule her out. Why should she give you the opportunity?"

"Is she afraid of me?"

He smiled: "I don't think so." And his smile angered his sister.

"Very well," she said, biting her lip.

For a few moments she sat there deliberating, her pointed patent-leather toe tapping the polished floor. Then she stood up, with decision:

"There is no use in our quarreling, Louis — until the time comes when some outsider forces us into an unhappy mis-understanding. Kiss me good-bye, dear."

She lifted her face; he kissed her; and her hand closed impulsively on his arm:

"Louis! Louis! I love you. I am so proud of you — I — you know I love you, don't you?"

"Yes — I think so."

"You *know* I am devoted to your happiness! — your *real* happiness — which those blinded eyes in that obstinate head of yours refuse to see. Believe me — believe me, dear, that your *real* happiness is not in this pretty, strange girl's keeping. No, no, no! You are wrong, Louis — terribly and hopelessly wrong! Because happiness for you lies in the keeping of another woman — a woman of your own world, dear — of your own kind — a gently-bred, lovable, generous girl whom you, deep in your heart and soul, love, unknowingly — have always loved!"

He shook his head, slowly, looking down into his sister's eyes.

She said, almost frightened:

"You — you won't do it — suddenly — without letting us know — will you, Louis?"

"What?"

"Marry this girl!"

"No," he said, "it is not likely."

"But you — you mean to marry her?"

"I want to. . . . But it is not likely to happen — for a while."

"How long?"

"I don't know."

She drew a tremulous breath of relief, looking up into his face. Then her eyes narrowed; she thought a moment, and her gaze became preoccupied and remote, and her lips grew firm with the train of thought she was pursuing.

He put his arms around her and kissed her again; and she felt the boyish appeal in it and her lip quivered. But she could not respond, could not consider for one moment, could not permit her sympathy for him to enlist her against what she was devoutly convinced were his own most vital interests — his honor, his happiness, the success of his future career.

She said with tears in her eyes: "Louis, I love you dearly. If God will grant us all a little patience and a little wisdom there will be a way made clear to all of us. Good-bye."

Whether it was that the Almighty did not grant Mrs. Collis the patience to wait until a way was made clear, or whether another letter from her father decided her to clear that way for herself, is uncertain; but one day in March Valerie received a letter from Mrs. Collis; and answered it; and the next morning she shortened a séance with Querida, exchanged her costume for her street-clothes, and hastened to her apartments, where Mrs. Collis was already awaiting her in the little sitting room.

Valerie offered her hand and stood looking at Lily Collis, as though searching for some resemblance to her brother in the pretty, slightly flushed features. There was a very indefinite family resemblance.

"Miss West," she said, "it is amiable of you to overlook the informality —"

"I am not formal, Mrs. Collis," she said, quietly. "Will you sit here?" indicating an armchair near the window, — "because the light is not very good and I have some mending to do on a costume which I must pose in this afternoon."

Lily Collis seated herself, her bewitched gaze following Valerie as she moved lightly and gracefully about, collecting sewing materials and the costume in question, and bringing them to a low chair under the north window.

"I am sure you will not mind my sewing," she said, with a slight upward inflection to her voice, which made it a question.

"Please, Miss West," said Lily, hastily.

"It is really a necessity," observed Valerie threading her needle and turning over the skirt. "Illustrators are very arbitrary gentlemen; a model's failure to keep an engagement sometimes means loss of a valuable contract to them, and that isn't fair either to them or to their publishers, who would be forced to hunt up another artist at the last moment."

"Your — profession — must be an exceedingly interesting one," said Lily in a low voice.

Valerie smiled: "It is a very exacting one."

There was a silence. Valerie's head was bent over her sewing; Mrs. Collis, fascinated, almost alarmed by her beauty, could not take her eyes from her. Outwardly Lily was pleasantly reserved, perfectly at ease with this young girl; inwardly all was commotion approaching actual consternation.

She had been prepared for youth, for a certain kind of charm and beauty — but not for this kind — not for the loveliness, the grace, the composure, the exquisite simplicity of this young girl who sat sewing there before her.

She was obliged to force herself to recollect that this girl was a model hired to pose for men — paid to expose her young, unclothed limbs and body! Yet — could it be possible! Was this the girl hailed as a comrade by the irrepressible Ogilvy and Annan — the heroine of a score of unconventional and careless gaieties recounted by them? Was this the coquette who, it was rumored, had flung over Querida, snapped her white fingers at Penrhyn Cardemon, and laughed disrespectfully at a dozen respected pillars of society, who appeared to be willing to support her in addition to the entire social structure?

Very quietly the girl raised her head. Her sensitive lips were edged with a smile, but there was no mirth in her clear eyes:

"Mrs. Collis, perhaps you are waiting for me to say something about your letter and my answer to it. I did not mean to embarrass you by not speaking of it, but I was not certain that the initiative lay with me."

Lily reddened: "It lies with *me*, Miss West — the initiative. I mean —" She hesitated, suddenly realizing how difficult it had become to go on, — how utterly unprepared she was to encounter passive resistance from such composure as this young girl already displayed.

"You wrote to me about your anxiety concerning Mr. Neville," said Valerie, gently.

"Yes — I did, Miss West. You will surely understand — and forgive me — if I say to you that I am still a prey to deepest anxiety."

"Why?"

The question was so candid, so direct that for a moment Lily remained silent. But the dark, clear, friendly eyes were asking for an answer, and the woman of the world who knew how to meet most situations and how to dominate them, searched her experience in vain for the proper words to use in this one.

After a moment Valerie's eyes dropped, and she resumed her sewing; and Lily bit her lip and composed her mind to its delicate task:

"Miss West," she said, "what I have to say is not going to be very agreeable to either of us. It is going to be painful perhaps — and it is going to take a long while to explain —"

"It need not take long," said Valerie, without raising her eyes from her stitches; "it requires only a word to tell me that you and your father and mother do not wish your brother to marry me."

She looked up quietly, and her eyes met Lily's:

"I promise not to marry him," she said. "You are perfectly right. He belongs to his own family; he belongs in his own world."

She looked down again at her sewing with a faint smile:

"I shall not attempt to enter that world as his wife, Mrs. Collis, or to draw him out of it. . . . And I hope that you will not be anxious anymore."

She laid aside her work and rose to her slender height, smilingly, as though the elder woman had terminated the interview; and Lily, utterly confounded, rose, too, as Valerie offered her hand in adieu.

"Miss West," she began, not perfectly sure of what she was saying, "I — scarcely dare thank you — for what you have said — for — my — brother's — sake —"

Valerie laughed: "I would do much more than that for him, Mrs. Collis. . . . Only I must first be sure of what is really the best way to serve him."

Lily's gloved hand tightened over hers; and she laid the other one over it:

"You are so generous, so sweet about it!" she said unsteadily. "And I look into your face and I know you are good — *good* — all the way through —"

Valerie laughed again:

"There isn't any real evil in me. . . . And I am not astonishingly generous — merely sensible. I knew from the first that I couldn't marry him — if I really loved him," she added, under her breath.

They were at the door now. Lily passed out into the entry, halted, turned impulsively, the tears in her eyes, and put both arms tenderly around the girl.

"You poor child," she whispered. "You dear, brave, generous girl! God knows whether I am right or wrong. I am only trying to do my duty — trying to do what is best for him."

Valerie looked at her curiously:

"Yes, you cannot choose but think of him if you really love him. . . . That is the way it is with love."

Afterward, sewing by the window, she could scarcely see the stitches for the clinging tears. But they dried on her lashes; not one fell. And when Rita came in breezily to join her at luncheon she was ready, her costume mended and folded in her hand-satchel, and there remained scarcely even a redness of the lids to betray her.

That evening she did not stop for tea at Neville's studio; and, later, when he telephoned, asking her to dine with him, she pleaded the feminine prerogative of tea in her room and going to bed early for a change. But she lay awake until midnight trying to think out a *modus vivendi* for Neville and herself which, would involve no sacrifice on his part and no unhappiness for anybody except, perhaps, for herself.

The morning was dull and threatened rain, and she awoke with a slight headache, remembering that she had dreamed all night of weeping.

In her mail there was a note from Querida asking her to stop for a few moments at his studio that afternoon, several business communications, and a long letter from Mrs. Collis which she read lying in bed, one hand resting on her aching temples:

"MY DEAR MISS WEST:

"Our interview this morning has left me with a somewhat confused sense of indebtedness to you and an admiration and respect for your character which I wished very much to convey to you this morning, but which I was at a loss to express.

"You are not only kind and reasonable, but so entirely unselfish that my own attitude in this unhappy matter has seemed to me harsh and ungracious.

"I went to you entertaining a very different idea of you, and very different sentiments from the opinion which I took away with me. I admit that my call on you was not made with any agreeable anticipations; but I was determined to see you and learn for myself what manner of woman had so disturbed us all.

"In justice to you — in grateful recognition of your tact and gentleness, I am venturing to express to you now my very thorough respect for you, my sense of deep obligation, and my sympathy — which I am afraid you may not care for.

"That it would not be suitable for a marriage to take place between my brother and yourself is, it appears, as evident to you as it is to his own family. Yet, will you permit me to wish that it were otherwise? I do wish it; I wish that the circumstances had made such a marriage possible. I say this to you in spite of the fact that we have always expected my brother to marry into a family which has been intimate with our own family for many generations. It is a tribute to your character which I am unwilling to suppress; which I believe I owe to you, to say that, had circumstances been different, you might have been made welcome among us.

"The circumstances of which I speak are of an importance to us, perhaps exaggerated, possibly out of proportion to the fundamental conditions of the situation. But they are conditions which our family has never ignored. And it is too late for us to learn to ignore them now.

"I think that you will feel — I think that a large part of the world might consider our attitude toward such a woman as you have shown yourself to be, narrow, prejudiced, provincial. The modern world would scarcely arm us with any warrant for interfering in a matter which a man nearly thirty is supposed to be able to manage for himself. But my father and mother are old, and they will never change in their beliefs and prejudices inherited from their parents, who, in turn, inherited their beliefs.

"It was for them more than for myself — more even than for my brother — that I appealed to you. The latter end of their lives should not be made unhappy. And your generous decision assures me that it will not be made so.

"As for myself, my marriage permitted me an early enfranchisement from the obsolete conventional limits within which my brother and I were brought up.

"I understand enough of the modern world not to clash with, it unnecessarily, enough of ultra-modernity not to be too much afraid of it.

"But even I, while I might theoretically admit and even admire that cheerful and fearless courage which makes it possible for such a self-respecting woman as yourself to face the world and force it to recognize her right to earn her own living as she chooses — I could not bring myself to contemplate with equanimity my brother's marrying you. And I do not believe my father would survive such an event.

"To us, to me, also, certain fixed conventional limits are the basis of all happiness. To offend them is to be unhappy; to ignore them would mean destruction to our peace of mind and self-respect. And, though I do admire you and respect you for what you are, it is only just to you to say that we could never reconcile ourselves to those modern social conditions which you so charmingly represent, and which are embodied in you with such convincing dignity.

"Dear Miss West, have I pained you? Have I offended you in return for all your courtesy to me? I hope not. I felt that I owed you this. Please accept it as a tribute and as a sorrowful acquiescence in conditions which an old-fashioned family are unable to change.

"Very sincerely yours,

"LILLY COLLIS"

She lay for a while, thinking, the sheets of the letter lying loose on the bed. It seemed to require no answer. Nor had Mrs. Collis, apparently, any fear that Valerie would ever inform Louis Neville of what had occurred between his sister and herself.

Still, to Valerie, an unanswered letter was like a civil observation ignored.

She wrote that evening to Lily:

"DEAR MRS. COLLIS:

"In acknowledging your letter of yesterday I beg to assure you that I understand the inadvisability of my marrying your brother, and that I have no idea of doing it, and that, through me, he shall never know of your letters or of your visit to me in his behalf.

"With many thanks for your kindly expressions of good-will toward me, I am

"Very truly yours,

"VALERIE WEST"

She had been too tired to call at Querida's studio, too tired even to take tea at the Plaza with Neville.

Rita came in, silent and out of spirits, and replied in monosyllables to Valerie's inquiries.

It finally transpired that Sam Ogilvy and Harry Annan had been tormenting John Burleson after their own fashion until their inanity had exasperated her and she expressed herself freely to everybody concerned.

"It makes me very angry," she said, "to have a lot of brainless people believe that John Burleson is stupid. He isn't; he is merely a trifle literal, and far too intelligent to see any humor in the silly capers Sam and Harry cut."

Valerie, who was feeling better, sipped her tea and nibbled her toast, much amused at Rita's championship of the big sculptor.

"John is a dear," she said, "but even his most enthusiastic partisans could hardly characterize him as a humorist."

"He's not a clown — if that's what you mean," said Rita shortly.

"But, Rita, he *isn't* humorous, you know."

"He *is*. He has a sense of humor perfectly intelligible to those who understand it."

"Do you, dear?"

"Certainly . . . And I always have understood it."

"Oh, what kind of occult humor is it?"

"It is a quiet, cultivated, dignified sense of humor not uncommon in New England, and not understood in New York."

Valerie nibbled her toast, secretly amused. Burleson was from Massachusetts. Rita was the daughter of a Massachusetts clergyman. No doubt they were fitted to understand each other.

It occurred to her, too, that John Burleson and Rita Tevis had always been on a friendly footing rather quieter and more serious than the usual gay and irresponsible relations maintained between two people under similar circumstances.

Sometimes she had noticed that when affairs became too frivolous and the scintillation of wit and epigram too rapid and continuous, John Burleson and Rita were very apt to edge out of the circle as though for mutual protection.

"You're not posing for John, are you, Rita?" she asked.

"No. He has a bad cold, and I stopped in to see that he wore a red flannel bandage around his throat. A sculptor's work is so dreadfully wet and sloppy, and his throat has always been very delicate."

"Do you mean to say that you charge your mind with the coddling of that great big, pink-cheeked boy?" laughed Valerie,

"Coddling!" repeated Rita, flushing up. "I don't call it coddling to stop in for a moment to remind a friend that he doesn't know how to take care of himself, and never will."

"Nonsense. You couldn't kill a man of that size and placidity of character."

"You don't know anything about him. He is much more delicate than he looks."

Valerie glanced curiously at the girl, who was preparing oysters in the chafing dish.

"How do *you* happen to know so much about him, Rita?"

She answered, carelessly: "I have known him ever since I began to pose — almost."

Valerie set her cup aside, sprang up to rinse mouth and hands. Then, gathering her pink negligée around her, curled up in a big wing-chair, drawing her bare feet up under the silken folds and watching Rita prepare the modest repast for one.

"Rita," she said, "who was the first artist you ever posed for? Was it John Burleson — and did you endure the tortures of the damned?"

"No, it was not John Burleson. . . . And I endured — enough."

"Don't you care to tell me who it was?"

Rita did not reply at that time. Later, however, when the simple supper was ended, she lighted a cigarette and found a place where, with lamplight behind her, she could read a book which Burleson had sent her, and which she had been attempting to assimilate and digest all winter. It was a large, thick, dark book, and weighed nearly four pounds. It was called "Essays on the Obvious"; and Valerie had made fun of it until, to her surprise, she noticed that her pleasantries annoyed Rita.

Valerie, curled up in the wing-chair, cheek resting against its velvet side, was reading the Psalms again — fascinated as always by the noble music of the verse. And it was only by chance that, lifting her eyes absently for a moment, she found that Rita had laid aside her book and was looking at her intently.

"Hello, dear!" she said, indolently humorous.

Rita said: "You read your Bible a good deal, don't you?"

"Parts of it."

"The parts you believe?"

"Yes; and the parts that I can't believe."

"What parts can't you believe?"

Valerie laughed: "Oh, the unfair parts — the cruel parts, the inconsistent parts."

"What about faith?"

"Faith is a matter of temperament, dear."

"Haven't you any?"

"Yes, in all things good."

"Then you have faith in yourself that you are capable of deciding what is good and worthy of belief in the Scriptures, and what is unworthy?"

"It must be that way. I am intelligent. One must decide for one's self what is fair and what is unfair; what is cruel and what is merciful and kind. Intelligence must always evolve its own religion; sin is only an unfaithfulness to what one really believes."

"What *do* you believe, Valerie?"

"About what, dear?"

"Love."

"Loving a man?"

"Yes."

"You know what my creed is — that love must be utterly unselfish to be pure — to be love at all."

"One must not think of one's self," murmured Rita, absently.

"I don't mean that. I mean that one must not hesitate to sacrifice one's self when the happiness or welfare of the other is in the balance."

"Yes. Of course. . . ! Suppose you love a man."

"Yes," said Valerie, smiling, "I can imagine that."

"Listen, dear. Suppose you love a man. And you think that perhaps he is beginning — just beginning to care a little for you. And suppose — suppose that you are — have been — long ago — once, very long ago —"

"What?"

"Unwise," said Rita, in a low voice.

"Unwise? How?"

"In the — unwisest way that a girl can be."

"You mean any less unwise than a man might be — probably the very man she is in love with?"

"You know well enough what is thought about a girl's unwisdom and the same unwisdom in a man."

"I know what is thought; but *I* don't think it."

"Perhaps you don't. But the world's opinion is different."

"Yes, I know it. . . . What is your question again? You say to me, here's a man beginning to care for a girl who has been unwise enough before she knew him to let herself believe she cared enough for another man to become his mistress. Is that it, Rita?"

"Y-yes."

"Very well. What do you wish to ask me?"

"I wish to ask you what that girl should do."

"Do? Nothing. What is there for her to do?"

"Ought she to let that man care for her?"

"Has he ever made the same mistake she has?"

"I — don't think so."

"Are you sure?"

"Almost."

"Well, then, I'd tell him."

Rita lay silent, gazing into space, her blond hair clustering around the pretty oval of her face.

Valerie waited for a few moments, then resumed her reading, glancing inquiringly at intervals over the top of her book at Rita, who seemed disinclined for further conversation.

After a long silence she sat up abruptly on the sofa and looked at Valerie.

"You asked me who was the first man for whom I posed. I'll tell you if you wish to know. It was Penrhyn Cardemon. . . ! And I was eighteen years old."

Valerie dropped her book in astonishment.

"Penrhyn Cardemon!" she repeated. "Why, he isn't an artist!"

"He has a studio."

"Where?"

"On Fifth Avenue."

"What does he do there?"

"Deviltry."

Valerie's face was blank; Rita sat sullenly cradling one knee in her arms, looking at the floor, her soft, gold hair hanging over her face and forehead so that it shadowed her face.

"I've meant to tell you for a long time," she went on; "I would have told you if Cardemon had ever sent for you to — to pose — in his place."

"He asked me to go on *The Mohave.*"

"I'd have warned you if Louis Neville had not objected."

"Do you suppose Louis knew?"

"No. He scarcely knows Penrhyn Cardemon. His family and Cardemon are neighbors in the country, but the Nevilles and the Collises are snobs — I'm speaking plainly, Valerie — and they have no use for that red-faced, red-necked, stocky young millionaire."

Valerie sat thinking; Rita, nursing her knee, brooded under the bright tangle of her hair, linking and unlinking her fingers as she gently swayed her foot to and fro.

"That's how it is," she said at last. "Now you know."

Valerie's head was still lowered, but she raised her eyes and looked straight at Rita where she sat on the sofa's edge, carelessly swinging her foot to and fro.

"Was it — Penrhyn Cardemon?" she asked.

"Yes. . . . I thought it had killed any possibility of ever caring — that way — for any other man."

"But it hasn't?"

"No."

"And — you are in love?"

"Yes."

"With John Burleson?"

Rita looked up from the burnished disorder of her hair:

"I have been in love with him for three years," she said, "and you are the only person in the world except myself who knows it."

Valerie rose and walked over to Rita and seated herself
beside her. Then she put one arm around her; and Rita bit
her lip and stared at space, swinging her slender foot.

"You poor dear," said Valerie. Rita's bare foot hung inert;
the silken slipper dropped from it to the floor; and then her
head fell, sideways, resting on Valerie's shoulder, showering
her body with its tangled gold.

Valerie said, thoughtfully: "Girls don't seem to have a very
good chance. . . . I had no idea about Cardemon — that he
was that kind of a man. A girl never knows. Men can be so
attractive and so nice. . . . And so many of them are merciless. . . . I suppose you thought you loved him."

"Y — yes."

"We all think that, I suppose," said Valerie, thoughtfully.
"Other girls have thought it of Penrhyn Cardemon."

"Other *girls?*"

"Yes."

Valerie's face expressed bewilderment.

"I didn't know that there were really such men."

Rita closed her disillusioned eyes.

"Plenty," she said wearily.

"I don't care to believe that."

"You may believe it, Valerie. Men are almost never single-
minded; women are — almost always. You see what chance for
happiness we have? But it's the truth, and the world has been
made that way. It's a man's world, Valerie. I don't think there's
much use for us to fight against it. . . . She sat very silent for
a while, close to Valerie, her hot face on the younger girl's
shoulder. Suddenly she straightened up and dried her eyes
naïvely on the sleeve of her kimono.

"Goodness!" she said, "I almost forgot!"

And a moment later Valerie heard her at the telephone:

"Is that you, John?"

"*H*ave you remembered to take your medicine?"

*

"How perfectly horrid of you! Take it at once! It's the one
in the brown bottle — six drops in a wineglass of water —"

Chapter XII

Mrs. Hind-Willet, born to the purple — or rather entitled to a narrow border of discreet mauve on all occasions of ceremony in Manhattan, was a dreamer of dreams. One of her dreams concerned her hyphenated husband, and she put him away; another concerned Penrhyn Cardemon; and she woke up. But the persistent visualization, which had become obsession, of a society to be formed out of the massed intellects of Manhattan regardless of race, morals, or previous condition of social servitude — a gentle intellectual affinity which knew no law of art except individual inspiration, haunted her always. And there was always her own set to which she could retreat if desirable.

She had begun with a fashionable and semi-fashionable nucleus which included Mrs. Atherstane, the Countess d'Enver, Latimer Varyck, Olaf Dennison, and Pedro Carrillo, and then enlarged the circle from those perpetual candidates squatting anxiously upon the social step-ladder all the way from the bottom to the top.

The result was what Ogilvy called intellectual local option; and though he haunted this agglomeration at times, particularly when temporarily smitten by a pretty face or figure, he was under no illusions concerning it or the people composing it.

Returning one afternoon from a reception at Mrs. Atherstane's he replied to Annan's disrespectful inquiries and injurious observations:

"You're on to that joint, Henry; it's a saloon, not a salon; and Art is the petrified sandwich. Fix me a very, ve-ry high one, dearie, because little sunshine is in love again."

"Who drew the lucky number?" asked Annan with a shrug.

"The Countess d'Enver. She's the birdie."

"Intellectually?"

"Oh, she's an intellectual four-flusher, bless her heart! But she was the only woman there who didn't try to mentally frisk me. We lunch together soon, Henry."

"Where's Count hubby?"

"Aloft. She's a bird," he repeated, fondly reminiscent over his high-ball — "and I myself am the real ornithological thing — the species that Brooklyn itself would label 'boid' . . . She has such pretty, confiding ways, Harry."

"You'd both better join the Audubon Society for Mutual Protection," observed Annan dryly.

"I'll stand for anything she stands for except that social Tenderloin; I'll join anything she joins except the 'classes now forming' in that intellectual dance hall. By the way, who do you suppose was there?"

"The police?"

"Naw — the saloon wasn't raided, though 'Professor' Carrillo's poem was *assez raide.* Mek-mek-k-k-k! But oh, the ginky pictures! Oh, the Art Beautiful! Aniline rainbows exploding in a physical culture school couldn't beat that omelet. . . ! And guess who was pouring tea in the center of the olio, Harry!"

"You?" inquired Annan wearily.

"Valerie West."

"What in God's name has that bunch taken her up for?"

*F*or the last few weeks Valerie's telephone had rung intermittently summoning her to conversation with Mrs. Hind-Willet.

At first the amiable interest displayed by Mrs. Hind-Willet puzzled Valerie until one day, returning to her rooms for luncheon, she found the Countess d'Enver's brougham standing in front of the house and that discreetly perfumed lady about to descend.

"How do you do?" said Valerie, stopping on the sidewalk and offering her hand with a frank smile.

"I came to call on you," said the overdressed little countess; "may I?"

"It is very kind of you. Will you come upstairs? There is no elevator."

The pretty bejeweled countess arrived in the living room out of breath, and seated herself, flushed, speechless, overcome, her little white gloved hand clutching her breast.

Valerie, accustomed to the climb, was in nowise distressed; and went serenely about her business while the countess was recovering.

"I am going to prepare luncheon; may I hope you will remain and share it with me?" she asked.

The countess nodded, slowly recovering her breath and glancing curiously around the room.

"You see I have only an hour between poses," observed Valerie, moving swiftly from cupboard to kitchenette, "so luncheon is always rather simple. Miss Tevis, with whom I live, never lunches here, so I take what there is left from breakfast."

A little later they were seated at a small table together, sipping chocolate. There was cold meat, a light salad, and fruit. The conversation was as haphazard and casual as the luncheon, until the pretty countess lighted a cigarette and tasted her tiny glass of Port — the latter a gift from Querida. "Do you think it odd of me to call on you uninvited?" she asked, with that smiling abruptness which sometimes arises from embarrassment.

"I think it is very sweet of you," said Valerie, "I am very happy to know that you remember me."

The countess flushed up: "Do you really feel that way about it?"

"Yes," said Valerie, smiling, "or I would not say so."

"Then — you give me courage to tell you that since I first met you I've been — quite mad about you."

"About *me!*" in smiling surprise.

"Yes. I wanted to know you. I told Mrs. Hind-Willet to ask you to the club. She did. But you never came. . . . And I *did* like you so much."

Valerie said in a sweet, surprised way: "Do you know what I am?"

"Yes; you sit for artists."

"I am a professional model," said Valerie. "I don't believe you understood that, did you?"

"Yes, I did," said the countess. "You pose for the ensemble, too."

Valerie looked at her incredulously:

"Do you think you would really care to know me? I, an artist's model, and you, the Countess d'Enver?"

"I was Nellie Jackson before that." She leaned across the table, smiling, with heightened color; "I believe I'd never have to pretend with you. The minute I saw you I liked you. Will you let me talk to you?"

"Y — yes."

There was a constrained silence; Hélène d'Enver touched the water in the bowl with her fingertips, dried them, looked up at Valerie, who rose. Under the window there was a tufted seat; and here they found places together.

"Do you know why I came?" asked Hélène d'Enver. "I was lonely."

"*You!*"

"My dear, I am a lonely woman; I'm lonely to desperation. I don't belong in New York and I don't belong in France, and I don't like Pittsburgh. I'm lonely! I've always been lonely ever since I left Pittsburgh. There doesn't seem to be any definite place anywhere for me. And I haven't a real woman friend in the world!"

"How in the world can you say that?" exclaimed Valerie, astonished.

The countess lighted another cigarette and wreathed her pretty face in smoke.

"You think because I have a title and am presentable that I can go anywhere?" She smiled. "The society I might care for hasn't the slightest interest in me. There is in this city a kind of society recruited largely from the fashionable hotels and from among those who have no fixed social position in New

York — people who are never very far outside or inside the edge of things — but who never penetrate any farther." She laughed. "This society camps permanently at the base of the Great Wall of China. But it never scales it."

"Watch the men on Fifth Avenue," she went on. "Some walk there as though they do not belong there; some walk as though they do belong there; some, as though they lived there. I move about as though I belonged where I am occasionally seen; but I'm tired of pretending that I live there."

She leaned back among the cushions, dropping one knee over the other and tossing away her cigarette. And her little suede shoe swung nervously to and fro.

"You're the first girl I've seen in New York who, I believe, really doesn't care what I am — and I don't care what she is. Shall we be friends? I'm lonely."

Valerie looked at her, diffidently:

"I haven't had very much experience in friendship — except with Rita Tevis," she said.

"Will you let me take you to drive sometimes?"

"I'd love to, only you see I am in business."

"Of course I mean after hours."

"Thank you. . . . But I usually am expected — to tea — and dinner —"

Hélène lay back among the cushions, looking at her.

"Haven't you any time at all for me?" she asked, wistfully.

Valerie was thinking of Neville: "Not — very — much I am afraid —"

"Can't you spare me an hour now and then?"

"Y — yes; I'll try."

There was a silence. The mantel clock struck, and Valerie glanced up. Hélène d'Enver rose, stood still a moment, then stepped forward and took both of Valerie's hands:

"Can't we be friends? I do need one; and I like you so much. You've the eyes that make a woman easy. There are none like yours in New York."

Valerie laughed, uncertainly.

"Your friends wouldn't care for me," she said. "I don't believe there is any real place at all for me in this city except among the few men and women I already know."

"Won't you include me among the number? There is a place for you in my heart."

Touched and surprised, the girl stood looking at the older woman in silence.

"May I drive you to your destination?" asked Hélène gently.

"You are very kind. . . . It is Mr. Burleson's studio — if it won't take you too far out of your way."

By the end of March Valerie had driven with the Countess d'Enver once or twice; and once or twice had been to see her, and had met, in her apartment, men and women who were inclined to make a fuss over her — men like Carrillo and Dennison, and women like Mrs. Hind-Willet and Mrs. Atherstane. It was her unconventional profession that interested them.

To Neville, recounting her experiences, she said with a patient little smile:

"It's rather nice to be liked and to have some kind of a place among people who live in this city. Nobody seems to mind my being a model. Perhaps they *have* taken merely a passing fancy to me and are exhibiting me to each other as a wild thing just captured and being trained —" She laughed — "but they do it so pleasantly that I don't mind. . . . And anyway, the Countess d'Enver is genuine; I am sure of that."

"A genuine countess?"

"A genuine woman, sincere, lovable, and kind — I am becoming very fond of her. . . . Do you mind my abandoning you for an afternoon now and then? Because it *is* nice to have as a friend a woman older and more experienced."

"Does that mean you're going off with her this afternoon?"

"I *was* going. But I won't if you feel that I'm deserting you."

He laid aside his palette and went over to where she was standing.

"You darling," he said, "go and drive in the Park with your funny little friend."

"She was going to take me to the Plaza for tea. There are to be some very nice women there who are interested in the New Idea Home." She added, shyly, "I have subscribed ten dollars."

He kissed her, lightly, humorously. "And what, sweetheart, may the New Idea Home be?"

"Oh, it's an idea of Mrs. Hind-Willet's about caring for wayward girls. Mrs. Willet thinks that it is cruel and silly to send them into virtual imprisonment, to punish them and watch them and confront them at every turn with threats and the merciless routine of discipline. She thinks that the thing to do is to give them a chance for sensible and normal happiness; not to segregate them one side of a dead line; not to treat them like criminals to be watched and doubted and suspected."

She linked her arms around his neck, interested, earnest, sure of his sympathy and approval:

"We want to build a school in the country — two schools, one for girls who have misbehaved, one for youths who are similarly delinquent. And, during recreation, we mean to let them meet in a natural manner — play games together, dance, mingle out of doors in a wholesome and innocent way — of course, under necessary and sympathetic supervision — and learn a healthy consideration and respect for one another which the squalid, crowded, irresponsible conditions of their former street life in the slums and tenements made utterly impossible."

He looked into the pretty, eager face with its honest, beautiful eyes and sensitive mouth — and touched his lips to her hair.

"It sounds fine, sweetheart," he said: "and I won't be lonely if you go to the Plaza and settle the affairs of this topsy-turvy world. . . . Do you love me?"

"Louis! Can you ask?"

"I do ask."

She smiled, faintly; then her young face grew serious, and a hint of passion darkened her eyes as her arms tightened around his neck and her lips met his.

"All I care for in the world, or out of it, is you, Louis. If I find pleasure in anything it is because of you; if I take a little pride in having people like me, it is only for your sake — for the sake of the pride you may feel in having others find me agreeable and desirable. I wish it were possible that your, own world could find me agreeable and desirable — for your sake, my darling, more than for mine. But it never will — never could. There is a wall around your world which I can never scale. And it does not make me unhappy — I only wish you to know that I want to be what you would have me — and if I can't be all that you might wish, I love and adore you nonetheless — am nonetheless willing to give you all there is to me — all there is to a girl named Valerie West who finds this life a happy one because you have made it so for her."

She continued to see Hélène d'Enver, poured tea sometimes at the Five-Minute-Club, listened to the consultations over the New Idea Home, and met a great many people of all kinds, fashionable women with a passion for the bizarre and unconventional, women of gentle breeding and no social pretence, who worked to support themselves; idle women, ambitious women, restless women; but the majority formed part of the floating circles domiciled in apartments and at the great hotels — people who wintered in New York and were a part of its social and civic life to that extent, but whose duties and responsibilities for the metropolitan welfare were self-imposed, and neither hereditary nor constant.

As all circles in New York have, at certain irregular periods, accidental points of temporary contact, Valerie now and then met people whom she was scarcely ever likely to see again. And it was at a New Idea Home conference, scheduled for five o'clock in the red parlor of the ladies' waiting room in the great Hotel Imperator, that Valerie, arriving early as delegated substitute for Mrs. Hind-Willet, found herself among a small group of beautifully gowned strangers — the sort of women whom she had never before met in this way.

They all knew each other; others who arrived seemed to recognize with more or less intimacy everybody in the room excepting herself.

She was sitting apart by the crimson-curtained windows, perfectly self-possessed and rather interested in watching the arrivals of women whose names, as she caught them, suggested social positions which were vaguely familiar to her, when an exceedingly pretty girl detached herself from the increasing group and came across to where Valerie was sitting alone.

"I was wondering whether you had met any of the new committee," she said pleasantly.

"I *had* expected to meet the Countess d'Enver here," said Valerie, smiling.

The girl's expression altered slightly, but she nodded amiably; "May I sit here with you until she arrives? I am Stephanie Swift."

Valerie said: "It is very amiable of you. I am Valerie West."

Stephanie remained perfectly still for a moment; then, conscious that she was staring, calmly averted her gaze while the slow fire died out in her cheeks. And in a moment she had decided:

"I have heard so pleasantly about you through Mrs. Collis," she said with perfect composure. "You remember her, I think."

Valerie, startled, lifted her brown eyes. Then very quietly:

"Mrs. Collis is very kind. I remember her distinctly."

"Mrs. Collis retains the most agreeable memories of meeting you. . . . I —" she looked at Valerie, curiously — "I have heard from others how charming and clever you are — from Mr. Ogilvy? — and Mr. Annan?"

"They are my friends," said Valerie briefly.

"And Mr. Querida, and Mr. Burleson, and — Mr. Neville."

"They are my friends," repeated Valerie. . . . After a second she added: "They also employ me."

Stephanie looked away: "Your profession must be most interesting, Miss West."

"Yes."

"But — exacting."

"Very."

Neither made any further effort. A moment later, however, Hélène d'Enver came in. She knew some of the women very slightly, none intimately; and, catching sight of Valerie, she came across the room with a quick smile of recognition:

"I'm dreadfully late, dear — how do you do, Miss Swift" — to Stephanie, who had risen. And to Valerie: "Mr. Ogilvy came; just as I had my furs on — and you know how casually a man takes his leave when you're in a tearing hurry!"

She laughed and took Valerie's gloved hands in her own; and Stephanie, who had been looking at the latter, came to an abrupt conclusion that amazed her; and she heard herself saying:

"It has been most interesting to meet you, Miss West. I have heard of you so pleasantly that I had hoped to meet you some time. And I hope I shall again."

Valerie thanked her with a self-possession which she did not entirely feel, and turned away with Hélène d'Enver.

"That's the girl who is supposed to be engaged to Louis Neville," whispered the pretty countess.

Valerie halted, astounded.

"Didn't you know it?" asked the other, surprised.

For a moment Valerie remained speechless, then the wild absurdity of it flashed over her and she laughed her relief.

"No, I didn't know it," she said.

"Hasn't anybody ever told you?"

"No," said Valerie, smiling.

"Well, perhaps it isn't so, then," said the countess naïvely. "I know very few people of that set, but I've heard it talked about — outside."

"I don't believe it is so," said Valerie demurely. Her little heart was beating confidently again and she seated herself beside Hélène d'Enver in the prim circle of delegates intent upon their chairman, who was calling the meeting to order.

The meeting was interesting and there were few feminine clashes — merely a smiling and deadly exchange of amenities between a fashionable woman who was an ardent advocate of suffrage, and an equally distinguished lady who was scornfully opposed to it. But the franchise had nothing at all to do with the discussion concerning the New Idea Home, which is doubtless why it was mentioned; and the meeting of delegates proceeded without further debate.

After it was ended Valerie hurried away to keep an appointment with Neville at Burleson's studio, and found the big sculptor lying on the sofa, neck swathed in flannel, and an array of medicine bottles at his elbow.

"Can't go to dinner with you," he said; "Rita won't have it. There's nothing the matter with me, but she made me lie down here, and I've promised to stay here until she returns."

"John, you don't look very well," said Valerie, coming over and seating herself by his side.

"I'm all right, except that I catch cold now and then," he insisted obstinately.

Valerie looked at the pink patches of color burning in his cheeks. There was a transparency to his skin, too, that troubled her. He was one of those big, blond, blue-eyed fellows whose vivid color and fine-grained, delicate skin caused physicians to look twice.

He had been reading when Valerie entered; now he laid his ponderous book away, doubled his arms back under his head and looked at Valerie with the placid, bovine friendliness which warmed her heart but always left a slight smile in the corner of her mouth.

"Why do you always smile at me, Valerie?" he asked.

"Because you're good, John, and I like you."

"I know you do. You're a fine woman, Valerie. . . . So is Rita."

"Rita is a darling."

"She's all right," he nodded. A moment later he added: "She comes from Massachusetts."

Valerie laughed: "The sacred codfish smiled on your cradle, too, didn't it, John?"

"Yes, thank God," he said seriously. . . . "I was born in the old town of Hitherford."

"How funny!" exclaimed the girl.

"What is there funny about that?" demanded John.

"Why, Rita was born in Hitherford."

"Hitherford Center," corrected John. "Her father was a clergyman there."

"Oh; so you knew it?"

"I knew, of course, that she was from Massachusetts," said John, "because she speaks English properly. So I asked her where she was born and she told me. . . . My grandfather knew hers."

"Isn't it — curious," mused the girl.

"What's curious?"

"Your meeting this way — as sculptor and model."

"Rita is a very fine girl," he said. "Would you mind handing me my pipe? No, don't. I forgot that Rita won't let me. You see my chest is rather uncomfortable."

He glanced at the clock, leaned over and gulped down some medicine, then placidly folding his hands, lay back:

"How's Kelly?"

"I haven't seen him today, John."

"Well, he ought to be here very soon. He can take you and Rita to dinner."

"I'm so sorry you can't come."

"So am I."

Valerie laid a cool hand on his face; he seemed slightly feverish. Rita came in at that moment, smiled at Valerie, and went straight to Burleson's couch:

"Have you taken your medicine?"

"Certainly."

She glanced at the bottles. "Men are so horridly untruthful," she remarked to Valerie; "and this great, lumbering six-footer hasn't the sense of a baby —"

"I have, too!" roared John, indignantly; and Valerie laughed but Rita scarcely smiled.

"He's always working in a puddle of wet clay and he's always having colds and coughing, and there's always more or less fever," she said, looking down at the huge young fellow. "I know that he ought to give up his work and go away for a while —"

"Where?" demanded Burleson indignantly.

"Oh, somewhere — where there's plenty of — air. Like Arizona, and Colorado."

"Do you think there's anything the matter with my lungs?" he roared.

"No! — you perfect idiot!" said Rita, seating herself; "and if you shout that way at me again I'll go to dinner with Kelly and Valerie and leave you here alone. I will not permit you to be uncivil, John. Please remember it."

Neville arrived in excellent spirits, greeted everybody, and stood beside Valerie, carelessly touching the tip of his fingers to hers where they hung at her side.

"What's the matter with *you*, John? Rita, isn't he coming? I've a taxi outside ruining me."

"John has a bad cold and doesn't care to go —"

"Yes, I do!" growled John.

"And he doesn't care to risk contracting pneumonia," continued Rita icily, "and he isn't going, anyway. And if he behaves like a man instead of an overgrown baby, I have promised to stay and dine with him here. Otherwise I'll go with you."

"Sure. You'd better stay indoors, John. You ought to buck up and get rid of that cold. It's been hanging on all winter."

Burleson rumbled and grumbled and shot a mutinous glance at Rita, who paid it no attention.

"Order us a nice dinner at the Plaza, Kelly — if you don't mind," she said cheerfully, going with them to the door. She added under her breath: "I wish he'd see a doctor, but the idea enrages him. I don't see why he has such a cold all the time — and such flushed cheeks —" Her voice quivered and she checked herself abruptly.

"Suppose I ring up Dr. Colbert on my own hook?" whispered Neville.

"Would you?"

"Certainly. And you can tell John that I did it on my own responsibility."

Neville and Valerie went away together, and Rita returned to the studio. Burleson was reading again, and scowling; and he scarcely noticed her. She seated herself by the fire and looked into the big bare studio beyond where the electric light threw strange shadows over shrouded shapes of wet clay and blocks of marble in the rough or partly hewn into rough semblance of human figures.

It was a damp place at best; there were always wet sponges, wet cloths, pails of water, masses of moist clay about. Her blue eyes wandered over it with something approaching fear — almost the fear of hatred.

"John," she said, "why won't you go to a dry climate for a few months and get rid of your cold?"

"Do you mean Arizona?"

"Or some similar place: yes."

"Well, how am I to do any work out there? I've got commissions on hand. Where am I going to find anyplace to work out in Arizona?"

"Build a shanty."

"That's all very well, but there are no models to be had out there."

"Why don't you do some Indians?"

"Because," said John wrathfully, "I haven't any commissions that call for Indians. I've two angels, a nymph and a Diana to do; and I can't do them unless I have a female model, can I?"

After a silence Rita said carelessly:

"I'll go with you if you like."

"You! Out there!"

"I said so."

"To Arizona! You wouldn't stand for it!"

"John Burleson!" she said impatiently, "I've told you once that I'd go with you if you need a model! Don't you suppose I know what I am saying?"

He lay placidly staring at her, the heavy book open across his chest. Presently he coughed and Rita sprang up and removed the book.

"You'd go with me to Arizona," he repeated, as though to himself — "just to pose for me. . . . That's very kind of you, Rita. It's thoroughly nice of you. But you couldn't stand it. You'd find it too cruelly stupid out there alone — entirely isolated in some funny town. I couldn't ask it of you —"

"You haven't. I've asked it — of you."

But he only began to grumble and fret again, thrashing about restlessly on the lounge; and the tall young girl watched him out of lowered eyes, silent, serious, the lamplight edging her hair with a halo of ruddy gold.

*T*he month sped away very swiftly for Valerie. Her companionship with Rita, her new friendship for Hélène d'Enver, her work, filled all the little moments not occupied with Neville. It had been a happy, exciting winter; and now, with the first days of spring, an excitement and a happiness so strange that it even resembled fear at moments, possessed her, in the imminence of the great change.

Often, in these days, she found herself staring at Neville with a sort of fixed fascination almost bordering on terror;

— there were moments when alone with him, and even while with him among his friends and hers, when there seemed to awake in her a fear so sudden, so inexplicable, that every nerve in her quivered apprehension until it had passed as it came. What those moments of keenest fear might signify she had no idea. She loved, and was loved, and was not afraid.

In early April Neville went to Ashuelyn. Ogilvy was there, also Stephanie Swift.

His sister Lily had triumphantly produced a second sample of what she could do to perpetuate the House of Collis, and was much engrossed with nursery duties; so Stephanie haunted the nursery, while Ogilvy, Neville, and Gordon Collis played golf over the April pastures, joining them only when Lily was at liberty.

Why Stephanie avoided Neville she herself scarcely knew; why she clung so closely to Lily's skirts seemed no easier to explain. But in her heart there was a restlessness which no ignoring, no self-discipline could suppress — an unease which had been there many days, now — a hard, tired, ceaseless inquietude that found some little relief when she was near Lily Collis, but which, when alone, became a dull ache.

She had grown thin and spiritless within the last few months. Lily saw it and resented it hotly.

"The child," she said to her husband, "is perfectly wretched over Louis and his ignominious affair with that West girl. I don't know whether she means to keep her word to me or not, but she's with him every day. They're seen together everywhere except where Louis really belongs."

"It looks to me," said Gordon mildly, "as though he were really in love with her."

"Gordon! How *can* you say such a thing in such a sympathetic tone!"

"Why — aren't you sorry for them?"

"I'm sorry for Louis — and perfectly disgusted. I *was* sorry for her; an excess of sentimentality. But she hasn't kept her word to me."

"Did she promise not to gad about with him?"

"That was the spirit of the compact; she agreed not to marry him."

"Sometimes they — don't marry," observed Gordon, twirling his thumbs.

Lily looked up quickly; then flushed slightly.

"What do you mean, Gordon?"

"Nothing specific; anything in general."

"You mean to hint that — that Louis — Louis Neville could be — permit himself to be so common — so unutterably low —"

"Better men have taken the half-loaf."

"Gordon!" she exclaimed, scarlet with amazement and indignation.

"Personally," he said, unperturbed, "I haven't much sympathy with such affairs. If a man can't marry a girl he ought to leave her alone; that's my idea of the game. But men play it in a variety of ways. Personally, I'd as soon plug a loaded shot-gun with mud and then fire it, as block a man who wants to marry."

"I *did* block it!" said Lily with angry decision; "and I am glad I did."

"Look out for the explosion then," he said philosophically, and strolled off to see to the setting out of some young hemlocks, headed in the year previous.

Lily Collis was deeply disturbed — more deeply than her pride and her sophistication cared to admit. She strove to believe that such a horror as her husband had hinted at so coolly could never happen to a Neville; she rejected it with anger, with fear, with a proud and dainty fastidiousness that ought to have calmed and reassured her. It did not.

Once or twice she reverted to the subject, haughtily; but Gordon merely shrugged:

"You can't teach a man of twenty-eight when, where, and how to fall in love," he said. "And it's all the more hopeless when the girl possesses the qualities which you once told me this girl possesses."

Lily bit her lip, angry and disconcerted, but utterly unable to refute him or find anything in her memory of Valerie to criticize and condemn, except the intimacy with her brother which had continued and which, she had supposed, would cease on Valerie's promise to her.

"It's very horrid of her to go about with him under the circumstances — knowing she can't marry him if she keeps her word," said Lily.

"Why? Stephanie goes about with him."

"Do you think it is good taste to compare those two people?"

"Why not. From what you told me I gather that Valerie West is as innocent and upright a woman as Stephanie — and as proudly capable of self-sacrifice as any woman who ever loved."

"Gordon," she said, exasperated, "do you actually wish to see my brother marry a common model?"

"*Is* she common? I thought you said —"

"You — you annoy me," said Lily; and began to cry.

Stephanie, coming into the nursery that afternoon, found Lily watching the sleeping children and knitting a tiny sweater. Mrs. Collis was pale, but her eyes were still red.

"Where have you been, Stephanie?"

"Helping Gordon set hemlocks."

"Where is Louis?"

The girl did not appear to hear the question.

"I thought I heard him telephoning a few minutes ago," added Lily. "Look over the banisters, dear, and see if he's still there."

"He is," said Stephanie, not stirring.

"Telephoning all this time? Is he talking to somebody in town?"

"I believe so."

Lily suddenly looked up. Stephanie was quietly examining some recently laundered clothing for the children.

"To whom is Louis talking; do you happen to know?" asked Lily abruptly.

Stephanie's serious gaze encountered hers.

"Does that concern us, Lily?"

After a while, as Mrs. Collis sat in silence working her ivory needles, a tear or two fell silently upon the little white wool garment on her lap.

And presently Stephanie went over and touched her forehead with gentle lips; but Lily did not look up — could not — and her fingers and ivory needles flew the faster.

"Do you know," said Stephanie in a low voice, "that she is a modest, well-bred, and very beautiful girl?"

"What!" exclaimed Lily, staring at her in grief and amazement. "Of whom are you speaking, Stephanie?"

"Of Valerie West, dear."

"W-what do you know about her?"

"I have met her."

"You!"

"Yes. She came, with that rather common countess, as substitute delegate for Mrs. Hind-Willet, to a New Idea meeting. I spoke to her, seeing she was alone and seemed to know nobody; I had no suspicion of who she was until she told me."

"Mrs. Hind-Willet is a busybody!" said Lily, furious. "Let her fill her own drawing room with freaks if it pleases her, but she has no right to send them abroad among self-respecting people who are too unsuspicious to protect themselves!"

Stephanie said: "Until one has seen and spoken with Valerie West one can scarcely understand how a man like your brother could care so much for her —"

"How do you know Louis cares for her?"

"He told me."

Lily looked into the frank, grey eyes in horror unutterable. The crash had come. The last feeble hope that her brother might come to his senses and marry this girl was ended forever.

"How — could he!" she stammered, outraged. "How could he tell — tell *you* —"

"Because he and I are old and close friends, Lily. . . . And will remain so, God willing."

Lily was crying freely now.

"He had no business to tell you. He knows perfectly well what his father and mother think about it and what I think. He can't marry her! He shall not. It is too cruel — too wicked — too heartless! And anyway — she promised me not to marry him —"

"What!"

Lily brushed the tears from her eyes, heedless now of how much Stephanie might learn.

"I wrote her — I went to see her in behalf of my own family as I had a perfect right to. She promised me not to marry Louis."

"Does Louis know this?"

"Not unless she's told him. . . . I don't care whether he does or not! He has disappointed me — he has embittered life for me — and for his parents. We — I — I had every reason to believe that he and — you —"

Something in Stephanie's grey eyes checked her. When breeding goes to pieces it makes a worse mess of it than does sheer vulgarity.

"If I were Louis I would marry her," said Stephanie very quietly. "I gave him that advice."

She rose, looking down at Lily where she sat bowed over her wool-work, her face buried in her hands.

"Think about it; and talk patiently with Louis," she said gently.

Passing the stairs she glanced toward the telephone. Louis was still talking to somebody in New York.

*I*t was partly fear of what her husband had hinted, partly terror of what she considered worse still — a legal marriage — that drove Lily Collis to write once more to Valerie West:

"Dear Miss West:

"It is not that I have any disposition to doubt your word to me, but, in view of the assurance you have given me, do you consider it wise to permit my brother's rather conspicuous attentions to you?

"Permit me, my dear Miss West, as an older woman with wider experience which years must bring, to suggest that it is due to yourself to curtail an intimacy which the world — of course mistakenly in your case — views always uncharitably.

"No man — and I include my brother as severely as I do any man — has a right to let the world form any misconception as to his intentions toward any woman.

If he does he is either ignorant or selfish and ruthless; and it behooves a girl to protect her own reputation.

"I write this in all faith and kindliness for your sake as well as for his. But a man outlives such things, a woman never. And, for the sake of your own future I beg you to consider this matter and I trust that you may not misconstrue the motive which has given me the courage to write you what has caused me deepest concern.

"Very sincerely yours,

"LILY COLLIS"

To which Valerie replied:

"MY DEAR, MRS. COLLIS:

"I have to thank you for your excellent intentions in writing me. But with all deference to your wider experience I am afraid that I must remain the judge of my own conduct. Pray, believe that, in proportion to your sincerity, I am grateful to you; and that I should never dream of being discourteous to Mr. Neville's sister if I venture to suggest to her that liberty of conscience is a fundamental scarcely susceptible of argument or discussion.

"I assume that you would not care to have Mr. Neville know of this correspondence, and for that reason I am returning to you your letter so that you may be assured of its ultimate destruction.

"Very truly yours,

"VALERIE WEST"

Which letter and its reply made Valerie deeply unhappy; and she wrote Neville a little note saying that she had gone to the country with Hélène d'Enver for a few days' rest.

The countess had taken a house among the hills at Estwich; and as chance would have it, about eight miles from Ashuelyn and Penrhyn Cardemon's great establishment, El Naúar.

Later Valerie was surprised and disturbed to learn of the proximity of Neville's family, fearing that if Mrs. Collis heard of her in the neighborhood she might misunderstand.

But there was only scant and rough communication between Ashuelyn and Estwich; the road was a wretched hill-path passable only by buck-boards; Westwich was the nearest town to Ashuelyn and El Naúar and the city of Dartford, the county seat most convenient to Estwich.

Spring was early; the Estwich hills bloomed in May; and Hélène d'Enver moved her numerous household from the huge Castilione Apartment House to Estwich and settled down for a summer of mental and physical recuperation.

Valerie, writing to Neville the first week in May, said:

"Louis, the country here is divine. I thought the shaggy, unkempt hills of Delaware County were heavenly — and they *were* when you came and made them so — but this rich, green, well-ordered country with its hills and woods and meadows of emerald — its calm river, its lovely little brooks, its gardens, hedges, farms, is to me the most wonderful land I ever looked upon.

"Hélène has a pretty house, white with green blinds and verandas, and the loveliest lawns you ever saw — unless the English lawns are lovelier.

"To my city-wearied eyes the region is celestial in its horizon-wide quiet. Only the ripple of water in leafy ravines — only the music of birds breaks the silence that is so welcome, so blessed.

"Today Hélène and I picked strawberries for breakfast, then filled the house with great fragrant peonies, some of which are the color of Brides' roses, some of water-lilies.

"I'm quite mad with delight; I love the farm with its ducks and hens and pigeons; I adore the cattle in the meadow. They are fragrant. Hélène laughs at me because I follow the cows about, sniffing luxuriously. They smell like the clover they chew.

"Louis, dear, I have decided to remain a week here, if you don't mind. I'm a little tired, I think. John Burleson, poor boy, does not need me. I'm terribly worried about him. Rita writes that there is no danger of pneumonia, but that Dr. Colbert is making a careful examination. I hope it is not lung trouble. It would be too tragic. He is only twenty-seven. Still, they cure such things now, don't they? Rita is hoping he will go to Arizona, and has offered to go with him as his model.

That means — if she does go — that she'll nurse him and take care of him. She is devoted to him. What a generous girl she is!

"Dear, if you don't need me, or are not too lonely without seeing me come fluttering into your studio every evening at teatime, I would really like to remain here a few days longer. I have arranged business so that I can stay if it is agreeable to you. Tell me exactly how you feel about it and I will do exactly as you wish — which, please God — I shall always do while life lasts.

"Sam came up over Sunday, lugging Harry Annan and a bulldog — a present for Hélène. Sam is *so* sentimental about Hélène!

"And he's so droll about it. But I've seen him that way before; haven't you? And Hélène, bless her heart, lets him make eyes at her and just laughs in that happy, wholesome way of hers.

"She's a perfect dear, Louis; so sweet and kind to me, so unaffected, so genuine, so humorous about herself and her funny title. She told me that she would gladly shed it if she were not obliged to shed her legacy with it. I don't blame her. What an awful title — when you translate it!

"Sam is temporarily laid up. He attempted to milk a cow and she kicked him; and he's lying in a hammock and Hélène is reading to him, while Harry paints her portrait. Oh, dear — I *love* Harry Annan, but he can't paint!

"Dearest — as I sit here in my room with the chintz curtains blowing and the sun shining on the vines outside my open windows, I am thinking of you; and my girl's heart is very full — very humble in the wonder of your love for me — a miracle ever new, ever sweeter, ever holier.

"I pray that it be given to me to see the best way for your happiness and your welfare; I pray that I may not be confused by thought of self.

"Dear, the spring is going very swiftly. I can scarcely believe that May is already here — is already passing — and that the first of June is so near.

"Will you *always* love me? Will you always think tenderly of me — happily — ! Alas, it is a promise nobody can honestly make. One can be honest only in wishing it may be so.

"Dearest of men, the great change is near at hand — nearer than I can realize. Do you still want me? Is the world impossible without me? Tell me so, Louis; tell me so now — and in the years to come — very often — very, very often. I shall need to hear you say it; I understand now how great my need will be to hear you say it in the years to come."

Writing to him in a gayer mood a week later:

"It is perfectly dear of you to tell me to remain. I *do* miss you; I'm simply wild to see you; but I am getting so strong, so well, so deliciously active and vigorous again. I *was* rather run down in town. But in the magic of this air and sunshine I have watched the reincarnation of myself. I swim, I row, I am learning to sit a horse; I play tennis — *and* I flirt, Monsieur — shamelessly, with Sam and Harry. Do you object —

"We had such a delightful time — a week-end party, perfectly informal and crazy; Mrs. Hind-Willet — who is such a funny woman, considering the position she might occupy in society — and José Querida — just six of us, until — and this I'm afraid you may not like — Mrs. Hind-Willet telephoned Penrhyn Cardemon to come over.

"You know, Louis, he *seems* a gentleman, though it is perfectly certain that he isn't. I hate and despise him; and have been barely civil to him. But in a small company one has to endure such things with outward equanimity; and I am sure that nobody suspects my contempt for him and that my dislike has not caused one awkward moment."

She wrote again:

"I beg of you not to suggest to your sister that she call on me. Try to be reasonable, dear. Mrs. Collis does not desire to know me. Why should she? Why should you wish to have me meet her? If you have any vague ideas that my meeting her might in any possible way alter a situation which must always exist between your family and myself, you are utterly mistaken, dearest.

"And my acquaintance with Miss Swift is so slight — I never saw her but once, and then only for a moment! — that it would be only painful and embarrassing to her if you asked her to call on me. Besides, you are a man and you don't understand such things. Also, Mrs. Collis and Miss Swift have only the slightest and most formal acquaintance with Hélène;

and it is very plain that they are as content with that acquaintance as is Hélène. And in addition to that, you dear stupid boy, your family has carefully ignored Mr. Cardemon for years, although he is their neighbor; and Mr. Cardemon is here. And to cap the climax, your father and mother are at Ashuelyn. *Can't* you understand?

"Dearest of men, don't put your family and yourself — and me — into such a false position. I know you won't when I have explained it; I know you trust me; I know you love me dearly.

"We had a straw ride. There's no new straw, of course, so we had a wagon filled with straw from one of the barns and we drove to Lake Gentian and Querida was glorious in the moonlight with his guitar.

"He's so nice to me now — so like himself. But I *hate* Penrhyn Cardemon and I wish he would go; and he's taken a fancy to me, and for Hélène's sake I don't snub him — the unmitigated cad!

"However, it takes all kinds to make even the smallest of house parties; and I continue to be very happy and to write to you every day.

"Sam is queer. I'm beginning to wonder whether he is really in love with Hélène. If he isn't he ought to have his knuckles rapped. Of course, Hélène will be sensible about it. But, Louis, when a really nice man behaves as though he were in love with a woman, no matter how gaily she laughs over it, it is bound to mean *something* to her. And men don't seem to understand that."

"Mrs. Hind-Willet departs tomorrow. Sam and Harry go to Ashuelyn; Mr. Cardemon to his rural palace, I devoutly trust; which will leave José to Hélène and me; and he's equal to it.

"How long may I stay, dear? I am having a heavenly time — which is odd because heaven is in New York just now."

Another letter in answer to one of his was briefer:

"My Darling:

"Certainly you must go to Ashuelyn if your father and mother wish it. They are old, dear; and it is a heartless thing to thwart the old.

"Don't think of attempting to come over here to see me. The chances are that your family would hear of it and it would only pain them. Any happiness that you and I are ever to have must not be gained at any expense to them.

"So keep your distance, Monsieur; make your parents and your sister happy for the few days you are to be there; and on Thursday I will meet you on the 9.30 train and we will go back to town together.

"I am going anyway, for two reasons; I have been away from you entirely too long, and — the First of June is very, very near.

"I love you with all my heart, Louis.

"Valerie West"

Chapter XIII

He never doubted that, when at length the time came for the great change — though perhaps not until the last moment — Valerie would consent to marry him. Because, so far in his life of twenty-eight years, everything he had desired very much had come true — everything he had really believed in and worked for, had happened as he foresaw it would, in spite of the doubts, the fears, the apprehensions that all creators of circumstances and makers of their own destiny experience.

Among his fellow-men he had forged a self-centered, confident way to the front; and had met there not ultimate achievement, but a young girl, Valerie West. Through her, somehow, already was coming into his life and into his work that indefinite, elusive quality — that *something*, the existence of which, until the last winter, he had never even admitted. But it was coming; he first became conscious of it through his need of it; suspected its existence as astronomers suspect the presence of a star yet uncharted and unseen. Suddenly it had appeared in his portrait of Valerie; and he knew that Querida had recognized it.

In his picture "A Bride," the pale, mysterious glow of it suffused his canvas. It was penetrating into his own veins, too, subtle, indefinable, yet always there now; and he was sensitive to its presence not only when absorbed in his work but, more or less in his daily life.

And it was playing tricks on him, too, as when one morning, absorbed by the eagerness of achievement, and midway in the happiness of his own work, suddenly and unbidden the memory of poor Annan came to him — the boy's patient, humorous face bravely confronting failure on the canvas, before him, from which Neville had turned away without a word, because he had no good word to say of it.

And Neville, scarcely appreciating the reason for any immediate self-sacrifice, nevertheless had laid aside his brushes as at some unheard command, and had gone straight to Annan's studio. And there he had spent the whole morning giving the discouraged boy all that was best in him of strength and wisdom and cheerful sympathy, until, by noon, an almost hopeless canvas was saved; and Annan, going with him to the door, said unsteadily, "Kelly, that is the kindest thing one man ever did for another, and I'll never forget it."

Yes, the *something* seemed to have penetrated to his own veins now; he felt its serene glow mounting when he spent solemn evenings in John Burleson's room, the big sculptor lying in his morris-chair, sometimes irritable, sometimes morose, but always now wearing the vivid patch of color on his flat and sunken cheeks.

Once John said: "Why on earth do you waste a perfectly good afternoon dawdling in this place with me?"

And Neville, for a second, wondered, too; then he laughed:

"I get all that I give you, John, and more, too. Shut up and mind your business."

"*What* do you get from me?" demanded the literal one, astonished.

"All that you are, Johnny; which is much that I am not — but ought to be — may yet be."

"That's some sort of transcendental philosophy, isn't it?" grumbled the sculptor.

"You ought to know better than I, John. The sacred codfish never penetrated to the Hudson. *Inde irae!*"

Yes, truly, whatever it was that had crept into his veins had imperceptibly suffused him, enveloped him — and was working changes. He had a vague idea, sometimes, that Valerie had been the inception, the source, the reagent in the chemistry which was surely altering either himself or the world of men around him; that the change was less a synthesis than a catalysis — that he was gradually becoming different because of her nearness to him — her physical and spiritual nearness.

He had plenty of leisure to think of her while she was away; but thought of her was now only an active ebullition of the ceaseless consciousness of her which so entirely possessed him. When a selfish man loves — if he *really* loves — his disintegration begins.

Waking, sleeping, in happiness, in perplexity, abroad, at home, active or at rest, inspired or weary, alone or with others, an exquisite sense of her presence on earth invaded him, subtly refreshing him with every breath he drew. He walked abroad amid the city crowds companioned by her always; at rest the essence of her stole through and through him till the very air around seemed sweetened.

He heard others mention her, and remained silent, aloof, wrapped in his memories, like one who listens to phantoms in a dream praising perfection.

Lying back in his chair before his canvas, he thought of her often — of odd little details concerning their daily life — details almost trivial — gestures, a glance, a laugh — recollections which surprised him with the very charm of their insignificance.

He remembered that he had never known her to be ungenerous — had never detected in her a willfully selfish motive. In his life he had never before believed in a character so utterly unshackled by thought of self.

He remembered that he had never known her to fail in sympathy for any living thing; had never detected in her an indifference to either the happiness or the sorrow of others. In his life he had never before believed that the command to love one's neighbor had in it anything more significant than the beauty of an immortal theory. He believed it now because, in her, he had seen it in effortless practice. He was even beginning to understand how it might be possible for him to follow where she led — as she, unconsciously, was a follower of a precept given to lead the world through eternities.

Leaning on the closed piano, thinking of her in the still, sunny afternoons, faintly in his ears her voice seemed to sound; and he remembered her choice of ballads: —

— "For even the blind distinguisheth
    The king with his robe and crown;

But only the humble eye of faith
Beholdeth Jesus of Nazareth
   In the beggar's tattered gown.

"I saw Him not in the mendicant
   And I heeded not his cry;
Now Christ in His infinite mercy grant
   That the prayer I say in my day of want,
Be not in scorn put by."

No; he had never known her to be unkind, uncharitable, unforgiving; he had never known her to be insincere, untruthful, or envious. But the decalogue is no stronger than its weakest link. Was it in the heart of such a woman — this woman he loved — was it in the heart of this young girl to shatter it?

He went on to Ashuelyn, confident of her and of himself, less confident of his sister — almost appalled at the prospect of reconciling his father and mother to this marriage that must surely be. Yet — so far in life — life had finally yielded to him what he fought for; and it must yield now; and in the end it would surely give him the loyalty and sympathy of his family. Which meant that Valerie would listen to him; and, in the certainty of his family's ultimate acquiescence, she would wear his ring and face with him the problems and the sorrows that must come to all.

Cameron drove down to the station in the motorcar to meet him:

"Hello, Genius," he said, patting Neville on the back with a pudgy hand. "How's your twin brother, Vice?"

"Hello, you large and adipose object!" retorted Neville, seating himself in the tonneau. "How is that overworked, money-grubbing intellect of yours staggering along?"

"Handicapped with precious thoughts; Ogilvy threw 'em into me when he was here. How's the wanton Muse, Louis? Sitting on your knees as usual?"

"One arm around my neck," admitted Neville, "and the band playing 'Sweethearts.'"

"Waiting for you to order inspiration cocktails. You're looking fit."

"Am I? I haven't had one."

"Oh, I thought you threw one every time you painted that pretty model of yours —" He looked sideways at Neville, but seeing that he was unreceptive, shrugged.

"You're a mean bunch, you artists," he said. "I'd like to meet that girl, but because I'm a broker anybody'd think I had rat-plague from the way you all quarantine her — yes, the whole lot of you — Ogilvy, Annan, Querida. Why, even Penrhyn Cardemon has met her; he told me so; and if he has why can't I —"

"For heaven's sake let up!" said Neville, keeping his temper, "and tell me how everybody is at Ashuelyn."

"Huh! I'm ridden off as usual," grunted Cameron. "All right, then; I'll fix it myself. What was it you were gracious enough to inquire of me?"

"How the people are at Ashuelyn?" repeated Neville.

"How they are? How the deuce do I know? Your mother embroiders and reads *The Atlantic Monthly*; your father tucks his hands behind him and critically inspects the landscape; and when he doesn't do that he reads Herbert Spencer. Your efficient sister nourishes her progeny and does all things thoroughly and well; Gordon digs up some trees and plants others and squirts un-fragrant mixtures over the shrubbery, and sits on fences talking to various Rubes. Stephanie floats about like a well-fed angel, with a fox-terrier, and makes a monkey of me at tennis whenever I'm lunatic enough to let her, and generally dispenses sweetness, wholesomeness, and light upon a worthy household. I wouldn't mind marrying that girl," he added casually. "What do you think?"

Neville laughed: "Why don't you? She's the nicest girl I ever knew — almost."

"I'd ask her to marry me," said Cameron facetiously; "only I'm afraid such a dazzling prospect would turn her head and completely spoil her."

He spoke gaily and laughed loudly — almost boisterously. Neville glanced at him with a feeling that Cameron was slightly overdoing it — rather forcing the mirth without any particular reason.

After a moment he said: "Sandy, you don't have to be a clown if you don't want to be, you know."

"Can't help it," said Cameron, reddening; "everybody expects it now. When Ogilvy was here we played in a double ring to crowded houses. Every seat on the veranda was taken; we turned 'em away, my boy. *What* was it you started to say about Stephanie?"

"I didn't start to say anything about Stephanie."

"Oh, I thought you were going to" — his voice died into an uncertain grumble. Neville glanced at him again, thoughtfully.

"You know, Sandy," he said, "that there's another side to you — which, for some occult reason you seem to hide — even to be ashamed of."

"Sure I'm ashamed to be a broker with all you highbrows lining out homers for the girls while I have to sit on the bleachers and score 'em up. If I try to make a hit with the ladies it's a bingle; and it's the bench and the bush-league for muh —"

"You great, overgrown kid! It's a pity people can't see you down town. Everybody knows you're the cleverest thing south of Broad and Wall. Look at all the boards, all the committees, all the directorates you're mixed up with! Look at all the time you give freely to others — look at all your charities, all your: civic activities, all —"

"All the hell I raise!" said Cameron, very red. "Don't forget that, Louis!"

"You never did — that's the wonder and the eternal decency of you, Cameron. You're a good citizen and a good man, and you do more for the world than we painters ever could do! That's the real truth of it; and why you so persistently try to represent yourself as a commonplace something else is beyond me — and probably beyond Stephanie Swift," he added carelessly.

They whizzed along in silence for some time, and it was only when Ashuelyn was in sight that Cameron suddenly turned and held out his hand:

"Thank you, Louis; you've said some very kind things."

Neville shrugged: "I hear you are financing that New Idea Home. I tell you that's a fine conception."

But Cameron only looked modest. At heart he was a very shy man and he deprecated any idea that he was doing anything unusual in giving most of his time to affairs that paid dividends only in happiness and in the consciousness of moral obligation fulfilled.

The household was occupying the pergola as they arrived and sprang out upon the clipped lawn.

Neville kissed his mother tenderly, shook hands cordially with his father, greeted Lily with a fraternal hug and Stephanie with a firm grasp of both hands.

"How perfectly beautiful it is here!" he exclaimed, looking out over the green valley beyond — and unconsciously his gaze rested on the Estwich hills, blue and hazy and soft as dimpled velvet. Out there, somewhere, was Valerie; heart and pulse began to quicken. Suddenly he became aware that his mother's eyes were on him, and he turned away toward the south as though there was also something in that point of the compass to interest him.

Gordon Collis, following a hand-cart full of young trees wrapped in burlap, passed across the lawn below and waved a greeting at Neville.

"How are you, Louis!" he called out. "Don't you want to help us set these hybrid catalpas?"

"I'll be along by and by," he replied, and turned to the group under the pergola who desired to know how it was in town — the first question always asked by New Yorkers of anybody who has just arrived from that holy spot.

"It's not too warm," said Neville; "the Park is charming, most of the houses on Fifth Avenue are closed —"

"Have you chanced to pass through Tenth Street?" asked his father solemnly.

But Neville confessed that he had not set foot in those sanctified precincts, and his father's personal interest in Manhattan Island ceased immediately.

They chatted inconsequentially for a while; then, in reply to a question from Stephanie, he spoke of his picture, "A Bride," and, though it was still unfinished, he showed them a photograph of it.

The unmounted imprint passed from hand to hand amid various comments.

"It is very beautiful, Louis," said his mother, with a smile of pride; and even as she spoke the smile faded and her sad eyes rested on him wistfully.

"Is it a sacred picture?" asked his father, examining it through his glasses without the slightest trace of interest.

"It is an Annunciation, isn't it?" inquired Lily, calmly. But her heart was failing her, for in the beauty of the exquisite, enraptured face, she saw what might have been the very soul of Valerie West.

His father, removing his spectacles, delivered himself of an opinion concerning mysticism, and betrayed an illogical tendency to drift toward the Concord School of Philosophy. However, there seemed to be insufficient incentive; he glanced coldly toward Cameron and resumed Herbert Spencer and his spectacles.

"Mother, don't you want to stroll on the lawn a bit?" he asked presently. "It looks very inviting to a city man's pavement-worn feet."

She drew her light wool shawl around her shoulders and took her tall son's arm.

For a long while they strolled in silence, passed idly through the garden where masses of peonies hung over the paths, and pansies, iris, and forget-me-nots made the place fragrant.

It was not until they came to the plank bridge where the meadow rivulet, under its beds of cress and mint, threaded a shining way toward the woods, that his mother said in a troubled voice:

"You are not happy, Louis."

"Why, mother — what an odd idea!"

"Am I mistaken?" she asked, timidly.

"Yes, indeed, you are. I am very happy."

"Then," she said, "what is it that has changed you so?"

"Changed me?"

"Yes, dear."

"I am not changed, mother."

"Do you think a mother can be mistaken in her only son? You are so subdued, so serious. You are like men who have known sorrow. . . . What sorrow have you ever known, Louis?"

"None. No great one, mother. Perhaps, lately, I have developed — recognized — become aware of the somber part of life — become sensitive to it — to unhappiness in others — and have cared more —"

"You speak like a man who has suffered."

"But I haven't, mother," he insisted. "Of course, every painter worries. I did last winter — last winter —" He hesitated, conscious that last winter — on the snowy threshold of the new year — sorrow and pain and happiness and pity had, in an instant, assumed for him a significance totally new.

"Mother," he said slowly, "if I have changed it is only in a better understanding of the world and those who live in it. I have cared very little about people; I seem to have come to care more, lately. What they did, what they thought, hoped, desired, endured, suffered, interested me little except as it concerned my work. And somehow, since then, I am becoming interested in people for their own sakes. It's a — new sensation."

He smiled and laid his hand over hers:

"Do you know I never even appreciated what a good man Alexander Cameron is until recently. Why, mother, that man is one of the most generous, modest, kind, charitable, unselfish fellows in the world!"

"His behavior is sometimes a little extraordinary," said his mother — "isn't it?"

"Oh, that's all on the surface! He's full of boyish spirits. He dearly loves a joke — but the greater part of that interminable funny business is merely to mask the modesty of a man whose particular perversity is a fear that people might discover how kind and how clever he really is!"

They walked on in silence for a while, then his mother said:

"Mr. Querida was here. Is he a friend of yours?"

Neville hesitated: "I'll tell you, mother," he said, "I don't find Querida personally very congenial. But I have no doubt he's an exceedingly nice fellow. And he's far and away the best painter in America. . . . When did he go back to town?"

"Last week. I did not care for him."

"You and father seldom do care for new acquaintances," he rejoined, smiling. "Don't you think it is about time for you to emerge from your shells and make up your minds that a few people have been born since you retired?"

"People have been born in China, too, but that scarcely interests your father and me."

"Let it interest you, mother. You have no idea how amusing new people are. That's the way to keep young, too."

"It is a little too late for us to think of youth — or to think as youth thinks — even if it were desirable."

"It *is* desirable. Youth — which will be age tomorrow — may venture to draw a little consideration in advance —"

"My children interest me — and I give their youth my full consideration. But I can scarcely be expected to find any further vital interest in youth — and in the complexity of its modern views and ideas. You ask impossibilities of two very old people."

"I do not mean to. I ask only, then, that you and father take a vital and intelligent interest in me. Will you, mother?"

"Intelligent? What do you mean, Louis?"

"I mean," he said, "that you might recognize my right to govern my own conduct; that you might try to sympathize with views which are not your own — with the ideas, ideals, desires, convictions which, if modern, are nonetheless genuine — and are mine."

There was a brief silence; then:

"Louis, are you speaking with any thought of — that woman in your mind?" she asked in a voice that quivered slightly.

"Yes, mother."

"I knew it," she said, under her breath; "I knew it was that — I knew what had changed you — was changing you."

"Have I altered for the worse?"

"I don't know — I don't know, Louis!" She was leaning heavily on his elbow now; he put one arm around her and they walked very slowly over the fragrant grass.

"First of all, mother, please don't call her, 'that woman.' Because she is a very sweet, innocent, and blameless girl. . . . Will you let me tell you a little about her?"

His mother bent her head in silence; and for a long while he talked to her of Valerie.

The sun still hung high over the Estwich hills when he ended. His mother, pale, silent, offered no comment until, in his trouble, he urged her. Then she said:

"Your father will never consent."

"Let me talk to father. Will *you* consent?"

"I – Louis – it would break our hearts if –"

"Not when you know her."

"Lily knows her and is bitterly opposed to her –"

"What!" he exclaimed, astounded. "You say that my sister knows Valerie West?"

"I – forgot," faltered his mother; "I ought not to have said anything."

"Where did Lily meet her?" he asked, bewildered.

"Don't ask me, Louis. I should not have spoken –"

"Yes, you should have! It is my affair; it concerns me – and it concerns Valerie – her future and mine – our happiness. Where did Lily meet her?"

"You must ask that of Lily. I cannot and will not discuss it. I will say only this: I have seen the – this Miss West. She is at present a guest at the villa of a – countess – of whom neither your father nor I ever before heard – and whom even Lily knows so slightly that she scarcely bows to her. And yesterday, while motoring, we met them driving on the Estwich road and your sister told us who they were."

After a moment he said slowly: "So you have actually seen the girl I am in love with?"

"I saw – Miss West."

"Can't you understand that I *am* in love with her?"

"Even if you are it is better for you to conquer your inclination –"

"Why?"

"Because all your life long you will regret such a marriage."

"Why?"

"Because nobody will care to receive a woman for whom you can make no explanation – even if you are married to her."

He kept his patience.

"Will *you* receive her, mother?"

She closed her eyes, drew a quick, painful breath: "My son's wife — whoever she may be — will meet with no discourtesy under my roof."

"Is that the best you can offer us?"

"Louis! Louis! — if it lay only with me — I would do what you wished — even this — if it made you happy —"

He took her in his arms and kissed her in silence.

"You don't understand," she said, — "it is not I — it is the family — our entire little world against her. It would be only an eternal, hopeless, heart-breaking struggle for you, and for her; — pain for you — deep pain and resentment and bitterness for those who did not — perhaps could not — take your views of —"

"I don't care, mother, as long as you and father and Lily stand by her. And Valerie won't marry me unless you do. I didn't tell you that, but it is the truth. And I'm fighting very hard to win her — harder than you know — or will ever know. Don't embitter me; don't let me give up. Because, if I do, it means desperation — and things which you never could understand. . . . And *I* want you to talk to father. Will you? And to Lily, too. Its fairer to warn her that I have learned of her meeting Valerie. Then I'll talk to them both and see what can be done. . . . And, mother, I am very happy and very grateful and very proud that you are going to stand by me — and by the loveliest girl in all the world."

That night Lily came to his room. Her eyes were red, but there was fire in them. She seated herself and surveyed her brother with ominous self-possession.

"Well, Lily," he said pleasantly, prepared to keep his temper at all hazards.

"Well, Louis, I understand from mother that you have some questions to ask me."

"No questions, little sister; only your sympathetic attention while I tell you how matters stand with me."

"You require too much!" she said shortly.

"If I ask for your sympathy?"

"Not if you ask it for yourself, Louis. But if you include that —"

"Please, dear!" he interrupted, checking her with a slight gesture — for an instant only; then she went on in a determined voice:

"Louis, I might as well tell you at once that I have no sympathy for her. I wrote to her, out of sheer kindness, for her own good — and she replied so insolently that — that I am not yet perfectly recovered —"

"What did you write?"

Mrs. Collis remained disdainfully silent, but her eyes sparkled.

"Won't you tell me," he asked, patiently, "what it was you wrote to Valerie West?"

"Yes, I'll tell you if you insist on knowing! — even if you do misconstrue it! I wrote to her — for her own sake — and to avoid ill-natured comment, — suggesting that she be seen less frequently with you in public. I wrote as nicely, as kindly, as delicately as I knew how. And her reply was a practical request that I mind my business. . . ! Which was vulgar and outrageous, considering that she had given me her promise —" Mrs. Collis checked herself in her headlong and indignant complaint; then she colored painfully, but her mouth settled into tight, uncompromising lines.

"What promise had Valerie West made you?" he asked, resolutely subduing his amazement and irritation.

For a moment Mrs. Collis hesitated; then, realizing that matters had gone too far for concealment, she answered almost violently:

"She promised me not to marry you, — if you must know! I can't help what you think about it; I realized that you were infatuated — that you were making a fatal and terrible mistake — ruining life for yourself and for your family — and I went to her and told her so! I've done all I could to save you. I suppose I have gained your enmity by doing it. She promised me not to marry you — but she'll probably break her word. If you mean to marry her you'll do so, no doubt. But, Louis, if you do, such a step will sever all social relations between you and your family. Because I will *not* receive her! Nor will my friends — nor yours — nor father's and mother's friends! And that settles it."

He spoke with great care, hesitating, picking and choosing his words:

"Is it — possible that you did — such a thing — as to write to Valerie West — threatening her with my family's displeasure if she married me?"

"I did not write her at first. The first time I went to see her. And I told her kindly but plainly what I had to tell her! It was my duty to do it and I didn't flinch."

Lily was breathing fast; her eyes narrowed unpleasantly.

He managed to master his astonishment and anger; but it was a heavy draught on his reserve of self-discipline, good temper, and common sense to pass over this thing that had been done to him and to concentrate himself upon the main issue. When he was able to speak again, calmly and without resentment, he said:

"The first thing for us to do, as a family, is to eliminate all personal bitterness from this discussion. There must be no question of our affection for one another; no question but what we wish to do the best by each other. I accept that as granted. If you took the step which you did take it was because you really believed it necessary for my happiness —"

"I still believe it!" she insisted; and her lips became a thin, hard line.

"Then we won't discuss it. But I want to ask you one thing; have you talked with mother about it?"

"Yes — naturally."

"Has she told you all that I told her this afternoon?"

"I suppose so. It does not alter my opinion one particle," she replied, her pretty head obstinately lowered.

He said: "Valerie West will not marry me if my family continues hostile to her."

Lily slowly lifted her eyes:

"Then will you tell me why she permits herself to be seen so constantly with you? If she is not going to marry you what *is* she going to do? Does she care what people are saying about her? — and about you?"

"No decent people are likely to say anything unpleasant about either of us," he said, keeping a tight rein on himself — but the curb was biting deeply now. "Mother will stand by me, Lily. Will you?"

His sister's face reddened: "Louis," she said, "I am married; I have children, friends, a certain position to maintain. You are unmarried, careless of conventions, uninterested in the kind of life that I and my friends have led, and will always lead. The life, the society, the formalities, the conventional observances are all part of our lives, and make for our happiness and self-respect; but they mean absolutely nothing to you. And you propose to invade our respectable and inoffensive seclusion with a conspicuous wife who has been a notorious professional model; and you demand of your family that they receive her as one of them! Louis, I ask you, is this fair to us?"

He said very gravely: "You have met Valerie West. Do you really believe that either the dignity or the morals of the family circle would suffer by her introduction to it?"

"I know nothing about her morals!" said his sister, excitedly.

"Then why condemn them?"

"I did not; I merely reminded you that she is a celebrated professional model."

"It is not necessary to remind me. My mother knows it and will stand by her. Will you do less for your own brother?"

"Louis! You are cruel, selfish, utterly heartless —"

"I am trying to think of everybody in the family who is concerned; but, when a man's in love he can't help thinking a little of the woman he loves — especially if nobody else does." He turned his head and looked out of the window. Stars were shining faintly in a luminous sky. His face seemed to have grown old and grey and haggard:

"I don't know what to do," he said, as though speaking to himself; — "I don't know where to turn. She would marry me if you'd let her; she will never marry me if my family is unkind to her —"

"What *will* she do, then?" asked Lily, coolly.

For a moment he let her words pass, then, turned around. The expression of his sister's brightly curious eyes perplexed him.

"What do you mean?" he asked, disturbed.

"What I say, Louis. I asked you what Miss West means to do if she does not marry you? Discontinue her indiscreet intimacy with you?"

"Why should she?"

Lily said, sharply: "I would not have to put that question to a modest girl."

"I have to put it to *you!*" he retorted, beginning to lose his self-command. "Why should Valerie West discontinue her friendship with me because my family's stupid attitude toward her makes it impossible for a generous and proud girl to marry me?"

Lily, pale, infuriated, leaned forward in her chair.

"Because," she retorted violently, "if that intimacy continues much longer a stupid world and your stupid family will believe that the girl is your mistress! But in that event, thank God, the infamy will rest where it belongs — not on us!"

A cold rage paralyzed his speech; she saw its ghastly reflection on his white and haggard face — saw him quiver under the shock; rose involuntarily, terrified at the lengths to which passion had scourged her:

"Louis," she faltered — "I — I didn't mean that! — I was beside myself; forgive me, please! Don't look like that; you are frightening me —"

She caught his arm as he passed her, clung to it, pallid, fearful, imploring, — "W-what are you going to do, Louis! Don't go, dear, please. I'm sorry, I'm very, very humble. Won't you speak to me? I said too much; I was wrong; — I — I will try to be different — try to reconcile myself to — to what — you — wish —"

He looked down at her where she hung to him, tearful face lifted to his:

"I didn't know women could feel that way about another woman," he said, in a dull voice. "There's no use — no use —"

"But — but I love you dearly, Louis! I couldn't endure it to have anything come between us — disrupt the family —"

"Nothing will, Lily. . . . I must go now."

"Don't you believe I love you?"

He drew a deep, unconscious breath.

"I suppose so. Different people express love differently. There's no use in asking you to be different —"

She said, piteously: "I'm trying. Don't you see I'm trying? Give me time, Louis! Make allowances. You can't utterly change people in a few hours."

He gazed at her intently for a moment.

"You mean that you are trying to be fair to — her?"

"I — if you call it that; — yes! But a family can not adapt itself, instantaneously, to such a cataclysm as threatens — I mean — I mean — oh, Louis! Try to understand us and sympathize a little with us!"

His arms closed around her shoulders:

"Little sister, we both have the family temper — and beneath it, the family instinct for cohesion. If we are also selfish it is not individual but family selfishness. It is the family which has always said to the world, *'Noli me tangere!'* while we, individually, are really inclined to be kinder, more sympathetic, more curious about the neighbors outside our gate. Let it be so now. Once inside the family, what can harm Valerie?"

"Dearest, dearest brother," she murmured, "you talk like a foolish man. Women understand better. And if it is a part of your program that this girl is to be accepted by an old-fashioned society, now almost obsolete, but in which this family is merely a single superannuated unit, that program can never be carried out."

"I think you are mistaken," he said.

"I know I am not. It is inevitable that if you marry this girl she will be more or less ignored, isolated, humiliated, overlooked outside our own little family circle. Even in that limited mob which the newspapers call New York Society — in that modern, wealthy, hard-witted, overjeweled, self-sufficient league which is yet too eternally uncertain of its own status to assume any authority or any responsibility for a stranger without credentials, — it would not be possible to make Valerie West acceptable in the slightest sense of the word. Because she is too well known; her beauty is celebrated; she has become famous. Her only chance there — or with us — would have been in her absolute anonymity. Then lies *might* have done the rest. But lying is now useless in regard to her."

"Perfectly," he said. "She would not permit it."

In his vacant gaze there was something changed — a fixed-ness born of a slow and hopeless enlightenment.

"If that is the case, there is no chance," he said thought-fully. "I had not considered that aspect."

"I had."

He shook his head slightly, gazing through the window at the starry luster overhead.

"I wouldn't care," he said, "if she would only marry me. If she'd do that I'd never bother anybody — nor embarrass the family —"

"Louis!"

"I mean make any social demands on you. . . . And, as for the world —" He slowly shook his head again: "We could make our own friends and our own way — if she would only consent to do it. But she never will."

"Do you mean to say she will not marry you if you ask her?" began Lily incredulously.

"Absolutely."

"Why?"

"For your sakes — yours, and mother's, and father's — and for mine."

There was a long silence, then Lily said unsteadily:

"There — there seems to be a certain — nobility — about her. . . . It is a pity — a tragedy — that she is what she is!"

"It is a tragedy that the world is what it is," he said. "Good night."

*H*is father sent for him in the morning; Louis found him reading the *Tribune* in his room and sipping a bowl of hot milk and toast.

"What have you been saying to your mother?" he asked, looking up through his gold-rimmed spectacles and munch-ing toast.

"Has she not told you, father?"

"Yes, she has. . . . I think you had better make a trip around the world."

"That would not alter matters."

"I differ with you," observed his father, leisurely employing his napkin.

"There is no use considering it," said his son patiently.

"Then what do you propose to do?"

"There is nothing to do."

"By that somewhat indefinite expression I suppose that you intend to pursue a waiting policy?"

"A waiting policy?" His son laughed, mirthlessly. "What am I to wait for? If you all were kind to Valerie West she might, perhaps, consent to marry me. But it seems that even our own family circle has not sufficient authority to protect her from our friends' neglect and humiliation. . . .

"She warned me that it would be so, long ago. I did not believe it; I could not comprehend it. But, somehow, Lily has made me believe it. And so have you. I guess it must be true. And if that's all I have to offer my wife, it's not enough to compensate her for her loss of freedom and happiness and self-respect among those who really care for her."

"Do you give me to understand that you renounce all intentions of marrying this girl?" asked his father, breaking more toast into his bowl of milk.

"Yes," said his son, listlessly.

"Thank God!" said his father; "come here, my son."

They shook hands; the son's lifeless arm fell to his side and he stood looking at the floor in silence. The father took a spoonful of hot milk with satisfaction, and, after the younger man had left the room, he resumed his newspaper. He was particularly interested in the "Sunshine Column," which dispensed sweetness and light under a poetic caption too beautiful to be true in a coldly humorous world.

*T*hat afternoon Gordon Collis said abruptly to Neville:

"You look like the devil, Louis."

"Do I?"

"You certainly do." And, in a lower voice: "I guess I've heard what's the matter. Don't worry. It's a thing about which nobody ever ought to give anybody any advice — so I'll give you some. Marry whoever you damn please. It'll be all the same after that oak I planted this morning is half grown."

"Gordon," he said, surprised, "I didn't suppose *you* were liberal."

"Liberal! Why, man alive! Do you think a fellow can live out of doors as I have lived, and see germs sprout, and see mountain ranges decay, and sit on a few glaciers, and swing a pick into a mother-lode — and *not* be liberal? Do you suppose ten-cent laws bother me when I'm up against the blind laws that made the law-makers? — laws that made life itself before Christ lived to conform to them. . . ? I married where I loved. It chanced that my marriage with your sister didn't clash with the sanctified order of things in Manhattan town. But if your sister had been the maid who dresses her, and I had loved her, I'd have married her all the same and have gone about the pleasures and duties of procreation and conservation exactly as I go about 'em now. . . . I wonder how much the Almighty was thinking about Tenth Street when the first pair of anthropoids mated? *Nobilitas sola est atque unica virtus.* If you love each other — *Noli pugnare duobus.* . . . And I'm going into the woods to look for ginseng. Want to come?"

Neville went. Cameron and Stephanie, equipped with buckskin gloves, a fox terrier, and digging apparatus, joined them just where the slender meadow brook entered the woods.

"There are mosquitoes here!" exclaimed Cameron wrathfully. "All day and every day I'm being stung down town, and I'm not going to stand for it here!"

Stephanie let him aid her to the top of a fallen log, glancing back once or twice toward Neville, who was sauntering forward among the trees, pretending to look for ginseng.

"Do you notice how Louis has changed?" she said, keeping her balance on the log. "I cannot bear to see him so thin and colorless."

Cameron now entertained a lively suspicion how matters stood, and knew that Stephanie also suspected; but he only said, carelessly: "It's probably dissipation. You know what a terrible pace he's been going from the cradle onward."

She smiled quietly. "Yes, I know, Sandy. And I know, too, that you are the only man who has been able to keep up that devilish pace with him."

"I've led a horrible life," muttered Cameron darkly.

Stephanie laughed; he gave her his hand as she stood balanced on the big log; she laid her fingers in his confidently, looked into his honest face, still laughing, then sprang lightly to the ground.

"What a really good man you are!" she said tormentingly.

"Oh, heaven! If you call me that I'm really done for!"

"Done for?" she exclaimed in surprise. "How?"

"Done for as far as you are concerned."

"I? Why how, and with what am I concerned, Sandy? I don't understand you."

But he only turned red and muttered to himself and strolled about with his hands in his pockets, kicking the dead leaves as though he expected to find something astonishing under them. And Stephanie glanced at him sideways once or twice, thoughtfully, curiously, but questioned him no further.

Gordon Collis pottered about in a neighboring thicket; the fox terrier was chasing chipmunks. As for Neville he had already sauntered out of sight among the trees.

Stephanie, seated on a dry and mossy stump, preoccupied with her own ruminations, looked up absently as Cameron came up to her bearing floral offerings.

"Thank you, Sandy," she said, as he handed her a cluster of wild blossoms. Then, fastening them to her waist, she glanced up mischievously:

"How funny you are! You look and act like a little boy at a party presenting his first offering to the eternal feminine."

"It's my first offering," he said coolly.

"Oh, Sandy! With *your* devilish record!"

"Do you know," he said, "that I'm thirty-two years old? And that you are twenty-two? And that since you were twelve and I was twenty odd I've been in love with you?"

She looked at him in blank dismay for a moment, then forced a laugh:

"Of course I know it, Sandy. It's the kind of love a girl cares most about —"

"It's really love," said Cameron, un-smiling — "the kind I'm afraid she doesn't care very much about."

She hesitated, then met his gaze with a distressed smile: "You don't really mean that, Sandy —"

"I've meant it for ten years. . . . But it doesn't matter —"

"Sandy. . . ! It *does* matter — if —"

"No, it doesn't. . . . Come on and kick these leaves about and we'll make a million dollars in ginseng!"

But she remained seated, mute, her gaze a sorrowful interrogation which at length he could not pretend to ignore:

"Stephanie child, don't worry. I'm not worrying. I'm glad I told you. . . . Now just let me go on as I've always gone —"

"How *can* we?"

"Easily. Shut your eyes, breathe deeply, lifting both arms and lowering them while counting ten in German —"

"Sandy, don't be so foolish at — such a time."

"Such a time? What time is it?" pretending to consult his watch with great anxiety. Then a quick smile of relief spread over his features: "It's all right, Stephanie; it's my hour to be foolish. If you'll place a lump of sugar on my nose, and say 'when,' I'll perform."

There was no answering smile on her face.

"It's curious," she said, "how a girl can make a muddle of life without even trying."

"But just think what you might have done if you'd tried! You've much to be thankful for," he said gravely.

She raised her eyes, considering him:

"I wonder," she said, under her breath.

"Sure thing, Stephanie. You might have done worse; you might have married me. Throw away those flowers — there's a good girl — and forget what they meant."

Slowly, deliberately, blossom by blossom she drew them from her girdle and laid them on the moss beside her.

"There's one left," he said cheerfully. "Raus mit it!"

But she made no motion to detach it; appeared to be unconscious of it and of him as she turned her face and looked silently toward the place where Neville had disappeared.

An hour or two later, when Gordon was ready to return to the house, he shouted for Neville. Cameron also lifted up his voice in a series of prolonged howls.

But Neville was far beyond earshot, and still walking through woods and valleys and pleasant meadows in the general direction of the Estwich hills.

Somewhere there amid that soft rolling expanse of green was the woman who would never marry him. And it was now, at last, he decided that he would never take her on any other terms even though they were her own terms; that he must give her up to chance again as innocent as chance had given her into his brief keeping. No, she would never accept his terms and face the world with him as his wife. And so he must give her up. For he believed that, in him, the instinct of moral law had been too carefully developed ever to be deliberately ignored; he still believed marriage to be not only a rational social procedure, not only a human compromise and a divine convention, but the only possible sanctuary where love might dwell, and remain, and permanently endure inviolate.

Chapter XIV

The Countess Hélène had taken her maid and gone to New York on business for a day or two, leaving Valerie to amuse herself until her return.

Which was no hardship for Valerie. The only difficulty lay in there being too much to do.

In the first place she had become excellent friends with the farmer and had persuaded him to delegate to her a number of his duties. She had to collect the newly laid eggs, hunt up stolen nests, inspect and feed the clucking, quacking, gobbling personnel of the barnyard which came crowding to her clear-voiced call.

As for the cattle, she was rather timid about venturing to milk since the Ogilvy's painful and undignified début as an amateur Strephon.

However, she assisted at pasture call accompanied by a fat and lazy collie; and she petted and salted the herd to her heart's content.

Then there were books and magazines to be read, leisurely; and hammocks to lie in, while her eyes watched the sky where clouds sailed in snowy squadrons out of the breezy west.

And what happier company for her than her thoughts — what tenderer companionship than her memories; what more absorbing fellowship than the little busy intimate reflections that came swarming around her, more exciting, more impetuous, more exquisitely disturbing as the hurrying, sunny hours sped away and the first day of June drew nigh?

She spent hours alone on the hill behind the house, lying full length in the fragrant, wild grasses, looking across a green and sunlit world toward Ashuelyn.

She had told him not to attempt to come to Estwich; and, though she knew she had told him wisely, often and often there on her breezy hilltop she wished that she hadn't — wished that he would disregard her request — hoped he would — lay there, a dry grass stem between her lips, thinking how it would be if, suddenly, down there by — well, say down by that big oak, for example, a figure should stroll into view along the sheep-path. . . . And at first — just to prolong the tension — perhaps she wouldn't recognize him — just for a moment. Then, suddenly —

But she never got beyond that first blissful instant of recognition — the expression of his face — his quick spring forward — and she, amazed, rising to her feet and hastening forward to meet him. For she never pictured herself as standing still to await the man she loved.

When Hélène left, Valerie had the place to herself; and, without any disloyalty to the little countess, she experienced a new pleasure in the liberty of an indolence which exacted nothing of her.

She prowled around the library, luxuriously, dipping into inviting volumes; she strolled at hazard from veranda to garden, from garden to lawn, from lawn to farmyard.

About luncheon time she arrived at the house with her arms full of scented peonies, and spent a long while selecting the receptacles for them.

Luncheon was a deliciously lazy affair at which she felt at liberty to take her own time; and she did so, scanning the morning paper, which had just been delivered; making several bites of every cherry and strawberry, and being good to the three cats with asparagus ends and a saucer of chicken bouillon.

Later, reclining in the hammock, she mended a pair of brier-torn stockings; and when that thrifty and praiseworthy task was finished, she lay back and thought of Neville.

But at what moment in any day was she ever entirely unconscious of him? Besides, she could always think of him better — summon him nearer — visualize him more clearly, when she was afield, the blue sky above her, the green earth under foot, and companioned only by memory.

So she went to her room, put on her stout little shoes and her walking skirt; braided her hair and made of it a soft, light, lustrous turban; and taking her dog-whip, ran down stairs.

The fat old collie came wagging up to the whistle, capered clumsily as in duty bound; but before she had entirely traversed the chestnut woods he basely deserted her and waddled back to the kitchen door where a thoughtful cook and a succulent bone were combinations not unknown.

Valerie missed him presently, and whistled; but the fat sybarite, if within earshot, paid no attention; and she was left to swing her dog-whip and stroll on alone.

Her direction lay along the most inviting by-roads and paths; and she let chance direct her feet through this friendly, sunny land where one little hill was as green as another, and one little brook as clear and musical as another, and the dainty, ferny patches of woodlands resembled one another.

It was a delight to scramble over stone walls; she adored lying flat and wriggling under murderous barbed-wire, feeling the weeds brush her face. When a brook was a little too wide to jump, it was ecstasy to attempt it. She got both shoes wet and loved it. Brambles plucked boldly at her skirt; wild forest blossoms timidly summoned her aside to kneel and touch them, but to let them live; squirrels threatened her and rushed madly up and down trees defying her; a redstart in vermilion and black, fussed about her where she sat, closing and spreading its ornamental tail for somebody's benefit — perhaps for hers.

She was not tired; she did not suppose that she had wandered very far, but, glancing at her watch, she was surprised to find how late it was. And she decided to return.

After she had been deciding to return for about an hour it annoyed her to find that she could not get clear of the woods. It seemed preposterous; the woods could not be very extensive. As for being actually lost it seemed too absurd. Life is largely composed of absurdities.

There was one direction which she had not tried, and it lay along a bridle path, but whether north or south or east or west she was utterly unable to determine. She felt quite certain that Estwich could not lie either way along that bridle-path which stretched almost a straight, dark way under the trees as far as she could see.

Vexed, yet amused, at her own stupid plight, she was standing in the road, trying to make up her mind to try it, when, far down the vista, a horseman appeared, coming on at a leisurely canter; and with a sigh of relief she saw her troubles already at an end.

He drew bridle abreast of her, stared, sprang from his saddle and, cap in hand, came up to her holding out his hand:

"Miss West!" he exclaimed. "How on earth did you ever find your way into my woods?"

"I don't know, Mr. Cardemon," she said, thankful to encounter even him in her dilemma. "I must have walked a great deal farther than I meant to."

"You've walked at least five miles if you came by road; and nobody knows how far if you came across country," he said, staring at her out of his slightly prominent eyes.

"I did come across country. And if you will be kind enough to start me toward home —"

"You mean to *walk* back!"

"Of course I do."

"I won't permit it!" he exclaimed. "It's only a little way across to the house and we'll just step over and I'll have a car brought around for you —"

"Thank you, I am not tired —"

"You are on my land, therefore you are my guest," he insisted. "I am not going to let you go back on foot —"

"Mr. Cardemon, if you please, I very much prefer to return in my own way."

"What an obstinate girl you are!" he said, with his uncertain laugh, which never came until he had prejudged its effect on the situation; but the puffy flesh above his white riding-stock behind his lobeless ears reddened, and a slow, thickish color came into his face and remained under the thick skin.

"If you won't let me send you back in a car," he said, "you at least won't refuse a glass of sherry and a biscuit —"

"Thank you — I haven't time —"

"My housekeeper, Mrs. Munn, is on the premises," he persisted.

"You are very kind, but —"

"Oh, don't turn a man down so mercilessly, Miss West!"

"You are exceedingly amiable," she repeated, "but I must go at once."

He switched the weeds with his crop, then the uncertain laugh came:

"I'll show you a short cut," he said. His prominent eyes rested on her, passed over her from head to foot, then wandered askance over the young woodland.

"In which direction lies Estwich?" she asked, lifting her gaze to meet his eyes; but they avoided her as he answered, busy fumbling with a girth that required no adjustment:

"Over yonder," — making a slight movement with his head. Then taking his horse by the head he said heartily:

"Awfully sorry you won't accept my hospitality; but if you won't you won't, and we'll try to find a short cut."

He led his horse out of the path straight ahead through the woods, and she walked beside him.

"Of course you know the way, Mr. Cardemon?" she said pleasantly.

"I ought to — unless the undergrowth has changed the looks of things since I've been through."

"How long is it since you've been through?"

"Oh, I can't just recollect," he said carelessly. "I guess it will be all right."

For a while they walked steadily forward among the trees; he talking to her with a frank and detached amiability, asking about the people at Estwich, interested to hear that the small house-party had disintegrated, surprised to learn that the countess had gone to town.

"Are you entirely alone in the house?" he asked; and his eyes seemed to protrude a little more than usual.

"Entirely," she said carelessly; "except for Binns and his wife and the servants."

"Why didn't you 'phone a fellow to stop over to lunch?" he asked, suddenly assuming a jovial manner which their acquaintance did not warrant. "We country folk don't stand on ceremony you know."

"I did not know it," she said quietly.

His bold gaze rested on her again; again the uncertain laugh followed:

"If you'd ask me to dine with you tonight I'd take it as a charming concession to our native informality. What do you say, Miss West?"

She forced a smile, making a sign of negation with her head, but he began to press her until his importunities and his short, abrupt laughter embarrassed her.

"I couldn't ask anybody without permission from my hostess," she said, striving to maintain the light, careless tone which his changing manner toward her made more difficult for her.

"Oh, come, Miss West!" he said in a loud humorous voice; "don't pass me the prunes and prisms but be a good little sport and let a fellow come over to see you! You never did give me half a chance to know you, but you're hands across the table with that Ogilvy artist and José Querida —"

"I've known them rather longer than I have you, Mr. Cardemon."

"That's my handicap! I'm not squealing. All I want is to start in the race —"

"What race?" she asked coolly, turning on him a level gaze that, in spite of her, she could not maintain under the stare with which he returned it. And again the slight uneasiness crept over her and involuntarily she looked around her at the woods.

"How far is it now?" she inquired.

"Are you tired?"

"No. But I'm anxious to get back. Could you tell me how near to some road we are?"

He halted and looked around; she watched him anxiously as he tossed his bridle over his horse's neck and walked forward into a little glade where the late rays of the sun struck ruddy and warm on the dry grass.

"That's singular," he said as she went forward into the open where he stood; "I don't seem to remember this place."

"But you know about where we are, don't you?" she asked, resolutely suppressing the growing uneasiness and anxiety.

"Well — I am not perfectly certain." He kept his eyes off her while he spoke; but when she also turned and gazed helplessly at the woods encircling her, his glance stole toward her.

"You're not scared, are you?" he asked, and then laughed abruptly.

"Not in the slightest."

"Sure! You're a perfectly good sport. . . . I'll tell you — I'll leave my horse for one of my men to hunt up later, and we'll start off together on a good old-fashioned hike! Are you game?"

"Yes — if I only knew — if you were perfectly sure how to get to the edge of the woods. I don't see how you *can* be lost in your own woods —"

"I don't believe I am!" he said, laughing violently. "The Estwich road *must* be over in that direction. Come ahead, Miss West; the birds can cover us up if worst comes to worst!"

She went with him, entering the thicker growth with a quick, vigorous little stride as though energy and rapidity of motion could subdue the misgiving that threatened to frighten her sooner or later.

Over logs, boulders, gulleys, she swung forward, he supporting her from time to time in spite of her hasty assurance that she did not require aid.

Once, before she could prevent it, he grasped her and fairly swung her across a gulley; and again, as she gathered herself to jump, his powerful arm slipped around her body and he lowered her to the moss below, leaving her with red cheeks and a rapid heart to climb the laurel-choked ravine beside him.

It was breathless work; again and again, before she could prevent it, he forced his assistance on her; and in the abrupt, almost rough contact there was something that began at last to terrify her — weaken her — so that, at the top of the slope, she caught breathless at a tree and leaned against the trunk for a moment, closing her eyes.

"You poor little girl," he breathed close to her ear; and as her startled eyes flew open, he drew her into his arms.

For a second his congested face and prominent, pale eyes swam before her; then with a convulsive gasp she wrenched herself partly free and strained away from his grasp, panting.

"Let me go, Mr. Cardemon!"

"Look here, Valerie, you know I'm crazy about you —"

"Will you let me go?"

"Oh, come, little girl, I know who you are, all right! Be a good little sport and —"

"Let me go," she whispered between her teeth. Then his red, perspiring features — the prominent eyes and loose mouth drew nearer — nearer — and she struck blindly at the face with her dog-whip — twice with the lash and once with the stag-horn handle. And the next instant she was running.

He caught her at the foot of the slope; she saw blood on his cheek and puffy welts striping his distorted features, strove to strike him again, but felt her arm powerless in his grasp.

"Are you mad!" she gasped.

"Mad about *you!* For God's sake listen to me, Valerie! Batter me, tear me to pieces — and I won't care, if you'll listen to me a moment —"

She struggled silently, fiercely, to use her whip, to wrench herself free.

"I tell you I love you!" he said; "I'd go through hell for you. You've got to listen — you've got to *know* —"

"You coward!" she sobbed.

"I don't care what you say to me if you'll listen a moment —"

"As Rita Tevis listened to you!" she said, white to the lips — "you murderer of souls!" And, as his grasp relaxed for a second, she tore her arm free, sprang forward and slashed him across the mouth with the lash.

Behind her she heard his sharp cry of pain, heard him staggering about in the underbrush. Terror winged her feet and she fairly flew along the open ridge and down through the dead leaves across a soft, green, marshy hollow, hearing him somewhere in the woods behind her, coming on at a heavy run.

For a long time she ran; and suddenly collapsed, falling in a huddled desperate heap, her slender hands catching at her throat.

At the foot of the hill she saw him striding hither and thither, examining the soft forest soil or halting to listen — then as though scourged into action, running aimlessly toward where she lay, casting about on every side like a burly dog at fault.

Once, when he stood not very far away, and she had hidden her face in her arms, trembling like a doomed thing — she heard him call to her — heard the cry burst from him as though in agony:

"Valerie, don't be afraid! I was crazy to touch you; — I'll let you cut me to pieces if you'll only answer me."

And again he shouted, in a voice made thin by fright: "For God's sake, Valerie, think of *me* for a moment. Don't run off like that and let people know what's happened to you!"

Then, in a moment, his heavy, hurried tread resounded; and he must have run very near to where she crouched, because she could hear him whimpering in his fear; but he ran on past where she lay, calling to her at intervals, until his frightened voice sounded at a distance and she could scarcely hear the rustle of the dead leaves under his hurrying tread.

Even then terror held her chained, breathing fast like a wounded thing, eyes bright with the insanity of her fear. She lay flat in the leaves, not stirring.

The last red sunbeams slanted through the woods, painting tree trunks crimson and running in fiery furrows through, the dead leaves; the sky faded to rose-color, to mauve; faintly a star shone.

For a long time now nothing had stirred in the woodland silence. And, as the star glimmered brighter through the branches, she shivered, moved, lay listening, then crawled a little way. Every sound that she made was a terror to her, every heart beat seemed to burst the silence.

It was dusk when she crept out at last into a stony road, dragging her limbs; a fine mist had settled over the fields; the air grew keener. Somewhere in the darkness cowbells tinkled; overhead, through the damp sheet of fog, the veiled stars were still shining.

Her senses were not perfectly clear; she remembered falling once or twice — remembered seeing the granite posts and iron gates of a drive, and that lighted windows were shining dimly somewhere beyond. And she crept toward them, still stupid with exhaustion and fright. Then she was aware of people, dim shapes in the darkness — of a dog barking — of voices, a quick movement in the dusk — of a woman's startled exclamation.

Suddenly she heard Neville's voice — and a door opened, flooding her with yellow light where she stood swaying, dazed, deathly pale.

"Louis!" she said.

He sprang to her, caught her in his arms

"Good God! What is the matter?"

She rested against him, her eyes listlessly watching the people swiftly gathering in the dazzling light.

"Where in the world — how did you get here! — where have you been —" His stammered words made him incoherent as he caught sight of the mud and dust on her torn waist and skirt.

Her eyes had closed a moment; they opened now with an effort. Once more she looked blindly at the people clustering around her — recognized his sister and Stephanie — divined that it was his mother who stood gazing at her in pallid consternation — summoned every atom of her courage to spare him the insult which a man's world had offered to her — found strength to ignore it so that no shadow of the outrage should fall through her upon him or upon those nearest to him.

"I lost my way," she said. Her white lips tried to smile; she strove to stand upright, alone; caught mechanically at his arm, the fixed smile still stamped on her lips. "I am sorry to — disturb anybody. . . . I was lost — and it grew dark. . . . I don't know my way — very well —"

She turned, conscious of someone's arm supporting her; and Stephanie said, in a low, pitiful voice:

"Lean back on me. You must let me help you to the house."

"Thank you — I won't go in. . . . If I could rest — a moment — perhaps somebody — Mr. Neville — would help me to get home again —"

"Come with me, Miss West," whispered Stephanie, "I *want* you. Will you come to my room with me for a little while?"

She looked into Stephanie's eyes, turned and looked at Neville.

"Dearest," he whispered, putting his arm around her, "you must come with us."

She nodded and moved forward, steadily, between them both, and entered the house, head-carried high on the slender neck, but her face was colorless under the dark masses of her loosened hair, and she swayed at the foot of the stairs, reaching out blindly at nothing — falling forward.

It was a dead weight that Neville bore into Stephanie's room. When his mother turned him out and closed the door behind him he stood stupidly about until his sister, who had gone into the room, opened the door and bade him telephone for Dr. Ogilvy.

"What has happened to her?" he asked, as though dazed.

"I don't know. I think you'd better tell Quinn to bring around the car and go for Dr. Ogilvy yourself."

It was a swift rush to Dartford through the night; bare-headed he bent forward beside the chauffeur, teeth set, every nerve tense and straining as though his very will power was driving the machine forward. Then there came a maddening slowing down through Dartford streets, a nerve-racking delay until Sam Ogilvy's giant brother had stowed away himself and his satchel in the tonneau; then slow speed to the town limits; a swift hurling forward into space that whirled blackly around them as the great acetylenes split the darkness and chaos roared in their ears.

Under the lighted windows the big doctor scrambled out and stamped upstairs; and Neville waited on the landing.

His father appeared below, looking up at him, and started to say something; but apparently changed his mind and went back into the living room, rattling his evening paper and coughing.

Cameron passed through the hallway, looked at him, but let him alone.

After a while the door opened and Lily came out.

"I'm not needed," she said; "your mother and Stephanie have taken charge."

"Is she going to be very ill?"

"Billy Ogilvy hasn't said anything yet."

"Is she conscious?"

"Yes, she is now."

"Has she said anything more?"

"No."

Lily stood silent a moment, gazing absently down at the lighted hall below, then she looked at her brother as though she, too, were about to speak, but, like her father, she reconsidered the impulse, and went away toward the nursery.

Later his mother opened the door very softly, let herself and Stephanie out, and stood looking at him, one finger across her lips, while Stephanie hurried away downstairs.

"She's asleep, Louis. Don't raise your voice —" as he stepped quickly toward her.

"Is it anything serious?" he asked in a low voice.

"I don't know what Dr. Ogilvy thinks. He is coming out in a moment. . . ." She placed one hand on her son's shoulder, reddening a trifle. "I've told William Ogilvy that she is a friend of — the family. He may have heard Sam talking about her when he was here last. So I thought it safer."

Neville brought a chair for his mother, but she shook her head, cautioning silence, and went noiselessly downstairs.

Half an hour later Dr. Ogilvy emerged, saw Neville — walked up and inspected him, curiously.

"Well, Louis, what do you know about this?" he asked, buttoning his big thick rain-coat to the throat.

"Absolutely nothing, Billy, except that Miss West, who is a guest of the Countess d'Enver at Estwich, lost her way in the woods. How is she now?"

"All right," said the doctor, dryly.

"Is she conscious?"

"Perfectly."

"Awake?"

"Yes. She won't be — long."

"Did she talk to you?"

"A little."

"What *is* the matter?"

"Fright. And I'm wondering whether merely being lost in the woods is enough to have terrified a girl like that? Because, apparently, she is as superb a specimen of healthy womanhood as this world manufactures once in a hundred years. How well do you know her?"

"We are very close friends."

"H'm. Did you suppose she was the kind of woman to be frightened at merely being lost in a civilized country?"

"No. She has more courage — of all kinds — than most women."

"Because," said the big doctor thoughtfully, "while she was unconscious it took me ten minutes to pry open her fingers and disengage a rather heavy dog-whip from her clutch. . . . And there was some evidences of blood on the lash and on the bone handle."

"What!" exclaimed Neville, amazed.

The doctor shrugged: "I don't know of any fierce and vicious dogs between here and Estwich, either," he mused.

"No, Cardemon keeps none. And its mostly his estate."

"Oh . . . Any — h'm! — vicious *men* — in his employment?"

"My God!" whispered Neville, "what do you mean, Billy?"

"Finger imprints — black and blue — on both arms. Didn't Miss West say anything that might enlighten *you?*"

"No . . . She only said she had been lost. . . . Wait a moment; I'm trying to think of the men Cardemon employs —"

He was ashy white and trembling, and the doctor laid a steadying hand on his arm.

"Hold on, Louis," he said sharply, "it was no *worse* than a fright. *Do you understand?*. . . And do you understand, too, that an innocent and sensitive and modest girl would rather die than have such a thing made public through your well-meant activity? So there's nothing for anybody to do — yet."

Neville could scarcely speak.

"Do you mean — she was attacked by some — man!"

"It looks like it. And — you'd better keep it from your family — because *she* did. She's game to the core — that little girl."

"But she — she'll tell me!" stammered Neville — she's *got* to tell me — "

"She won't if she can help it. Would it aid her any if you found out who it was and killed him? — ran for a gun and did a little murdering some pleasant morning — just to show your chivalrous consideration and devotion to her?"

"Are you asking me to let a beast like that go unpunished?" demanded Neville violently.

"Oh, use your brains, Louis. He frightened her and she slashed him well for it. And, womanlike — after there was no more danger and no more necessity for pluck — she got scared and ran; and the farther she ran the more scared she became. Look here, Louis; look at me — squarely." He laid both ponderous hands on Neville's shoulders:

"Sam has told me all about you and Miss West — and I can guess how your family takes it. Can't you see why she had the pluck to remain silent about this thing? It was because she saw in it the brutal contempt of the world toward a woman who stood in that world alone, unsupported, unprotected. And she would not have you and your family know how lightly the world held the woman whom you love and wish to marry — not for her own sake alone — but for the sake of your family's pride — and yours."

His hands dropped from Neville's shoulders; he stood considering him for a moment in silence.

"I've told *you* because, if you are the man I think you are, you ought to know the facts. Forcing her to the humiliation of telling you will not help matters; filling this pup full of lead means an agony of endless publicity and shame for her, for your family, and for you. . . . He'll never dare remain in the same county with her after this. He's probably skedaddled by this time anyway." . . . Dr. Ogilvy looked narrowly at Neville. "Are you pretty sane, now?"

"Yes."

"You realize that gun-play is no good in this matter?"

"Y-yes."

"And you really are going to consider Miss West before your own natural but very primitive desire to do murder?"

Neville nodded.

"Knowing," added the doctor, "that the unspeakable cur who affronted her has probably taken to his heels?"

Neville, pale and silent, raised his eyes:

"Do you suspect anybody?"

"I don't know," said the doctor carelessly; — "I'll just step over to the telephone and make an inquiry of Penrhyn Cardemon —"

He walked to the end of the big hall, unhooked the receiver, asked for Cardemon's house, got it.

Neville heard him say:

"This is Dr. Ogilvy. Is that you, Gelett? Isn't your master at home?"

"What? Had to catch a train?"

*

"Oh! A sudden matter of business."

*

"I see. He's had a cable calling him to London. How long will he be away, Gelett?"

*

"Oh, I see. You don't know. Very well. I only called up because I understood he required medical attention."

*

"Yes — I understood he'd been hurt about the head and face, but I didn't know he had received such a — battering."

*

"You say that his horse threw him in the big beech-woods? Was he really very much cut up?"

"Pretty roughly handled, eh! All right. When you communicate with him tell him that Dr. Ogilvy and Mr. Neville, Jr., were greatly interested to know how badly he was injured. Do you understand? Well, don't forget. And you may tell him, Gelett, that as long as the scars remain, he'd better remain, too. Get it straight, Gelett; tell him it's my medical advice to remain away as long as he can — and a little longer. This climate is no good for him. Good-bye."

He turned from the telephone and sauntered toward Neville, who regarded him with a fixed stare.

"You see," he remarked with a shrug; and drew from his pocket a slightly twisted scarf pin — a big horse-shoe set with sapphires and diamonds — the kind of pin some kinds of men use in their riding-stocks.

"I've often seen him wearing it," he said carelessly. "Curious how it could have become twisted and entangled in Miss West's lace waist."

He held out the pin, turning it over reflectively as the facets of the gems caught and flashed back the light from the hall brackets.

"I'll drop it into the poor-box I think," he mused. "Cardemon will remain away so long that this pin will be entirely
out of fashion when he returns."

After a few moments Neville drew a long, deep breath, and
his clenched hands relaxed.

"Sure," commented the burly doctor. "That's right — feeling better — rush of common sense to the head. Well, I've got
to go."

"Will you be here in the morning?"

"I think not. She'll be all right. If she isn't, send over for
me."

"You don't think that the shock — the exhaustion —"

"Naw," said the big doctor with good-natured contempt;
"she's going to be all right in the morning. . . . She's a lovely
creature, isn't she? Sam said so. Sam has an eye for beauty.
But, by jinks! I was scarcely prepared for such physical perfection — h'm! — or such fine and nice discrimination — or
for such pluck. . . . God knows what people's families want
these days. If the world mated properly our best families
would be extinct in another generation. . . . You're one of 'em;
you'd better get diligent before the world wakes up with a
rush of common sense to its doddering old head." He gave
him both hands, warmly, cordially: "Good-bye, Louis."

Neville said: "I want you to know that I'd marry her
tomorrow if she'd have me, Billy."

The doctor lifted his eyebrows.

"Won't she?"

"No."

"Then probably you're not up to sample. A girl like that
is no fool. She'll require a lot in a man. However, you're
young; and you may make good yet."

"You don't understand, Billy —"

"Yes, I do. She wears a dinky miniature of you against her
naked heart. Yes, I guess I understand. . . . And I guess she's
that kind of a girl all unselfishness and innocence, and
generous perversity and — quixotic love. . . . It's too bad,
Louis. I guess you're up against it for fair."

He surveyed the younger man, shook his head:

"They can't stand for her, can they?"

"No."

"And she won't stand for snaking you out of the fold. That's it, I fancy?"

"Yes."

"Too bad — too bad. She's a fine woman — a very fine little woman. That's the kind a man ought to marry and bother the Almighty with gratitude all the rest of his life. Well — well! Your family is your own after all; and I live in Dartford, thank God! — not on lower Fifth Avenue or Tenth Street."

He started away, halted, came back:

"Couldn't you run away with her?" he asked anxiously.

"She won't," replied Neville, unsmiling.

"I mean, violently. But she's too heavy to carry, I fancy — and I'll bet she's got the vigor of little old Diana herself. No — you couldn't do the Sabine act with her — only a club and the cave-man's gentle persuasion would help either of you. . . . Well — well, if they see her at breakfast it may help some. You know a woman makes or breaks herself at breakfast. That's why the majority of woman take it abed. I'm serious, Louis; no man can stand 'em — the majority."

Once more he started away, hesitated, came back.

"Who's this Countess that Sam is so crazy about?"

"A sweet little woman, well-bred, and very genuine and sincere."

"Never heard of her in Dartford," muttered the doctor.

Neville laughed grimly:

"Billy, Tenth Street and lower Fifth Avenue and Greenwich Village and Chelsea and Stuyvesant Square — and Syringa Avenue, Dartford, are all about alike. Bird Center is just as stupid as Manhattan; and there never was and never will be a republic and a democracy in any country on the face of this snob-cursed globe."

The doctor, very red, stared at him.

"By jinks!" he said, "I guess I'm one after all. Now, who in hell would suspect that! — after all the advice I've given you!"

"It was another fellow's family, that's all," said Neville wearily. "Theories work or they don't; only few care to try them on themselves or their own families — particularly when they devoutly believe in them."

"Gad! That's a stinger! You've got me going all right," said the doctor, wincing, "and you're perfectly correct. Here I've been practically counseling you to marry where your inclination led you, and let the rest go to blazes; and when it's a question of Sam doing something similar, I retire hastily across the river and establish a residence in Missouri. What a rotten, custom-ridden bunch of snippy-snappy-snobbery we are after all. . . ! All the same — who *is* the Countess?"

Neville didn't know much about her.

"Sam's such an ass," said his brother, "and it isn't all snobbery on my part."

"The safest thing to do," said Neville bitterly, "is to let a man in love alone."

"Right. Foolish — damned foolish — but right! There is no greater ass than a wise one. Those who don't know anything at all are the better asses — and the happier."

And he went away down the stairs, muttering and gesticulating.

Mrs. Neville came to the door as he opened it to go out. They talked in low voices for a few moments, then the doctor went out and Mrs. Neville called to Stephanie.

The girl came from the lighted drawing room, and, together, the two women ascended the stairs.

Stephanie smiled and nodded to Neville, then continued on along the hall; but his mother stopped to speak to him.

"Go and sit with your father a little while," she said. "And don't be impatient with him, dear. He is an old man — a product of a different age and a simpler civilization — perhaps a narrower one. Be patient and gentle with him. He really is fond of you and proud of you."

"Very well, mother. . . . Is anybody going to sit up with Valerie?"

"Stephanie insists on sleeping on the couch at the foot of her bed. I offered to sit up but she wouldn't let me. . . . You'll see that I'm called if anything happens, won't you?"

"Yes. Good-night, mother."

He kissed her, stood a moment looking at the closed door behind which lay Valerie — tried to realize that she did lie there under the same roof tree that sheltered father, mother, and sister — then, with a strange thrill in his heart, he went downstairs.

Cameron passed him, on his upward way to slumberland.

"How's Miss West?" he asked cheerfully.

"Asleep, I think. Billy Ogilvy expects her to be all right in the morning."

"Good work! Glad of it. Tell your governor; he's been inquiring."

"Has he?" said Neville, with another thrill, and went into the living room where his father sat alone before the whitening ashes of the fire.

"Well, father!" he said, smiling.

The older man turned his head, then turned it away as his son drew up a chair and laid a stick across the andirons.

"It's turned a little chilly," he said.

"I have known of many a frost in May," said his father.

There was a silence; then his father slowly turned and gazed at him.

"How is — Miss West?" he asked stiffly.

"Billy Ogilvy says she will be all right tomorrow, father."

"Was she injured by her unfortunate experience?"

"A little briar-torn, I'm afraid. Those big beech woods are rather a puzzle to anybody who is not familiar with the country. No wonder she became frightened when it grew dark."

"It was — very distressing," nodded his father.

They remained silent again until Mr. Neville rose, took off his spectacles, laid aside *The Evening Post,* and held out his hand.

"Good-night, my son."

"Good-night, father."

"Yes — yes — good-night — good-night — to many, many things, my son; old-fashioned things of no value anymore — of no use to me, or you, or anybody anymore."

He retained his son's hand in his, peering at him, dim-eyed, without his spectacles:

"The old order passes — the old ideas, the old beliefs — and the old people who cherished them — who know no others, needed no others. . . . Good-night, my son."

But he made no movement to leave, and still held to his son's hand:

"I've tried to live as blamelessly as my father lived, Louis — and as God has given me to see my way through life. . . .

But — the times change so — change so. The times are perplexing; life grows noisier, and stranger and more complex and more violent every day around us — and the old require repose, Louis. Try to understand that."

"Yes, father."

The other looked at him, wearily:

"Your mother seems to think that your happiness in life depends on — what we say to you — this evening. Stephanie seems to believe it, too. . . . Lily says very little. . . . And so do I, Louis — very little . . . only enough to — to wish you — happiness. And so — good-night."

Chapter XV

*I*t was barely daylight when Valerie awoke. She lay perfectly still, listening, remembering, her eyes wandering over the dim, unfamiliar room. Through thin silk curtains a little of the early light penetrated; she heard the ceaseless chorus of the birds, cocks crowing near and far away, the whimpering flight of pigeons around the eaves above her windows, and their low, incessant cooing.

Suddenly, through the foot-bars of her bed she caught sight of Stephanie lying sound asleep on the couch, and she sat up — swiftly, noiselessly, staring at her out of wide eyes from which the last trace of dreams had fled.

For a long while she remained upright among her pillows, looking at Stephanie, remembering, considering; then, with decision, she slipped silently out of bed, and went about her dressing without a sound.

In the connecting bathroom and dressing-room beyond she found her clothing gathered in a heap, evidently to be taken away and freshened early in the morning. She dared not brush it for fear of awakening Stephanie; her toilet was swift and simple; she clothed herself rapidly and stepped out into the hall, her rubber-soled walking shoes making no noise.

Below, the sidelights of the door made unbolting and unchaining easy; it would be hours yet before even the servants were stirring, but she moved with infinite caution, stepping out onto the veranda and closing the door behind her without making the slightest noise.

Dew splashed her shoes as she hastened across the lawn. She knew the Estwich road even if there had been no finger-posts to point out her way.

The sun had not yet risen; woods were foggy; the cattle in the fields stood to their shadowy flanks in the thin mist; and everywhere, like the cheery rush of a stream, sounded the torrent of bird-music from bramble patch and alder-swale, from hedge and orchard and young woodland.

It was not until she had arrived in sight of Estwich Corners that she met the first farmer afield; and, as she turned into the drive, the edge of the sun sent a blinding search-light over a dew-soaked world, and her long-shadow sprang into view, streaming away behind her across the lawn.

To her surprise the front door was open and a harnessed buck-board stood at the gate; and suddenly she recollected with a hot blush that the household must have been amazed and probably alarmed by her non-appearance the night before.

Hélène's farmer and her maid came out as she entered the front walk, and, seeing her, stood round-eyed and gaping.

"I got lost and remained over night at Mrs. Collis's," she said, smiling. "Now, I'd like a bath if you please and some fresh clothing for traveling, because I am obliged to go to the city, and I wish to catch the earliest train."

When at last it was plain to them that she was alive and well, Hélène's maid, still trembling, hastened to draw a bath for her and pack the small steamer trunk; and the farmer sat down on the porch and waited, still more or less shaken by the anxiety which had sent him pottering about the neighboring woods and fields with a lantern the night before, and had aroused him to renewed endeavor before sunrise.

Bathed and freshly clothed, Valerie hastened into the pretty library, seated herself at the desk, pushed up her veil, and wrote rapidly:

"MY DEAR MRS. COLLIS:
	"My gratitude to you, to Mrs. Neville, and to Miss Swift is nonetheless real because I am acknowledging it by letter. Besides, I am very certain that you would prefer it so.

"You and your family have been kindness itself to me in my awkward and painful dilemma; you have sheltered me and provided medical attendance; and I am deeply in your debt.

"Had matters been different I need scarcely say that it would have been a pleasure for me to personally acknowledge to you and your family my grateful appreciation.

"But I am very sure that I could show my gratitude in no more welcome manner than by doing what I have done this morning and by expressing that obligation to you in writing.

"Before I close may I ask you to believe that I had no intention of seeking shelter at your house? Until I heard Mr. Neville's voice I had no idea where I was. I merely made my way toward the first lighted windows that I saw, never dreaming that I had come to Ashuelyn.

"I am sorry that my stupid misadventure has caused you and your family so much trouble and annoyance. I feel it very keenly — more keenly because of your kindness in making the best of what must have been to you and your family a most disagreeable episode.

"May I venture to express to you my thanks to Miss Swift who so generously remained in my room last night? I am deeply sensible of her sweetness to an unwelcome stranger — and of Mrs. Neville's gentle manner toward one who, I am afraid, has caused her much anxiety.

"To the very amiable physician who did so much to calm a foolish and inexcusable nervousness, I am genuinely grateful. If I knew his name and address I would write and properly acknowledge my debt.

"There is one thing more before I close: I am sorry that I wrote you so ungraciously after receiving your last letter. It would have been perfectly easy to have thanked you courteously, whatever private opinion I may have entertained concerning a matter about which there may be more than my own opinion.

"And now, please believe that I will never again voluntarily cause you and your family the slightest uneasi-

ness or inconvenience; and believe me, too, if you care
to. Very gratefully yours,

"VALERIE WEST"

She directed and sealed the letter, then drew toward her
another sheet of paper:

"DEAREST:
    "I could die of shame for having blundered into your
family circle. I dare not even consider what they must
think of me now. *You* will know how innocently and
unsuspiciously it was done — how utterly impossible it
would have been for me to have voluntarily committed
such an act even in the last extremity. But what *they* will
think of my appearance at your door last night, I don't
know and I dare not surmise. I have done all I could; I
have rid them of me, and I have written to your sister
to thank her and your family for their very real kindness
to the last woman in the world whom they would have
willingly chosen to receive and entertain.
    "Dear, I didn't know I had nerves; but this experience
seems to have developed them. I am perfectly well, but
the country here has become distasteful to me, and I am
going to town in a few minutes. I want to get away — I
want to go back to my work — earn my living again —
live in blessed self-respect where, as a worker, I have the
right to live.
    "Dearest, I am sorry about not meeting you at the
station and going back to town with you. But I simply
cannot endure staying here after last night. I suppose it
is weak and silly of me, but I feel now as though your
family would never be perfectly tranquil again until I
am out of their immediate vicinity. I cannot convey to
you or to them how sorry and how distressed I am that
this thing has occurred.
    "But I can, perhaps, make you understand that I love
you, dearly — love you enough to give myself to you —
love you enough to give you up forever.
    "And it is to consider what is best, what to do, that I
am going away quietly somewhere by myself to think it

all out once more — and to come to a final decision before the first of June.

"I want to search my heart, and let God search it for any secret selfishness and unworthiness that might sway me in my choice — any overmastering love for you that might blind me. When I know myself, you shall know me. Until then I shall not write you; but sometime before the first of June — or on that day, you shall know and I shall know how I have decided wherein I may best serve you — whether by giving or withholding — whether by accepting or refusing forever all that I care for in the world — you, Louis, and the love you have given me.

"VALERIE WEST"

She sealed and directed this, laid it beside the other, and summoned the maid:

"Have these sent at once to Ashuelyn," she said; "let Jimmy go on his bicycle. Are my things ready? Is the buck-board still there? Then I will leave a note for the Countess."

And she scribbled hastily:

"HÉLÈNE DEAR:

"I've got to go to town in a hurry on matters of importance, and so I am taking a very unceremonious leave of you and of your delightful house.

"They'll tell you I got lost in the woods last night, and I did. It was too stupid of me; but no harm came of it — only a little embarrassment in accepting a night's shelter at Ashuelyn among people who were everything that was hospitable, but who must have been anything but delighted to entertain me.

"In a few weeks I shall write you again. I have not exactly decided what to do this summer. I may go abroad for a vacation as I have saved enough to do so in an economical manner; and I should love to see the French cathedrals. Perhaps, if I so decide, you might be persuaded to go with me.

"However, it is too early to plan yet. A matter of utmost importance is going to keep me busy and se-

cluded for a week or so. After that I shall come to some
definite decision; and then you shall hear from me.

"In the meanwhile — I have enjoyed Estwich and you
immensely. It was kind and dear of you to ask me. I shall
never forget my visit.

"Good-bye, Hélène dear.

                                        "Valerie West"

This note she left on Hélène's dresser, then ran downstairs
and sprang into the buck-board.

They had plenty of time to catch the train; and on the train
she had plenty of leisure for reflection. But she could not
seem to think; a confused sensation of excitement invaded
her mind and she sat in her velvet armed chair alternately
shivering with the memory of Cardemon's villainy, and quivering under the recollection of her night at Ashuelyn.

Rita was not at home when she came into their little
apartment. The parrot greeted her, flapping his brilliant
wings and shrieking from his perch; the goldfish goggled his
eyes and swam 'round and 'round. She stood still in the center
of her room looking vacantly about her. An immense, over-
whelming sense of loneliness came over her; she turned as
the rush of tears blinded her and flung herself full length
among the pillows of her bed.

*H*er first two or three days in town were busy ones; she
had her accounts to balance, her inventories to take, her
mending to do, her modest summer wardrobe to acquire,
letters to write and to answer, engagements to make, to fulfill,
to postpone; friends to call on and to receive, duties in regard
to the New Idea Home to attend to.

Also, the morning after her arrival came a special delivery
letter from Neville:

"It was a mistake to go, dear, because, although you
could not have known it, matters have changed most
happily for us. You were a welcome guest in my sister's
house; you would have been asked to remain after your

visit at Estwich was over. My family's sentiments are changing — have changed. It requires only you yourself to convince them. I wish you had remained, although your going so quietly commanded the respect of everybody. They all are very silent about it and about you, yet I can see that they have been affected most favorably by their brief glimpse of you.

"As for your wishing to remain undisturbed for a few days, I can see no reason for it now, dear, but of course I shall respect your wishes.

"Only send me a line to say that the month of June will mean our marriage. Say it, dear, because there is now no reason to refuse."

To which she answered:

"Dearest among all men, no family's sentiments change over night. Your people were nice to me and I have thanked them. But, dear, I am not likely to delude myself in regard to their real sentiments concerning me. Too deeply ingrained, too basic, too essentially part of themselves and of their lives are the creeds, codes, and beliefs which, in spite of themselves, must continue to govern their real attitude toward such a girl as I am.

"It is dear of you to wish for us what cannot be; it is kind of them to accept your wish with resignation.

"But I have told you many times, my darling, that I would not accept a status as your wife at any cost to you or to them — and I can read between the lines, even if I did not know, what it would cost them and you. And so, very gently, and with a heart full of gratitude and love for you, I must decline this public honor.

"But, God willing, I shall not decline a lifetime devoted to you when you are not with them. That is all I can hope for; and it is so much more than I ever dreamed of having, that, to have you at all — even for a part of the time — even for a part of my life, is enough. And I say it humbly, reverently, without ignoble envy or discontent for what might have been had you and I been born to the same life amid the same surroundings.

"Don't write to me again, dear, until I have determined what is best for us. Before the first day of summer, or on that day, you will know. And so will I.

"My life is such a little thing compared to yours — of such slight value and worth that sometimes I think I am considering matters too deeply — that if I simply fling it in the scales the balance will scarcely be altered — the splendid, even tenor of your career will scarcely swerve a shade.

"Yet my life is already something to you; and besides it is all I have to give you; and if I am to give it — if it is adding an iota to your happiness for me to give it — then I must truly treat it with respect, and deeply consider the gift, and the giving, and if it shall be better for you to possess it, or better that you never shall.

"And whatever I do with myself, my darling, be certain that it is of you I am thinking and not of the girl, who loves you.

"V."

By degrees she cleared up her accounts and set her small house in order.

Rita seemed to divine that something radical was in progress of evolution, but Valerie offered no confidence, and the girl, already deeply worried over John Burleson's condition, had not spirit enough to meddle.

"Sam Ogilvy's brother is a wonder on tubercular cases," she said to Valerie, "and I'm doing my best to get John to go and see him at Dartford."

"Won't he?"

"He says he will, but you know how horridly untruthful men are. And now John is slopping about with his wet clay again as usual — an order for a tomb in Greenwood — poor boy, he had better think how best to keep away from tombs."

"Why, Rita!" said Valerie, shocked.

"I can't help it; I'm really frightened, dear. And you know well enough I'm no flighty alarmist. Besides, somehow, I feel certain that Sam's brother would tell John to go to Arizona" — she pointed piteously to her trunk: "It's packed; it has been packed for weeks. I'm all ready to go with him. Why can't a man mold clay and chip marble and cast bronze as well in Arizona as in this vile pest-hole?"

Valerie sat with folded hands looking at her.

"How do you think *you* could stand that desolation?"

"Arizona?"

"Yes."

"There is another desolation I dread more."

"Do you really love him so?"

Rita slowly turned from the window and looked at her.

"Yes," she said.

"Does he know it, Rita?"

"No, dear."

"Do you think — if he did —"

"No. . . . How could it be — after what has happened to me?"

"You would tell him?"

"Of course. I sometimes wonder whether he has not already heard — something — from that beast —"

"Does John know him?"

"He has done two fountains for his place at El Naúar. He had several other things in view —" she shrugged — "but *The Mohave* sailed suddenly with its owner for a voyage around the world — so John was told; — and — Valerie, it's the first clear breath of relief I've drawn since Penrhyn Cardemon entered John's studio."

"I didn't know he had ever been there."

"Yes; twice."

"Did you see him there?"

"Yes. I nearly dropped. At first he did not recognize me — I was very young — when —"

"Did he speak to you?"

"Yes. I managed to answer. John was not looking at me, fortunately. . . . After that he wrote to me — and I burned the letter. . . . It was horrible; he said that José Querida was his guest at El Naúar, and he asked me to get you because you knew Querida, and be his guest for a week end. . . . I cried that night; you heard me."

"Was *that* it!" asked Valerie, very pale.

"Yes; I was too wretched to tell you,"

Valerie sat silent, her teeth fixed in her lower lip. Then:

"José could not have known what kind of a man the — other — is."

"I hope not."

"Oh, he *couldn't* have known! Rita, he wouldn't have let him ask us —"

"Men seldom deceive one another."

"You *don't* think José Querida *knew?*"

"I — don't — think. . . . Valerie, men are very — very unlike women. . . . Forgive me if I seem to be embittered. . . . Even you have had your experience with men — the men that all the world seems to like — kind, jolly, generous, jovial, amusing men — and clever men; men of attainment, of distinction. And they — the majority of them — are, after all, just men, Valerie, just men in a world made for men, a world into which we come like timid intruders; uncertain through generations of uncertainty — innocently stupid through ages of stupid innocence, ready to please though not knowing exactly how; ready to be pleased, God knows, with pleasures as innocent as the simple minds that dream of them.

"Valerie, I do not believe any evil first came into this world of men through any woman."

Valerie looked down at her folded hands — small, smooth, white hands, pure of skin and innocent as a child's.

"I don't know," she said, troubled, "how much more unhappiness arises through men than through women, if any more . . . I like men. Some are unruly — like children; some have the sense and the morals of marauding dogs.

"But, at worst, the unruly and the marauders seem so hopelessly beneath one, intellectually, that a girl's resentment is really more of contempt than of anger — and perhaps more of pity than of either."

Rita said: "I cannot feel as charitably. . . . *You* still have that right."

"Rita! Rita!" she said softly, "we both have loved men, you with the ignorance and courage of a child — I with less ignorance and with my courage as yet untested. Where is the difference between us — if we love sincerely?"

Rita leaned forward and looked at her searchingly:

"Do you mean to do — what you said you would?"

"Yes."

"Why?"

"Because he wants me."

Rita sprang to her feet and began pacing the floor.

"I will not have it so!" she said excitedly, "I will not have it so! If he is a man — a real man — he will not have it so, either. If he will, he does not love you; mark what I say, Valerie — he does not love you enough. No man can love a woman enough to accept that from her; it would be a paradox, I tell you!"

"He loves me enough," said Valerie, very pale. "He could not love me as I care for him; it is not in a man to do it, nor in any human being to love as I love him. You don't understand, Rita. I *must* be a part of him — not very much, because already there is so much to him — and I am so — so unimportant."

"You are more important than he is," said Rita fiercely — "with all your fineness and loyalty and divine sympathy and splendid humility — with your purity and your loveliness; and in spite of his very lofty intellect and his rather amazing genius, and his inherited social respectability — *you* are the more important to the happiness and welfare of this world — even to the humblest corner in it!"

"Rita! Rita! What wild, partisan nonsense you are talking!"

"Oh, Valerie, Valerie, if you only knew! If you only knew!"

Querida called next day. Rita was at home but flatly refused to see him.

"Tell Mr. Querida," she said to the janitor, "that neither I nor Miss West are at home to him, and that if he is as nimble at riddles as he is at mischief he can guess this one before his friend Mr. Cardemon returns from a voyage around the world."

Which reply slightly disturbed Querida.

All during dinner — and he was dining alone — he considered it; and his thoughts were mostly centered on Valerie.

Somehow, some way or other he must come to an understanding with Valerie West. Somehow, some way, she must be brought to listen to him. Because, while he lived, married or single, poor or wealthy, he would never rest, never be satisfied, never wring from life the last drop that life must pay him, until this woman's love was his.

He loved her as such a man loves; he had no idea of letting that love for her interfere with other ambitions.

Long ago, when very poor and very talented and very confident that the world, which pretended to ignore him, really knew in its furtive heart that it owed him fame and fortune and social position, he had determined to begin the final campaign with a perfectly suitable marriage.

That was all years ago; and he had never swerved in his determination — not even when Valerie West surprised his life in all the freshness of her young beauty.

And, as he sat there leisurely over his claret, he reflected, easily, that the time had come for the marriage, and that the woman he had picked out was perfectly suitable, and that the suitable evening to inform her was the present evening.

Mrs. Hind-Willet was prepossessing enough to interest him, clever enough to stop gaps in a dinner table conversation, wealthy enough to permit him a liberty of rejecting commissions, which he had never before dared to exercise, and fashionable enough to carry for him what could not be carried through his own presentable good looks and manners and fame.

This last winter he had become a frequenter of her house on Sixty-third Street; and so carelessly assiduous, and so delightfully casual had become his attentions to that beautifully groomed widow, that his footing with her was already an intimacy, and his portrait of her, which he had given her, had been the sensation of the loan exhibition at the great Interborough Charity Bazaar.

He was neither apprehensive nor excited as he calmly finished his claret. He was to drop in there after dinner to discuss with her several candidates as architects for the New Idea Home.

So when he was entirely ready he took his hat and stick and departed in a taxicab, pleasantly suffused with a gentle glow of anticipation. He had waited many years for such an evening as this was to be. He was a patient and unmoral man. He could wait longer for Valerie, — and for the first secret blow at the happiness and threatened artistic success of Louis Neville.

So he rolled away in his taxi very comfortably, savoring his cigarette, indolently assured of his reception in a house which it would suit him perfectly to inhabit when he cared to.

Only one thing worried him a little — the short note he had received from his friend Penrhyn Cardemon, saying rather brusquely that he'd made up his mind not to have his portrait painted for five thousand dollars, and that he was going off on *The Mohave* to be gone a year at least.

Which pained Querida, because Cardemon had not only side-stepped what was almost a commission, but he had, also, apparently forgotten his invitation to spend the summer on *The Mohave* — with the understanding that Valerie West was also to be invited.

However, everything comes in its season; and this did not appear to be the season for ripe commissions and yachting enterprises; but it certainly seemed to be the season for a judicious matrimonial enterprise.

And when Mrs. Hind-Willet received him in a rose-tinted reception corner, audaciously intimate and secluded, he truly felt that he was really missing something of the pleasures of the chase, and that it was a little too easy to be acutely enjoyable.

However, when at last he had gently retained her hand and had whispered, "Alma," and had let his big, dark, velvet eyes rest with respectful passion upon her smaller and clearer and blacker ones, something somewhere in the machinery seemed to go wrong — annoyingly wrong.

Because Mrs. Hind-Willet began to laugh — and evidently was trying not to — trying to remain very serious; but her little black eyes were glistening with tears of suppressed mirth, and when, amazed and offended, he would have withdrawn his hand, she retained it almost convulsively:

"José! I *beg* your pardon! — I truly do. It is perfectly horrid and unspeakable of me to behave this way; but listen, child! I am forty; I am perfectly contented not to marry again; *and* I don't love you. So, my poor José, what on earth am I to do if I don't laugh a little. I *can't* weep over it you know."

The scarlet flush faded from his olive skin. "Alma," he began mournfully, but she only shook her head, vigorously.

"Nonsense," she said. "You like me for a sufficient variety of reasons. And to tell you the truth I suspect that I am quite as madly in love with you as you actually are with me. No, no, José. There are too many — discrepancies — of various kinds. I have too little to gain! — to be horribly frank — and you — alas! — are a very cautious, very clever, and admirably sophisticated young man. . . . There, there! I am not really accusing you — or blaming you — very much. . . . I'd have tried the same thing in your place — yes, indeed I would. . . . But, José dear, if you'll take the mature advice of fair, plump, and forty, you'll let the lesser ambition go.

"A clever wealthy woman nearer your age, and on the edge of things — with you for a husband, ought to carry you and herself far enough to suit you. And there'd be more amusement in it, believe me. . . . And now — you may kiss my hand — very good-humoredly and respectfully, and we'll talk about those architects. Shall we?"

*F*or twenty-four hours Querida remained a profoundly astonished man. Examine, in retrospective, as he would, the details of the delicately adjusted machinery which for so many years had slowly but surely turned the interlocking cog-wheels of destiny for him, he could not find where the trouble had been — could discover no friction caused by neglect of lubricants; no overoiling, either; no flaw.

Wherein lay the trouble? Based on what error was his theory that the average man could marry anybody he chose? Just where had he miscalculated?

He admitted that times changed very fast; that the world was spinning at a rate that required nimble wits to keep account of its revolutions. But his own wits were nimble, almost feminine in the rapid delicacy of their intuition — *almost* feminine, but not quite. And he felt, vaguely, that there lay his mistake in engaging a woman with a woman's own weapons; and that the only chance a man has is to perplex her with his own.

The world was spinning rapidly; times changed very fast, but not as fast as women were changing in the Western World. For the self-sufficient woman — the self-confident, self-sustaining individual, not only content but actually preferring autonomy of mind and body, was a fact in which José Querida had never really ever believed. No sentimentalist does or really can. And all creators of things artistic are, basically, sentimentalists.

Querida's almond-shaped, velvet eyes had done their share for him in his time; they were merely part of a complex machinery which, included many exquisitely adjusted parts which could produce at will such phenomena as temporary but genuine sympathy and emotion: a voice controlled and modulated to the finest nuances; a grace of body and mind that resembled inherent delicacy; a nervous receptiveness and intelligence almost supersensitive in its recognition of complicated ethical problems. It was a machinery which could make of him any manner of man which the opportunism of the particular moment required. Yet, with all this, in every nerve and bone and fiber he adored material and intellectual beauty, and physical suffering in others actually distressed him.

Now, reviewing matters, deeply interested to find the microscopic obstruction which had so abruptly stopped the machinery of destiny for him, he was modest enough and sufficiently liberal-minded to admit to himself that Alma Hind-Willet was the exception that proved this rule. There *were* women so constructed that they had become essentially unresponsive. Alma was one. But, he concluded that if he lived a thousand years he was not likely to encounter another.

And the following afternoon he called upon Mrs. Hind-Willet's understudy, the blue-eyed little Countess d'Enver.

Hélène d'Enver was superintending the definite closing of her beautiful duplex apartments — the most beautiful in the great châteaulike, limestone building. And José Querida knew perfectly well what the rents were.

"Such a funny time to come to see me," she had said laughingly over the telephone; "I'm in a dreadful state with skirts pinned up and a motor-bonnet over my hair, but I will *not* permit my maids to touch the porcelains; and if you really wish to see me, come ahead."

He really wished to. Besides he adored her Ming porcelains and her Celedon, and the idea of any maid touching them almost gave him heart-failure. He himself possessed one piece of Ming and a broken fragment of Celedon. Women had been married for less.

She was very charming in her pinned-up skirts and her dainty headgear, and she welcomed him and entrusted him with specimens which sent pleasant shivers down his flexible spine.

And, together, they put away many scores of specimens which were actually priceless, inasmuch as any rumor of a public sale would have excited amateurs to the verge of lunacy, and almost any psychopathic might have established a new record for madness at an auction of this matchless collection.

They breathed easier when the thrilling task was ended; but emotion still enchained them as they seated themselves at a tea-table — an emotion so deep on Hélène's part that she suffered Querida to retain the tips of her fingers for an appreciable moment when transferring sugar to his cup. And she listened, with a smile almost tremulous, to the fascinating music of his voice, charmingly attuned and modulated to a pitch which, somehow, seemed to harmonize with the very word, Celedon.

"I am so surprised," she said softly — but his dark eyes noted that she was still busy with her tea paraphernalia — "I scarcely know what to think, Mr. Querida —"

"Think that I love you —" breathed Querida, his dark and beautiful head very near to her blond one.

"I — am — thinking of it. . . . But —"

"Hélène," he whispered musically; — and suddenly stiffened in his chair as the maid came clattering in over the rugless and polished parquet to announce Mr. Ogilvy, followed *san façon* by that young man, swinging a straw hat and a Malacca stick.

"Sam!" said the pretty Countess, changing countenance.

"Hello, Hélène! How-do, Querida! I heard you were temporarily in town, dear lady —" He kissed a hand that was as faltering and guilty as the irresolute eyes she lifted to his.

Ten minutes later Querida took his leave. He dismissed the expensive taxi which had been devouring time outside, and walked thoughtfully away down the fashionable street.

Because the machinery had chanced to clog twice did not disturb his theory; but the trouble with him was local; he was intensely and personally annoyed, nervous, irritated unspeakably. Because, except for Valerie, these two, Alma Hind-Willet and Hélène d'Enver, were the only two socially and financially suitable women in whom he took the slightest physical interest.

There is, in all women, one moment — sometimes repeated — in which a sudden yielding to caprice sometimes overturns the logical plans laid out and inexorably followed for half a lifetime. And there was much of the feminine about Querida.

And it chanced to happen on this day — when no doubt all unsuspected and unperceived some lurking jettatura had given him the evil eye — that he passed by hazard through the block where Valerie lived, and saw her mounting the steps.

"Why, José!" she exclaimed, a trifle confused in her smiling cordiality as he sprang up the steps behind her — for Rita's bitterness, if it had not aroused in her suspicions, had troubled her in spite of her declaration of unbelief.

He asked for a cup of tea, and she invited him. Rita was in the room when they entered; and she stood up coolly, coolly returned Querida's steady glance and salutation with a glance as calm, as detached, and as intelligent as a surgeon's.

Neither he nor she referred to his recent call; he was perfectly self-possessed, entirely amiable with that serene and level good-humor which sometimes masks a defiance almost contemptuous.

But Rita's engagements required her to leave very shortly after his advent; and before she went out she deliberately waited to catch Valerie's eye; and Valerie colored deeply under her silent message.

Then Rita went away with a scarcely perceptible nod to Querida; and when, by the clock, she had been gone twenty minutes, Querida, without reason, without preparation, and perfectly aware of his moment's insanity, yielded to a second's flash of caprice — the second that comes once in the lives of all women — and now, in the ordered symmetry of his life, had come to him.

"Valerie," he said, "I love you. Will you marry me?"

She had been leaning sideways on the back of her chair, one hand supporting her cheek, gazing almost listlessly out of the open window.

She did not stir, nor did her face alter, but, very quietly she turned her head and looked at him.

He spoke, breathlessly, eloquently, persuasively, and well; the perfect machinery was imitating for him a single-minded, ardent, honorable young man, intelligent enough to know his own mind, manly enough to speak it. The facsimile was flawless.

He had finished and was waiting, long fingers gripping the arms of his chair; and her face had altered only to soften divinely, and her eyes were very sweet and untroubled.

"I am glad you have spoken this way to me, José. Something has been said about you — in connection with Mr. Cardemon — which disturbed me and made me very sad and miserable, although I would not permit myself to believe it. . . . And now I know it was a mistake — because you have asked me to be your wife."

She sat looking at him, the sadness in her eyes emphasized by the troubled smile curving her lips:

"I couldn't marry you, José, because I am not in love with you. If I were I would do it. . . . But I do not care for you that way."

For an instant some inner flare of madness blinded his brain and vision. There was, in his face, something so terrible that Valerie unconsciously rose to her feet, bewildered, almost stunned.

"I want you," he said slowly.

"José! What in the world —"

His dry lips moved, but no articulate sound came from them. Suddenly he sprang to his feet, and out of his twisted, distorted mouth poured a torrent of passion, of reproach, of half-crazed pleading — incoherency tumbling over incoherency, deafening her, beating in upon her, till she swayed where she stood, holding her arms up as though to shield herself.

The next instant she was straining, twisting in his arms, striving to cry out, to wrench herself free to keep her feet amid the crash of the overturned table and a falling chair.

"José! Are you insane?" she panted, tearing herself free and springing toward the door. Suddenly she halted, uttered a cry as he jumped back to block her way. The low window-ledge caught him under both knees; he clutched at nothing, reeled backward and outward and fell into space.

For a second she covered her white face with both hands, then turned, dragged herself to the open window, forced herself to look out.

He lay on his back on the grass in the rear yard, and the janitor was already bending over him. And when she reached the yard Querida had opened both eyes.

Later the ambulance came, and with its surgeon came a policeman. Querida, lying with his head on her lap, opened his eyes again:

"I was — seated — on the window-ledge," he said with difficulty — "and overbalanced myself. . . . Caught the table — but it fell over. . . . That's all."

The eyes in his ghastly face closed wearily, then fluttered:

"Awfully sorry, Valerie — make such a mess — in your house."

"Oh-h — José," she sobbed.

After that they took him away to the Presbyterian Hospital; and nobody seemed to find very much the matter with him except that he'd been badly shocked.

But the next day all sensation ceased in his body from the neck downward.

And they told Valerie why.

For ten days he lay there, perfectly conscious, patient, good-humored, and his almond-shaped and hollow eyes rested on Valerie and Rita with a fatalistic serenity subtly tinged with irony.

John Burleson came to see him, and cried. After he left, Querida said to Valerie:

"John and I are destined to remain near neighbors; his grief is well meant, but a trifle premature."

"You are not going to die, José!" she said gently.

But he only smiled.

Ogilvy came, Annan came, the Countess Hélène, and even Mrs. Hind-Willet. He inspected them all with his shadowy and mysterious smile, answered them gently deep in his sunken eyes a somber amusement seemed to dwell. But there was in it no bitterness.

Then Neville came. Valerie and Rita were absent that day but their roses filled the private ward-room with a hint of the coming summer.

Querida lay looking at Neville, the half smile resting on his pallid face like a slight shadow that faintly waxed and waned with every breath he drew.

"Well," he said quietly, "you are the man I wished to see."

"Querida," he said, deeply affected, "this thing isn't going to be permanent —"

"No; not permanent. It won't last, Neville. Nothing does last. . . . unless you can tell me whether my pictures are going to endure. Are they? I know that you will be as honest with me as I was — dishonest with you. I will believe what you say. Is my work destined to be permanent?"

"Don't you know it is?"

"I thought so. . . . But *you* know. Because, Neville, you are the man who is coming into what was mine, and what will be your own; — and you are coming into more than that, Neville, more than I ever could have attained. Now answer me; will my work live?"

"Always," said Neville simply.

Querida smiled:

"The rest doesn't matter then. . . . Even Valerie doesn't matter. . . . But you may hand me one of her roses. . . . No, a bud, if you don't mind — unopened."

When it was time for Neville to go Querida's smile had faded and the pink rose-bud lay wilted in his fingers.

"It is just as well, Neville," he said. "I couldn't have endured your advent. Somebody *has* to be first; I was — as long as I lived. . . . It is curious how acquiescent a man's mind becomes — when he's like this. I never believed it possible that a man really could die without regret, without some shadow of a desire to live. Yet it is that way, Neville. . . . But a man must lie dying before he can understand it."

A highly tinted uncle from Oporto arrived in New York just in time to see Querida alive. He brought with him a parrot.

"Send it to Mrs. Hind-Willet," whispered Querida with stiffening lips; *"uno lavanta la caça y otro la nata."*

A few minutes later he died, and his highly colored uncle from Oporto sent the bird to Mrs. Hind-Willet and made the thriftiest arrangement possible to transport what was mortal of a great artist to Oporto — where a certain kind of parrot comes from.

Chapter XVI

On the morning of the first day of June Neville came into his studio and found there a letter from Valerie:

"DEAREST:

"I am not keeping my word to you; I am asking you for more time; and I know you will grant it.

"José Querida's death has had a curious effect on me. I was inclined to care very sincerely for him; I comprehended him better than many people, I think. Yet there was much in him that I never understood. And I doubt that he ever entirely understood himself.

"I believe that he was really a great painter, Louis — and have sometimes thought that his character was mediæval at the foundations — with five centuries of civilization thinly deposited over the bed-rock. . . . In him there seemed to be something primitive; something untamable, and utterly irreconcilable with, the fundamental characteristics of modern man.

"He was my friend. . . . Friendship, they say, is a record of misunderstandings; and it was so with us But may I tell you something? José Querida loved me — in his own fashion.

"What kind of a love it was — of what value — I can not tell you. I do not think it was very high in the scale. Only he felt it for me, and for no other woman, I believe.

"It never was a love that I could entirely understand or respect; yet, — it is odd but true — I cared something for it — perhaps because, in spite of its unfamiliar and sometimes repellent disguises — it *was* love after all.

"And now, as at heart and in mind you and I are one; and as I keep nothing of real importance from you — perhaps *can* not; I must tell you that José Querida came that day to ask me to marry him.

"I tried to make him understand that I could not think of such a thing; and he lost his head and became violent. That is how the table fell: — I had started toward the door when he sprang back to block me, and the low windowsill caught him under the knees, and he fell outward into the yard.

"I know of course that no blame could rest on me, but it was a terrible and dreadful thing that happened there in one brief second; and somehow it seems to have moved in me depths that have never before been stirred.

"The newspapers, as you know, published it merely as an accident — which it really was. But they might have made it, by innuendo, a horror for me. However, they put it so simply and so unsuspiciously that José Querida might have been any nice man calling on any nice woman.

"Louis, I have never been so lonely in my life as I have been since José Querida died; alas! not because he has gone out of my life forever, but because, somehow, the manner of his death has made me realize how difficult it is for a woman alone to contend with men in a man's own world.

"Do what she may to maintain her freedom, her integrity, there is always, — sometimes impalpable, sometimes not — a steady, remorseless pressure on her, forcing her unwillingly to take frightened cognizance of men; — take into account their inexorable desire for domination; the subtle cohesion existent among them which, at moments, becomes like a wall of adamant barring, limiting, enclosing and forcing women toward the deepworn grooves which women have trodden through the sad centuries; — and which they tread still — and will tread perhaps for years to come before the real enfranchisement of mankind begins.

"I do not mean to write bitterly, dear; but, somehow, all this seems to bear significantly, ominously, upon my situation in the world.

"When I first knew you I felt so young, so confident, so free, so scornful of custom, so wholesomely emancipated from silly and unjust conventions, that perhaps I overestimated my own vigor and ability to go my way, unvexed, unfettered in this man's world, and let the world make its own journey in peace. But it will not.

"Twice, now, within a month, — and not through any conscious fault of mine — this man's world has shown its teeth at me; I have been menaced by its innate scorn of woman, and have, by chance, escaped a publicity which would have damned me so utterly that I would not have cared to live.

"And dear, for the first time I really begin to understand now what the shelter of a family means; what it is to have law on my side, — and a man who understands his man's world well enough to fight it with its own weapons; — well enough to protect a woman from things she never dreamed might menace her.

"When that policeman came into my room, — dear, you will think me a perfect coward — but suddenly I seemed to realize what law meant, and that it had power to protect me or destroy me. . . . And I was frightened, — and the table lay there with the fragments of broken china — and there was that dreadful window — and I — I who knew how he died! — Louis! Louis! guiltless as I was, — blameless in thought and deed — I died a thousand deaths there while the big policeman and the reporters were questioning me.

"If it had not been for what José was generous enough to say, I could never have thought out a lie to tell them; I should have told them how it had really happened. . . . And what the papers would have printed about him and about me, God only knows.

"Never, never had I needed you as I needed you at that moment. . . . Well; I lied to them, somehow; I said to them what José had said — that he was seated on the window-ledge, lost his balance, clutched at the table, overturned it, and fell. And they believed me. . . . It is the first lie since I was a little child, that I have ever knowingly told. . . . And I know now that I could never contrive to tell another.

"Dear, let me try to think out what is best for us. . . . And forgive me, Louis, if I can not help a thought or two of self creeping in. I am so terribly alone. Somehow I am beginning to believe that it may sometimes be a weakness to totally ignore one's self. . . . Not that I consider myself of importance compared to you, my darling; not that I would fail to set aside any thought of self where your welfare is concerned. You know that, don't you?

"But I have been wondering how it would be with you if I passed quietly and absolutely out of your life. That is what I am trying to determine. Because it must be either that or the tie unrecognized by civilization. And which would be better for you? I do not know yet. I ask more time. Don't write me. Your silence will accord it.

"You are always in my thoughts.

"VALERIE"

Ogilvy came into the studio that afternoon, loquacious, in excellent humor, and lighting a pipe, detailed what news he had while Neville tried to hide his own deep perplexity and anxiety under a cordial welcome.

"You know," said Ogilvy, "that all the time you've given me and all your kindness and encouragement has made a corker of that picture of mine."

"You did it yourself," said Neville. "It's good work, Sam."

"Sure it's good work — being mostly yours. And what do you think, Kelly; it's sold!"

"Good for you!"

"Certainly it's good for me. I need the mazuma. A courteous multi purchased it for his Long Branch cottage — said cottage costing a million. What?"

"Oh, you're doing very well," laughed Neville.

"I've *got* to. . . . I've — h'm! — undertaken to assume obligations toward civilization — h'm! — and certain duties to my — h'm — country —"

"What on earth are you driving at?" asked Neville, eying him.

"Huh! Driving single just at present; practicing for tandem — h'm! — and a spike — h'm — some day — I hope — of course —"

"Sam!"

"Hey?"

"Are you trying to say something?"

"Oh, Lord, no! Why, Kelly, did you suspect that I was really attempting to convey anything to you which I was really too damned embarrassed to tell you in the patois of my native city?"

"It sounded that way," observed Neville, smiling.

"Did it?" Ogilvy considered, head on one side. "Did it sound anything like a — h'm! — a man who was trying to — h'm! — to tell you that he was going to — h'm! — to try to get somebody to try to let him try to tell her that he wanted to — marry her?"

"Good heavens!" exclaimed Neville, bewildered, "what do you mean?"

Ogilvy pirouetted, picked up a mahl-stick, and began a lively fencing bout with an imaginary adversary.

"I'm going to get married," he said amiably.

"What!"

"Sure."

"To whom?"

"To Hélène d'Enver. Only she doesn't know it yet."

"What an infernal idiot you are, Sam!"

"Ya-as, so they say. Some say I'm an ass, others a bally idiot, others merely refer to me as imbecile. And so it goes, Kelly, — so it goes."

He flourished his mahl-stick, neatly punctured the air, and cried "Hah!" very fiercely.

Then he said:

"I've concluded to let Hélène know about it this afternoon."

"About what? — you monkey?"

"About our marriage. *Won't* it surprise her though! Oh, no! But I think I'll let her into the secret before some suspicious gink gets wind of it and tells her himself."

Neville looked at the boy, perplexed, undecided, until he caught his eye. And over Sam's countenance stole a vivid and beauteous blush.

"Sam! I — upon my word I believe you mean it!"

"Sure I do!"

Neville grasped his hand:

"My dear fellow!" he said cordially, "I was slow, not unsympathetic. I'm frightfully glad — I'm perfectly delighted. She's a charming and sincere woman. Go in and win and God bless you both!"

Ogilvy wrung his hand, then, to relieve his feelings, ran all over the floor like a spider and was pretending to spin a huge web in a corner when Harry Annan and Rita Tevis came in and discovered him.

"Hah!" he exclaimed, "flies! Two nice, silly, appetizing flies. Pretend to fall into my web, Rita, and begin to buzz like mad!"

Rita's dainty nose went up into the air, but Annan succumbed to the alluring suggestion, and presently he was buzzing frantically in a corner while Sam spun an imaginary web all over him.

Rita and Neville looked on for a while.

"Sam never will grow up," she said disdainfully.

"He's fortunate," observed Neville.

"*You* don't think so."

"I wish I knew what I did think, Rita. How is John?"

"I came to tell you. He has gone to Dartford."

"To see Dr. Ogilvy? Good! I'm glad, Rita. Billy Ogilvy usually makes people do what he tells them to do."

The girl stood silent, eyes lowered. After a while she looked up at him; and in her unfaltering but sorrowful gaze he read the tragedy which he had long since suspected.

Neither spoke for a moment; he held out both hands; she laid hers in them, and her gaze became remote.

After a while she said in a low voice:

"Let me be with you now and then while he's away; will you, Kelly?"

"Yes. Would you like to pose for me? I haven't anything pressing on hand. You might begin now if it suits you."

"May I?" she asked gratefully.

"Of course, child. . . . Let me think —" He looked again into her dark blue eyes, absently, then suddenly his attention became riveted upon something which he seemed to be reading in her face.

Long before Sam and Harry had ended their puppylike scuffling and had retired to woo their respective deputy-muses, Rita was seated on the model-stand, and Neville had already begun that strange and somber picture afterward so famous, and about which one of the finest of our modern poets wrote:

"Her gold hair, fallen about her face
　Made light within that shadowy place,
　　But on her garments lay the dust
　Of many a vanished race.

"Her deep eyes, gazing straight ahead,
　Saw years and days and hours long dead,
　　While strange gems glittered at her feet,
　Yellow, and green, and red.

"And ever from the shadows came
　Voices to pierce her heart like flame,
　　The great bats fanned her with their wings,
　The voices called her name.

"But yet her look turned not aside
　From the black deep where dreams abide,
　　Where worlds and pageantries lay dead
　Beneath that viewless tide.

"Her elbow on her knee was set,
　Her strong hand propped her chin, and yet
　　No man might name that look she wore,
　Nor any man forget."

All day long in the pleasant June weather they worked together over the picture; and if he really knew what he was about, it is uncertain, for his thoughts were of Valerie; and he painted as in a dream, and with a shadowy splendor that seemed even to him unreal.

They scarcely spoke; now and then Rita came silently on sandaled feet to stand behind him and look at what he had done.

The first time she thought to herself, "Querida!" But the second time she remained mute; and when the daylight was waning to a golden gloom in the room she came a third time and stood with one hand on his arm, her eyes fixed upon the dawning mystery on the canvas — spellbound under the somber magnificence already vaguely shadowed forth from infinite depth of shade.

Gladys came and rubbed and purred around his legs; the most recent progeny toddled after her, ratty tails erect; sportive, casual little optimists frisking unsteadily on wavering legs among the fading sunbeams on the floor.

The sunbeams died out on wall and ceiling; high through the glass roof above, a shoal of rosy clouds paled to saffron, then to a cinder grey. And the first night-hawk, like a huge, erratic swallow, sailed into view, soaring, tumbling aloft, while its short raucous cry sounded incessantly above the roofs and chimneys.

Neville was still seated before his canvas, palette flat across his left arm, the sheaf of wet brushes held loosely.

"I suppose you are dining with Valerie," he said.

"No."

He turned and looked at her, inquiringly.

"Valerie has gone away."

"Where?"

"I don't know, Kelly. . . . I was not to know."

"I see." He picked up a handful of waste and slowly began to clean the brushes, one by one. Then he drove them deep into a bowl of black soap.

"Shall we dine together here, Rita?"

"If you care to have me."

"Yes, I do."

He laid aside his palette, rang up the kitchen, gave his order, and slowly returned to where Rita was seated.

Dinner was rather a silent affair. They touched briefly and formally on Querida and his ripening talent prematurely annihilated; they spoke of men they knew who were to come after him — a long, long way after him.

"I don't know who is to take his place," mused Neville over his claret.

"You."

"Not his place, Rita. He thought so; but that place must remain his."

"Perhaps. But you are carving out your own niche in a higher tier. You are already beginning to do it; and yesterday his niche was the higher. . . . Yet, after all — after all —"

He nodded. "Yes," he said, "what does it matter to him, now? A man carves out his resting place as you say, but he carves it out in vain. Those who come after him will either place him in his proper sepulcher . . . or utterly neglect him. . . . And neglect or transfer will cause him neither happiness nor pain. . . . Both are ended for Querida; — let men exalt him above all, or bury him and his work out of sight — what does he care about it now? He has had all that life held for him, and what another life may promise him no man can know. All reward for labor is here, Rita; and the reward lasts only while the pleasure in labor lasts. Creative work — even if well done — loses its savor when it is finished. Happiness in it ends with the final touch. It is like a dead thing to him who created it; men's praise or blame makes little impression; and the aftertaste of both is either bitter or flat and lasts but a moment."

"Are you a little morbid, Kelly?"

"Am I?"

"It seems to me so."

"And you, Rita?"

She shook her pretty head in silence.

After a while Gladys jumped up into her lap, and she lay back in her armchair smoothing the creature's fur, and gazing absently into space.

"Kelly," she said, "how many, many years ago it seems when you came up to Delaware County to see us."

"It seems very long ago to me, too."

She lifted her blue eyes:

"May I speak plainly? I have known you a long while. There is only one man I like better. But there is no woman in the world whom I love as I love Valerie West. . . . May I speak plainly?"

"Yes."

"Then — be fair to her, Kelly. Will you?"

"I will try."

"Try very hard. For after all it *is* a man's world, and she doesn't understand it. Try to be fair to her, Kelly. For — whether or not the laws that govern the world are man-made and unjust — they are, nevertheless, the only laws. Few men can successfully fight them; no woman can — yet. . . . I am not angering you, am I?"

"No. Go on."

"I have so little to say — I who feel so deeply — deeply. . . . And the laws are always there, Kelly, always there — fair or unfair, just or unjust — they are always there to govern the world that framed them. And a woman disobeys them at her peril."

She moved slightly in her chair and sat supporting her head on one pretty ringless hand.

"Yet," she said, "although a woman disobeys any law at her peril — laws which a man may often ignore with impunity — there is one law to which no woman should dare subscribe. And it is sometimes known as 'The Common Law of Marriage.'"

She sat silent for a while, her gaze never leaving his shadowy face.

"That is the only law — if it is truly a law — that a woman must ignore. All others it is best for her to observe. And if the laws of marriage are merely man-made or divine, I do not know. There is a din in the world today which drowns the voices preaching old beliefs. . . . And a girl is deafened by the clamor. . . . And I don't know.

"But, it seems to me, that back of the laws men have made — if there be nothing divine in their inspiration — there is another foundation solid enough to carry them. Because it seems to me that the world's laws — even when unjust — are built on natural laws. And how can a girl say that these natural laws are unjust because they have fashioned her to bear children and feed them from her own body?

"And another thing, Kelly; if a man breaks a man-made law — founded, we believe, on a divine commandment — he suffers only in a spiritual and moral sense. . . . And with us it may be more than that. For women, at least, hell is on earth."

He stirred in his chair, and his somber gaze rested on the floor at her feet.

"What are we to do?" he said dully.

Rita shook her head:

"I don't know. I am not instructing you, Kelly, only recalling to your mind what you already know; what all men know, and find so convenient to forget. Love is not excuse enough; the peril is unequally divided. The chances are uneven; the odds are unfair. If a man really loves a woman, how can he hazard her in a game of chance that is not square? How can he let her offer more than he has at stake — even if she is willing? How can he permit her to risk more than he is even able to risk? How can he accept a magnanimity which leaves him her hopeless debtor? But men have done it, men will continue to do it; God alone knows how they reconcile it with their manhood or find it in their hearts to deal so unfairly by us. But they do. . . . And still we stake all; and proudly overlook the chances against us; and face the contemptible odds with a smile, dauntless and — damned!"

He leaned forward in the dusk; she could see his bloodless features now only as a pale blot in the twilight.

"All this I knew, Rita. But it is just as well, perhaps, that you remind me."

"I thought it might be as well. The world has grown very clever; but after all there is no steadier anchor for a soul than a platitude."

Ogilvy and Annan came mincing in about nine o'clock, disposed for flippancy and gossip; but neither Neville nor Rita encouraged them; so after a while they took their unimpaired cheerfulness and horse-play elsewhere, leaving the two occupants of the studio to their own silent devices.

It was nearly midnight when he walked back with Rita to her rooms.

And now day followed day in a sequence of limpid dawns and cloudless sunsets. Summer began with a clear, hot week in June, followed by three days' steady downpour which freshened and cooled the city and unfolded, in square and park, everything green into magnificent maturity.

Every day Neville and Rita worked together in the studio; and every evening they walked together in the park or sat in the cool, dusky studio, companionably conversational or permitting silence to act as their interpreter.

Then John Burleson came back from Dartford after remaining there ten days under Dr. Ogilvy's observation; and Rita arrived at the studio next day almost smiling.

"We're' going to Arizona," she said. "*What* do you think of that, Kelly?"

"You poor child!" exclaimed Neville, taking her hands into his and holding them closely.

"Why, Kelly," she said gently, "I knew he had to go. This has not taken me unawares."

"I hoped there might be some doubt," he said.

"There was none in my mind. I foresaw it. Listen to me: twice in a woman's life a woman becomes a prophetess. That fatal clairvoyance is permitted to a woman twice in her life — and the second time it is neither for herself that she foresees the future, nor for him whom she loves. . . ."

"I wish — I wish —" he hesitated; and she flushed brightly.

"I know what you wish, Kelly dear. I don't think it will ever happen. But it is so much for me to be permitted to remain near him — so much! — Ah, you don't know, Kelly! You don't know!"

"Would you marry him?"

Her honest blue eyes met his:

"If he asked me; and if he still wished it — after he knew."

"Could you ever be less to him — and perhaps more, Rita?"

"Do you mean —"

He nodded deliberately.

She hung her head.

"Yes," she said, "if I could be no more I would be what I could."

"And you tell *me* that, after all that you have said?"

"I did not pretend to speak for men, Kelly. I told you that women had, and women still would overlook the chances menacing them and face the odds dauntlessly. . . . Because, whatever a man is — if a woman loves him enough — he is worth to her what she gives."

"Rita! Rita! Is it *you* who content yourself with such sorry philosophy?"

"Yes, it is I. You asked me and I answer you. Whatever I said — I know only one thing now. And you know what that is."

"And where am I to look for sympathy and support in my own decision? What can I think now about all that you have said to me?"

"You will never forget it, Kelly — whatever becomes of the girl who said it. Because it's the truth, no matter whose lips uttered it."

He released her hands and she went away to dress herself for the pose. When she returned and seated herself he picked up his palette and brushes and began in silence.

*T*hat evening he went to see John Buries on and found him smoking tranquilly in the midst of disorder. Packing cases, trunks, bundles, boxes were scattered and piled up in every direction, and the master of the establishment, apparently in excellent health, reclined on a lounge in the center of chaos, the long clay stem of a church-warden pipe between his lips, puffing rings at the ceiling.

"Hello, Kelly!" he exclaimed, sitting up; "I've got to move out of this place. Rita told you all about it, didn't she? Isn't it rotten hard luck?"

"Not a bit of it. What did Billy Ogilvy say?"

"Oh, I've got *it* all right. Not seriously yet. What's Arizona like, anyway?"

"Half hell, half paradise, they say."

"Then me for the celestial section. Ogilvy gave me the name of a place" — he fumbled about — "Rita has it, I believe. . . . Isn't she a corker to go? My conscience, Kelly, what a Godsend it will be to have a Massachusetts girl out there to talk to!"

"Isn't she going as your model?"

"My Lord, man! Don't you talk to a model? Is a nice girl who poses for a fellow anything extra-human or superhuman or — or unhuman or inhuman — so that intelligent conversation becomes impossible?"

"No," began Neville, laughing, but Burleson interrupted excitedly:

"A girl can be anything she chooses if she's all right, can't she? And Rita comes from Massachusetts, doesn't she?"

"Certainly."

"Not only from Massachusetts, but from Hitherford!" added Burleson triumphantly. "I came from Hitherford. My grandfather knew hers. Why, man alive, Rita Tevis is entitled to do anything she chooses to do."

"That's one way of looking at it, anyway," admitted Neville gravely.

"I look at it that way. *You* can't; you're not from Massachusetts; but you have a sort of a New England name, too. It's Yankee, isn't it?"

"Southern."

"Oh," said Burleson, honestly depressed; "I *am* sorry. There were Nevilles in Hitherford Lower Falls two hundred years ago. I've always liked to think of you as originating, somehow or other, in Massachusetts Bay."

"No, John: unlike McGinty, I am unfamiliar with the cod-thronged ocean deeps. . . . When are you going?"

"Day after tomorrow. Rita says you don't need her any longer on that picture —"

"Lord, man! If I did I wouldn't hold you up. But don't worry, John; she wouldn't let me. . . . She's a fine specimen of girl," he added casually.

"Do you suppose that is news to me?"

"Oh, no; I'm sure you find her amusing —"

"What!"

"Amusing," repeated Neville innocently. "Don't you?"

"That is scarcely the word I would have chosen, Kelly. I have a very warm admiration and a very sincere respect for Rita Tevis —"

"John! You sound like a Puritan making love!"

Burleson was intensely annoyed:

"You'd better understand, Kelly, that Rita Tevis is as well born as I am, and that there would be nothing at all incongruous in any declaration that any decent man might make her!"

"Why, I know that."

"I'm glad you do. And I'm gratified that what you said has given me the opportunity to make myself very plain on the subject of Rita Tevis. It may amaze you to know that her great grandsire carried a flintlock with the Hitherford Minute Men, and fell most respectably at Boston Neck."

"Certainly, John. I knew she was all right. But I wasn't sure you knew it —"

"Confound it! Of course I did. I've always known it. Do you think I'd care for her so much if she wasn't all right?"

Neville smiled at him gravely, then held out his hand:

"Give my love to her, John. I'll see you both again before you go."

For nearly two weeks he had not heard a word from Valerie West. Rita and John Burleson had departed, cheerful, sure of early convalescence and a complete and radical cure.

Neville went with them to the train, but his mind was full of his own troubles and he could scarcely keep his attention on the ponderous conversation of Burleson, who was admonishing him and Ogilvy impartially concerning the true interpretation of creative art.

He turned aside to Rita when opportunity offered and said in a low voice:

"Before you go, tell me where Valerie is."

"I can't, Kelly."

"Did you promise her not to?"

"Yes."

He said, slowly: "I haven't had one word from her in nearly two weeks. Is she well?"

"Yes. She came into town this morning to say good-bye to me."

"I didn't know she was out of town," he said, troubled.

"She has been, and is now. That's all I can tell you, Kelly dear."

"She *is* coming back, isn't she?"

"I hope so."

"Don't you know?"

She looked into his anxious and miserable face and gently shook her head:

"I *don't* know, Kelly."

"Didn't she say — intimate anything —"

"No. . . . I don't think she knows — yet."

He said, very quietly: "If she ever comes to any conclusion that it is better for us both never to meet again — I might be as dead as Querida for any work I should ever again set hand to.

"If she will not marry me, but will let things remain as they are, at least I can go on caring for her and working out this miserable problem of life. But if she goes out of my life, life will go out of me. I know that now."

Rita looked at him pitifully:

"Valerie's mind is her own, Kelly. It is the most honest mind I have ever known; and nothing on earth — no pain that her decision might inflict upon her — would swerve it a hair's breath from what she concludes is the right thing to do."

"I know it," he said, swallowing a sudden throb of fear.

"Then what can I say to you?"

"Nothing. I must wait."

"Kelly, if you loved her enough you would not even wait."

"What!"

"Because her return to you will mean only one thing. Are you going to accept it of her?"

"What can I do? I can't live without her!"

"*Her* problem is nobler, Kelly. She is asking herself not whether she can live life through without *you* — but whether you can live life well, and to the full, without *her*?"

Neville flushed painfully.

"Yes," he said, "*that is* Valerie. I'm not worth the anxiety, the sorrow that I have brought her. I'm not worth marrying; and I'm not worth a heavier sacrifice. . . . I'm trying to think less of myself, Rita, and more of her. . . . Perhaps, if I knew she were happy, I could stand — losing her. . . . If she could be — without me —" He checked himself, for the struggle was unnerving him; then he set his face firmly and looked straight at Rita.

"Do you believe she could forget me and be contented and tranquil — if I gave her the chance?"

"Are *you* talking of self-sacrifice for *her* sake?"

He drew a deep, uneven breath:

"I — suppose it's — that."

"You mean that you're willing to eliminate yourself and give her an opportunity to see a little of the world — a little of its order and tranquility and quieter happiness? — a chance to meet interesting women and attractive men of her own age — as she is certain to do through her intimacy with the Countess d'Enver?"

"Yes," he said, "that is what must be done. . . . I've been blind — and rottenly selfish. I did not mean to be. . . . I've tried to force her — I have done nothing else since I fell in love with her, but force her toward people whom she has a perfect right not to care for — even if they happen to be my own people. She has felt nothing but a steady and stupid pressure from me; — heard from me nothing except importunities — the merciless, obstinate urging of my own views — which, God forgive me, I thought were the only views because they were respectable!"

He stood, head lowered, nervously clenching and unclenching his hands.

"It was not for her own sake — that's the worst of it! It was for my sake — because I've had respectability inculcated until I can't conceive of my doing anything not respectable. . . . Once, something else got away with me — and I gave it rein for a moment — until checked. . . . I'm really no different from other men."

"I think you are beginning to be, Kelly."

"Am I? I don't know. But the worst of it was my selfishness — my fixed idea that her marrying me was the *only* salvation for her. . . . I never thought of giving her a chance of seeing other people — other men — better men — of seeing a tranquil, well-ordered world — of being in it and of it. I behaved as though my world — the fragment inhabited by my friends and family — was the only alternative to this one. I've been a fool, Rita; and a cruel one."

"No, only an average man, Kelly. . . . If I give you Valerie's address, would you write and give her her freedom — for her own sake? — the freedom to try life in that well-ordered world we speak of. . . ? Because she is very young. Life is all before her. Who can foretell what friends she may be destined to make; what opportunities she may have. I care a great deal for you, Kelly; but I love Valerie. . . . And, there *are* other men

in the world after all; — but there is only one Valerie. . . . And
— *how truly do you love her?*"

"Enough," he said under his breath.

"Enough to — leave her alone?"

"Yes."

"Then write and tell her so. Here is the address."

She slipped a small bit of folded paper into Neville's land.

"We must join the others, now," she said calmly.

Annan had come up, and he and Ogilvy were noisily
baiting Burleson amid shouts of laughter and a protesting
roar from John.

"Stop it, you wretches," said Rita amiably, entering the
little group. "John, are you never going to earn not to pay
any attention to this pair of infants?"

"Are you going to kiss me good-bye, Rita, when the train
departs?" inquired Sam, anxiously.

"Certainly; I kissed Gladys good-bye —"

"Before all this waiting room full of people?" persisted
Sam. *"Are* you?"

"Why I'll do it now if you like, Sammy dear."

"They'll take you for my sister," said Sam, disgusted.

"Or your nurse; John, what *is* that man bellowing through
the megaphone?"

"Our train," said Burleson, picking up the satchels. He
dropped them again to shake the hands that were offered:

"Good-bye, John, dear old fellow! You'll get all over this
thing in a jiffy out there You'll be back in no time at all! Don't
worry, and get well!"

He smiled confidently and shook all their hands Rita's
pretty face was pale; she let Ogilvy kiss her cheek, shook hands
with Annan, and then, turning to Neville, put both hands
on his shoulders and kissed him on the mouth.

"Give her her chance, Kelly," she whispered . . . "And it
shall be rendered unto you seven-fold."

"No, Rita; it never will be now."

"Who knows?"

"Rita! Rita!" he said under his breath, "when I am ending,
she must begin. . . . You are right: this world needs her. Try
as I might, I never could be worth what she is worth without
effort. It is my life which does not matter, not hers. I will do

what ought to be done. Don't be afraid. I will do it. And thank God that it is not too late."

That night, seated at his desk in the studio, he looked at the calendar. It was the thirteenth day since he had heard from her; the last day but two of the fifteen days she had asked for. The day after tomorrow she would have come, or would have written him that she was renouncing him forever for his own sake. Which might it have been? He would never know now.

He wrote her:

"Dearest of women, Rita has been loyal to you. It was only when I explained to her for what purpose I wished your address that she wisely gave it to me.

"Dearest, from the beginning of our acquaintance and afterward when it ripened into friendship and finally became love, upon you has rested the burden of decision; and I have permitted it.

"Even now, as I am writing here in the studio, the burden lies heavily upon your girl's shoulders and is weighting your girl's heart. And it must not be so any longer.

"I have never, perhaps, really meant to be selfish; a man in love really doesn't know what he means. But now I know what I have done; and what must be undone.

"You were perfectly right. It was for you to say whether you would marry me or not. It was for you to decide whether it was possible or impossible for you to appear as my wife in a world in which you had had no experience. It was for you to generously decide whether a rupture between that world and myself — between my family and myself — would render me — and yourself — eternally unhappy.

"You were free to decide; you used your own intellect, and you so decided. And I had no right to question you — I have no right now. I shall never question you again.

"Then, because you loved me, and because it was the kind of love that ignored self, you offered me a supreme sacrifice. And I did not refuse; I merely continued to fight for what I thought ought to be — distressing, confusing, paining you with the stupid, obstinate reiterations of my importunities. And you stood fast by your colors.

"Dear, I *was* wrong. And so were you. Those were not the only alternatives. I allowed them to appear so because of selfishness. . . . Alas, Valerie, in spite of all I have protested and professed of love and passion for you, today, for the first time, have I really loved you enough to consider you, alone. And with God's help I will do so always.

"You have offered me two alternatives: to give yourself and your life to me without marriage; or to quietly slip out of my life forever.

"And it never occurred to you — and I say, with shame, that it never occurred to me — that I might quietly efface myself and my demands from *your* life: leave you free and at peace to rest and develop in that new and quieter world which your beauty and goodness has opened to you.

"Desirable people have met you more than half-way, and they like you. Your little friend, Hélène d'Enver is a genuine and charming woman. Your friendship for her will mean all that you have so far missed in life all that a girl is entitled to.

"Through her you will widen the circle of your acquaintances and form newer and better friendships You will meet men and women of your own age and your own tastes which is what ought to happen.

"And it is right and just and fair that you enter into the beginning of your future with a mind unvexed and a heart untroubled by conflicts which can never solve for you and me any future life together.

"I do not believe you will ever forget me, or wish to, wholly. Time heals — otherwise the world had gone mad some centuries ago.

"But whatever destiny is reserved for you, I know you will meet it with the tranquility and the sweet courage which you have always shown.

"What kind of future I wish for you, I need not write here. You know. And it is for the sake of that future —

for the sake of the girl whose unselfish life has at last taught me and shamed me, that I give you up forever.

"Dear, perhaps you had better not answer this for a long, long time. Then, when that clever surgeon, Time, has effaced all scars — and when not only tranquility is yours but, perhaps, a deeper happiness is in sight, write and tell me so. And the great god Kelly, nodding before his easel, will rouse up from his Olympian reverie and totter away to find a sheaf of blessings to bestow upon the finest, truest, and loveliest girl in all the world.

"*Halcyonii dies! Fortem posce animum! Forsan et haec olim meminisse juvabit. Vale!*

"Louis Neville"

Chapter XVII

*T*he fifteenth day of her absence had come and gone and there had been no word from her.

Whether or not he had permitted himself to expect any, the suspense had been nonetheless almost unendurable. He walked the floor of the studio all day long, scarcely knowing what he was about, insensible to fatigue or to anything except the dull, ceaseless beating of his heart. He seemed older, thinner: — a man whose sands were running very swiftly.

With the dawn of the fifteenth day of her absence a grey pallor had come into his face; and it remained there. Ogilvy and Annan sauntered into the studio to visit him, twice, and the second time they arrived bearing gifts — favorite tonics, prescriptions, and pills.

"You look like hell, Kelly," observed Sam with tactful and characteristic frankness. "Try a few of this assorted dope. Harry and I dote on dope:

"*'After the bat is over,*
    After the last cent's spent,
And the pigs have gone from the clover
    And the very last gent has went;
After the cards are scattered,
    After I've paid the bill,
Weary and rocky and battered
    I swallow my liver pill!'"

— he sang, waltzing slowly around the room with Annan until, inadvertently, they stepped upon the tail of Gladys who went off like a pack of wet fire-crackers; whereupon they retired in confusion to their respective abodes above.

Evening came, and with evening, letters; but none from her. And slowly the stealthy twilight hours dragged their heavy minutes toward darkness; and night crawled into the room like some sinister living thing, and found him still pacing the floor.

Through the dusky June silence far below in the street sounded the clatter of wheels; but they never stopped before his abode. Voices rose faintly at moments in the still air, borne upward as from infinite depths; but her voice would never sound again for him: he knew it now — never again for him. And yet he paced the floor, listening. The pain in his heart grew duller at intervals, benumbed by the tension; but it always returned, sickening him, almost crazing him.

Late in the evening he gave way under the torture — turned coward, and started to write to her. Twice he began letters — pleading with her to forget his letter; begging her to come back. And destroyed them with hands that shook like the hands of a sick man. Then the dull insensibility to pain gave him a little respite, but later the misery and terror of it drove him out into the street with an insane idea of seeking her — of taking the train and finding her.

He throttled that impulse; the struggle exhausted him; and he returned, listlessly, to the door and stood there, vacant-eyed, staring into the lamp-lit street.

Once he caught sight of a shadowy, graceful figure crossing the avenue — a lithe young silhouette against the gas-light — and his heart stood still for an instant but it was not she, and he swayed where he stood, under the agony of reaction, dazed by the rushing recession of emotion.

Then a sudden fear seized him that she might have come while he had been away. He had been as far as the avenue. Could she have come?

But when he arrived at his door he had scarce courage enough to go in. She had a key; she might have entered. Had she entered: was she there, behind the closed door? To go in and find the studio empty seemed almost more than he could endure. But, at last, he went in; and he found the studio empty.

Confused, shaken, tortured, he began again his aimless tour of the place, ranging the four walls like a wild creature dulled to insanity by long imprisonment — passing backward, forward, to and fro, across, around his footsteps timing the dreadful monotone of his heart, his pulse beating, thudding out his doom.

She would never come; never come again. She had determined what was best to do; she had arrived at her decision. Perhaps his letter had convinced her, — had cleared her vision; — the letter which he had been man enough to write — fool enough — God! — perhaps brave enough. . . . But if what he had done in his madness was bravery, it was an accursed thing; and he set his teeth and cursed himself scarce knowing what he was saying.

It promised to be an endless night for him; and there were other nights to come — interminable nights. And now he began to watch the clock — strained eyes riveted on the stiff gilded hands — and on the little one jerkily, pitilessly recording the seconds and twitching them one by one into eternity.

Nearer and nearer to midnight crept the gilded, flamboyant hour-hand; the gaunter minute-hand was slowly but inexorably overtaking it. Nearer, nearer, they drew together; then came the ominous click; a moment's suspense; the high-keyed gong quivered twelve times under the impact of the tiny steel hammer.

And he never would hear her voice again. And he dropped to his knees asking mercy on them both.

In his dulled ears still lingered the treble ringing echo of the bell — lingered, reiterated, repeated incessantly, until he thought he was going mad. Then, of a sudden, he realized that the telephone was ringing; and he reeled from his knees to his feet, and crept forward into the shadows, feeling his way like a blind man.

"Louis?"

But he could not utter a sound.

"Louis, is it you?"

"Yes," he whispered.

"What is the matter? Are you ill? Your voice is so strange. *Are* you?"

"No! — Is it *you*, Valerie?"

"You know it is!"

"Where — are you?"

"In my room — where I have been all day."

"You have been — *there!* You have been *here* — in the city — all this time —"

"I came in on the morning train. I wanted to be sure. There *have* been such things as railroad delays you know."

"Why — *why* didn't you let me know —"

"Louis! You will please to recollect that I had until midnight . . . I — was busy. Besides, midnight has just sounded — and here I am."

He waited.

"I received your letter." Her voice had the sweet, familiar, rising inflection which seemed to invite an answer.

"Yes," he muttered, "I wrote to you."

"Do you wish to know what I thought of your letter?"

"Yes," he breathed.

"I will tell you some other time; not now. . . . Have you been perfectly well, Louis? But I heard all about you, every day, — through Rita. Do you know I am quite mad to see that picture you painted of her, — the new one — 'Womanhood.' She says it is a great picture — really great. Is it?"

He did not answer.

"Louis!"

"Yes."

"I would like to see that picture."

"Valerie?"

"Yes?" — sweetly impatient.

"Are we to see each other again?"

She said calmly: "I didn't ask to see *you,* Louis: I asked to see a picture which you recently painted, called 'Womanhood.'"

He remained silent and presently she called him again by name: "You say that you are well — or rather Rita said so two days ago — and I'm wondering whether in the interim you've fallen ill? Two days without news from you is rather disquieting. Please tell me at once exactly how you are?"

He succeeded in forcing something resembling a laugh: "I am all right," he said.

"I don't see how you could be — after the letter you wrote me. How much of it did you mean?"

He was silent.

"Louis! Answer me!"

"All — of it," he managed to reply.

"*All!*"

"Yes."

"Then — perhaps you scarcely expected me to call up tonight. Did you?"

"No."

"Suppose I had not done so."

He shivered slightly, but remained mute.

"Answer me, Louis?"

"It would have been — better."

"For you?"

"For — both."

"Do you believe it?"

"Yes."

"Then — have I any choice except to say — good-night?"

"No choice. Good-night."

"Good-night."

He crept, shaking, into his bedroom, sat down, resting his hands on his knees and staring at vacancy.

Valerie, in her room, hung up the receiver, buried her face in her hands for a moment, then quietly turned, lowering her hands from her face, and looked down at the delicate, intimate garments spread in order on the counterpane beside her. There was a new summer gown there, too — a light, dainty, fragile affair on which she had worked while away. Beside it lay a big summer hat of white straw and white lilacs.

She stood for a moment, reflecting; then she knelt down beside the bed and covered her eyes again while she said whatever prayer she had in mind.

It was not a very short petition, because it concerned Neville. She asked nothing for herself except as it regarded him or might matter to his peace of mind. Otherwise what she said, asked, and offered, related wholly to Neville.

Presently she rose and went lightly and silently about her ablutions; and afterward she dressed herself in the fragile

snowy garments ranged so methodically upon the white counterpane, each in its proper place.

She was longer over her hair, letting it fall in a dark lustrous
cloud to her waist, then combing and gathering it and bringing it under discipline.

She put on her gown, managing somehow to fasten it, her
lithe young body and slender arms aiding her to achieve the
impossible between neck and shoulders. Afterward she
pinned on her big white hat.

At the door she paused for a second; took a last look at
the quiet, white little room tranquil and silent in the lamp-
light; then she turned off the light and went out, softly,
holding in her hands a key which fitted no door of her own.

One o'clock sounded heavily from Saint Hilda's as she left
her house; the half hour was striking as she stooped in the
dark hallway outside the studio and fitted the key she held —
the key that was to unlock for her the mystery of the world.

He had not heard her. She groped her way into the un-
lighted studio, touched with caressing fingertips the vague
familiar shapes that the starlight, falling through the glass
above, revealed to her as she passed.

In the little inner room she paused. There was a light
through the passageway beyond, but she stood here a moment, looking around her while memories of the place deepened the color in her cheeks.

Then she went forward, timidly, and stood at his closed
door, listening.

A sudden fright seized her; one hand flew to her breast,
her throat — covered her eyes for a moment — and fell limp
by her side.

"Louis!" she faltered. She heard him spring to his feet and
stand as though transfixed.

"Louis," she said, "it is I. Will you open your door to me?"

The sudden flood of electric light dazzled her; then she
saw him standing there, one hand still resting on the door
knob.

"I've come," she said, with a faint smile.

"Valerie! My God!"

She stood, half smiling, half fearful, her dark eyes meeting his, two friendly little hands outstretched. Then, as his own caught them, almost crushed them:

"Oh, it was *your* letter that ended all for me, Louis! It settled every doubt I had. I *knew* then — you darling!"

She bent and touched his hands with her lips, then lifted her sweet, untroubled gaze to his:

"I had been away from you so long, so long. And the time was approaching for me to decide, and I didn't know what was best for us, anymore than when I went away. And *then!* — your letter came!"

She shook her head, slowly:

"I don't know what I might have decided if you never had written that letter to me; probably I would have come back to you anyway. I think so; I can't think of my doing anything else: though I *might* have decided — against myself. But as soon as I read your letter I *knew*, Louis. . . . And I am here."

He said with drawn lips quivering:

"Did you read in that letter one single word of cowardly appeal? — one infamous word of self? If you did, I wrote in vain."

"It was because I read nothing in it of self that I made up my mind, Louis." She stepped nearer. "Why are you so dreadfully pale and worn? Your face is so haggard — so terrible —"

She laid one hand on his shoulder, looking up at him; then she smoothed his forehead and hair, lightly.

"As though I could ever live without you," she said under her breath. Then she laughed, releasing her hands, and went over to the dresser where there was a mirror.

"I have come, at one in the morning, to pay you a call," she said, withdrawing the long pins from her hat and taking it off. "Later I should like a cup of chocolate, please. . . . Oh, there is Gladys! You sweet thing!" she cried softly, kneeling to embrace the cat who came silently into the room, tail waving aloft in gentle greeting.

The girl lifted Gladys onto the bed and rolled her over into a fluffy ball and rubbed her cheeks and her ears until her furry toes curled, and her loud and grateful purring filled the room.

Valerie, seated sideways on the edge of the bed, looked up at Neville, laughing:

"I *must* tell you about Sam and Hélène," she said. "They are too funny! Hélène was furious because Sam wrote her a letter saying that he intended to marry her but had not the courage to notify her, personally, of his decision; and Hélène was wild, and wrote him that he might save himself further trouble in the matter. And they've been telephoning to each other at intervals all day, and Sam is so afraid of her that he dare not go to see her; and Hélène was in tears when I saw her — and I *think* it was because she was afraid Sam wouldn't come and resume the quarrel where she could manage it and him more satisfactorily."

She threw back her head and laughed at the recollection, stroking Gladys the while:

"It will come out all right, of course," she added, her eyes full of laughter; "she's been in love with Sam ever since he broke a Ming jar and almost died of fright. But isn't it funny, Louis? — the way people fall in love, and their various manners of informing each other!"

He was trying to smile, but the grey constraint in his face made it only an effort. Valerie pretended not to notice it, and she rattled on gaily, detailing her small budget of gossip and caressing Gladys — behaving as irresponsibly and as capriciously as though her heart were not singing a ceaseless hymn of happiness too deep, too thankful to utter by word or look.

"Dear little Rita," she exclaimed, suddenly and tenderly solemn — "I saw her the morning of the day she departed with John. And first of all I asked about you of course — you spoiled thing! — and then I asked about John. And we put our arms around each other and had a good, old-fashioned cry. . . . But — *don't* you think he is going to get well, Louis?"

"Sam's brother — Billy Ogilvy — wrote me that he would always have to live in Arizona. He *can* live there. But the East would be death to him."

"Can't he ever come back?" she asked pitifully.

"No, dear."

"But — but what will Rita do?"

He said: "I think that will depend on Rita. I think it depends on her already."

"Why?" she asked, wide-eyed. "Do you believe that John cares for her?"

"I know he does. . . . And I haven't much doubt that he wants to marry her."

"Do you think so? Oh, Louis — if that is true, what a heavenly future for Rita!"

"Heavenly? Out in that scorching desert?"

"Do you think she'd care *where* she was? Kelly, you're ridiculous!"

"Do you believe that any woman could stand that for the rest of her life, Valerie?"

She smiled, head lowered, fondling the cat who had gone ecstatically to sleep.

She said, still smiling: "If a girl is loved she endures some things; if she loves she endures more. But to a girl who is loved, and who loves, nothing else matters . . . And it would be that way with Rita" — she lifted her eyes — "as it is with me."

He was standing beside her now; she made room on the side of the bed for him with a little gesture of invitation:

"People who die for each other are less admirable than people who live for each other. The latter requires the higher type of courage . . . If I go out of your life I am like a dead person to you — a little worse in fact. Besides, I've shown the white feather and run away. That's a cowardly solution of a problem, isn't it?"

"Am I a coward if I decide to stand back and give you a chance?"

"You haven't decided to do it," she said cheerfully, lifting the somnolent cat and hugging it.

"I'm afraid I have, dear."

"Why?"

"You read my letter?"

"Yes and kissed every line in it."

He retained sufficient self-control to keep his hands off her — but that was all; and her eyes, which were looking into his, grew serious and beautiful.

"I love you so," she breathed.

"I love you, Valerie."

"Yes. . . . I know it. . . . I know you do. . . ." She sat musing a moment, then: "And I thought that I knew what it was to love, before you wrote that letter." She shook her head, murmuring something to herself. Then the swift smile curved her lips again, she dumped Gladys out of her lap without ceremony, and leaned her shoulder on Neville's, resting her cheek lightly against his:

"It doesn't seem possible that the problem of life has really been solved for us, Louis. I can scarcely realize it — scarcely understand what this heavenly relief means — this utterly blissful relaxation and untroubled confidence. There isn't anything in the world that can harm me, now; is there?"

"Nothing."

"Nor my soul?"

"It has always been beyond danger."

"There are those who might tell me differently."

"Let them talk. I *know*."

"Do you? — you darling!" Her soft, fragrant mouth touched his cheek, lingered, then she laughed to herself for the very happiness of living.

"Isn't it wonderful how a word sometimes shatters the fixed ideas that a girl has arrived at through prayer and fasting? I am beginning to think that no real intelligence can remain very long welded to anyone fixed belief."

"What do you mean, Valerie?" She rested her head on his shoulder and sat considering, eyes remote; then her white fingers crept into his:

"We won't talk about it now. I was wrong in some ways. You or common sense — or something — opened my eyes. . . . But we won't talk about it now. . . . Because there are still perplexities — some few. . . . We'll go over them together — and arrange matters — somehow."

"What matters?"

But she placed a soft hand over his lips, imposing silence, and drew his arm around her with a little sigh of content.

Presently she said: "Have you noticed my gown? I made it."

He smiled and bent forward to look.

"I made *everything* that I am wearing — except the shoes and stockings. But they are perfectly new. . . . I wanted to come to you — perfectly new. There was a Valerie who didn't really love you. She thought she did, but she didn't. . . . So I left her behind when I came — left everything about her behind me. I am all new, Louis. . . . Are you afraid to love me?"

He drew her closer; she turned, partly, and put both arms around his neck, and their lips touched and clung.

Then, a little pale, she drew away from him, a vague smile tremulous on her lips. The confused sweetness of her eyes held him breathless with their enchantment; the faint fragrance of her dazed him.

In silence she bent her head, remained curbed, motionless for a few moments, then slowly lifted her eyes to his.

"How much do you want me, Louis?"

"You know."

"Enough to — give me up?"

His lips stiffened and refused at first, then:

"Yes," they motioned. And she saw the word they formed.

"I knew it," she breathed; "I only wanted to hear you say it again. . . . I don't know why I'm crying; — do you. . . ? What a perfect ninny a girl can be when she tries to. . . . *All* over your 'collar, too. . . . And now you're what Mr. Mantalini would call 'demned moist and unpleasant!' . . . I — I don't want to — s-sob — this way! I do-don't wish to . . . M-make me stop, Louis. . . ! I'd like a handkerchief — anything — give me Gladys and I'll staunch my tears on her!"

She slipped from the bed's edge to the floor, and stood with her back toward him. Then she glanced sideways at the mirror to inspect her nose.

"Thank goodness *that* isn't red," she said gaily. . . . "Kelly, I'm hungry. . . . I've fasted since dawn — on this day — because I wanted to break bread with you on the first day of our new life together."

He looked at her, appalled, but she laughed and went into the studio. There was a beautiful old sideboard there always well stocked.

He turned on the lights, brought peaches and melons and strawberries and milk from the ice-chest, and found her already preparing chocolate over the electric grill and buttering immense slices of peasant bread.

"It's after two o'clock," she said, delighted. "Isn't this divinely silly? I wonder if there happens to be any salad in the ice-chest?"

"Cold chicken, too," he nodded, watching her set the table.

She glanced at him over her shoulder from time to time:

"Louis, are you going to enjoy all this? *All of* it? You — somehow — don't look entirely happy —"

"I am. . . . All I wanted was to see you — hear your voice. . . . I shall be contented now."

"With just a view of me, and the sound of my voice?"

"You know there is — nothing more for us."

"I know nothing of the kind. The idea! And don't you dare struggle and kick and scream when I kiss you. Do you hear me, Louis?"

He laughed and watched her as she went swiftly and gracefully about the table arrangement, glancing up at him from moment to moment.

"The idea," she repeated, indignantly. "I guess I'll kiss you when I choose to. You are not in holy orders, are you? You haven't made any particular vows, have you — ?"

"One."

She halted, looked at him, then went on with her labors, a delicate color flushing face and neck.

"Where in the world is that salad, Louis? A hungry girl asks you! Don't drive me to desperation —"

"Are we going to have coffee?"

"No, it will keep us awake all night! I believe you *are* bent on my destruction." And, as she hovered over the table, she hummed the latest popular summer-roof ballad:

"'Stand back! Go 'way!
  I can no longer stay
    Although you are a Marquis or a Earl!
You may tempt the upper classes
With your villainous demitasses
But —
    Heaven will protect the Working Girl!'"

At length everything was ready. He had placed two chairs opposite one another, but she wouldn't have it, and made him lug up a bench, lay a cushion on it, and sit beside her.

They behaved foolishly; she fed him strawberries at intervals, discreetly, on a fork — and otherwise.

"Think of it! Fruit — at three in the morning, Louis! I hope Heaven will protect *this* working girl. . . . No, dear, I'd rather not have any champagne. . . . You forget that this is a brand-new girl you're supping with . . . And, for reasons of her own — perhaps as an example to you — there is never again to be anything like that — not even a cigarette."

"Nonsense —"

"Oh, it's on account of my voice, not my morals, goose! I have rather a nice voice you know, and, if we can afford it, it would be a jolly good idea to have it cultivated . . . Isn't this melon divine! What fun, Louis. . . ! I believe you *are* a little happier. That crease between your eyes has quite disappeared — There! Don't dare let it come back! It has no business there I tell you. I *know* it hasn't — and you must trust my word. Will you?"

She leaned swiftly toward him, placed both hands on his shoulders.

"You've a perfectly new girl to deal with," she said, looking him in the eyes; — "a miracle of meekness and patience that is rather certain to turn into a dreadful, frowsy old hausfrau some day. But that's the kind you wanted. . . . It's none of my doings —"

"Valerie!"

"What?"

"You darling! — do you mean —"

She closed his lips with hers.

"Silence," she said; "we have plenty to talk over before the hour arrives for me to be a door-mat. I *won't* be a door-mat when I'm trying to be happy over a perfectly good supper. . . ! Besides I want to torture you while there's still time. I want to make you miserable by reminding you how disgracefully unmoral we are, here in your studio together at three in the morning —" She stretched out a slim, white ringless hand, and lifted the third finger for his inspection:

"Not a sign of a ring! Shame!" She turned her pretty, daring face to his, eyes sparkling with audacity:

"Besides, I'm not going back tonight."

He said tranquilly: "I should think not."

"I mean it, Kelly, I simply won't go. And you may ring up the police and every ambulance in town — and the fire department —"

"I've done it," he said, "but the fire department refuses to put you out. . . . You don't mean to say you've finished! — after fasting all day like a little idiot," he exclaimed as she sprang to her feet and pushed away her chair.

"I have. I am *not* an anaconda!" . . . She passed swiftly into the outer room where her own toilet necessaries were always ready, and presently came back, leisurely, her hands behind her back, sauntering toward, him with a provoking smile edging her lips:

"You may retire when you like, Kelly, and tie your red cotton nightcap under your chin. *I* shall sit up for the sun. It's due in about an hour, you know."

"Nonsense," he said. "We'll both, be dead in the morning."

"You offer me your guest-room?" she said in pretence of surprise. "How *very* nice of you, Mr. Neville. I — ah — will condescend to occupy it — for this evening only —" Her eyes brightened into laughter: "Oh, isn't it delicious, Louis! Isn't it perfectly heavenly to *know* that we are utterly and absolutely all right, — and to know that the world outside would be perfectly certain that we are not? What a darling you are!"

Still holding her hands behind her back she bent forward and touched her lips to his, daintily, fastidious in the light contact,

"Where is that picture of 'Womanhood'?" she asked.

He drew out the easel, adjusting the canvas to the light, and rolled a big chair up in front of it.

"Please sit there," she said; and seated herself on the padded arm, still keeping her hands behind her back.

"Are you concealing anything from me?" he asked.

"Never mind. I want to look at your picture," she added slowly as her eyes fell upon the canvas.

Minute after minute she sat there in silence, neither stirring nor offering comment. And after a long time he moved restlessly in the depths of the chair beside her.

Then she turned and looked down at him:

"Yes," she said, "it is really great. . . . And, *somehow*, I am lonely. Take me, Louis."

He drew her into his arms. She lay very silent against his breast for a while, and at last raised her curiously troubled eyes.

"You are going to be a very, very great painter, aren't you, Louis?"

He laughed and kissed her, watching her face.

"Don't be too great — so great that I shall feel too — too lonely," she whispered.

Then his eyes fell upon the ring which he had given her — and which she had gently put aside. She was wearing it on her betrothal finger.

"Where did you — find it?" he said unsteadily.

"In its box on your dresser."

"Do you realize what it means?"

"Yes. . . . And I am wearing it."

"Valerie!"

Her head nestled closer:

"Because I am going to marry you, Louis. . . . You were right. . . . If I fail, as your wife, to win my way in your world, then it will be because I have attempted the impossible. Which is no crime. . . . Who was it said 'Not failure, but low aim is crime'?"

She sighed, nestling closer like a child seeking rest:

"I am not coward enough to run away from you and destiny. . . . And if I stay, only two ways remain. . . . And the lawful is the better for us both. . . ." She laid her flushed cheek against his: "Because," she said dreamily, "there is one thing of which I never thought — children. . . . And I don't, perhaps, exactly understand, but I realize that — such things have happened; — and that it could happen to — us."

She lay silent for a while, her fingers restless on his shoulder; then she spoke again in the same dreamy voice of a half-awakened child:

"Each for the other's sake is not enough. It must be broader, wider, more generous . . . it must be for the sake of all. . . . I have learned this. . . . We can learn it better together. . . . Louis, can you guess what I did the day your letter came to me at Estwich?"

"What did you do, my darling?"

"I went to Ashuelyn."

"What?"

"Yes, dear. If it had not been for your letter which I could feel against my breast I should have been frightened. . . . Because all your family were together under the pergola. . . . As it was I could scarcely speak; I gave your mother the letter, and when she had read it and your father and your sister had read it, I asked them what I was to do.

"It was so strange and still there under the pergola; and I scarcely knew what I was saying — and I didn't realize that there were tears in my eyes — until I saw them in your mother's, too.

"Louis! Louis! I wonder if she can really ever care for me! — she was so good — so sweet to me. . . . And Mrs. Collis took me away to her own room — after your father had shaken hands with me — very stiffly but I think kindly — and I behaved very badly, dear — and your sister let me cry — all that I needed to."

She said nothing more for a while, resting in his arms, dark eyes fixed on space. Then:

"They asked me to remain; your brother-in-law is a dear! — but I still had a long day of self-examination before me. Your father and mother walked with me to the gate. Your mother kissed me."

His eyes, blinded by tears, scarcely saw her; and she turned her head and smiled at him.

"What they said to me was *very* sweet and patient, Louis. . . . I believe — I sometimes believe that I may, in time, win more than their consent, I believe that, some day, they will care to think of me as your wife — and think of me as such, kindly, without regret for what might have been if I had never known you."

Chapter XVIII

*H*élène d'Enver had gone back to the country, and Ogilvy dared not pursue her thither.

From her fastness at Estwich she defied him in letters, but every letter of hers seemed to leave some loophole open for further argument, and Ogilvy replied valiantly from a perfectly safe distance, vowing that he meant to marry her some day in spite of herself and threatening to go up and tell her so to her face, until she became bored to death waiting for him to fulfill this threat.

"There's a perfectly good inn here," she wrote, — "for of course, under the circumstances, you would scarcely have the impudence to expect the hospitality of my own roof. But if you are determined to have a final 'No' for your answer, I am entirely competent to give it to you by word of mouth —"

"And such a distractingly lovely mouth," sighed Ogilvy, perusing the letter in his studio. He whistled a slow waltz, thoughtfully, and as slowly and solemnly kept step to it, turning round and round, buried in deepest reflection. He had a habit of doing this when profoundly perplexed.

Annan discovered him waltzing mournfully all by himself:

"What's up?" he inquired cheerfully.

"It's all up, I suppose."

"With you and your countess?"

"Yes, Harry."

"Rot! Why don't you go and talk to her?"

"Because if I remain invisible she might possibly forget my face. I stand a better chance by letter, Harry."

"Now you're not bad-looking," insisted Annan, kindly. "And besides, a man's face doesn't count with a girl. Half of 'em are neurotics, anyway, and they adore the bizarre —"

"Damn it," snapped Sam, "do you mean that my countenance resembles a gargoyle? If you do, say so in English."

"No, no, no," said Annan soothingly, — "I've seen more awful mugs — married mugs, too. What woman has done woman may do again. Buck up! Beauty and the beast is no idle jest —"

"I'll punch you good and plenty," began Sam wrathfully, but Annan fled, weak with laughter.

"There's no vainer man than an ugly one!" he called back, and slammed the door to escape a flight of paint brushes hurled by a maddened man.

"I'll go! By jinks, I'll go, anyway!" he exclaimed; "and I don't care what she thinks of my face . . . only I think I'll take Annan with me — just for company — or — dummy bridge on the way up. . . . Harry!" he shouted.

Annan cautiously appeared, ready for rapid flight.

"Aw come on in! My face suits me. Besides, thank Heaven I've got a reputation back of it; but yours breaks the speed laws. Will you go up there with me — like a man?"

"Where?"

"To Estwich?"

"When?" inquired Annan, skeptically.

"Now! — b' jinks!"

"Have *you* sufficient nerve, *this* time?"

"Watch me."

And he dragged out a suit-case and began wildly throwing articles of toilet and apparel into it,

"Come on, Harry!" he shouted, hurling a pair of tennis shoes at the suit-case; "I've got to go while I'm excited or I'll never budge!"

But when, ten minutes later, Annan arrived, suit-case in hand, ready for love's journey, he could scarcely contrive to kick and drag Sam into the elevator, and, later, into a taxicab.

Ogilvy sat there alternately shivering and attempting to invent imperative engagements in town which he had just remembered, but Annan said angrily:

"No, you don't. This makes the seventh time I've started with you for Estwich, and I'm going to put it through or perish in a hand-to-hand conflict with you."

And he started for the train, dragging Sam with him, talking angrily all the time.

He talked all the way to Estwich, too, partly to reassure Ogilvy and give him no time for terrified reflection, partly because he liked to talk. And when they arrived at the Estwich Arms he shoved Ogilvy into a room, locked the door, and went away to telephone to the Countess d'Enver.

"Yes?" she inquired sweetly, "who is it?"

"Me," replied Annan, regardless of an unpopular grammatical convention. "I'm here with Ogilvy. May we come to tea?"

"Is Mr. Ogilvy *here?*"

"Yes, here at the Estwich Arms. May I — er — may *he* bring *me* over to call on you?"

"Y-yes. Oh, with pleasure, Mr. Annan. . . . When may I expect hi — you?"

"In about ten minutes," replied Annan firmly.

Then he went back and looked into Ogilvy's room. Sam was seated, his head clasped in his hands.

"I thought you *might* tear up your sheets and let yourself out of the window," said Annan sarcastically. "You're a fine specimen! Why you're actually lantern-jawed with fright. But I don't care! Come on; we're expected to tea! Get into your white flannels and pretty blue coat and put on your dinkey rah-rah, and follow me. Or, by heaven! — I'll do murder right now!"

Ogilvy's knees wavered as they entered the gateway.

"Go on!" hissed Annan, giving him a violent shove.

Then, to Ogilvy, came that desperate and hysterical courage that comes to those whose terrors have at last infuriated them.

"By jinks!" he said with an unearthly smile, "I *will* come on!"

And he did, straight through the door and into the pretty living room where Hélène d'Enver rose in some slight consternation to receive this astonishingly pale and rather desperate-faced young man.

"Harry," said Ogilvy, calmly retaining Hélène's hand, "you go and play around the yard for a few moments. I have something to tell the Countess d'Enver; and then we'll all have tea."

"Mr. Ogilvy!" she said, amazed.

But Annan had already vanished; and she looked into a pair of steady eyes that suddenly made her quail.

"Hélène," he said, "I really do love you."

"Please —"

"No! I love you! Are you going to let me?"

"I — how on earth — what a perfectly senseless —"

"I know it. I'm half senseless from fright. Yes, I am, Hélène! Now! here! at this very minute, I am scared blue. That's why I'm holding on to your hand so desperately; I'm afraid to let go."

She flushed brightly with annoyance, or something or other — but he held fast to her hand and put one arm around her waist.

"Sam!" she said, exasperated. That was the last perfectly coherent word she uttered for several minutes. And, later, she was too busy to say very much.

When Annan returned, Hélène rose from the couch where she and Ogilvy had been seated and came across the floor, blushing vividly.

"I don't know what on earth you think of me, Mr. Annan, and I suppose I will have to learn to endure the consequences of Mr. Ogilvy's eccentricities —"

"Oh, I'm terribly glad!" said Annan, grinning, and taking her hand in both of his.

They had tea on the veranda. Ogilvy was too excited and far too happy to be dignified, and Hélène was so much embarrassed by his behavior and so much in love that she made a distractingly pretty picture between the two young men who, as Rita had said, would never, never be old enough to grow up.

"Do you know," said Hélène, "that your friends the Nevilles have recently been very nice to me? They have called, and have returned my call, and have asked me to dinner. I suppose cordiality takes longer to arrive at maturity in New York State than in any other part of the Union. But when New York people make up their minds to be agreeable, they certainly are delightful."

"They're a bunch of snobs," said Ogilvy, calmly.

"Oh!" said Hélène with a distressed glance at Annan.

"He's one, too," observed her affianced, coolly nodding toward Annan. "We're a sickening lot, Hélène — until some charming and genuine person like you comes along to jounce us out of our smiling and imbecile self-absorption."

"I," said Annan gravely, "am probably the most frightful snob that ever wandered, in a moment of temporary aberration, north of lower Fifth Avenue."

"I'm worse," observed Sam gloomily. "Help us, Hélène, toward loftier aspirations. Be our little uplift girl —"

"You silly things!" she said indignantly.

Later two riders passed the house, Cameron and Stephanie Swift, who saluted Hélène most cordially, and waved airy recognition to the two men.

"More snobs," commented Sam.

"They are very delightful people!" retorted Hélène hotly.

"Most snobs are when they like you."

"Sam! I won't have you express such sentiments!"

He bent nearer to her:

"Dearest, I never had any sentiments except for you. And only the inconvenient propinquity of that man Annan prevents me from expressing them."

"Please, Sam —"

"Don't be afraid; I won't. He wouldn't care; — but I won't. . . . Hello! Why look who's here!" he exclaimed, rising. "Why it's the great god Kelly and little Sunshine!" — as Neville and Valerie sprang out of Mrs. Collis's touring car and came up the walk.

Hélène went forward to meet them, putting one arm around Valerie and holding out the other to Neville.

"When did you arrive, darling?" she exclaimed. "How do you do, Mr. Neville? Valerie, child, I'm perfectly enchanted to see you. But where in the world are you stopping?"

"At Ashuelyn," said the girl, looking straight into Hélène's eyes. A faint flash of telepathy passed between them; then, slowly, Hélène turned and looked at Neville.

"Will you wish us happiness?" he said, smiling.

"Oh-h," whispered Hélène under her breath — "I do — I do — God knows. I wish you everything that makes for happiness in all the world!" she stammered, for the wonder of it was still on her.

Then Sam's voice sounded close at hand:

"Why," he said admiringly, "it *looks* like lovey and dovey!"

"It is," said Valerie, laughing.

"You! — *and* Kelly!"

"We two."

Sam in his excitement became a little wild and incongruous:

"'My wife's gone to the country!
    Hooray! Hooray!'"

he shouted, holding hands with Annan and swinging back and forth.

"Sam!" exclaimed Hélène, mortified.

"Darling? — oh, gee! I forgot what is due to decorum! Please, *please* forgive me, Hélène! And kindly inform these ladies and gentlemen that you have consented to render me eternally and supremely happy; because if I tried to express to them that delirious fact I'd end by standing on my head in the grass —"

"You dear!" whispered Valerie, holding tightly to Hélène's hands.

"Isn't it dreadful?" murmured Hélène, turning her blue eyes on the man who never would grow old enough to grow up. "I had no such intention, I can assure you; and I don't even understand myself yet."

"Don't you?" said Valerie, laughing tenderly; — "then you are like all other women. What is the use of our ever trying to understand ourselves?"

Hélène laughed, too:

"No use, dear. Leave it to men who say *they* understand us. It's a mercy somebody does."

"Isn't it," nodded Valerie; and they kissed each other, laughing.

"My goodness, it's like the embrace of the two augurs!" said Ogilvy. "They're laughing at *us*, Kelly! — at you, and me and Harry! — and at man in general! — innocent man! — so charmingly and guilelessly symbolized by us! Stop it, Hélène! You make me shiver. You'll frighten Annan so that he'll *never* marry if you and Valerie laugh that way at each other."

"I wonder," said Hélène, quieting him with a fair hand laid lightly on his sleeve, "whether you all would remain and dine with me this evening — just as you are I mean; — and I won't dress —"

"I insist *proh pudeur*," muttered Sam. "I can't countenance any such saturnalia —"

"Oh, Sam, do be quiet, dear —" She caught herself up with a blush, and everybody smiled.

"What do we care!" said Sam. "I'm tired of convention! If I want to call you darling in public, b'jinks! I will! Darling — darling — darling — there! —"

"Sam!"

"Dearest —"

"*Sam!*"

"Ma'am?"

Hélène looked at Valerie:

"There's no use," she sighed, "is there?"

"No use," sighed Valerie, smiling at the man she loved.

THE END

Lightning Source UK Ltd.
Milton Keynes UK
UKOW05f2325021213

222267UK00002B/350/A